Sally Stewart

A London childhood was dominated at home by the mixed pleasure of having four elder brothers. Unused to the country, I declined to stay there more than a month or two as an evacuee, and returned in good time for the Blitz. Later schooldays were spent watching doodlebugs flying overhead or ducking those that failed to fly overhead.

Working life was, first, a long connection with the *Reader's Digest*. I worked for its chairman, travelled to other *Digest* companies in Europe and America, and learned from my boss anything I know about the writing of English.

Marriage eventually meant separation from London. My husband and I moved out of the shelter of a huge concern, to try running our own small one. We missed the boom, caught the backwash, and finally failed . . . back to being employed again. This time, to broaden our experience if not our minds, we entered the groves of Academe.

Then I entered a magazine story competition and, astonishingly, won it. Now, many stories later (published by *Woman's Weekly, Woman & Home*, Mills & Boon, Piatkus, and Corgi) I am an addict, and reach for my pen as an alcoholic reaches for a glass.

My husband's and my retirement from Oxford University brought us to the green hills of Somerset, and the pleasurable oddities of village life. We like to roam about Europe, or contentedly apply ourselves to the other good things of life – friends, food, wine, music, and our garden.

Also by Sally Stewart

ECHOES IN THE SQUARE
THE WOMEN OF PROVIDENCE

and published by Corgi Books

THE BIRD OF HAPPINESS

Sally Stewart

CORGI BOOKS

THE BIRD OF HAPPINESS
A CORGI BOOK   0 552 13850 9

First publication in Great Britain

PRINTING HISTORY
Corgi edition published 1991

This book is set in 10pt Plantin by
County Typesetters, Margate, Kent

Corgi Books are published by Transworld Publishers Ltd,
61–63 Uxbridge Road, Ealing, London W5 5SA, in Australia
by Transworld Publishers (Australia) Pty Ltd, 15–23 Helles
Avenue, Moorebank, NSW 2170, and in New Zealand by
Transworld Publishers (NZ) Ltd, Cnr Moselle and
Waipareira Avenues, Henderson, Auckland.

Made and printed in Great Britain by
BPCC Hazell Books
Aylesbury, Bucks., England
Member of BPCC Ltd.

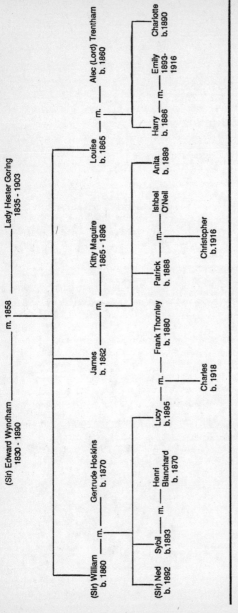

(Sir) Edward Wyndham —— m. 1858 —— Lady Hester Goring
1830 - 1890   1835 - 1903

(Sir) William ——m.—— Gertrude Hoskins
b. 1860   b. 1870

James —— m. —— Kitty Maguire
b. 1862   1865 - 1896

Louise —— m. —— Alec (Lord) Trentham
b. 1865   b. 1860

(Sir) Ned   Sybil —— m. —— Henri   Lucy
b. 1892   b.1893   Blanchard   b.1895
                                b. 1870

Frank Thornley —— m. —— Patrick   Ishbel —— m. —— Anita
b. 1880   b. 1888   O'Neil   b. 1889

Charles   Christopher
b. 1918   b.1916

Harry —— m. —— Emily   Charlotte
b. 1886   1893 -   b.1890
                1916

George Hoskins —— m. —— Emma Rostell   Daniel Maguire (Visited UK 1869)
b. 1846   1869   1848 - 1886   d. 1912

Gertrude (Hoskins)   Kitty Maguire
b. 1870   1865 - 1896

1920

Chapter One

The summer had been unusually hot, but now September sunshine fell softly over the pasture-meadows and stubbled cornfields of the countryside. Its patchwork of green and gold was seamed with the deeper green of hedgerows, and blurred with the shadows thrown by huge, old trees. Hay Wood, last remnant of the Forest of Arden, climbed the hillsides to the north, shutting the valley away from the noise and stench of Birmingham. Encircled by the greenness that flowed around it like water, the village of Haywood's End faced towards its ancient protector – a manor house called Providence. Village and house had shared the valley for the past five hundred years, mostly undisturbed since Yorkists and Lancastrians had fought the Wars of the Roses. There'd been a more recent clash between Roundheads and Cavaliers, but it had been far to the south at Edge Hill, and only faint echoes of the battle had troubled the sleep of Haywood's End. Something terrible had happened since then – the war to end all wars, finished a mere two years ago – but it hadn't been fought over peaceful English soil; only peaceful English lives had been changed by it, uprooted, and shattered for ever.

Providence, sashed by the silver ribbon of its moat, seemed to belong as naturally to the landscape as the trees and meadows that surrounded it. Three miles away as the crow flew, but nearer six by the road to Birmingham, a different kind of house had been imposed on the valley by a successful Victorian ironmaster. Its present châtelaine, Jane Thornley, doubted whether any amount of time would make Bicton look as if it belonged to the country-side. She'd allowed herself to be moved without complaint from a comfortable villa in Birmingham when her husband insisted that it was time they went up in the world, but her first sight of Bicton had nearly given her heart failure. Even now, though she'd long since come to terms with it, she still tried to go in and out of the house without staring at its forest of gables and turrets and curlicues – hideous in themselves, and the stuff of nightmare when rendered in brick of a peculiar yellowish-grey. To be fair to Arthur, it was Providence, the home of the Wyndhams, that he'd wanted to own; he'd had to make do with Bicton.

Twenty years later, Jane still smiled at the memory of her first afternoon visitor. A Birmingham upbringing hadn't accustomed her to formal calls, and the news that Lady Wyndham was at the door had all but paralysed her with fright. She'd waited in her vast, ugly drawing-room to be patronized or snubbed by some blue-blooded county matron, and found herself instead being advised by a friendly, smiling young woman to laugh at Bicton, as its previous mistress had done. That was unexpected enough; but over the years more remarkable things had happened. Gertrude Wyndham had become her dearest friend, and the Wyndhams' younger daughter had married Jane's son, Frank. Even Arthur had had to admit that the Thornleys had gone up in the world, as the world counted such things.

Of the whole monstrous Victorian-Gothic pile she'd been installed in, Jane really only enjoyed the conservatory attached to its southern end. Here, especially on sunlit mornings like the present one, she snipped and sniffed and watered her plants with the contentment of a woman who felt at home.

'Might've known I'd find you here with your fingers covered in muck.' Her husband's voice from the doorway behind her sounded slightly aggrieved. 'Why not leave the dirty work to Fitton? It's what he's paid for.'

'I prefer to muddle along on my own,' Jane said serenely. 'He doesn't approve of my efforts; he knows how ignorant I am, and reckons that any self-respecting plant in here ought to die immediately. For some reason neither of us can understand, instead of dying, everything flourishes beautifully!'

10

She smiled at Arthur, expecting him to smile back, but his heavy, square face looked preoccupied. It was early for him to have put aside the morning's newspapers which he normally sifted, with the diligence of a terrier chasing rabbits, for every sign of Government sloth, trades union stupidity, or foreign wickedness. Something was troubling him, and she suspected that she knew what it was.

'Didn't mention it, but I looked in at Providence on my way home yesterday. Our grandson was in the stable yard bellowing fit to bust because the fool of a girl who looks after him had let Daft Artie sit him on a horse again.'

'Pony, I expect, dear . . . just a *little* horse,' Jane suggested excusingly.

'Big or little . . . what's it matter? Charlie doesn't *like* horses, and she ought to know that by now.'

Jane's thoughts swooped backwards again. They'd gone to Bicton so that, in the right surroundings, Frank would grow up a country gentleman. He'd grown up stubbornly true to himself instead, an industrial genius, just like his father. Arthur couldn't help but be proud of *that*, but he hadn't bargained for a small grandson *born* at Providence to be so reluctant to acquire the traditional habits of the gentry. Jane thought that it accounted for some of her husband's irritation now.

'Arthur dear, Artie means well, and you *know* he wouldn't let the boy fall off,' she offered by way of comfort.

'That's not the point, Janey. A child needs a bit of attention from its *mother* occasionally, and where was Lucy yesterday? Over at Barham again, playing tennis or some such foolery.'

Jane put down her watering-can, aware that the matter had become serious. The trouble was that in her heart of hearts she agreed with him about a girl she loved as the daughter she'd never had; but to admit that anything was wrong at all was to begin admitting that a great deal more might be wrong as well. She *wouldn't* admit to it because, apart from a threat to Arthur himself, the only thing that could destroy her universe would be for Frank and Lucy's life together to fail of happiness.

'Listen, my dearie, we won't wrap the truth up in fine linen,' she said bravely. 'Lucy's fifteen years younger than Frank, and he only knows one way of living, the same as you did . . . to work all the hours God sends. If it's not Thornley factories, it's work for the Government. Can you wonder that a girl of twenty-six gets bored and lonely?'

'She's got a child to raise and servants to run, and a family that lives in the other half of Providence; what more company does she need?'

'People of her own age, Arthur. There's no-one at Haywood's End she can make a friend of, and her brother's as bad as Frank, always working about the gardens or the farms. She's bound to go looking for companionship.'

It was the truth of Jane's opinion as far as it went, but she could have added more – that Frank ought to let Lloyd George's problems wait while he made time for his wife, and gave her another child. It was an indelicate thing for a woman born in Victoria's reign to think, and impossible to say, but Arthur said it for her. 'There ought to be several more children in the nursery – then Lucy wouldn't feel lonely.'

He saw the troubled expression in his wife's eyes, and leaned forward to kiss her cheek. 'No need to worry, love. I know better than to go putting my clumsy feet in Frank's affairs, and I shan't worry Gertrude Wyndham, either, next time she asks us to eat our dinner at Providence. Quiet as a mouse I'll be, same as I always am.'

Jane smiled at him with forgiving tenderness. 'You mean you'll only roar at William because the French have got things all wrong *again*, and ask Ned what his American cousin thinks he's doing, mixing with a lot of Irish murderers in Dublin!'

'Just making conversation,' Arthur pointed out guilelessly. 'A man's got to say *something*, Janey.'

She agreed that this was so, knowing that he chafed enough under the self-imposed discipline of leaving the running of things to his son. Frank did very well by Thornley's . . . but that left the rest of the world unattended to, and Arthur couldn't help thinking it would be a tidier place if they'd let *him* have the ordering of it. By and large Jane agreed with him.

'Come and help me bully Fitton,' she suggested. 'He's planting spring bulbs again, and *this* time, Arthur, I'm determined to have daffodils and tulips in lovely fat clumps, just the way Ned grows them at Providence. Each year I explain it to Fitton, and each year he gets out his tape-measure again and plants them in straight rows, one every six inches.'

Arthur saw nothing wrong himself in keeping the upper hand over Nature, but if Janey wanted clumps, that was what she should have, and be damned to the most cantankerous gardener in Warwickshire. He was perfectly well aware that she wanted to occupy him with something other than the worry that had taken him to look for her in the conservatory; but she *hadn't* said what he'd hoped she'd say – that he was daft to imagine there was anything wrong with little Lucy.

In the Rectory garden at Haywood's End Maud Roberts was deep in the tangled depths of the herbaceous border when Lucy Thornley rode over from Providence to find her. A battered Panama hat nodding among the huge heads of bronze and crimson dahlias signalled that she might be hidden there, and a moment later she could be heard as well, recommending a purple- and white-striped giant to hold still, for pity's sake, if it expected to be safely staked up.

For once Lucy found herself content to stand and stare. The urge that troubled her frequently nowadays to rush on somewhere else from wherever she happened to be seemed to lose itself in the peace and late-summer beauty of Maud's garden. She had come on an impulse, with no excuse to offer for disturbing her old friend, but one of Miss Roberts' more notable traits was not to appear to notice if other people didn't behave rationally. For a

13

moment or two, Lucy thought, she need do nothing but feel the sun's warmth on her face, and watch a bee quartering a nearby clump of lavender for every last grain of sweetness.

'Happy bee,' she said out loud, and gave away the fact that she was there.

'Who's that? Lucy?' Maud's rump, clothed in a pair of her brother's old tweed trousers, backed slowly out of the foliage. Then she turned and smiled at her visitor. 'I could have done with another pair of hands ten minutes ago. Don't know why I bother growing these great, vulgar things that can't even hold up their own heads.'

'So that you can beat Ned and old Biddle at the autumn Show!'

'There is *that*,' Maud acknowledged, 'though I trust you won't tell them so.' She walked towards a tree-shaded seat, stopping to pick a handful of plums on the way. They shared them in silence, while a curious robin perched himself three feet away, watching them with bright, expectant eyes.

'I'm interrupting your work,' Lucy said finally.

'True, but it's a kindness to interrupt a gardener of my great age occasionally . . . gives her an excuse to sit down.' Maud nibbled at a plum, then asked a casual question. 'What made you say the bee was happy?'

'Buzzing merrily about its allotted task, I suppose; knowing what its task *is*,' Lucy muttered. She was staring down at the fruit in her hands, as if its soft purple bloom needed careful inspection. A bar of sunlight gleamed on the brightness of her hair but her beautiful face was shadowed by the tree. It looked withdrawn and sad, and Maud wished she knew for certain what ailed a girl who had once been happy.

'Is that *your* difficulty now . . . knowing what your task is?' she asked gently.

Lucy gave a little shrug, learned not at Haywood's End but from the sophisticated people she mixed with nowadays in London. 'Why shouldn't I know? My job is to be the wife of a successful man, to entertain his important friends, to raise his son to inherit the Thornley empire . . . There's nothing difficult about *knowing*; the only trouble is in doing it. My father-in-law thinks I don't do it very well.'

'My dear Lucy, Arthur Thornley adores you.'

'I know . . . *that* makes it worse, don't you think?'

She spoke so calmly that her friend was almost trapped into agreeing, but before the mistake could be made Lucy had begun again. 'I can't ask anyone else . . . that's why I'm bothering you. What's wrong with me? I used to love Providence more than anywhere else on earth – now I feel buried there. Haywood's End is still firmly rooted in the Dark Ages but I even enjoyed *that* years ago; now it just makes me want to scream.'

She had spoken only of places, Maud noticed; the family on whom she had once lavished all her love hadn't been mentioned, nor the man she'd married and the child they'd created between them.

'Nothing's wrong with you,' Miss Roberts said, after a moment's careful thought, 'except some painful after-effects of the war. Don't smile . . . I'm sure I'm right, even though opinionated old women like me always *do* think they're right. Those four years swallowed up *your* youth as certainly as they did Ned's, and the youth of millions like him. You did the hard, physical work of a man, shared your grandfather's worries over keeping the estate going, and supported your parents through harrowing anxieties. Now that it's all over there seems nothing left to do. It's still your mother's job, rather than yours, to cherish Providence, and Ned is more and more able to take charge again. You are Frank's wife, *not* a farm-hand toiling in the fields from dawn to dusk.'

It was perfectly true, but Maud knew that she had left out the most relevant fact of all: Lucy had chosen to marry a rich man she didn't love in order to keep Providence safe for her parents and for Ned. After two years in the trenches of Flanders he'd been invalided out of the army, a shell-shocked ghost trapped in a private hell they couldn't share. Gertrude Wyndham had fought the military ruling that would have condemned him indefinitely to a psychiatric hospital, certain that if anything could reach and save him, it would be the healing grace of Providence. It had begun to do so when the worst that could have happened to them *did* happen: the bank foreclosed on the mortgaged house during the closing stages of the war. Had anyone else in the world but Frank Thornley bought it, the Wyndhams would have lost their home and Ned his refuge, but Frank took over the mortgage as the price for getting Lucy as his wife. They made one wing of it their country home, and left William, Gertrude and Ned undisturbed in the rest of it.

Maud stretched out a brown, scratched hand and laid it over Lucy's soft one. 'Be patient, my dear. Life has a way of providing the cures we need, but it's not a particle of good saying "I insist on being cured *now*, please"; the adjustments take time.'

Lucy's taut face relaxed into a smile because she suddenly felt full of affection for the woman beside her. Maud's faith in God was the rock on which her life was built, but she never confused eternal verities with short-term human wants and needs. He was all-powerful but not all-responsible, and full-grown men and women had to learn to live with the choices they made.

'Lucky Ned and Syb to have you as their godmother,' Lucy said suddenly. 'I was given Aunt Louise, who terrified me as a child and still does. What's more, I think she has the same effect on Father!'

It was Maud's turn to smile. 'She's a trifle formidable, I grant you – unlike your dear parents. It probably comes of years spent in India with Alec Trentham. Women like her served Victoria's Empire just as surely as their menfolk did.'

'Well, according to Hodges, she was what he calls a "reg'lar tartar" long before that! He should know because he had the job of teaching her to ride.' Amusement touched Lucy's face, but quickly faded because she remembered the old man's outspoken regret at Charlie's refusal to have anything to do with horses.

'How's my dear Ned?' Maud asked quickly, noticing her change of expression. 'I haven't catched sight of him, as they say at Haywood's End, for days and days.'

'He's all right – working hard again; *too* hard, Mama thinks but is careful not to say.' Lucy stared at her friend's tranquil face, suddenly envying with all her heart the serenity of a woman who seemed immune to the emotional tangles that beset her own family. 'My mother has convinced herself that Ned continues to improve, because she can't bear to think that he won't get completely better.'

'You *don't* think so?' Maud asked quietly.

'He's got better at hiding his nightmares, that's all, so as not to worry her. If you're not right about time bringing its cures, I think the sight of Ned's trembling hands will one day break her heart.' Lucy stared sombrely at the garden, not seeing its glowing beauty. 'We still miss Syb, you know . . . probably Father and Ned most of all. She's *rotten* to stay in France and never come near us.'

The childish adjective made Maud smile, but it seemed apt. However happy Sybil Wyndham might be, living in Paris with the man who had been her father's friend, it was time she remembered that she had a family at Providence. The war had been over for two years, and William and Gertrude hadn't seen their elder daughter since even before that, when she'd last come home on leave from her VAD unit in France. Maud missed her god-daughter too, because however much Sybil infuriated those who knew her, she had the knack of enchanting them as well.

'She'll wake up one morning and decide that she must leave for England that very day,' Maud ventured hopefully. 'Plans and arrangements made in advance, with due consideration for this and that, aren't for the Syb I remember. She'll just turn up, grinning, as if she'd never been away.'

'I don't think so,' Lucy commented after a moment's thought. 'She knows Papa well enough to guess the truth. He misses her dreadfully, but he's deeply shocked as well that a daughter of his could live with a man old enough to be her father and not marry him.'

'He might blame Henri Blanchard for that, rather than Sybil.'

'Yes, but it makes matters even worse because Henri was his friend. He never mentions him now. When there are paintings to be sold he sends Jem Martin up to London with them. He hasn't been to the Blanchard Gallery himself since the war ended. Sybil must know the reason for that. She won't come until we beg her to on bended knee, and she might not come even then.'

Maud found herself unable to repeat the comforting maxim that time, left to itself, healed all things. She knew much more than Lucy knew about the complicated relationship between Henri Blanchard and the Wyndhams. He hadn't only been the art-dealer who had launched William on his successful career as a painter; in times past he'd seduced William's sister Louise, and fallen in love with William's wife. Maud had had to guess what it cost Gertrude long ago to stay with William, and what it had cost her since to know that Henri's present mistress was her own daughter.

Maud's painful train of thought was interrupted by Lucy, getting to her feet. 'Time I went home, I think. Your dahlias are being sadly neglected, and Charles will have exhausted the patience of both his nursemaids by now. It will be my turn to try and exhaust *him* sufficiently for them to put him to bed. Grandpa Thornley lives again in my small son!'

'You might be glad of that one day.'

'So I might. In the meanwhile I just wish . . .' Lucy stopped, smiled ruefully, and began again. 'No, I'm not to wish, am I, but to wait patiently for time to readjust me! All the same, dearest Maud, I doubt if time is going to make any difference to the problems of Ned and Sybil.'

She kissed Miss Roberts goodbye and rode slowly home, unaware that she was wrong about both of them. A month later Aunt Louise's son, Harry Trentham, told Ned about a hospital in Edinburgh where the analytical techniques pioneered by Dr Sigmund Freud were being used successfully on men whose minds had been hurt by the war. Ned knew perfectly well that he wasn't healed, but another piece of self-knowledge, shared with his mother, insisted that only cowardice kept him from giving the new treatment a try.

'It's not that I mind admitting that I'm still a bit queer in the attic,' he explained to her, 'or even that I can't make myself walk back inside a mental hospital – dreadful though that would be. The really desperate possibility is that I might come out worse than I went in! What do you say to that, Mama?'

His hands were hidden inside the pockets of his shabby tweed jacket so that she shouldn't see them tremble. She loved him more than anyone else in the world, but there was nothing more that she could do to help him.

'Dear Ned, I can't make you any promises, and nor can the doctors at Craiglockhart. I'm prepared to believe that they can help you, but you don't have to subject yourself to still *more* punishment in order to prove that you aren't afraid of it. That's the sort of stupid logic that only men are capable of.'

A ripple of amusement wiped away the strain in his face. 'Spoken just like Aunt Louise! I'll have a think about it, shall I?'

It was her turn to smile at the familiar turn of phrase, and she wasn't surprised when he left a week later to take the train north to Edinburgh.

At almost the same time Harry Trentham's sister walked into the Blanchard Gallery in Bond Street, and found herself side by side with a girl who hadn't been seen in London, or in her home at Providence, for the past three years.

Chapter Two

Charlotte Trentham had made almost a complete circuit of the room before one painting in particular caught her eye – a canvas by Alfred Sisley, entitled 'A Small Meadow in Spring'. It could have been better described 'Girl with Beech Trees' perhaps, but the painting was charming – a spring sky blobbed with soft white clouds, and a girl in a blue dress framed by trees that were just coming into golden leaf.

With her mind made up, Charlotte turned away and almost cannoned into a small, dark-haired girl who was absorbed in a neighbouring canvas. After one glance a different exclamation escaped her, instead of the apology on her lips.

'Good Lord above, it's Syb!' Then, more doubtfully, 'It *is* you, isn't it?'

The girl smiled, then nodded, but Charlotte was already sure – no-one else had quite the grin that lifted a short upper lip over very white, slightly uneven, front teeth. There was no reason why it should have been particularly attractive, but on Sybil Wyndham it always had been, and still was. She was vividly attractive altogether, even without any of her sister Lucy's regular-featured, golden beauty. Short black hair curved in glossy wings against cheeks as smooth and pale as ivory. Her eyes were very dark, and her red mouth demanded that *men*, especially, should take notice of it. Charlotte surprised herself by recognizing the fact, because her own vague intention was that men shouldn't notice her at all.

'Nobody mentioned that you were coming,' she said next, seeing that her cousin seemed in no hurry to speak.

'Nobody knew . . . Henri had to come to London for a

day or two and I refused to be left behind. We shall be leaving again as soon as this morning's vital consultation with his tailor is over.'

'Without going to Providence?' Charlotte asked doubtfully. Her voice laid no stress on the question, but Sybil heard it as an accusation.

'I'm being tactful! An erring daughter does better to stay away from her family, especially if they live in a place like Haywood's End. Now that I come to think of it, perhaps *you* should have swept past me with a distant, disapproving nod!'

'Dear Syb, don't be a fool.' For a moment Charlotte managed to sound so like her mother that Sybil smiled with complete naturalness; but her cousin's next blunt question wiped amusement from her face. 'What am I supposed to say to Aunt Gertrude?'

'Nothing at all . . . *please*, Lottie. I'd never have come to the gallery if I'd thought there was the slightest chance of any of you being here. Why on earth *did* you come, anyway?'

'Wedding anniversary present for my parents . . . *that*, I rather thought,' she explained, pointing to the Sisley painting. 'A relief for Mama from too many Trentham ancestors glaring at her out of heavy gold frames; on the other hand, not too "modern" to frighten my father.'

'Whose taste in art, *my* father used to say, hasn't progressed beyond the Early Victorian!' Her glance wandered back to the wall beside them, and Charlotte registered what it was her cousin had been staring at a few minutes ago – a painting of the lake at Providence, caught at a moment of autumn when the surface of the water wore a patina of bronze and gold leaves. The signature of William Wyndham was written in one corner, in small, meticulously neat lettering.

'He's got rather good,' Sybil said abruptly. Then she turned to look at Charlotte again. 'My mother writes an occasional, dutiful letter. Do you see them? Is Ned really getting better?'

'He's certainly better than he was, but there's a chance

21

now that he can be completely cured. Harry heard about a neurasthenic hospital in Edinburgh offering a new treatment, and Ned decided to go . . . he's there now, as a matter of fact.'

'I haven't seen him since his regiment was sent out of the Line for a week's rest . . . a whole *week*, such was the generosity of Staff officers housed in comfort at a safe distance from the trenches! Ned cadged a lift and came to the hospital at Etaples to see me. I didn't even recognize my darling Ned until he smiled . . .' She looked away from her cousin, and after a moment Charlotte filled the pause.

'You might not recognize *Lucy* now, either. Frank seems to be a kind of unofficial consultant for the Government, so they spend a lot of time in London. She's changed . . . got very sophisticated-looking, like you!'

'Don't tell me her husband's changed as well, and lost his delightful Birmingham uncouthness?'

'I don't think he was ever uncouth,' Charlotte said fairly, 'just not quite one of us. He *still* isn't, but that hasn't stopped him becoming rather an impressive man in his own way.'

'Generous of you, coz; he sounds perfectly grim to me. By the way, Harry won't have told you because I asked him not to, but I met *him* when he was in Paris a year or so ago. It was lovely to see him, but saddening as well; I hadn't quite expected him to look so old and stern. I got the impression that he hated what he was doing. Poor Harry . . . sickened by soldiering, and then obliged to follow Uncle Alec into politics.'

'He doesn't hate political life *now* – in fact he revels in it, having left the Liberal Party. It was on his mind for ages, but he only took the plunge six months ago.'

'Into *what*, may I ask?'

'Socialism, of course. He's out of Parliament at the moment because he had to resign the Somerton seat, but he'll be a Labour Party candidate at the next General Election.'

'Mama's letters have never mentioned *that*, and no

22

wonder! A Trentham turned anything but Liberal is enough to make your forbears gyrate in their graves, but a *Socialist* . . . lumme!'

'I'm one too,' Charlotte confessed with simple pride, 'at least, a Fabian; we advocate *peaceful* change, not revolution.'

'How nice!' Sybil said faintly. 'That must be a *great* comfort to Aunt Louise.'

Her cousin's long, plain face was lit by a charming smile. 'You haven't changed much after all; I was bemused for a bit by the Parisian gloss. Syb . . . don't stay away for ever from Providence – they miss you; in fact, we all do.'

For a moment she thought she saw the shine of tears in her cousin's dark eyes, then decided she was mistaken, because Sybil was smiling brightly again.

'Nothing's for ever, Lottie dear. Henri may get tired of me before long and send me home!' A glance at the little fob-watch pinned to the emerald-green jacket of her suit ended the conversation. 'I must go . . . I'm supposed to be back at the Ritz by now, and the boat-train leaves at midday.' She reached up to kiss her taller cousin's cheek, started to walk towards the door, and then turned round again.

'Don't forget you were going to buy the Sisley. Henri would approve the choice. *Au revoir*, coz.'

Charlotte walked to the window to watch her slender figure merge with the passers-by on the pavement outside. Then she gave a little sigh, and went towards the elegant young man who sat at a desk in the corner of the room. By now, without Sybil's reminder, she would certainly have forgotten what she'd come there to buy. It was going to be hard not to tell Lucy about the morning's meeting, and even harder to conceal from Harry the fact that his favourite cousin had been in London.

A fortnight later Frank Thornley chose, for once, to walk from Westminster to his London home in St James's Place. It was a waste of working time, and therefore a luxury he didn't normally allow himself, but the empty peacefulness of the park was all about him, and he walked into its quiet heart thankfully. He was an urban man who was learning to hate cities. The stale air of Whitehall offices clogged his lungs and he moved slowly, not only because he was very tired. Depression weighed him down as well, and not all of it was to do with the country's problems that he was required to help grapple with. *They* were bad enough, God knew, and the worthy gentlemen of the Coalition cabinet had precious little idea what to do about them. It seemed to Frank that even Lloyd George himself, so dynamic a leader during the latter part of the war, was relying on time and pious hope to revive world trade, full employment, and outworn, failing industries. People found comfort in the general idea that the good old pre-war times were bound to come again, because prosperity was only what England deserved. Frank found himself unable to believe in it; problems didn't disappear, in his experience, simply because their sufferers' cause was righteous.

He stopped to watch the antics of a family of ducks on the lake because the sunlit water reminded him of the moat at home and Charlie laughing as he fed the creatures there. It was strange to feel so out of place still at Providence and yet to miss it painfully when he wasn't there. It was stranger still that Lucy, bred up to its peaceful beauty, now seemed to crave nothing but the noisy turmoil of London.

He walked on again, telling himself that for once he might find her quietly alone, sipping tea, or sewing, or doing anything which a wife would be glad to put aside simply because her husband was home again after being away. She was young – he repeated it often, like a lesson that had to be constantly relearned; she was beautiful, sociable, and vividly alive. He was nearly middle-aged, and at this moment tired and unusually depressed. The Duke of York's Steps reared up in front of him, requiring a huge effort to be climbed, and beyond them Pall Mall stretched interminably. Still, at the end of it he was nearly home . . . just the slope up St James's Street and into his own turning; odd that it should take extreme tiredness to make him notice that there were hills in London.

Five minutes later he unlocked the front door of his small, elegant house and heard the sound of Lucy's laughter from the drawing-room on the first floor. She *wasn't* alone . . . but he hadn't really expected that she would be. Instead of going upstairs, he hid himself in the small room behind the dining-room that served as his study. There was always work to fill in time, and at least its problems were impersonal ones that he'd had no hand in causing.

He was frowning over a file of papers when she came into the room. Without hearing her he knew she was there because the air was suddenly touched with the faint sweetness of the perfume she always used. He looked up and was struck, as usual, by the lightness and grace that seemed to belong naturally to her. It had something to do with the brightness of her hair, and perfect skin, or perhaps it was simply the way she moved; he could never be sure. He wanted to hold her close and be held, to kiss her and be kissed, but he hesitated too long and the moment when it would have been natural to take her in his arms was lost. She offered him a cool, smooth cheek instead.

'Frank, why didn't you say you were here? I knew you were back in London because a minion arrived from the Ministry with your luggage, but I expected Sir Robert to keep you talking for hours.'

'He's got a report to study before we can talk, and it will take him most of the night. I am dismissed until tomorrow.'

The jaded tone of his voice made her stare more carefully at him. 'For once you look and sound very tired . . . as if you hadn't enjoyed wrestling with problems and setting them to rights.'

'No, I didn't enjoy myself. Unfortunately the problems aren't dealt with that easily, but I won't bore you with the details, my dear – you're obviously entertaining upstairs.'

'Only Biddy Carslake having tea with me. Shall I let you off joining us?'

A gleam of humour lightened Frank's face. 'I think you'd better. *I'm* quite unable to discuss Massine's leaps and bounds in *Petrouschka*, and your Hon. friend can't seem to talk about anything else!'

Lucy's smile was suddenly warm and amused. 'Poor Biddy . . . she does rather run *on* about the Russian Ballet. Still, you could always have your revenge. Try *her* on the economic consequences of the Great War, or expansion versus deflation as a cure for unemployment!'

His burden of weariness eased for a second or two; even to laugh with her was something . . . much better than nothing at all. 'It takes another woman to hit on something so devilishly simple! My dear, shall we go home as soon as I can escape from tomorrow's meeting? Charlie will have forgotten us if we stay away much longer.'

Lucy turned away to fidget with a card on the mantelpiece. 'You mean you can't wait to get back to Birmingham, in case Thornley's haven't been managing well enough without you.'

He walked over to her and laid his hands on her shoulders. 'I mean what I say. It's time we saw our son again. Apart from that, I'm tired to death of cities and travelling and listening to people who only tell me what they want done for them, not what they're prepared to do for themselves.'

'Very well,' she agreed flatly. It sounded ungracious, even to her, and she twisted round to smile at him. 'Of course . . . we'll go as soon as you're ready. Now, though, I must go back to poor Biddy upstairs.'

Frank released her, and she was almost at the door when she remembered something. 'By the way – it's Charlotte's birthday and we're dining with her this evening. Not a party; just Harry and the Brasteads apart from ourselves. You'll be safe from the Ballet!'

'But not from a dissertation on the glories of the Russian Revolution. My dear girl, *must* we go? Desmond Brastead is a fool of an intellectual in love with a Marxist dream,

26

and his wife is still *more* daft. Your cousin Harry, who should know better, encourages them *both* in their lunacy.'

His contempt made her own anger flare. 'It's lunacy to *you*. I'm sorry you find my cousins and my friends so uncongenial, but we *do* have to go; I told Charlotte we'd be there. If you think the evening is going to be wasted, you could redeem it by converting them to *your* point of view.'

'I shouldn't even try . . . they're not open to rational argument.'

'You mean you'd rather despise them in silence and say nothing at all . . . Your usual form, in fact,' she flashed. Even as the words left her mouth she regretted them. A moment ago she'd felt genuinely sorry for his tiredness; now, she was at her usual pointless game of trying to jolt him out of cold self-control, even if it was only to be angry with her.

'I'm sorry you find my usual form uncongenial.' He offered her back the words she had used almost indifferently, and the blankness of his expression seemed to say that he wasn't troubled by her opinion. But she knew it wasn't so; she had an immense and unfair capacity to hurt him.

'I'm . . . I'm sorry, Frank,' she stammered. 'I didn't mean that . . . spoke without thinking.' The light from the window fell on his face, showing her the lines etched into it from nostril to chin, and the flecks of white in his sandy hair. She couldn't remember that he'd ever looked young, but now that he was forty-one he could have been taken for a man ten years older. Pity for him stirred again, but she felt helpless to dismantle the barrier that nowadays seemed to be rearing itself, brick by brick, between them.

'Shall I ask Mrs Knightly to bring you some tea?' she suggested desperately.

'Thank you . . . just what I need.'

She smiled, hearing no irony, and escaped out of the room. Frank stared at the emptiness she'd left behind. He wanted many things, but must be grateful that she'd remembered to offer him tea.

*

27

Charlotte's dinner-party that evening obstinately refused to become a success. Her guests looked prosperous, well-dressed, well-fed; they were typical representatives of their kind, cushioned by class, education, or sufficient wealth against the hardships of post-war life that most people were suffering. The dinner jackets the men wore were generally acceptable now for anything but grand occasions, and more comfortable than formal evening wear. The women's dresses had departed much more profoundly from pre-war fashions, suggesting that some physiological change had occurred in their bodies as well. The voluptuous, corset-induced curves of an Edwardian belle had disappeared into Lucy Thornley's modern kind of beauty.

Her almost boyish slenderness was emphasized by a tunic of dark-blue chiffon, scattered with sequins; it was as lovely as a fragment of starlit sky, Charlotte thought. Beside her, she knew herself to look adequate but ordinary in lavender-coloured silk. Unity Brastead, whose ambition was to look anything but ordinary, had ventured into a peasant blouse and vividly patterned skirt fringed with tiny bells that tinkled when she moved. After one disbelieving glance Frank was careful not to look at her; nor did he appear to notice that his wife's appearance was attracting more of Harry Trentham's attention than social conventions allowed.

Charlotte struggled to keep the conversation afloat on subjects that wouldn't lead them into hostilities. She was accustomed to Frank having little to say, but it was something new for Harry to retreat into an abstracted silence instead of taking his usual dashing charge of the evening. *He* was unlike himself, and Lucy seemed on edge. Unity did her best, and pelted Frank with questions about the dying industries he'd been inspecting in the north, but monosyllabic answers gave her so little encouragement that she finally gave him up and turned to Harry instead.

'Harry dear . . . I'm *longing* to know . . . have you made up your mind? What's the future to be – inheriting the role of Lord of the Manor at Somerton, or doing a real job of work again in the House of Commons?'

She could be relied upon, Charlotte thought, to phrase a question not unreasonable in itself with the maximum lack of tact. She was a well-meaning, foolish woman whom more intelligent members of the Independent Labour Party seemed to have agreed to tolerate. A sprinkling of upper-class disciples like herself helped persuade nervous Liberals that there was nothing dangerous about reformist zeal. She also contributed generously to Party funds, and to shelters for the homeless in London. Remembering it, Charlotte amended her thoughts . . . Unity was a *good* but foolish woman.

'My parents run Somerton,' Harry said, answering her question, 'with the aid of an agent and a small army of estate-workers and servants. They don't need me, and I shall certainly offer myself as a candidate at the next General Election.'

'You mean a *Labour* candidate, Harry?' Lucy asked.

The direct question gave him another excuse to stare at her, and yet again that evening he wondered why it had taken him so long to notice that she was well worth staring at. She was the little cousin who'd grown up in Sybil's shadow, and latterly the indulged wife of a man he didn't like; but he'd been slow to realize that she was beautiful.

'Of course, a Labour candidate . . . what else?' he said, smiling at her. 'I can work for the Socialist cause outside Parliament, but there's a great deal to be done, and I find I want a hand in the running of things!'

For the first time that evening he'd succeeded in making Frank challenge him directly.

'You seem confident of getting power for yourself and the Party you now belong to, but at the moment Labour members are outnumbered in the House by ten to one, and those that *are* there are pigmies compared with a giant like the Prime Minister.'

Charlotte listened, impressed in spite of herself. It wasn't often that Frank Thornley declared himself so openly, with that ring of conviction in his voice.

'Giants and pigmies . . . labels, my dear Frank, attached by men according to where their own interests lie,' Harry said contemptuously. 'Your "giant" is being propped up by a party not his own. For all that he still calls himself a Liberal, Lloyd George wouldn't have survived the last election without the Tories, and he certainly won't survive the next one because even *they* are sick of him. The sooner he goes and takes a corrupt, incompetent Government with him, the better.'

'And then *that* will be our chance,' Desmond Brastead fluted excitedly. 'The old order has had its day, Thornley, whether you like it or not. We shall see a fresh beginning – the common ownership of wealth, State control of national industries, and such peaceful collaboration abroad that war becomes impossible and standing armies unnecessary.'

'The new Jerusalem!' Frank commented dryly. 'I'm sure our enemies would be happy to agree with you. Your peaceful collaboration – which, by the way, I prefer to call pacifism – would have left us yoked to Germany's cart-tail. If that is *your* idea of where this country ought to be, it isn't mine. The shared ownership of wealth has a fine ring to it, but it's nothing but a dangerous myth, incapable of being realized; and State interference in industry can be justified *only* in the extreme conditions of total war.'

He glanced round the table . . . Unity and her husband looked ruffled, Charlotte thoughtful but convinced of the rightness of the Socialist cause, and Harry bright-eyed and belligerent. It was more difficult to complete the circle and look at Lucy. She met his eyes coolly for a moment, then looked away – his wife was another of those present, it seemed, who didn't agree with him. He deliberately stretched out a hand for his wine glass once more.

'Outnumbered, I see. Never mind, I shall toast my giant even if I have to do it alone. Here's to the Welsh Wizard, and to the confusion of all his enemies!'

He replaced the empty glass on the table, smiling with new-found elation. There was nothing like stepping out of character to disconcert people who thought they knew him. Even his wife's startled glance was on *him* once again, and he could see her considering the strange possibility that he might be drunk. Perhaps he was, but drunk or sober he knew what they were all thinking – prick the skin of men like Frank Thornley and what did you find? Not true gentlemen, as they could still be counted even among Socialist members of the upper class, but get-rich-quick johnnies who could never quite be trusted.

'Charlotte dear . . . forgive us if we say good night.' It was Lucy, bravely interrupting the silence that had fallen on the table. 'Frank has been travelling for days, and has to face a meeting with Sir Robert Horne tomorrow morning at the Board of Trade.' She turned to smile brilliantly at Harry. 'When the Labour Party gets into power I hope it manages to govern the country without devouring the private lives of men like Frank who aren't professional politicians!'

'I shall insist on it, if that is what you want,' he said gravely. 'Good night, dear coz.' His blue eyes had the further message for her that he thought she was coping beautifully with her loutish husband's behaviour. She wrenched her gaze away from his, and stood up to go, flushed and faintly smiling. Frank watched the exchange of glances, then got to his feet as well, with an ironic bow for Unity Brastead whom he despised, and a smile for Charlotte, whom he liked very well despite her unaccountable devotion to the Fabian Society.

They drove back to St James's Place in silence, Frank still gripped by the stimulus born of alcohol combined with extreme fatigue, and Lucy struggling with emotions of her own. He shed hat and scarf in the hall, and finally put into words the grievance that had been growing in him during the journey home.

'Why did you drag us away so early? I was beginning to enjoy myself. A few more minutes and that fool of a woman would have been telling me that we must do away with the navy, the monarchy, and the House of Lords – where, incidentally, her august father has occasionally been known to take his seat.'

31

'I preferred *not* to wait until you'd drunk enough wine to make you unbearable. On tonight's showing I would rather have you *not* talking. You don't discuss, or even argue . . . you lay down Thornley's law. Our fellow-guests at a dinner-party are not your unfortunate factory slaves, compelled to touch their caps and agree with everything you say.'

'Thank you for reminding me – it's the kind of nice distinction a Birmingham boor like me is apt to forget.'

For the second time that day she was aware of danger; the rules by which they normally played the game of living together seemed suddenly inadequate to keep them safely on the board. Earlier in the afternoon she'd felt sorry for him; now, pity was the last thing in her mind, and an unmanageable turmoil raged instead. The vague unhappiness of recent months had exploded into a ferment of joy, sadness, hope, and despair that now drove her beyond the limits normally set by natural kindness and caution.

'You forget nothing that you wish to remember,' she insisted breathlessly. 'You *want* people like the Brasteads to know you're different from them . . . you take *pride* in it.'

She turned away to climb the stairs, but the deliberate gesture of withdrawal lit the flame of rage that had been smouldering inside him all the evening. He could see the whiteness of her skin beneath the delicate material of her dress. She was beautiful and desirable, and he wasn't the only man who found her so, but he was the one who possessed her. His hands fastened on her shoulders, forcing her to turn and look at him.

'I intend your friends to know I'm different to *this* extent – I'm not one of the new breed of husbands who doesn't bother to hold on to what he owns.'

'*Owns*! . . . I thought we should come to it, sooner or later.'

The flick of her voice was like a lash against his skin. *If they prick us, do we not bleed?* – even the rough Birmingham-bred war profiteers among us, with no ancient estate to weigh against the good of the Socialist cause? He could feel the softness of her body and smell her delicate perfume. She was the only treasure he wanted in the whole wide world, and instead of loving him her eyes flashed defiance and disgust.

'I didn't expect to have to remind you that we made a bargain. Shall we go to bed, my dear?' He felt her shrink beneath his hands, but even if she'd implored him to leave her alone he was too far launched on this strange, new game of pretending he was someone else. *If you wrong us shall we not revenge?*

She didn't plead with him, because the bargain *had* been made. It had taken courage on their wedding night to accept his body thrust into hers. She must find courage again now, and only weep in her heart for a penance to be endured that should have been an act of mutual joy. Undressing in her room, and shivering with dread, she clung to the faint hope that exhaustion or wine might defeat his intention to make love to her. Tonight of all nights in her life, when she might have lain awake remembering Harry's face when he'd smiled at her . . .

Frank was usually a careful lover, afraid of hurting her. Tonight *that* was different too. Afterwards she stared into the darkness, listening to the sound of his breathing beside her. She felt empty of any emotion at all, but one conviction had taken hold of her mind. Maud Roberts had offered her the comfort of time that would adjust her back to former contentment. *That* was beyond her reach, but she'd discovered for herself something quite different – a boundary between past and future that, once passed, couldn't be recrossed. She and Frank had reached that boundary . . . it was what all the confused misery of recent months had been leading her to. Now, she was a traveller compelled to venture into unknown territory, and part of the dreadful excitement of it was the fact that she must venture into it alone.

Chapter Three

Gertrude Wyndham put away the diary she was frowning over and walked from her own bedroom through the east range of the house to the room known, for reasons long since forgotten, as the Great Parlour. It was William's childhood refuge and, nowadays, his studio. Everywhere else at Providence hot-water pipes, electricity, and modern plumbing had removed the familiar discomforts. She suspected that he would have preferred the rest of his home to remain as he remembered it – draughty, candle-lit, and shabbily beautiful; but at least the improvements had stopped short of the Great Parlour. He still painted there by the daylight that flooded the huge, mullioned window, or not at all, and when the cold numbed his hands he wore the mittens she had knitted for him. In this one room of the house he could forget that Providence, home of the Wyndhams for four hundred years, was no longer theirs.

When she went in William was standing idly at the window, staring out at a landscape whitened by the season's first hard frost. He smiled as she crossed the room towards him and tucked her hand inside his arm. After thirty years of marriage he still felt most at ease when she was somewhere near. He couldn't help suspecting that the other men who had loved her could have given her an easier life; his only certainty was that he had loved her quite as much as they and needed her a great deal more.

'Work not going well?' she asked.

'Nothing started . . . I was doing what old men always do – reliving the past! Forty years ago on a morning like this my father would have been striding up and down commanding Heaven to make the frost disappear because he wanted to go hunting. James and Louise would have been fretting beside him, while their unsporting elder brother hid in here, indifferent to the weather!'

She smiled at memories of her own evoked by his. Of days when she'd been obliged to drop a curtsey if the Squire rode by, of the humiliation caused by Louise Wyndham's pitying stare at her hated black boots and pinafores. It seemed a lifetime ago – her mother a querulous invalid lying on a couch all day, and little Gertrude Hoskins struggling to discover where she belonged among the village children who rejected her and the Wyndhams who pitied her.

Her mind travelled slowly back from the past to the errand that had brought her to the studio. 'I thought you might just have forgotten that Louise and Alec will be arriving after lunch, on their way back to Somerton.'

'Dearest love, I *had* forgotten, exactly as you'd known I would. What do you suppose my sister will feel obliged to take me to task for *this* time . . . not enough, or too many, pictures painted, the vulgar redness of Sid Moffat's new roof, or the deplorable shabbiness of my old smoking jacket?'

'I dare say they may be touched on,' Gertrude conceded. 'All *I* ask is that you are somewhere to be found when Louise and Alec arrive.'

William promised to do his best, and promptly forgot his relatives in trying to decide whether the frosted beauty of the park was capturable on canvas or not. Gertrude selected from the worries in her mind the one that would disturb her husband least.

'We haven't seen Alec and Louise since Harry resigned from Parliament. What *can* they make of it, do you think?'

William's shoulders lifted in a little shrug. 'You know my forthright sister; I expect she tells her son that he's misguided and disloyal. Alec probably understands better.'

'Because he's a man?'

'No, because he was a soldier before he was a politician. Men like Harry who survived the trenches came back

35

hating the ageing, incompetent generals who sent them to be slaughtered. Equally they hate the politicians who were in charge then and are *still* in charge. Harry wants to change the world, not accept an order of things that allowed his wife to be buried under the ruins of a French field hospital.'

William didn't add that the same barbaric world had sent their son back to them a trembling stranger imprisoned in memories from which there was no escape, but Gertrude knew what he was thinking. There were griefs that could scarcely be talked about and Ned was the greatest of theirs. She swung round to put her hands on William's shoulders.

'Dearest, I won't let you doubt that the doctors at Craiglockhart can do something to help Ned. You *must* believe it. They've been miraculously successful with shell-shock cases worse than his.' Her grey eyes, still luminous and beautiful, beseeched her husband to share her conviction, and William found himself praying to God Almighty that *she* might be proved right and he wrong.

'You've got the faith that moves mountains,' he said gently, 'and I'm an ineffectual relic of the world Harry rightly wants to change. I'm a Late-Victorian dinosaur soon to be extinct, and a very good thing too!'

Amusement lit her face, driving away strain. 'I have a particular fondness for dinosaurs, and in any case I refuse to allow an internationally known painter to call himself ineffectual.'

For the second time that morning the past was echoing in her mind again. She could hear the voice of Henri Blanchard insisting that William was a true artist who might become a great one. In those far-off days it had seemed strange enough that Sir William Wyndham should fill his time by painting pictures at all, but the delicate, light-drenched canvases he produced had mystified neighbours accustomed to the work of conventional Victorian artists. Only Blanchard, whose galleries in Paris and London were helping to bring the French Impressionists into fashion, had understood what William was learning to do. Gradually he'd begun to sell the paintings, and the money earned from them had bought back mortgaged Wyndham land, even if it hadn't been enough to redeem Providence itself.

Henri . . . the man who had become a precious friend, and now kept their entranced daughter a stranger to them in Paris. Gertrude jerked her mind away from the thought of him, bidding it fasten itself on *anything* but that . . . look instead at the dogwoods Ned had planted by the moat bridge below the window where she stood. He'd promised her that when the bare stems turned crimson in winter they would look especially beautiful against the silver water, and he was never wrong about such things. Even when he'd first come out of hospital he'd been able to remember that his joy lay in working for Providence. They had owed his slow recovery there to Frank, who'd simply left him free to do whatever he chose. Dear, difficult Frank . . . Gertrude often prayed that her daughter had learned to love an admirable man who didn't make it easy for others to approach him.

William's voice interrupted her tangled thoughts again, and his beautiful thin hand gestured to the frosty view outside.

'Your father is predicting a harsh winter – snow before Christmas. I rather hope he's right. I still haven't mastered the most difficult trick of all – painting white on white; but I like to think it's because there's usually a lack of whiteness to practise on!'

'Then you may have snow,' she agreed generously. 'I'm not in favour of it otherwise. Now, I must stop dawdling here and go down to the Rectory. Maud is away, and without her Hubert will have forgotten that he's to address the schoolchildren on the anniversary of the Armistice.'

'Well, I hope he can expunge from his mind Woodrow Wilson's confident forecast at the end of the war that we were entering "if not perhaps the golden age, an age which is at least brightening from decade to decade"! In the two years that have elapsed since then we've managed to unveil a memorial to the dead in Whitehall, and to de-ration sugar. Do you think Hubert will be able to tell the children that we're rushing towards a golden age?'

'We've done a little more than that,' Gertrude pointed out. 'The peace treaty finally got signed, and the League of Nations now exists – two *important* things accomplished for the future of the world.' But her husband's expression remained so unconvinced that she was obliged to go on. 'Don't you have faith in the League . . . or are you worried about all the talk of a revolution *here*? Father says Lord Northcliffe's wretched rag speaks of nothing else.'

This time William was positive. 'My dear, forget the Bolshevik bogeys drawn out of thin air by the *Daily Mail*. Of course agitators are ready and willing to stir up all the strife they can, and it's sadly true that there are people suffering bitter hardship, but we're conditioned by the past eight hundred years into letting our changes come temperately, not red and reeking with the blood of destruction.'

From a husband temperamentally inclined to pessimism, Gertrude thought it sounded almost confident. She smiled lovingly at him and promised to inform Hubert Roberts that he could offer the children at least a little hope for the future. Then her face sobered again at the recollection of a more immediate duty. 'Lucy and Frank aren't back from London, so I must pay a visit to the nursery. Do you suppose our grandson might have grown a *little* less wilful overnight? Whenever I let myself get depressed it occurs to me that he's the image of his paternal grandfather!'

William's rare laughter echoed in the bare spaces of the room. 'My dear . . . remember what Mama always used to say – "there's a great deal of good in Arthur Thornley"!'

'Of course there is,' Gertrude agreed readily, 'as a matter of fact, I've even grown fond of him in an odd kind of way! All the same, it would be easier to deal with Charles if he took after sweet-natured Jane just a little; easier still if he occasionally reminded me of Lucy. Even for a two-year-old, he has an unnatural will of iron.'

'I don't think we should blame it all on Arthur,' William

suggested with careful impartiality. 'Think of the stubborn Wyndhams – my father and Louise, to name but two!'

Gertrude went away, still smiling, along the corridor that ran round the three sides of the house. Halfway along it she stopped to look down into the courtyard garden lying within the two parallel wings that Providence held out to the world like welcoming arms. Once upon a time there had been a fourth side completing the quadrangle, but for a century or two it had been open, and the garden there had faced the moat. Old Biddle was outside, teaching his lad how to trim the small dark sentinel yews that bordered the paths. The beds in between would already have been planted with bulbs to produce a springtime flowering of white, blue, and gold – the colours in the Wyndham coat-of-arms. In common with every villager at Haywood's End, Biddle knew with his mind that the Squire no longer owned Providence; but money, mortgages, and banks made no impression on his stubborn heart. Spring-time and summer, back through all the years of his remembering, the Wyndham colours had filled the garden in the courtyard; he reckoned to see to it that they would do so even after he was dead. He wasn't minded to be carried to the churchyard yet, but before he went he'd make sure the new lad knew what was what in the matter of the mistress's special garden.

Gertrude watched the two of them down below considering a wayward branch of yew, but she saw in her mind's eye a different pair – Biddle less stooped than he was now, and a small boy whose greatest joy had been in 'helpin' Bi'll'. Not all the years of growing up, nor bloody war and mental hurt, had been enough to destroy Ned's passionate delight in growing things according to his own dream of beauty. Charlie, Frank's son, would inherit Providence now, but Gertrude had come to understand that whether Wyndham or Thornley owned it simply didn't matter; only its continuance mattered – not for what it contained, or because it was beautiful, or even because it was part of England's story. Its special, precious value lay in the fact that, time and again, it had been a place of refuge. For a couple of years past it had been *that* to Ned, but in times to come there might be someone else who would need it just as badly.

She went on along the corridor and turned into the chapel room, where William's mother had long ago taught her to bring whatever fears assailed her. It was the place above all others in the house to pray for Ned while he was away. Providence had made bearable the distress that still lay trapped inside his head, but she asked God to hear her in the sweet silence of the room, and let him come home from Craiglockhart finally mended.

It was mid-afternoon before Alec Trentham's motor-car emerged from the tree-shadowed dimness of the drive on to the gravel forecourt beside the moat. Watching for it, Hodges reckoned it a poor thing compared with arrivals he remembered in the past, when carriages and horses had swept, jingling and snorting, into the stable yard. In those days, with a dozen hunters and riding-horses in his care, he'd been an important man, all-powerful in his kingdom in the yard. Now, he was supposed to be retired, but he still lived above the stables in the only home he'd ever known. His one remaining 'lad', Daft Artie grown to middle age, tended the ponies kept for hacking about the estate, but that didn't stop Hodges whispering in their ears of the glories of days past.

It wouldn't have occurred to him not to be outside with Artie when the Trenthams arrived. Almost half a century ago he'd taught Miss Louise to ride, and in all the years since then it had been *his* job to be the first to welcome her whenever she returned to Providence. Headstrong piece she'd been, he remembered, and a neck-or-nothing rider, just like old Squire, her father.

Seeing him there on a cold afternoon, another woman might have told him kindly that he should have stayed indoors, but it wasn't a mistake Louise Trentham would have dreamed of making.

'You're looking well, Hodges,' she said instead, in the

decided voice that never encouraged argument. It had sounded just the same when she was eight years old . . . 'I can do it by *myself*, thank you . . . you may take the leading-rein *away*!' He smiled at the memory and she suddenly smiled with him – a proud, privileged lady and an old servant who understood one another. As soon as she'd nodded goodbye and walked across the bridge, he gave Artie an unnecessary instruction to help his lordship, and then stumped away. Honour had been satisfied, and now he could get back to his snug parlour upstairs.

William took his brother-in-law off for the ritual inspection which one landowner always seemed obliged to offer another, and Gertrude installed her guest by the fire in the Great Hall. The name had clung over centuries, suggesting size and armorial splendour. It was true that generations of Wyndham coats-of-arms and quarterings were blazoned in the windows, throwing down shafts of coloured light; it was true that a single huge tapestry glowed on a side wall but, even so, grace, not grandeur, was the key-note of the room.

'You don't come often enough,' Gertrude told Louise Trentham.

The same thing would have been difficult to say in the early years of her marriage. William's duty had been to find himself a rich wife – perhaps an American or, failing that, the daughter of an English manufacturer who might have to be admitted to the ranks of the gentry. Always out of step with expectation, he'd chosen instead the daughter of the Wyndhams' governess and the estate land-agent. Louise, five years older than her sister-in-law, had had no doubt about the other gaps that separated them. In adolescence she'd stared pityingly down from her horse as Gertrude plodded to the village school. Much later, in India with her husband she'd received, but scarcely believed, the news that her brother could find no more suitable a wife than George Hoskins' daughter. Time, and troubles survived together, had gradually brought mutual respect and finally true liking. It was long since Louise had needed convincing that her elder brother had done unexpectedly well for himself after all.

'Did you enjoy London . . . discover that you regretted no longer living at the centre of things?' Gertrude enquired.

'I regretted nothing, except the brashness of a city that used to be dignified.' As usual, Louise sounded firmly positive, but she went on to make a surprising admission. 'I was also made to feel like a country dowd . . . completely passée!'

'I don't believe it. You're always elegance personified.'

'Wrong, my dear Gertrude. My hair was uncropped, my skirts too long, and my mouth and nails unpainted. I was clearly an unemancipated woman, but I made the final mistake of dining out at a restaurant with my *own* husband!'

'Well, being a good deal more dowdy than you, I shall take care to remain here, vegetating happily!' Gertrude busied herself with the ritual of pouring tea, unaware that she was being inspected with her sister-in-law's usual thoroughness.

'You're looking hagged. Worrying about Ned, I suppose?'

'Yes, though I try not to look as if I am. We shall be so thankful to have him home. It's a strain at the moment, not knowing what's happening. William feels it especially.'

In his sister's view, William felt everything to be a strain. Her patience with him frequently wore thin, but for once she managed not to say so. Nor did she even hint at an anxiety of her own – that Ned might return from Craiglockhart *more* disturbed than when he went there. Three peaceful years at Providence had helped, even if they hadn't cured him. She had no faith in a remedy that forced him to confront the horrors hidden in his mind.

'We must believe that Harry's right,' Gertrude pointed out gently, correctly guessing what Louise hadn't said. 'Ned can only be freed from his nightmares by being made to look at the cause of them.' She saw her sister-in-law's expression change, and added after a moment, 'Are you thinking that Harry needs healing too?'

Louise stared at the glowing heart of the fire, seeing there a vision of the carefree professional soldier who had been her son. Women had been easily charmed by him, but men had loved him as well for his gaiety and kindness. His regiment had been among the first to go to France; four years later he had come home a different man.

'It's three years since Emily was killed,' Louise said slowly. 'I don't say it to Alec, but I'm becoming more and more afraid that Harry will never marry again.'

'Afraid for him, or for Somerton?'

'What does Somerton matter now, since it means nothing to him? I don't say *that* out loud either, but Alec knows it as well as I do.' Her voice, usually so brisk and firm, trembled with the pain that must be kept hidden from her husband. 'We shall never be rid of the effects of that damnable war.'

Gertrude would have given comfort if she could, but what was there to say about the embittered stranger Harry had now become?

'Sometimes I scarcely recognize *either* of my children,' Louise went on bleakly. 'Charlotte has been infected with Harry's ideas . . . calls herself a Fabian, if you please, and sits at the feet of that extraordinary creature, Beatrice Webb! Harry's chosen companions are grubby, wild-eyed agitators looking for the quickest means of sweeping away every tradition he spent four blood-soaked years fighting to preserve.' A wintry smile touched her mouth for a moment. 'You realize, I hope, that the first of their ambitions is to sweep away people like us?'

'I know . . . up with the red, new dawn, and down with the monarchy and especially the upper classes. William says it's like the tale told by the idiot, "full of sound and fury, signifying nothing", because the English are just not revolution-prone. We shall have to hope he's right. All the same, there are thousands of people without homes or work. If *that* injustice is what Harry wants to fight, how can any of us blame him?'

'I *don't* blame him; I merely ask him to leave the running of the country to its elected Government, and if

43

he'd stayed as Somerton's representative, he might have become part of it.' She lapsed into silence, but roused herself after a moment to talk of something else. 'We caught a glimpse of Lucy in London, with Charlotte . . . looking very pretty and, unlike me, obviously feeling quite at home. Marriage seems to have changed my country-loving niece.'

'Marriage to *Frank* has changed her,' Gertrude agreed. 'A country-loving husband might not have done. He got to know David Lloyd George well during the war, at his munitions committee meetings, and their respect for one another seems to have lasted. Frank insists that he only collaborates because the Government must hear the views of the industrialists, but I suspect him of also enjoying being close to the seat of power!'

Louise nodded, but abandoned the subject of a man she'd never been able to like. 'Does Jane still organize those sewing women of hers at Bicton?'

'Of course! Hand once set to plough, my dear friend doesn't falter, but the women are no longer taken to Bicton. When the house was turned into a military convalescent home during the war Jane persuaded Arthur to set up a small factory for them in Birmingham. The women seem to prefer to work close to home.'

'How do you "persuade" the Arthur Thornleys of this world? I should have thought brute force was the only argument.'

Gertrude smiled but shook her head. 'He's putty in Jane's hands. Even if he weren't, the success of the business would have convinced him. Arthur sees it as his duty to encourage anything that makes money, and Frank has inherited exactly the same philosophy.' She listened to what she'd just said and disliked the sound of it. 'Sorry . . . I didn't mean to seem so much holier than they! Heaven knows we have reason to be thankful for Thornley money.'

'Let us be thankful, but *not* hypocritical,' Louise suggested, having now regained her usual crispness. 'Jane Thornley seems to have succeeded in learning to love her

44

husband, but the rest of us, thank God, don't even have to try. No doubt Lucy's father-in-law is a genius in his way; he's also a thrusting, vulgar townee, whose factories made him rich enough to buy an estate and turn himself into something that passes for a country gentleman.'

'No, Louise,' Gertrude said firmly. 'Arthur Thornley remains himself, *not* an unsuccessful imitation of someone else. He has never mentioned it, but Jane told me that he'd refused a knighthood simply because he wouldn't pretend to be something he is *not*. I'll grant you that it's hard not to wince at times, but for all that he's a true patriot, and an immensely generous man to a dozen worthy causes.'

She was still feeling surprised at the warmth of her own defence when the door opened and William and Alec Trentham walked in. They brought with them a rush of cold air, and the glow of satisfaction which hangs about men when they have just completed some futile masculine exercise. Time was when Louise might have told them so, but not now; she had married thirty-five years ago because it was expected of her and she'd grown bored with being the Squire's unmarried daughter. She had chosen Alec Trentham because he was suitable, and believed that he had chosen her for the same reason. But life is often perverse and against all probability a cool woman and a shy man had gradually come to love each other. Now, her only desire was to lessen any hurt that life might do to him.

She smiled as he walked towards her, but what she said was, 'I hope you told William that Sid Moffat's new roof at the Home Farm looks simply dreadful!'

Chapter Four

When dinner was over that evening and the four of them were drinking coffee round the fire, Louise switched the conversation to a member of the family they hadn't seen for years. She frowned slightly because whenever she thought about her younger brother she always felt irritated, as she did now, that he'd managed to live in America so successfully without the rest of them.

'William, have you heard recently from James?'

'We don't regularly correspond. After all these years I can't imagine that his interest in *my* affairs is any more keen than mine in his! I hope his railways and shipping-lines still flourish, but I don't want to be kept informed about them. We exchange brotherly greetings occasionally and that's about all.'

Louise showed no surprise. Her brothers hadn't been friends even as children, and she could see no reason why a gap of forty years and three thousand miles should have done anything to improve things. Gertrude heard in her husband's voice the expected note of dryness which always sounded when he spoke of James, but her inward ear was distracted by the echo of other conversations that could still be made to sound across the years . . . young James Wyndham of the red-gold beard and laughing eyes, saying goodbye to a dazzled adolescent and telling her to take care of Providence for him; an older, more disturbing James coming back unexpectedly from New York to entice her into madness when she was already married to William. Strictly speaking, she hadn't been a wife when she and James spent their one night together, because William hadn't by then felt brave enough or passionate enough to share her bed – that had only come afterwards.

There was only one other conversation to remember, some years later still; by then James's American wife was dead and, once more at Providence, he'd begged Gertrude to abandon William and go to New York with him. She had refused, and James had never visited them again. The joy of the night they'd spent together was now simply a thread, brighter than most, in the pattern life had woven for her, but the memory of the moment when she'd refused him remained much sharper. It was almost the only time she would have chosen *not* to go on living. The pity of it was that memory was arranged thus . . . much better at preserving pain than gladness.

She was unaware of having missed any of the conversation until the name of James's son was mentioned.

'Patrick's still in Dublin, apparently,' Alec was saying, making no effort to hide his disapproval. 'Eamon de Valera's visit to New York after he escaped from Lincoln Gaol certainly paid dividends. The Republicans have the fervent support of the Irish-American Association, Clan na Gael. God knows what James makes of a son wedded to the cause of Irish independence at *any* price, violence and bloodshed included.' He stopped abruptly, remembering that his own son now disowned loyalties that had always been part of the Trentham tradition.

'Shouldn't we remember that Ireland is another victim of the war?' William suggested quietly. 'But for that, the Home Rule Bill would have been passed years ago and this tragedy could have been avoided.'

'I doubt it. The Republicans in the south aren't interested in compromise. They want *one* independent Ireland,' Alec objected. 'That's more than any British Government could concede, for reasons of military security alone; but even if that weren't so, it doesn't help . . . the people in Ulster reject any kind of independence that ties them to the south. The problem seems to have become almost insoluble.'

Alec was still sufficiently fascinated by politics, and William by history, for the two of them to go on talking principles all night, but Gertrude found herself thinking about Patrick Wyndham, the nephew who had come only once to Providence. As far as she knew, he and his sister had never been told the truth about her own complicated relationship with them. It was old history now, almost forgotten by the few people who had ever known that James's wife, Kitty Maguire, and Gertrude had been half-sisters. On a long-ago visit to Providence, their father – Daniel Maguire – had seduced the Wyndhams' governess and given her a child. George Hoskins, the Squire's land-agent, had married the governess and given his name to the daughter who was born to her. Even after she learned the truth, Gertrude had never ceased to think of George Hoskins as her father; but she still felt guilty that she hadn't been able to like her half-sister's son when he came to Providence.

'Do you suppose there's any chance of Patrick wanting to come here from Dublin?' she asked suddenly. 'I suppose not, if he's so very pro-Irish.'

William smiled at her. 'My love, what you obviously mean but are being so careful not to say, is that you *hope* he won't come! So do I. There are any number of old men here – your father for one – who would be outraged by his views, and have no hesitation in saying so.'

'Well, even if Patrick doesn't come to England, his sister wants to.' Louise made the startling announcement, then added what little else she knew. 'Anita wrote to Charlotte recently. She's planning a visit to Paris in the spring, but suggested coming to London afterwards.'

A silence fell on the people grouped around the fire. The past was never dead, even when time seemed to have given it a decent burial. The present moment was linked across all the intervening years of pain and bloodshed with a sunlit summer when no-one had dreamed of war, and the supremacy of the British Empire looked set to last for ever. While Patrick left them to study architecture in Paris, Anita had stayed behind at Providence, to fall in love with England and Ned Wyndham.

'We can't have Anita here,' Gertrude said too loudly for the quietness of the room. 'Ned has never mentioned her . . . perhaps doesn't even remember . . .'

There wasn't a great deal *to* remember. She had watched the frail, summer-time romance, knowing what Ned had known: that he must get a little older, and Providence a little less desperately poor, before he could ask his American cousin to marry him. Anita had gone home to wait. It wasn't in her mind to wait for very long – Ned couldn't help but get older, and it didn't matter to her that Providence would never be rich. But then the war had come and nothing had been the same again.

'Patrick didn't volunteer to fight . . . how do we know what Anita felt about the war?' Gertrude asked more quietly. '*She* may have learned to hate us as well by now. It's eight years ago, William . . . too long. I *won't* have Ned upset again just when we hope . . .' she had to stop because sudden tears were clogging her throat, making words impossible. There was already so much to be anxious about that Anita Wyndham seemed the final straw.

Louise stepped in to rescue her. 'Don't worry – there's no need for a visit here. She can stay in Thurloe Square, or Charlotte can bring her to Somerton.'

William fingered his beard, and Gertrude knew what was coming. Her husband rarely asserted himself, but when he did she was obliged to listen. 'If Anita *had* learned to hate us, she wouldn't want to come. So shall we wait and see, my dear? Everything depends on Ned, but if she is going to be in England I doubt if we have the right to hide the knowledge from him.'

Gertrude wanted to beg, beseech, and scream that right or wrong were meaningless words in the heart-breaking struggle for Ned's peace of mind. But the protest refused to make itself heard. A memory had come back to her of Ned at Providence just after he'd been released from the military hospital. He was still tense, and liable to be made frantic by any sudden noise, or even a voice that sounded too loud. She had asked her son-in-law never to refer to the war in front of him, but Frank had refused. He'd said that Ned himself must be allowed to test the limits of what he could bear. It had been true then, and she knew that it was true now.

She looked at William and tried to smile. 'Very well. We'll wait and see.' It seemed to sum up what was constantly required of her, stifling her with the sense of her own helplessness. She must wait and see if Ned could cope with life, if Sybil remembered they were still alive, and Lucy managed to find contentment again. Only in the matter of her own troubled memories need she not be helpless. *They* must be hidden in the furthest reaches of her mind and left to die of inattention.

The Trenthams left the following morning for their home in Gloucestershire, and a week later Ned walked across the forecourt at Providence five days before the date Gertrude had circled on the calendar. She was in the dining-room darning a worn place in the curtains when she looked out and saw old Biddle break into a painful run. Alarmed that something was wrong, she put down her needle and hurried outside. She swung open the great door and stepped on to the bridge in time to see a young man with his arms round Biddle's heaving shoulders.

'You stupid silly *dear* old man,' she heard Ned say. 'What do you mean by thinking you can gallop about like a two-year-old!'

'I gallop if I feels inclined . . . if not, I goes very slow, see?' Biddle pointed out with great dignity and only a little breathlessness. A singularly sweet smile lit his face but he did his best to sound severe. ''Bout time you were home . . . now p'raps we can get on.' He caught a glimpse of his mistress waiting behind Ned, smiled at her, and happily limped away towards the glass-houses where there was work waiting to be done. Gertrude walked forward, and a moment later was caught in the bear-hug of her son's arms.

'You bad one . . . why didn't we *know* you were coming?' She smiled through the tears trickling down her cheeks and tried to sound severe. 'Biddle might have died of joy a moment ago, and now so might I! Dearest, how did you even get here?'

'Cadged a lift . . . someone was bound to be coming this way, but I bumped into Hubert Roberts on Warwick station.' It was typical of her, he thought, that she didn't instantly demand to be told how he was, was he cured, ought he to be there? The only important thing was to know that he was home. For the very reason that she never drowned confidences in a waterfall of inappropriate questions, he could always talk to her.

'Your father will be so glad . . . and as for Grandpa Hoskins – he's eaten enough to keep a bird alive and pretended it was because Emmy cooked nothing he liked. *That* was particularly unkind when she tried to tempt his appetite with the *choicest* morsels! Dear Ned . . . welcome home . . . or have I said that six times already?'

'No, but I wouldn't mind even if you had.' His blue eyes under ruffled brown hair smiled lovingly at her. 'If you'll be good enough to take my arm, your ladyship, I'll be happy to conduct you inside!'

She let him go alone to his grandfather's room, and it wasn't until William was back and they were lingering over the dinner-table that Ned began to describe his stay at Craiglockhart.

'The doctors there were quite different from the other ones I remember,' he said finally. 'The army medicos seemed to believe we could be better if we stopped thinking about ourselves and *tried*; up there we were told to stop trying and start thinking! It was terribly hard to know where to begin, but they seemed to know which questions to ask.'

'No more nightmares now, dearest?' Gertrude asked diffidently.

'Less and less often, and I think eventually they'll stop altogether. But it doesn't matter now, because I know how to cope . . . even with the worst of them.' He stared at his parents across the candle-lit table. 'The worst one was always the same. My platoon sergeant, Tom Haskell, was ordered to be shot for cowardice because in the end he simply couldn't obey one more order to go over the top. He was the best and bravest of men, but something just broke in him. After the push was over I went a bit mad . . . shouted at everyone I could find that he needed help, but it didn't make any difference; he was shot all the same . . . as an example, you see.'

'Yes, I see,' Gertrude whispered, with her eyes full of sudden tears.

'For a long time I refused to remember . . . managed to blank it out completely, I thought. But it lay festering in my subconscious, apparently, and erupting into those terrible nightmares. Now, I understand the logic of what happened to Tom, even though I still can't condone it. Fear in those conditions is a terribly contagious thing.'

William watched his son's face, aware that people of his own generation would never be able to comprehend the horror of a war they hadn't taken part in. Gertrude watched Ned's hands and saw that for the first time in three years they were perfectly steady.

He smiled at her, knowing what she was thinking. 'Now I'm going to do what I should have thought of doing a long time ago . . . get in touch with Tom's family. There may be something I can do to help them.'

He helped himself to more coffee, then suddenly grinned again. 'Full of self-importance and resolution as I now am, Mama, there's another thing! I got a letter from Harry about Patrick being in Dublin, but it also mentioned a visit from Anita.'

'Your Aunt Louise mentioned it as well,' Gertrude admitted. 'Left to myself, I doubt if I should have told you, but Papa insisted that you would have to know.'

'Then I'm sure he also insisted that she must be invited here,' Ned said, now looking for confirmation at his father. There were times, she thought helplessly, when they were much alike – quietly, gently certain that what they knew to be right *was* right. She loved Ned so much that she would be capable of killing anyone who ever hurt him again, but she must now agree, as smilingly as she could manage, that Anita should come to Providence.

'All right, my dearest. But full of resolution as you are, please promise me one thing. Remember that Patrick's

Irish-American wife seems to have taught him to hate the English. Anita might have learned to hate us, too.'

'We shall have to wait and see . . . although we're not so *very* dislikable are we?' His eyes were smiling again, telling her that there was no need to worry. 'Hard on Uncle James, wouldn't it be, if *both* his children had taken against the land of their ancestors!'

Gertrude would have said that, with Ned home and healed, nothing could disturb her again, but she reckoned without the telegram which arrived for William one morning. Heaven's grace provided for her the one afternoon visitor with whom she could have discussed it, and Maud Roberts was almost immediately aware that her friend's mind was not on the burning question of the annual nativity play.

'Shall we invite local mayhem by deciding to let Daisy Martin's daughter play the Virgin Mary *again*, or would you rather tell me what else is disturbing you,' she suggested calmly.

'Dear Maud, could Daisy's daughter wait a moment? The most unexpected thing you could think of has happened. William heard from Henri Blanchard this morning . . . he's coming to London, wants to visit us next week.'

'With Sybil, do you mean?'

'No, he'll be alone. *She* still doesn't want to see us, it seems. I could almost hate my daughter, and I certainly *can* hate Henri, for the hurt they do to William.'

'How did William reply?'

'As you'd expect – telegraphed back that Henri must come, of course . . . *toujours la politesse*, you see. William would courteously thank the executioner who was about to cut off his head!' Maud was careful not to smile because her friend looked so fierce, and after a moment Gertrude spoke again. 'I can't think *why* Henri should choose to come after all this time, nor what we shall find to say when he gets here.' She was ashamed of the tell-tale panic in her voice, and grimaced at the sight of her hands clenched desperately in her lap. 'So much for the myth that self-control comes with age! My grandson must have more of me in him than I supposed. There's no need to tell me how ridiculous I'm being. Henri will talk to William about his paintings; we shall ask about the daughter we haven't seen for three years; and after breakfast the following morning Henri will thank us politely and return to London . . . end of visit . . . end of all this *absurd* commotion.'

Maud had watched with affection and pride the journey that Gertrude had made – from being the little Hoskins child, persecuted by the village children because she didn't belong, to the serenely beautiful and brave woman who shared William Wyndham's life. There had been more costs along the way than William was aware of, and Maud knew that *one* of them still complicated Gertrude's relationship with her elder daughter. She knew it, but chose not to mention it, because there were privacies that even an old friend wasn't privileged to invade.

'My dear girl, the commotion isn't exactly absurd, but perhaps it isn't necessary,' she suggested quietly. 'You and William have been made unhappy about the ruin Sybil might be making of her life, but she isn't *obliged* to find her happiness in a way that makes her parents happy! Has my dear but difficult god-daughter ever done what was expected of her if it didn't happen to coincide with what *she* wanted?'

'Not that I can recall!'

'Nor I, but it hasn't stopped us loving her, or brought her to much harm. William's friendship with Henri *has* suffered, but perhaps this visit will help to mend that as well.'

A tremulous smile touched Gertrude's face, wiping away anxiety. 'The voice of sweet reason, as usual! Dear Maud, promise me that we can die together, because I shall never be able to manage without you!'

'You might have to, seeing that I am somewhat past my prime. In any case, it's nonsense because you manage better on your own than anyone else I know.'

It was true that Miss Roberts had just celebrated her

sixty-fifth birthday but to Gertrude, at least, the passing years seemed to make no difference to her friend. Maud's attraction was of a kind that didn't wear away with age; it made intelligence, humour, and compassion for the idiocies of mankind seem much more desirable than conventional beauty.

'I'm in a state of agitation all round, as a matter of fact,' Gertrude wasn't surprised to hear herself confessing. 'It seems to me life's like the game of hopscotch the children play in the schoolyard. One moment you're safely in a square, thinking that all you ask is to be allowed to stay there. But it's no good; there's someone waiting behind you, the pebble must be thrown again, and off you have to hop!'

'Who else, apart from Henri and Sybil, are forcing you to hop away from safety at the moment, may I ask?'

'Lucy troubles me, but won't let me help. Anita Wyndham is going to come, and that will probably disturb Ned again. She will bring with her memories of James and, with Henri coming as well, that will be two skeletons rattling in my *own* cupboard! Whatever Hubert claims for the comforts of religion, there's no denying the fact that life's a very dangerous business!'

'My dear, he has more sense than to disagree with you,' conceded Maud.

Chapter Five

Ned's working day usually began with an early-morning visit to Sid Moffat at the Home Farm. With livestock to look after, Sid was always up and about hours before townsmen thought of crawling out of bed, and after a chat with him in sheds full of contentedly snuffling beasts there was still time before breakfast back at Providence to call on Grandpa Hoskins and share the pot of tea Ethel always brought him.

It seemed to Ned that his grandfather had seen the wheel of fortune turn a complete circle for men who worked the land. After the boom years when Victoria had first come to the throne, a decline spread over nearly half a century had set in. Then had come the war, and farmers were important again. German submarines sank a devastating tonnage of merchant shipping and, faced with the possible starvation of its population, the Government recollected that farmers grew *food*! They might even be able to influence the outcome of the war. Encouragement in the form of subsidies was given; land left idle for years was reclaimed so that it could produce wheat again, and farmers produced the food that was required of them. They were desperately short of skilled men, but allowed a motley collection of helpers – old men, boys, unskilled women, and even German prisoners of war, who had to be taught the difference between a sword and a plough-share.

Farmers prospered as they deserved to during the war. Now, three years into peace, the Government was ready to forget them again, and imported wheat and frozen meat were once more swamping the home market.

'Moffat says Andy Blake is giving up,' Ned reported to his grandfather. 'When the Endicotts sold the Grange estate he took out a bank mortgage to buy his land . . . Now, with prices falling all the time, he can't find enough money for the repayments.'

'And thousands like him,' George Hoskins muttered. 'Blake's a good tenant-farmer, but he had no business to go trying to turn himself into a gentleman or a land-owner.' It was the stubbornly held conviction of a man who reckoned that the framework holding England together throughout the old Queen's long reign had been the right one. People had known where they belonged then; now, war and the mirage of the wealth that was supposed to pave the streets of hellish cities had come to unsettle them.

'You mustn't blame Andy Blake,' Ned said gently. 'He expected to have two sons to help him. One of them didn't come back from France, and the other one listened to too many stories told by Canadian soldiers . . . he's emigrating to Manitoba.'

George met his grandson's eye and smiled ruefully. 'All right . . . You put me in mind of your grandmother just then. Even after fifty years I can remember her being just like that – quiet but firm – correcting your Uncle James!'

Ned had heard that sort of remark before, but he didn't mind listening again, in fact rather liked the idea that they all, generation after generation, handed down to each other family habits and quirks that were immediately recognizable.

'Gramps . . . the Blake farm adjoins our western boundary; I'm going to ask Father if we can make a bid for it . . . Perhaps develop it for more market-gardening. It would do nicely for Sid Moffat's grandson, and he'll be wanting to strike out on his own in a few years' time.'

George examined the idea and finally gave an approving nod. 'So he will. I don't see *him* standing on the same spot for eight hours a day in a factory in Birmingham.'

He stared at Ned's quiet face, and thanked his Maker for a miracle. They'd expected too much originally . . . couldn't wait for the boy to grow up and save Providence for them. Now, it seemed miracle enough that he was there at all, alive when millions weren't, and at peace with himself again.

'Mama's a bit agitated,' Ned reported next. 'Seems we're to have a visit from Henri Blanchard, but not from Sybil. It's queer to think I haven't seen her for more than three years. I cadged a lift to the hospital when we were having a week's rest and scarcely recognized her. Her hair had been cut as short as a boy's and she looked tired and thin. But she was the same girl after all – funny and sharp and sweet, all mixed up together. I don't suppose living with Father's friend will have changed that, do you?'

'Doubt it, lad . . . seems to me people just get more of what they were to begin with. I dare say the maid'll be lonely on her own if Mr Blanchard's coming here.'

'Yes . . . she might, at that,' Ned agreed slowly. He smiled at his grandfather, but went away without referring to the idea that had just crept into his mind.

When he announced casually at the breakfast-table that he thought of going to France for a few days, his mother looked startled but managed to say, 'A little holiday, Ned, before you start working too hard again? What a good idea.'

'If you say France, I hope you mean Paris, my favourite city,' William put in shyly. 'When I was a young man I used to dream of living there – something paintable on every street corner, and exclusively inhabited, I liked to think, by artists who knew more about painting than I did!'

'I can't imagine you anywhere but here,' Ned said, smiling at the idea.

'Nor I, truthfully, but there was a slightly shameful pleasure in the idea of escaping from ancient traditions that governed everything we did and an ancient house prone to every ill, from rising damp in the cellars to death-watch beetle in the roof. I've got pretty well used to the traditions with the help of your dear mother!'

Gertrude shook her head. 'You mean you put up with harvest-home suppers, and Christmas parties for the estate children, and endure the unavoidable dinners with all your worthy neighbours who look blank when you mention a genius called Vincent Van Gogh!'

She didn't mention Ned's holiday again until she was alone with her husband. 'I don't believe it *is* a good idea, William . . . a lonely journey in November to the one place on earth you'd think Ned would want to avoid. Can you tell me why one's children have to be so strangely perverse?'

He had to admit that he could not, but made a suggestion of his own. 'Perhaps it's part of the cure. The doctors may even have recommended it – a trial of strength, you might say.'

'I shouldn't dream of saying anything so silly,' Gertrude insisted tartly. 'It's the kind of unnecessary ordeal that only *men* could confuse with bravery.' She saw William smile and guessed why he did so. 'I know what you're going to say – the female point of view in such matters is always suspect, and usually wrong!'

He leaned over and kissed her by way of answer. 'What I was actually going to say was that the time has come for you to stop worrying about Ned, and also that I love you very much, my dear one.'

'Comfort all round . . . what more could a woman ask!'

There were few preparations to be made for a brief trip abroad, and the most important of them was a ride round the estate to check that nothing was amiss with fences and farm buildings. On his way home Ned overtook Lucy, walking her own horse back to the stables. He hadn't seen her since he got back from Craiglockhart, and realized suddenly how very seldom he *did* see her nowadays.

'Why, if it isn't brother Ned returned to the fold,' she said brightly. 'Did you get tired of being in the nasty hospital and just decide to come home?'

'I decided that I'd been cured by the *nice* people and came home. How are *you*, and what's wrong with Polly here?'

'She has just had the pleasure of refusing a hedge and

chucking me off, so both of us are at less than our shining best.'

Ned dismounted, to run his hands over the horse. 'I don't wonder she refused. For one thing she's too old to jump, and for another she's walking lame. My dear good girl, what on earth were you *thinking* of?'

He sounded sharply severe for once, but when Lucy didn't answer he turned to stare at her and then spoke in a different tone of voice. '*You* all right, sis?'

'Undamaged except for where it hurts most – in my poor little pride!' She was the Lucy of recent months, bright and brittle as glass; but he was close enough to see the traces of tears on her face. Time was when she'd have told him what troubled her, but now they were bedevilled by much more than the fact that they were supposed to be grown up and able to manage on their own.

'Don't see much of you these days,' he said gently. 'It must be such a rotten bore having to keep going to London with Frank.'

'Dear Ned, will you be *very* shocked if I say that it's village life that is the bore? Same old pattern year in, year out: church fête, harvest festival, Bonfire Night, and the nativity play as the crowning excitement of the year. Deadly, if you ask me.'

'You didn't always think so.'

'No, but I'm a big girl now.'

'And not a very happy one,' he said slowly. 'If something's wrong, would you tell me . . . or has that changed as well?'

For a moment he saw her face quiver, thought he was almost inside the guard she hid behind; but the moment didn't last, and her smiling mask was in place again.

'Nothing's wrong, except that I'm going to be stiff tomorrow! *You'll* be on your way to France, I gather. Have a good time.'

'Thanks. I shan't tell Mama in case it doesn't come off, but I had the idea of looking in on Syb.'

'*Very* broad-minded of you, Ned. I thought we were supposed to wait for *her* to come home penitent. I suppose you know our charming neighbours pretend to believe she's working over there? The good women of Haywood's End aren't nearly so mealie-mouthed about it. If you do see her, give her my love.'

'I will, but only if you mean it.'

His eyes held hers in a glance that was puzzled and sad. She recognized the question it asked, and wanted to weep in his arms, wanted to hear him repeat the phrase that had always magically cured the woes of childhood . . . 'it's all right, you silly chump; Ned's here.' But she wasn't little Lucy Wyndham now, and the barrier between them seemed to equal the size and weight and permanence of Providence itself.

'Of *course* I mean it,' she said crossly.

'In that case you can ride my horse back and get into a hot bath, and Hodges shall have the pleasure of telling me it's time I knew how to ride an animal without laming it!'

A smile suddenly lit Lucy's strained face. 'Ned . . . I should have said it before . . . I'm very glad you're home again.'

The Channel looked an uninviting grey, and the wind stood anything but fair for France, but Ned enjoyed the crossing all the same. The journey *hadn't* been a test of whether or not he was confident enough to deal with memories of the embarkations that had led to Flanders mud, but he knew that he *had* secretly dreaded it Memories were all about him, but he could cope with them. Dear God . . . he *was* all right . . . blessedly normal, and in his own mind. He smiled for the sheer relief of it, exciting interest for a moment in the bored-looking girl who sat opposite him on the almost empty deck. But he was too deep in thought to notice her, and after a while she drifted away in search of some other man who would.

He enjoyed the journey to Paris, but not the afternoon and night he spent there. His father's recollections of it scarcely seemed to match a city that struck him as feverishly living on its nerves, filled with the sort of

61

artificial gaiety he'd known during the war in men suddenly released from too much strain. He was glad to take the train to Pont-sur-Seine the following morning.

The station-master there was over-helpful, pouring out a flood of rapid and mostly incomprehensible French. Yes, of a certainty he knew La Colomberie, and could without a doubt direct monsieur to it instantly. Ned watched the way the man's hands were pointing, and set out along the river. A converted mill shouldn't be all that hard to find.

He came upon it almost before he'd had time to think what he would say to Sybil if she were there, but at first glance he liked the look of Blanchard's home. Stone buildings were grouped round a paved courtyard, with just the same instinctive rightness that the masons of times past had known how to achieve at Providence. Shallow steps led up to a well in the centre of the open space, and a dovecote soared up in one corner, breaking the roof-line. Tubs and urns spilled greenery, and through an archway there was a glimpse of the willows that marked the curving line of the river. After the headlong pace of Paris it felt like paradise, but a peaceful backwater like this wasn't the setting he'd have expected Sybil to choose for herself.

He managed to announce himself to the servant who opened the door and was shown into an austerely simple room – white-washed walls and furniture of primitively carved dark wood. He had only a moment to realize that the simplicity was deliberate – a foil for the vivid beauty of the paintings on the walls – when Sybil herself walked into the room. She was smaller than he remembered, and fragile-looking compared with the village women at home. Her dress was a kind of loose kimono, silken and brilliantly coloured, that caught the light as she moved, and her short hair lay in a dark curving sweep against the whiteness of her forehead. She looked as exotic as a tropical bird, and seemed just as unfamiliar to him. He hadn't made much of a job of fathoming Lucy recently . . . *this* new Syb was certain to defeat him completely.

She stopped some way short of him, with a faint smile

on her mouth. 'Ned . . . a little foreign travel to broaden the mind, or have you come to reason with the prodigal daughter?'

The slightly mocking note in her voice *hadn't* changed, but an undertone of wariness warned him to be careful.

'I suppose I came because we miss you, and hoped you might be missing *us* a little, too,' he said simply.

'On those terms you're welcome.' She walked towards him and reached up to kiss him on both cheeks. 'French fashion, you see!' Her grin was suddenly real and familiar. 'What was it we used to say . . . ? "Oh frabjous day!" My beamish boy, it's so lovely to see you that for two pins I could weep real tears.'

'Me too,' Ned said truthfully. 'Silly that I can't think where to start when there's so much to say.'

'Never mind . . . you can stay for a bit, can't you? I suppose you know Henri's in England – even planning to visit Providence?'

'Yes . . . it's why I came now. Mama thinks I'm having a little holiday after the "ordeal" of getting myself investigated.'

'Investigated and *cured*, Ned?'

'Think so; sure so, in fact.' He nodded towards the prospect outside. 'It's lovely here, Syb. Is that why you've never come home?'

'I *couldn't* come, to begin with. Haywood's End was so safely detached from everything that had happened here that it seemed unreal.'

His eyebrow lifted in a gesture she remembered. 'There are six names engraved on just *our* small war-memorial, Sid Moffat's son among them. Chas Briggs is now a legless cripple in a wheelchair, and Hodges' nephew came back blind. If you ever do come home, for God's sake don't tell the people of Haywood's End that they were safely detached.'

'Sorry . . . sorry, Ned. What I *should* have said is that *I* grew detached from them. Apart from that, it was my only chance to be with Henri. He did his best to get rid of me, and that's really why I stayed . . . I was afraid he wouldn't let me come back if I went away.' Her mouth was smiling, but her eyes looked sombre in the lovely pallor of her face.

'Are you happy here?' Ned asked abruptly.

'If you mean here at Pont-sur-Seine, the answer is that I'm bored nearly to extinction. The difficulty is that while I was growing to love Paris, Henri was learning to hate it, so now we play an elaborate game of let's pretend – I try to look cheerful when we're here, and he smiles bravely when we're there.'

'It sounds a . . . a complicated way to live. Still, you obviously prefer it to anything else.'

'I prefer Henri to *anyone* else,' she agreed, still smiling, 'though I'm not sure he would truthfully say the same about me!'

There was so much they didn't know about each other now that Ned couldn't even decide whether she was serious or not. She still hadn't said whether she was happy, but he felt reluctant to ask the question again.

'I bumped into Charlotte a couple of months ago in the gallery in London,' Sybil confessed suddenly. 'Don't blame her for not mentioning it; I asked her not to.'

'You mean you got as far as London and still didn't bother to come home? Dammit, Syb . . . why ever not?'

'We only spent two nights there. In any case, an erring daughter does better to err away from a place like Haywood's End.'

'Rubbish, my dear girl; we're not living in the reign of Albert the Good. Can't you see how hurtful it is when you stay away?'

'Well, there *were* reasons . . .' she said defensively and cast around for something safer to talk about. 'Charlotte told me she and Harry had become Socialists. I can believe it of him after all that's happened, but it's hard to imagine prim, sweet Charlotte kicking over the traces . . . though she did assure me that she's working for a *peaceful* revolution!'

Ned's shout of laughter echoed round the room, making her join in. Once started, they couldn't stop. Laughter swept away strain, and they were friends, content to be together again.

'It's not really funny,' Ned said finally, wiping his eyes. 'Poor Aunt Louise pretends it's like a childish complaint caught later in life – the attack is virulent but hopefully not lasting. I don't think Harry *will* change again; he's committed to a fresh cause and there isn't room for anything else, even another wife.'

'I've been several times to visit Emily's grave,' Sybil muttered. 'It's with a lot of others, of course; all beautifully kept and heartbreaking.' She relapsed into silence, then touched on another painful subject. 'What about Providence, Ned? Surely it's unbearable to have Frank Thornley there; and now that you're well again Lucy must wonder why she rushed into marrying him.'

'She rushed because otherwise Providence would have been sold over our heads,' Ned said bluntly. 'Listen, Syb. It didn't help matters that I was half out of my mind, but we couldn't have redeemed the mortgage in any case. If Frank hadn't bought it, someone else would have done. When I was in a state to understand, I felt desperate about what Lucy had done, but gradually it seemed all right – it *wasn't* some ghastly kind of barter, after all. Frank clearly doted on her, and *she* seemed to be happy.'

Sybil saw a picture in her mind's eye, of Lucy dressed and ready to attend Harry's marriage to their friend, Emily Maynard. She had looked beautiful, being just old enough to wear her first grown-up hat and frock. She *hadn't* been quite old enough to know how to hide her feelings . . . but perhaps there'd been time since to learn how to deal with heartbreak.

'How is she now?' Sybil asked quietly.

'Changed a bit – laughs a lot and keeps rushing off to London. I have the feeling Mama worries about her, and Arthur Thornley nearly busts his braces trying *not* to ask her why she doesn't stay at home and look after young Charlie.'

Sybil stared out of the window at a distant glimpse of a slate-coloured steeple across the river. Simply because it was so different, it always reminded her of the square grey tower of Hubert's church at Haywood's End.

'How is Godmother Maud?'

'Ageing a little, but not prepared to take any notice of the fact!'

'Give her my love, please . . . give them *all* my love – stubborn old Biddle, and cantankerous Hodges, and . . .' Suddenly she couldn't go on with the rest of the list, because tears clogged her throat, stifling all the things she wanted to say.

Ned looked round the room for inspiration and found the glowing pictures on the walls. 'Father wouldn't mind an hour or two here. I'm an ignorant fool, but even I can see that these are marvellous.'

'Let me educate you, brother dear,' she said, trying to smile again, and beginning to steer him round the room. 'Orange flowers in a copper jug – Van Gogh, of course; Edouard Manet represented by scarlet rowing-boats reflected in blue water; and these sun-drenched Provençal landscapes could be by no-one but Cézanne. But here's something you *will* recognize.'

Ned saw his father's signature at the bottom of a small still-life – peaches heaped on a willow-pattern plate beside a flagon of blue Bristol glass; it was the essence of summer, caught on a canvas twelve inches square.

'Henri bought it for me from the gallery . . . it's my own small bit of Providence.'

Her eyes were fixed on the little painting and it was safe for Ned to stare at her shadowed face. He wondered what on earth he would say when they asked him at home if she was happy.

'Syb . . . don't stay away for ever,' he said impulsively. 'You always *did* get yourself into situations you didn't know how to retreat from! Promise me you'll not let it happen now.'

'I'll come when I can, but if you love me you'll have to hope that it isn't for a long time yet.'

He didn't understand what she meant, and when he said goodbye to her two days later, still hadn't puzzled out what she hadn't intended him to know.

Chapter Six

'Stop here a moment, if you please.'

Jem obediently braked the car, although he regretted the stop. He enjoyed swirling on to the forecourt with a good flourish and a spurt of gravel, and now there wouldn't be time to pick up speed again. Odd that his passenger should want to sit plumb in the middle of the drive, staring at the house, but then he *was* a foreigner, even if he did speak English that sounded just like Squire's.

'Am I right in thinking you were here when I came years ago?'

'Might have bin, sir. Jem Martin's the name . . . bin at Providence since I was a lad. I mind I went to London once with her ladyship, and I think it was to see *you* . . . place called Bond Street, she said it was.'

Henri Blanchard remembered the occasion even more clearly than his chauffeur did, but had no intention of talking about it. 'I expect you went to the war, Jem,' he said instead.

'Warwickshire Regiment, sir – same as Master Ned. Reckon I was one of the lucky ones , . . came home in one piece.'

Blanchard pointed to the house just visible through the bare branches of the lime trees bordering the drive. The winter light fell softly on the grey stone of Providence, and its twisted brick chimneys, weathered to rose-pink against the clear, pale sky.

'You must have feared you would never see *that* again.'

'We were feared of a lot of things, sir,' Jem agreed. The 'things' had mostly been the next night's wiring party in No Man's Land, or the relentless arrival of German shells, but it seemed a pity to disappoint his strange passenger by admitting that only survival had seemed important at the time.

At last the man beside him nodded in the direction of the house. 'Perhaps it's time we drove on, if you can persuade this machine to start again.'

'No trouble, sir. A flick of the handle and off she'll go, even though old Hodges *will* have it that God meant us to keep on using horses. Comes on very strong about motor-cars, does Hodges.'

'I remember *him*, too,' Blanchard said quietly. The truth was that he remembered everything about his first and only other visit to Providence. It remained imprinted, perfect and complete, on the retina of his mind's eye, so that he could recall it now in the minutest detail. William's mother, Lady Hester, had still been alive; he could have described the colour of the dress she wore, and the collar of stiffened lace about her throat, supported by tiny bones covered in black velvet. Sybil, her grand-daughter, had been four years old, and she'd conceived a violent attachment for him. Across all the years that lay between then and now he could hear himself saying to Sybil's mother, Gertrude Wyndham, 'there's every chance that she will grow up just like you'.

Time had proved him partly right, because in the matter of looks she often reminded him of her mother; but physical similarity only emphasized their other differences. The result had been a frequent sense of disappointment, and hiding *that* from Sybil had cost him more effort than he'd ever had to make before.

Jem coaxed the car into life again and five minutes later Henri stepped on to the bridge across the moat. Memory was playing not merely isolated notes but its full orchestra now. He was assailed by it. Time and space were annihilated and he could neither think nor move. But the great oak door swung open and a slender, silver-haired woman stood watching him. For a long moment he simply stared at her, and she at him.

'There are some changes, are there not?' he asked at last.

Changes in *them*, she understood him to mean, since they'd seen one another in Paris before the war. She should have remembered his habit of concentrating only on whatever happened to concern him most. There were social niceties that might have been observed, and certainly more important matters to be dealt with between them, but *not* in this first moment of recognition. His voice, like his directness, hadn't changed, but his black seal's cap of hair was now flecked with white, and the olive skin that had seemed so noticeable among English complexions was drawn tightly over jutting nose and cheek-bones. He looked tired, and rather ill, and it was quite impossible to remember that she had tried to hate him . . . *had* hated him for William's grief at losing Sybil and a friend.

'There are changes at *Providence*,' she agreed, warning him that their conversation was to be impersonal. 'The draughts and medieval plumbing have disappeared, and tonight you won't have to grope your way along the corridors by candle-light. But we still drink afternoon tea in the Great Hall. Will you come down when Ethel has shown you to your room?'

Her manner was politely remote, and so alien to his memory of her that he finally accepted the truth of something that had greatly troubled him. Sybil had been right, after all, to insist on staying away from Providence. Their unconventional behaviour had been too much for William to accept, and Gertrude had reasons of her own for doubting his attitude towards her daughter.

He followed the maid out of the hall, and Gertrude stared out unseeingly over the courtyard garden. The worst was over; she had accustomed herself to the fact that he was there, and the rest of his brief visit could be endured. When Blanchard reappeared she was the composed and courteous hostess again.

'I'm sorry . . . I should have apologized for William's absence – there was a meeting in Warwick that had to be attended, but he will be back in time for dinner. Our daughter Lucy and her husband should also have returned by then from a visit to London, and old friends you will remember – Maud and Hubert Roberts – will be dining with us as well.'

Henri accepted the information with a polite bow, then began a slow inspection of the room. Nothing important about it had been changed, although he knew from Sybil that her father no longer owned Providence. No doubt the woman in front of him had seen to it that the Great Hall remained the serene heart of the house, just as he remembered it. There was nothing to mark it out particularly – panelled walls, firelight glinting on old, polished furniture, and bronze and gold chrysanthemums adding their sharp sweetness to the scent of lavender and beeswax . . . these were things that could be found in a hundred other English country houses. But the quiet grace that surrounded him here belonged only to *this* house . . .

'I think the shade of William's mother still haunts this room,' Gertrude found herself confessing, because it was impossible to be with Blanchard and not share her thoughts with him. 'Ned swears that I even talk to her here! He can remember her very well and calls her his gentle lady.'

The thought of her son banished the last trace of stiffness from her face; she smiled and became the woman whose rare appearances in his life had left Henri with an aching sense of loss ever since.

'Ned is not here?' he asked quietly.

'Not at the moment . . . he's on the Continent, taking a little holiday. It would have been impossible only a short while ago, but now he's himself again, thanks to Dr Freud's new techniques. William wasn't hopeful, but I knew the treatment *had* to work.'

Henri thought it summed up the difference between them. William would probably die still fearing the worst about everything, while Gertrude took the habit of brave hope with her to the grave. She was very thin, and her face bore the marks of too much strain, but it was still beautiful – even more so now than before, with its arresting contrast of delicate black brows and silvered hair. He was a mere dealer in other men's paintings; if he'd been an artist he would have spent his days trying to capture her on canvas.

She saw his mouth twist into a smile that she remembered. 'Do you realize Sigmund Freud doesn't limit his investigations simply to the psyche of damaged soldiers? He's ready to interpret the fantasies we *all* conceal, in order to explain the dark secrets of our personalities!'

'Then I shall refuse to be investigated,' Gertrude said firmly. 'Our fantasies are probably the better for remaining cloaked in a little decent mystery, like ankles in Queen Victoria's time! It's almost unthinkable to someone who can remember bustles and whalebone corsets, but Louise Trentham tells me that women's *knees* in London are nearly visible.'

She poured tea, confused by her own unthinking mention of her sister-in-law. Dr Freud might have been intrigued by it, but Henri would think it had been intended to disconcert him.

'Mrs Trentham is well, I trust?' he enquired indifferently. There was nothing in his voice or expression to suggest that he was in the least disconcerted at being reminded of a woman who'd come close to wrecking her marriage for him years ago.

'Alec inherited his brother's title, which made him ineligible to remain in the House of Commons. Louise runs Somerton for him with the efficient perfection you might expect.' It seemed too curt a summary and she added something he probably knew already. 'Their son survived the war unhurt, but his wife was killed in France.'

'I know,' Blanchard said. 'I'm acquainted with as much of your lives as Sybil knows.'

'Of course,' she agreed calmly.

There was a moment of complete stillness in the room; even the logs on the hearth seemed reluctant to shift and resettle while his words still hung in the air.

'Gertrude, it's time to talk about your daughter, is it not? I should prefer to do it while William isn't here. You must both have been very hurt when Sybil didn't come back after the war.' He offered it as a fact, so self-evident that it didn't need commenting upon. 'It was one of those strange coincidences that seem to occur during the upheavals of war. I hadn't been at the gallery for months, hadn't even been in Paris, until the day Sybil came to the Boulevard Haussmann and knocked on the door. She still wore her VAD mackintosh and dreadful uniform hat . . . looked ill with exhaustion, and sickened by the experience of too much horror. I made her eat food, and then suddenly she began to talk. Words poured out of her . . . I *saw* that hospital at Etaples where Emily was killed, heard the sounds men made who had been hurt past bearing, smelled the stench of their poisoned wounds.'

'She wouldn't talk of those things here when she was given leave,' Gertrude murmured. 'Even the night the hospital was bombed was never referred to and we didn't dare ask . . . Perhaps we should have done.'

She watched him lift brown hands in an expressive gesture unknown to Englishmen. 'Perhaps it would have been the wrong time. She could only talk when she was ready to. When the talking was done she asked if she might stay in Paris, rather than go straight from that hellish place to the quietness of the English countryside. I could understand that she needed time to accustom herself to normal life again.' His eyes were fixed on Gertrude across the firelit space between them, asking *her* to understand. 'Sybil suggested working in the gallery in Paris, but she wasn't fit to work and I couldn't send her away. In the end I offered her a refuge at the mill. Life is unexciting there and I felt sure she'd get bored with it as soon as she felt strong again.'

Gertrude's expression changed, and sadness was briefly tinged with mockery. 'You had forgotten – because don't tell me you never knew! – that she began by appropriating you when she was four, then fell in love with you when she was a schoolgirl and you used to visit her in Lucerne.' It was impossible for him *not* to have learned early in life that women – young, respectably married, or blamelessly middle-aged – had no defence against loving him. The

72

Wyndham women, especially, seemed to have made a monotonous habit of it, but Sybil was the only one of them brave enough to have kicked convention in the face and *asked* for what she wanted.

Blanchard gave a little shrug. 'Schoolgirl passions are violent but brief. It didn't occur to me that she *wouldn't* want to go away. No doubt William blamed me for what inevitably happened. He might have blamed me less if I'd married Sybil immediately, but I was older by more than twenty years – determined that she should be free to leave whenever she wanted to.'

'Only, of course, she *didn't* want to.' Gertrude smiled ruefully. 'I'm afraid we certainly blamed you, although we shouldn't have done. It took Maud Roberts to point out to me that Sybil has gone through life doing only what *she* wanted. We should have been grateful for the kindness you offered her when she needed it . . . And now you've been kind enough to come and explain. Thank you, Henri.'

'I came to explain something else. She is expecting a child. There is no longer any question of her leaving, and we were married a fortnight ago.'

The words fell deliberately into the quietness of the room, while the invading dusk crept in a little further and Gertrude struggled with the shock of a discovery that was mainly about herself. He was *married* to Sybil. Almost the same age as herself, he was now her own son-in-law. It seemed absurdly impossible, except for one realization that seemed to be driving the blood from her heart. It had needed the unarguable fact that Sybil was pregnant to convince her body of something even her mind hadn't wanted to accept until now. He had been, still was, her daughter's lover.

'I should . . . should congratulate you,' she stammered at last. 'Congratulate you both. William will be so happy . . . Sybil might even feel able to visit us now . . .' She smiled to convince Henri that she wasn't on the verge of uncontrollable weeping, then confessed to it because the weeping seemed unavoidable. 'You must excuse me if I become tearful – it's always *good* news that seems to have that effect.'

In the dimness of the room his own expression was strangely sombre. 'Good news? Another child to be born into this frighteningly uncertain world . . . another hostage to fortune?'

'You sound as if you didn't want the child,' she said slowly.

'I don't – shocking, is it not, my dear?'

'You're like William, distrustful of the future. I understand the reason, of course, but we have a safeguard now. Today's children will be safe from the bloody carnage we have had to live through.'

'I doubt if you *do* understand my reason, Gertrude.' His smile glimmered strangely in the dusk. 'By all means let us put our faith in the League of Nations, but don't forget that I'm a Frenchman . . . we shall never do anything but distrust the German race with every drop of blood in our bodies.'

She was steadied by the discovery that his pessimism concerned mankind, not himself. 'I grant you the world's a dangerous place, but what is there to do but make the best we can of it? If there are ills, we must try to cure them, not stand wringing our hands, and thinking how much safer it would have been not to be born at all.

'In fact, we've only to "take arms against a sea of troubles and, by opposing, end them"!' Now he knew for certain that she was still the same Gertrude . . . older, but just as stubbornly courageous and beautiful as the girl who had walked into his London gallery years ago, determined to convince him that he wanted to buy William's paintings. Age might eventually cripple her body, but it would never touch her spirit, and he would love her for as long as he lived.

'Henri . . . Sybil is happy about the child, isn't she? *She* wanted it?'

'She intended to have it, let us say.' It wasn't quite the same thing, but Gertrude pretended to herself that it was. She was reminded of the women at Haywood's End, who

74

insisted that the having of babies 'settled' even the most troublesome of their daughters. The idea seemed strangely remote from the girl she'd known, but perhaps she no longer knew at all a daughter she hadn't seen for three years. In any case, Sybil was now Henri's *wife*. Realization swept over her again, drowning her in an emotion she couldn't bear to call by its real name. Pride alone wouldn't be enough to rescue her from the sin forbidden by the tenth commandment, and to covet what her own daughter possessed . . . the thought was unbearable; she must learn to accept pain with grace, or be utterly destroyed.

'Henri . . . while we wait for William, may I ask you to do something for me?' she suggested desperately. 'My father lives here with us now . . . Will you pay him a visit? In general he's content with his own company when he can't have Ned's, but he still misses Sybil. It would give him pleasure to hear you talk about her.' She was running on too much, could hear the sound of her own feverish voice echoing in her head; but, dear God, it was *hard* to appear normal when he behaved as if they were strangers meeting for the first time.

'I should like to meet your father,' he said calmly, and his very indifference to the past shocked her back into self-control again.

She led the way along the corridor into the south range of the house. For George Hoskins the long hours and exertions of being William's land-agent had now been replaced by the more gentle task of making an archive of the estate papers of the past fifty years. He smiled lovingly at Gertrude, and looked with placid interest at the visitor she had brought him. It was unusual for her to walk away leaving her guest behind, but he supposed she had domestic matters to attend to.

Henri exerted himself to talk, aware that he was being studied through the veil of the old man's pipe-smoke. Eventually he gestured to the volumes of estate history that already lined the shelves.

'You must feel sad, Monsieur: a story that has been long and continuous until now ends with William. After that it becomes a different story – Providence *not* owned by the Wyndhams, and a world changed out of all recognition from the one you used to know.'

With failing eyesight, George *listened* more carefully nowadays. He wondered why he should hear in the voice of this experienced, successful man a note of something that sounded like despair.

'You're right that the world has changed,' he conceded cautiously, 'but that's nothing new – it's been changing since the whole queer business began. It's true, as well, that Frank Thornley owns Providence now – but who owns this or that's a matter of chance, not worth a tinker's cuss.'

'Then you must tell me what *does* matter,' Henri suggested gravely.

'Why, the future of course . . . and it doesn't have to be the one *we'd* choose for ourselves. As long as Providence lasts, I don't mind whether Wyndham or Thornley or anyone else owns it. Same thing goes for the land; all we need for the future is to have *someone* working it – for love, you understand.'

He smiled shyly, giving Henri a glimpse of the young man who'd come to Providence fifty years before. 'Time was when I'd have seen things differently. In Victoria's reign we had the idea nothing would ever change . . . masters, men – they were all in their proper place! Now, as long as there's someone to cherish England, that's enough of a future for me.' He put down his pipe the better to stare at his visitor. 'I hope *your* future looks to be enough for you.'

Henri considered for a moment, then smiled with great sweetness. 'My dear Monsieur, now that you confront me with the idea, I shall have to make sure that it is!'

William returned from Warwick while Henri was still visiting George Hoskins. By then Gertrude had emerged from the peace of the Chapel Room in her right mind again. She phrased it thus to herself, and rehearsed the calm announcement she would make to her husband.

When he appeared in her room she blurted out something *not* rehearsed. 'Henri is talking to my father . . . he and Sybil were married two weeks ago, and she's expecting his child. Do you mind, William?'

'It's what I've prayed for,' he said simply. 'Now, she'll be safe and content . . . a young man wouldn't have done for her at all.'

Gertrude realized that, as usual, Maud had been right. William was not only relieved of anxiety about his daughter; he could now retrieve his friendship with Henri as well. All was for the best in the best of the worlds that were possible. She knew now that it was even true. Happiness for Sybil mattered a great deal more than anything she might have wanted for herself, and the certainty that this was so was enough to strengthen her and melt the coldness about her heart.

At dinner she could even enjoy listening to Maud and Henri sparring again with the ease of people who recognized each other as friends. With her usual disregard for appearances, Maud had unearthed from her wardrobe an evening dress of pre-war vintage. Beside Lucy's backless frock of gleaming satin it looked strange enough to be a museum-piece, but Henri gravely applauded her on an individual taste in dress that had only ripened with the years. Maud's delighted smile acknowledged her pleasure; it took conversational adroitness of a rare kind to make an insult sound like the most charming compliment!

Gertrude hoped she was imagining as the evening wore on that Lucy paid too little attention to her own husband, and too much to the man who was now her brother-in-law. Frank seemed not to notice, but it was a relief when Henri, deliberately she thought, contradicted Lucy's bright insistence on the excitement that it must be to live in Paris.

'You must remember my great age, chère madame,' he said solemnly. 'Cities are nowadays for what the war left of this generation. They live today as if tomorrow might never come, and we can scarcely blame them; but they and we no longer mix very well. They have a bright and brittle *style* of their own but, alas, no taste at all! That is also true, unfortunately, of the artists among them.'

'That from *you*,' William protested, 'the only art-dealer who has always understood the avant-garde painters, and helped prevent a good many of them from starving?'

Henri gave his characteristic little shrug. 'The artists you're talking about struggled to free themselves from the deadening conventions of the nineteenth century. Today's avant-garde are merely clever young men who ignore their fundamental duty.'

'To create beauty?'

It was Gertrude who suddenly answered William's question. 'No – to create something that comforts or enlightens those of us who are less gifted than they are.'

'Exactly.' For a moment the warmth of Henri's smile was for her alone; then his glance round the table gathered the rest of them in again. 'Dear people, a painting of a tree with human arms for branches tells us very little about a tree, and certainly nothing about humanity . . . so much for the Cubists, the Dadaists, the Surrealists and whatever "ists" come after them! It pains me to have to say it but I'm almost certain that the great days of painting in Paris are over.'

'What happens now, then?' William asked quietly. 'A gradual decline into different but equally deadening conventions?'

'I think so, unless we accept the *other*, simple alternative . . . which is to retrace our steps and go back to the beginning.'

'Duccio's Madonnas, Giotto's saints?' Maud hazarded.

'Exactly!' Henri said again. 'Timeless works of art, born of the faith and certainty *we* knew but lost, and the present generation has never known.' He stared at Hubert Roberts. 'Forgive me, Rector, if I feel bound to say that such faith and certainty have been lost for ever.'

'I understand why you think so, my dear Henri, but I refuse to share your pessimism. The rose breathes out its fragrance on the air whether anyone is there to savour it or not; the Kingdom of God exists even though the present

78

generation may not recognize it, or may deny it. Nothing that exists can be lost for ever.'

Henri smiled at him. 'Then I was wrong. *Perfect* faith is still to be found at Haywood's End.'

Going down to breakfast the following morning, Gertrude found Henri there alone. Already she was able to think of him as coupled with Sybil – 'paired', the village women would have called it – and it wasn't at all impossible to smile naturally at him.

'I expect William went into the studio on his way down, to decide whether he still likes what he painted yesterday!'

'He *must* do. He's painting so marvellously that I've made him promise to destroy nothing without my permission.'

While she poured coffee he fumbled in his jacket pocket and brought out a small wrapped packet which he laid beside her plate.

'I found it by chance in a second-hand bookshop in Florence, waiting for its rightful owner,' he said quietly. 'Don't thank me for it . . . It *had* to be yours.'

There was no time to say anything at all; Emmy bustled into the room with dishes, and then William appeared. After the meal was finished and Henri was due to leave, the three of them walked outside to the stable yard where Jem waited with the car. Gertrude held out her hand.

'Give our dearest love to Sybil. Say we shall be longing to see her and the child.'

'Of course.' His lips brushed her hand, then he climbed in beside Jem. She stayed beside William, but stared carefully at the ground while the car disappeared round a curve in the drive. When they walked back into the house together he noticed the packet still clutched in her hand.

'A little present Henri found in Florence . . . a book, I expect,' she murmured.

'A book, I'm certain,' William said with a smile. 'It's bound to be something you'll cherish – Henri's taste is never at fault.'

It wasn't. In the privacy of her own room she

79

unwrapped a small leather-bound volume of the poems of Robert Browning – the flyleaf inscribed in Browning's own hand to his 'beloved wife', Elizabeth. Gertrude found herself picturing the chance moment when Henri had come across such a treasure in some dingy bookshop, saw his brown hands turning the leaves until he left the little ribbon marker at the page it stood at now. It offered her a mere four lines of verse.

> . . . Nobody calls you a dunce,
> And people suppose me clever:
> This could have happened once,
> And we missed it, lost it for ever.

After a long while she moved the ribbon to a different page, and put the volume on her writing-desk where William could see it. He'd been right – she would cherish it for the rest of her life, and gradually out of terrible joy and pain, only the happiness of having been loved would remain.

The morning was too far advanced already for the list of duties that needed attending to, but if she concentrated very hard perhaps she would not only be able to remember what they were; she might actually succeed in applying herself to them.

Chapter Seven

William's American-born niece, Anita Wyndham, spent
the early spring of the following year in Paris, and reached
London later than expected. She finally arrived on April
the fifteenth, unaware that history would judge that
particular Friday of 1921 to have been in any way
noteworthy. Her cousin Charlotte's letters had promised
that Harry would be waiting to meet her off the boat-train.
Anita looked in vain for the man she vaguely remembered,
and was finally approached by a tall, thin young woman
whose face set up an echo of familiarity.

'I'm afraid it's the family nose,' Charlotte suggested
regretfully. 'Not a thing of beauty, but at least useful for
identifying long-lost cousins at railway stations! Welcome
back, Anita, and apologies from my brother . . . he fully
intended to be here himself, but today turns out to have
been rather crucial in our industrial affairs, and he's a
good deal involved in them.'

She was stared at in turn by a dark-haired girl who
resembled her very little in feature and not at all in
colouring; but something indefinable they certainly had in
common, Anita decided, as well as the Wyndham nose.

'I think you've changed more than I have,' she said, 'or
else I'm remembering you wrongly. You stood with Aunt
Louise welcoming guests to your birthday ball, looking as if
you longed to be anywhere but where you were. The rest of
us had a lovely time, but I always doubted whether *you* did.'

'You aren't remembering wrongly at all. I still hate
balls, but at least I can avoid them now when I choose.
There's that much to be said for being thirty instead of
twenty-one! Shall we go? We can do the rest of our
catching-up at home.'

She nodded to two porters already earmarked to deal with her cousin's luggage, then briskly led the way out of the station. Anita walked beside her, amused and wondering who needed Harry when they were being taken care of by his sister. Her remaining cousins might have other surprises in store, but surely none more remarkable than that shy, diffident Charlotte should have blossomed into another Aunt Louise! The managing streak might have surfaced late in her, but it was there after all.

The house they were driven to in Thurloe Square looked enormous for a young woman living on her own, but Charlotte explained that only the two top floors belonged to the Trenthams.

'Even that's more than I need, of course, but my parents stay here whenever they spend a night in London. It's *their* flat, really; I'm allowed to live here, under the eye of one of the servants from Somerton. The poor things take it in turns to endure the miseries of London!'

It was surely Aunt Louise's country home writ small, Anita decided; the first-floor drawing-room was full of polished mahogany and comfortable, chintz-covered armchairs, and the long windows opening on to useless but elegant wrought-iron balconies offered a view of greenness even in the heart of London.

'Harry doesn't share the apartment with you?'

'No; he sold his house in Chelsea after the war, and moved into a service flat in Arlington Street, just off Piccadilly.'

'It was a very dreadful tragedy,' Anita murmured. 'Poor Harry. Do you suppose he will ever marry again, or did lovely Emily spoil him for another wife?'

Charlotte frowned over the question. 'My mother continues to hope he'll remarry, but I'm bound to say I don't think he will. She hasn't quite given up hope of *me* yet, either, although she has to admit that, with suitable husband material in short supply now, I'm not likely to find a taker!'

'You don't sound worried,' Anita suggested smilingly.

'I'm not. I've got more interesting things to do than

82

pray that some man will be kind enough to marry me. It doesn't matter about me . . . I'm not supposed to produce an heir for Somerton. Harry *is*, but he's outgrown all that antiquated family nonsense.'

'*Has* he, indeed! Isn't that a little hard on your parents?'

'Well, yes . . . but we have to live our own lives, not simply prop up a decrepit system for another generation or two. Still, for different reasons, I rather wish Harry would remarry . . . men without wives seem to me to be such rudderless creatures.'

Anita stared at her cousin, still trying to recognize in this decided and composed young woman the Charlotte Trentham she remembered.

'Would you say the same about women without husbands – rudderless, too?' she ventured.

'Certainly not. The war taught us to manage on our own. Just as well, of course, since it left rather too many of *us* compared with them.'

Anita nodded, then asked another question. 'Is young Lucy going to take me by surprise as well? I met Sybil while I was in Paris and scarcely recognized *her*.'

'If you remember Lucy as a shy seventeen-year-old with a golden plait of hair hanging down her back, the answer is that you won't recognize *her* either. Presumably you know she married Frank Thornley before the end of the war? Harry disapproves of her rich husband on principle, and so do I; my brother *dislikes* Frank as well, but there's something about him I find admirable – his directness, I think. We don't normally see much of them even though they spend a lot of time in London, but you'll certainly meet them while you're here.'

'What's wrong in principle with a rich husband?' Anita feared that her conversation was becoming a succession of questions fired at point-blank range, but she was aware of being at a disadvantage. She knew as much as the rest of America knew about the political and economic conse-quences of the war in Europe. But what it had done to *people*, and in particular to the Wyndham family, she now realized she didn't know at all. Ned's mental sickness and the death of Harry's wife were facts, but the effects of such tragedies still had to be grappled with.

It had remained a life-long mystery to her that her father – deliberately, it seemed – should have almost lost touch with his elder brother, William. Now and then she would have sworn that he still missed Providence in his heart, but she'd given up trying to make him talk about it. Ned's letters had brought news for a while, but they became erratic as soon as he was sent to France, and ceased completely after he returned to England. Lost in thought, Anita had almost forgotten her own question and was startled when Charlotte eventually answered it.

'Nothing's wrong with a rich husband, I suppose, except that nowadays unless he's the Duke of Westminster he's likely to be what Frank is – a successful capitalist. As committed Socialists, Harry and I are bound to disapprove of that.'

Anita did her best not to stare round the comfortable room. It seemed an unlikely setting for a committed radical, but perhaps Socialists weren't required to renounce their background altogether. She was tempted to tease Charlotte about it, but remembered in time what her father said about all converts – they were apt to lose their sense of humour in the process of conversion.

'More accurately, I ought to call myself a Fabian,' Charlotte explained proudly. 'We advocate a *gradual* process of reform. Harry is more involved in the Parliamentary Labour Paty than I am. After the war he *tried* to follow in Father's footsteps – even represented Somerton as a conventional Trentham Liberal; but Lloyd George was more than he could bear. He hates the Prime Minister, and a Government that does nothing to remove the injustices of our society.'

'All right . . . so he hates Lloyd George, but what is personally wrong with Lucy's husband?'

'Frank's on good terms with the men in power – that's one thing against him. Another is that he made a second fortune out of the war. It wasn't his fault that he didn't go into the army; the Thornley factories were turned over to munitions and he was required to stay behind and run them, but Government contracts made him a good deal richer than he was before.'

'Someone had to provide guns. Why not Lucy's husband?'

'Well, preferably *not* her husband, in our view.'

It was said with a disdainful certainty worthy of Aunt Louise and might have made Anita smile if it hadn't irritated her instead.

'What does Frank Thornley think of Harry . . . or am I not supposed to make the enquiry that way round?'

'Why not? The question's valid,' Charlotte said fairly. 'It's hard to know *what* Frank thinks, because he prefers not to take people into his confidence. My *guess* is that he thinks Harry's a fool, playing with theories he doesn't understand.'

Anita's sympathies were with Frank, but she thought it too early in the re-acquaintance with her cousin to say so. 'Over here everything still seems to come back to the war,' she commented instead. 'I have to keep remembering that it explains why you all seem so changed. Women at home were scarcely aware of the war, unless they had men fighting in France, but there were comparatively few of those. Here, you were *all* involved, in a way it's hard for us to imagine.'

It was Charlotte's turn to exercise restraint. She had no great opinion of her uncle's adopted country, and considered that the American contribution to the war had come not only very late but also in the worst profiteering spirit of capitalism; America had done very well financially out of a war that had bankrupted everybody else, and damaged them almost irreparably in other ways as well.

'You were lucky to see Syb in Paris,' she said, tactfully changing the subject. 'She seems to have abandoned us for good. We miss her very much, and I can't imagine how *she's* getting on without Ned to keep her in order – no-one else ever could that I recall!'

'She has a husband now . . . perhaps Ned isn't needed.' Anita mentioned the name calmly, but it was the moment she had been waiting for . . . the chance to talk about him. Charlotte hadn't been much at Providence that golden, sunlit summer before the war, and it was the very reason Anita had written to *her* rather than to any other member of the family. She probably hadn't even been aware of a love-affair that had been sweet and brief and doomed. 'Sybil seemed to think Ned had recovered now . . . Do you see much of him?' she asked casually, as if the answer scarcely mattered at all.

'Only if I go to Providence. He still hates London, even though the noise doesn't seem to disturb him any longer. You'll recognize *him*, by the way. He doesn't laugh quite as readily as he did, but otherwise he's the same dear Ned.'

She had no idea how much or how little her cousin knew about the affairs of the Wyndhams. Presumably, though, she heard of them through Uncle James. Even if it had occurred to Charlotte that Anita *didn't* know the reason for Lucy's marriage to Frank, she would have taken for granted the fact that it was her uncle's, or Ned's, right to explain who now owned Providence.

'I may not see Ned at all, if he never comes here,' Anita murmured.

'Of course you will. There's a letter from Aunt Gertrude waiting for you in your room, and I can guess what it says – you're to go to Haywood's End as soon as the Great Wen becomes too much for you! She's just as convinced as Ned or Uncle William that no-one in her right mind chooses to stay long in London if she can escape to Providence.'

'But Lucy *isn't* convinced, if she spends a lot of time here?'

'As Mrs Frank Thornley, she seems to have acquired a different point of view. Time was when she never wanted to leave Haywood's End.' A little frown pulled Charlotte's thin, fair eyebrows together; then she gave a sudden smile. 'Isn't that enough about the family for the time being? We're probably better wrestled with in small doses until you've got used to us again. Why not go and unpack? Dinner's at eight, and by then Harry might be here, although I'm bound to say that politics have made him very unpunctual!'

Anita was conducted to the pleasant, white-draped bedroom that had been made ready for her, and left alone. Times had changed, she realized – unless it was her cousin's new egalitarian principles that drew the line at maids to empty visitors' suitcases and lay out their clothes. The bedroom lay at the back of the house and here, too, there was the greenness of a garden to look out on and – despite egalitarian principles – the seclusion that only money could buy.

Her aunt's letter lay on the dressing-table but Anita didn't make haste to open it. Charlotte's guess about its contents was likely to be correct, and the only important thing to know was that it hadn't come from Ned. *Nothing* had come from him even though he couldn't help but know she was in London. She opened suitcases, bestowed clothes in wardrobes and drawers, and forced herself to think calmly about the family Charlotte had advised her to get used to again in small doses.

She'd met them all on only one previous visit, but the visit had lasted six months while Patrick went to Paris to study. She'd been twenty-three, impressionable, shy, and fascinated by her father's English relatives. She'd liked them all, even sharp-tongued Sybil, but it was Ned she'd learned to love. No other man she'd met before or since had seemed one-half so charmingly kind, or one-quarter so quietly stubborn. He'd been three years younger than herself, and bound to explain that Providence was entangled in debt. For the moment he must wait, and grow a bit older, and do a lot of work, before he could afford to take a wife. Then the war had come to cut him off from her. She was trapped in America, looking after her father, while Patrick, more free to come if he'd wanted to, had *not* wanted to. England's fight wasn't his, he'd told James Wyndham. Anita had to guess what her cousins thought about that, because even Sybil had found tact enough not to say.

The war in Europe had seemed dreadful but remote,

even though she knew that Ned, Harry, Sybil, and Harry's wife were all serving in France. It remained remote until the arrival of a letter from Providence just before Christmas, 1916. Ned had been wounded in the head during the terrible Somme push required to relieve the French Army beleaguered at Verdun. His wounds were not desperate, but his shell-shocked condition was. She hadn't heard from him since . . . didn't even know whether past memories survived his illness. She had decided at last that she must come to Europe and find out.

With her clothes neatly put away, it was time to open Aunt Gertrude's letter. Its single sheet of paper quivered in her fingers but she smiled because its message resembled so nearly what Charlotte had predicted. The invitation was kindly phrased, as it would have been to any relative Gertrude Wyndham asked to Providence, but Anita's impression was that her aunt had had to labour over the wording. It carefully made no reference at all to the past. She might have been inviting a niece she'd never met to pay them an introductory visit. Anita read the note again, searching for something she might have missed the first time; there was nothing to be found, and after a while she folded it away and got ready for dinner.

She went downstairs at a quarter to eight, grateful for the confidence provided by a new dress bought in Paris; its dark-blue silk flattered her eyes and white skin, and she was aware of looking her best. It seemed necessary for a reunion with cousin Harry. He'd been a dashingly engaging young man, but she suspected she would like much less the embittered veteran who had returned from the war.

Charlotte, dressed in unadventurous beige, smiled approvingly as she went into the drawing-room.

'So elegant that you put me to shame! My mother and Aunt Gertrude have the same happy knack of knowing what to wear, but the talent wasn't passed on to me. I can't even manage Maud Roberts' trick at Haywood's End of looking interestingly eccentric; I'm a frump however hard I try, so now I don't even try.'

Perhaps frumpishness went with Fabianism? Anita was about to risk asking whether Beatrice Webb insisted on it when the door opened and Harry Trentham walked in. She supposed that the verbs 'to open' and 'to walk in' were factually correct, but they seemed inadequate to describe the eruption into the room of a tall, fair-headed man who strode forward to meet her and took her hand in a grip that hurt. A fighter for a cause, Sybil had said, and she was right; his face was taut with barely suppressed anger.

'Charlotte found you all right, then. I'm sorry . . . I meant to collect you myself.'

'She scooped me up with the greatest efficiency,' Anita informed him coolly. 'In any case, I gather it was my fault for choosing a bad day to arrive.'

If she expected a smile and a polite enquiry about her health, her journey, or anything else, she was disappointed. Harry only just managed not to shout his next remark. 'It was a disastrous day as it's turned out. *Today* we were going to make history. This time, for the first time, the trades union movement was going to play the only trump card it has, and the Government was going to be *forced* to listen.'

'*Was* going to?' Charlotte asked quietly.

'Yes. The chance has been thrown away, as usual. The miners were betrayed again because that . . . that infamous Welsh conjuror pulled out of his hat yet another "temporary" offer. It doesn't meet the real points of the miners' case and won't be honoured anyway; but it was enough to let Thomas withdraw his railwaymen from the strike. Ernest Bevin was then given all the excuse *he* needed to withdraw his transport workers as well, and the so-called Triple Alliance was in ruins again. When *will* they understand that concerted action is their only weapon against a system that has to be overthrown?'

'Overthrown? Harry dear . . . the Webbs don't approve of revolutionary action . . .'

'The Webbs are theorists,' he interrupted contemptuously. 'They could still be writing political tracts fifty years from now and nothing would have changed at all.'

Anita saw Charlotte steeling herself to defend her idols, even against 'Harry dear', and decided that it was time to throw herself into the fray. 'What do *you* advocate, cousin . . . That we should all join you at the barricades?'

It sounded more flippant than she'd intended, but it had the desired effect of directing Harry's fire away from Charlotte.

'You sound amused, Anita. *Does* it amuse you that men should work themselves into an early grave at the coal-face for forty shillings a week, and go home black with coal dust to hovels that don't even have running water to wash them clean? Are you going to tell me that a system which permits such conditions rather than have its employers forego an extra fraction of their profits is *not* evil?'

She had the feeling that anger acted on him like a dynamo, generating energy . . . or perhaps like a drug taken to blur the truth from himself – that he was angry at what life had done to *him* as well as to his miners. He *needed* opponents, and a cause to fight for; if they weren't forthcoming, he would probably invent them.

'You know about the miseries endured by men and their families, and I do not,' she agreed calmly, 'but their hardship doesn't necessarily mean that the *system* is evil, only that the way men choose to apply it is.'

He shook his head like a bull pricked by an impertinent dart – a powerful animal irritated, but not yet provoked to a final charge. 'You're chopping logic, my dear girl. Men who apply systems for their own benefit – mine-owners and all the other capitalists as well – *always* apply them without regard for the men and women who slave for them. That is what such systems inevitably boil down to.'

'But state ownership, which I assume you favour instead, is only another system which must also be applied by men – and *they* may be just as unfair, or incompetent, or ruthless as the private employers you hate.'

Harry's blue eyes flashed with the heat of his rage. At the end of a heartbreaking day this coolly combative girl infuriated him. It was something that she wasn't pretty as

90

well, but she *was* elegant and feminine, unlike the wives and sisters of his Socialist friends who gave deplorably little attention to their hair and the clothes they chose to wear. Anita Wyndham's mouth was humorous and at any othe time he might have liked it, but not when it seemed to be amused by *him*. She had no right to ignore her family for years and then arrive calmly prepared to do battle with him.

'The collective good, achieved by collective effort, makes no appeal to you?' he asked more quietly. 'You take the American view: that we live in a jungle where every man must fight for himself and the weak must go to the wall?'

'I take my father's view,' she said crisply. 'He's been in America for many years, but he was born English and remains so. His view is that we live in ugly, competitive, industrial societies, *not* pretty Arcadian communes inspired by the theories of Ruskin and William Morris. My father would say that an employer's duty is first of all to *employ*, and provide the jobs that workers certainly cannot provide for themselves. He cannot continue to do that unless he's allowed to make a profit. The level of profit might need to be regulated, but it's *he* who has to find his workers' wages, not some hot-headed shop steward who calls in question *everything* he chooses to do.'

Charlotte blinked at such cool temerity, and owned to a faint but secret pleasure in it. Harry struggled with the desire to resolve the argument by brute force and strangle his too-articulate cousin, but he made a great effort to speak calmly.

'You can't, or won't, understand. Men should not have to accept starvation wages and brutal working conditions for fear of losing their jobs. The State should employ them – in such a way that they can retain their self-respect.'

'Nationalization . . . the Socialist panacea? It doesn't seem to be working terribly well in Russia, but perhaps . . .'

'Damn it, *listen* to me, Anita . . .' Quietness had had its chance; Harry's infuriated roar filled the room, but was interrupted by the opening of the door. 'Great God in Heaven . . . *another* cousin come to help fight the capitalist cause. You've arrived just in time, my dear Lucy.'

She was so startled by the venom in his voice that the smile she was offering them all faded from her mouth. Charlotte hurriedly moved across the room to greet her.

'Take no notice of Harry . . . he's had a bad day. In any case I expect you came to welcome Anita, not to receive a political lecture from my dear brother.'

Lucy's smile reappeared as she walked towards the newcomer. 'No plaits and pinafores now, but surely you remember me?'

'Most surely I do, though there are rather more changes than the ones you mention,' Anita said truthfully. 'How very nice it is to see you again, even if you *do* make me feel about as old as Methuselah!'

'Frank isn't with you?' Charlotte asked Lucy. The question sounded absurd when clearly he wasn't there, but she thought it seemed necessary somehow to include him in the conversation.

'He had to rush off to Birmingham. I preferred to stay here until he gets back.'

Anita couldn't help but hear the note of defiance in her cousin's voice, reminding her of Jane Austen's appalling Mrs Elton: 'One has no great hopes from Birmingham. I always say there is something direful in the sound.'

Charlotte registered the defiance too, and guessed that Lucy had annoyed Frank by refusing to go with him. She felt sorry for him. Even an ardent Fabian clung to the old-fashioned idea that a wife should accompany her husband, whether or not it meant going to Birmingham.

'Anita dear . . . I'm going to look after *you*,' Lucy explained with entrancing warmth. 'Charlotte's always busy during the day, working in the offices of some dreary magazine, but you and I will have a marvellous time.' She turned on Harry a glance sparkling with provocation. 'Two sinners together,' she told him sweetly, '"raising capitalist Cain"!'

Chapter Eight

Frank's visit to Birmingham was brief, a routine check that all was well with the Thornley factories. He knew what awaited him back in London – a pressing, last-minute invitation to join a Government delegation to America. He'd refused when Sir Robert Horne first suggested it, knowing all the time that he would feel bound to go in the end. When he got home and told Lucy, he expected an indifferent shrug, or perhaps irritation at the most, but not the storm that suddenly broke about his head.

'Why *you*, Frank? Surely someone else could go – *would* go, if you refused and they were given the chance. But you never *do* refuse. Mr Lloyd George crooks his little finger and off you run.'

Unaccustomed anger began to burn in him, but he told himself that he mustn't let it get the upper hand. She was young, and she didn't understand.

'My dear girl, I'm not the Prime Minister's lap-dog. Horne relies on me because my life's been spent in manufacturing industries; my knowledge is practical. Civil servants who are otherwise useful don't have that experience.'

'Then let them find other industrialists. It doesn't always have to be you. Consider *me* for a change, instead of Sir Robert Horne.'

'I hope I'm considering England,' he said wearily. 'Listen, Lucy . . . we're a trading nation losing the battle for world trade, an industrial nation falling behind our competitors because our methods haven't changed since Victoria came to the throne. We *must* know what the Americans and the Japanese are doing.'

'*Your* factories flourish well enough – I can't see what all the fuss is about.'

Frank knew a terrible desire to shake her into acknowledging a truth she was quite capable of understanding if only she would allow herself to. 'You *know* what the fuss is about – more than a million men out of work because our old traditional industries are steadily declining. Go to South Wales, or Lancashire, or Scotland, and see what that means in terms of sheer human misery.'

'I'm sure it's very terrible,' she agreed reluctantly, 'but it doesn't always have to be *you* riding on your white horse to the rescue. Say just this once, Frank, that you're too tired, that Thornley's need you . . . say that *I* need you.'

He heard but didn't understand the note of desperation in her voice; all he could see was that she was merely being perverse again when he most needed her *not* to be.

'None of that would be true,' he said levelly. 'I have to leave the day after tomorrow . . . I hope you'll go back to Providence while I'm away and stay with Charlie.'

It sounded fatally like an order, and her pale face flushed with anger. 'He has too many people doting on him already. In any case, not being aware of *your* commitments, I promised to look after Anita while she's in London. I'll go to Haywood's End when she does.'

He wanted to rage at her, to command her to do as he said . . . No, he wanted to kneel before her and beg her to tell him what was wrong. But there wasn't time; there was never enough time, and because of it they stared at one another like enemies.

'Very well. Do as you please,' he said curtly, and walked out of the room.

By the time he sailed for New York Anita had finally made up her mind that she must accept her aunt's invitation and go to Providence. She had no trace of expectation left where Ned was concerned, but it was time for the past to be laid to rest. Until it was, she would never be able to look forward, instead of back at what might have been.

She needed to see Ned Wyndham once more, but there

were other reasons for going as well, and other people to relish for the last time – her aunt and uncle at Providence, their friends at the Rectory, and even Frank's parents at Bicton. She still smiled when she thought of the small, round, human dynamo that was Arthur Thornley, wrapped in tight, too-loud, 'country' tweeds, and Jane always beside him, to undo with her matter-of-fact sweetness the offence he often gave to people. Anita told herself that she couldn't go through life missing all of *them* as well as Ned. Another visit now that she was no longer young and impressionable would brush the magic off them.

There was still one other reason for going – the house itself, that had haunted her memory, just as she knew it had haunted her father's. Providence held within its green park and grey stone walls the spirit of generations of men and women who had learned to live with gentleness and unextravagant grace. They were people who had made laws and kept them and, because they belonged to the land, had understood the rhythm of the year's changing seasons.

She tried to put this feeling into words for Charlotte one morning and smiled ruefully at the result. 'I suppose that sounded stupidly idealized. Harry would certainly inform me that Providence and all it stands for is something England can well do without!'

Charlotte surprised herself by refusing to insist for once that what England needed was social reform and the sweeping away of all its traditional evils.

'I *know* what Harry would say,' she observed with perfect truth. 'It's more interesting to have *you* point out what *we* ought to find worth cherishing!'

Her cousin smiled, and thought not for the first time that Fabianism had done Charlotte no lasting harm. There was a core of sweet sanity about her which, for the moment at least, her brother seemed to lack.

'Nine years ago at Providence I thought I'd stumbled on paradise,' Anita slowly explained. 'You'd understand better if you knew the people I live among. Patrick and Ishbel's friends are all Irish-Americans – voluble men and women who excite each other into believing that bloody rebellion against the English is a just and sacred cause. They would think I was mad if I suggested that violence breeds nothing but more violence. But my memory of Providence is of blessed gentleness – do you remember Rupert Brooke's words? "Hearts at peace under an English Heaven".'

Charlotte watched Anita's face while she talked and came to the conclusion that her cousin was misleading: she seemed cool, but only because her warmth was kept hidden. Harry had found her obstinate, wrong-headed, and unattractive, but only because she had been tactless enough to hold views different from his own.

'It's odd to have an uncle we've never seen,' Charlotte said next. 'Do you realize James has never been back to England since we were all born? I suspect my mother of feeling that he had no right to be able to manage without us!'

The seriousness with which she said it suddenly convulsed Anita so much that, try as she would, a whoop of laughter couldn't be stifled. Charlotte looked astonished, smiled herself, and then joined in. At last, when Anita had wiped her streaming eyes, she was sober enough to consider what her cousin had said. 'I can't tell you why my father stays away, because he's never told *me*, but it's all the more odd when he remains stubbornly himself after more than forty years in America . . . so courteous that people are taken by surprise when he still manages to beat them to a business deal; so charming that they can't understand how it is they never get to know him!'

'The women must have expected him to marry again after your mother died.'

'They did much more than expect – I couldn't help noticing that some of them were *determined* he should marry again! He always eluded them, though, and took a certain pleasure in doing so, it seemed to me.'

She sometimes thought that he'd eluded his own children almost as successfully. Only once or twice had she been allowed to see behind the pleasant façade he presented to the world. There had been the time when she returned home after her first visit to England, sick with the unhappiness of missing Ned. James's smooth mask had slipped then, and she'd glimpsed his own tormented longing for something he couldn't have. She'd suspected it of being Providence itself, but even then he hadn't said. Years later, when the news of Ned's injury had come during the worst months of the war, she'd hidden in her room to weep in private. She'd still been able to hear the anguished sound of her father's voice ordering Patrick out of the house. She asked to be told why, and never forgot the expression on his face. 'Your brother and his precious friends would like to see England beaten.'

While Charlotte toiled daily in the offices of a radical review called *The New Statesman*, Anita would have preferred to be left alone, quietly waiting for the time settled upon with her aunt for the visit to Providence. London's museums and art galleries would have kept her perfectly content, but she couldn't convince Lucy that such a programme was even faintly bearable. Each day her cousin arrived in Thurloe Square to drag her on a round of shops, dressmakers, and luncheon parties.

'Don't you like my friends?' Lucy asked one morning. 'You're always beautifully polite, but sometimes I have the feeling that you find them frightful.'

It was uncomfortably close to a truth that Anita had to do her best with. 'My difficulty is that I don't seem to be able to tell them apart! You're kindness itself to take so much trouble with me, but there's really no need, and I'm beginning to feel guilty.'

'Dear coz, while Charlotte and Harry are busy saving England from itself, of *course* I must look after you. In any case, it's my excuse for staying here while Frank's in America.'

'Lucy . . . do you really want to?' Anita asked gravely. 'There's your small son at Providence, not to mention the rest of your family.'

'They'll still be waiting when I *have* to go back. Charlie's quite happy with a nice new nursemaid found by

Ned . . . the daughter of a man he knew in the war who was shot for cowardice. He tracked the family down when he came back from Craiglockhart, and found them in a desperate state. Mary Haskell's a good, competent girl, delighted to have a job at Providence. She's very welcome to it; personally I hate being there now.'

'What happened? I thought you loved Providence.'

'I did,' Lucy agreed flatly.

Almost defeated, Anita made her final effort. 'Well, Charles, then, don't you want to see *him*?' The moment the words were out of her mouth she wished them unsaid, suddenly afraid that Lucy might say she *didn't* want to see her own son.

'There are more than enough people at Providence and Bicton to look after a two-year-old child and spoil him. Why am I needed as well to coo and gurgle over a messy, self-willed scrap of humanity simply because it insisted on heaving itself out of *my* body?' There was a kind of horror in her cousin's face now, but Lucy swept on, consumed by the need to release the pent-up misery inside her. 'Are you about to tell me that I'm an unnatural monster for not adoring what Frank and I have created out of shared love and passion?'

Anita winced at the mockery in her voice. 'Something on those lines,' she mumbled, 'supposing that I could find anything to say at all.'

'Well, don't bother, coz. It wouldn't help me change my mind.'

There was a painful silence in the room while Anita dredged up other phrases of comfort and discarded them. What in the name of Heaven *could* safely be said to a girl who seemed to have discovered too late that she neither liked the man she'd married, nor the child she'd given birth to? Surely it had to be something positive and firm? She cleared her throat, and made a brave beginning. 'Now, Lucy dear . . .' then stuck again, bitterly regretting a life-long habit of self-discipline that had left her unable to deal with other people's emotions because she refused to examine her own. She stared desperately at Lucy and discovered that words weren't needed after all, because defiance had crumbled under the onslaught of tears. They were brimming over her cousin's eyelids and streaming down her cheeks – unstoppable and heartbreaking.

'My dear . . .' she said in a different tone of voice, then wrapped her arms about Lucy's trembling body.

When the storm of weeping seemed to be over she hurried from the room to find Charlotte's maid. She returned to find her cousin composed again, and attending to her tear-stained face.

'Sorry, Anita . . . embarrassing of me to spill angst all over you like that!'

'Coffee's coming, to restore us! Meanwhile, may I say what I think? Even if you only despise an inexperienced spinster's view of things, at least *that* should make you feel better! It seems to me you didn't have enough time for youth. The war, your marriage, your child, swallowed it up.' Now came the difficult bit, and Anita knew that she must needs be careful. 'I don't know your husband, although I think I should like him if I did, and so would my father. But I can see that it isn't much fun being married to a man with such a strongly developed sense of duty. Can't you persuade him to play a little more?'

She waited for an answer, and smiled gratefully on the maid who chose that moment to arrive with her tray of coffee. When they were alone again Lucy chose not to answer that question, but to ask one of her own.

'Have you ever wanted one thing in life so much that nothing else makes up for the lack of it? That's the trouble with *me*, you see, made worse by the fact that I'm not even sure what the *thing* is; all I'm sure of is that I haven't got whatever it is I need.'

'Nine years ago *I* wanted Ned,' Anita confessed gravely. 'If I hadn't believed then that one day I should be given him, I'd have done what you're doing now – refused to accept other ways of being happy. There are always alternatives – there *have* to be.'

Lucy sipped coffee and stared at her cousin, distracted for the moment from what they were discussing. 'Genes play the oddest tricks, it seems to me. I'm the one who *looks* like a Wyndham, but it's *you* who behave like one.'

'Cool-blooded and unexcitable, I suppose you mean?'

'Well, if I'd been you and wanted Ned, I wouldn't have waited this long to visit Providence again. That was carrying Wyndham coolness much too far.'

'I waited to be invited . . . no-one *did* invite me,' Anita pointed out with unusual sharpness. 'I'm only going now because Aunt Gertrude feels obliged to have me there. I am *not* going to throw myself at Ned, only to revisit a house that haunts my memory.'

Lucy looked unimpressed. 'Providence is lovely, ancient, peaceful . . . anything you like, but nowadays I hate the whole suffocating business of living there. Matthew Harris has tacked a garage on to his forge, and the village women, chattering like starlings, take a weekly motor-bus to Warwick instead of waiting for the carrier to call; but nothing's really changed. The children can still tell you which woman's pregnant again as soon as she knows herself, and the men still lay odds on how many more times Alf Parker will go home drunk from the alehouse before he falls in the village pond and drowns himself. Life at Haywood's End!'

'There's more to it than that . . . Lucy, I insist on believing it.'

'Then why not believe in the rest of what you want? For God's sake forget your upbringing – it's as dead as the dodo anyway. Go on and *throw* yourself at Ned! Haven't you heard that we're emancipated now, allowed to take what we want? My bold, brave sister can give you an example if you want one.'

Anita smiled with amusement and a hint of regret. 'I couldn't be like Sybil even if I tried. You'll have to let me cope with Ned in my own way.'

'Actually, you're much more like Charlotte,' Lucy observed, 'both of you diligently searching for someone else to give way to! I don't suppose she told you she fell in love during the war – with a wounded soldier she was helping in her Red Cross work. He wasn't in the least suitable, of course, but *she* wouldn't have minded that. My guess is that Aunt Louisa convinced her she wasn't suitable for *him*. That was enough to end her sad little love story.'

Anita thought it had the haunting ring of truth, and explained why Charlotte now worked for social reform and didn't want a husband.

'We aren't any nearer establishing what it is *you* want,' she reminded Lucy.

'No, but in the meantime we'll go out and buy something luxurious and useless. It's one pleasure, at least, that a rich man's wife can always permit herself!' She stared at Anita's expression, then said in a different tone of voice, 'Did that sound very brittle?'

'Well, rather *cheap*, since you ask me.'

Lucy flushed, but leaned over to kiss her cousin. 'I'm glad you came to England,' she said unexpectedly.

When Anita finally went to Providence, she travelled alone, because her cousin had hurried back two days previously, remembering that it was her father-in-law's birthday. The wistful hope that Ned might have come to meet the train died when she found Jem Martin waiting for her at the station. She couldn't remember him, or find anything to say to him as they drove along. Her trembling hands, and a heart that thudded like a schoolgirl's at her first evening dance, made her feel nervous and ashamed; at thirty-two it was pitiful to be in such a condition. She forced herself to concentrate on the landscape through which they drove, and was gradually calmed by the discovery that others had made before her. Nowhere else on earth could be more beautiful than the English countryside in spring-time. It was almost the end of April, and after a mild winter waterfalls of greenness poured themselves down the surrounding hills to merge with the greenness of the valley. The hedgerows were white with the blossom of blackthorn and wild cherry, and bluebells shimmered like water in the copse bordering the drive at Providence.

'Nearly there, Miss,' Jem shouted.

She closed her eyes so that the house should be there in front of her when she opened them again. The noise of the engine suddenly died into a stillness broken only by the scale a blackbird was rehearsing. She could see him perched on the top of a holly tree while he repeated his climbing phrase, then altered it by a single note, and tried again. Her life seemed to depend on concentrating on it so hard that she would be able to sing it for him; but she could see her aunt walking across the bridge to meet her. It was time to face the fact that, whatever might come of it, she was back at Providence.

'Anita, my dear . . . such a long, long time!'

Gertrude Wyndham's dark hair had silvered, and her face looked thin to the point of gauntness, but there was no mistaking her smile. The fear of being unwelcome dwindled and died.

'Dear Aunt . . . I'm so happy to be here . . . and everything looks so beautiful . . .' She could get no further for the tears clogging her throat, and gestured helplessly instead to an immediate loveliness – the great clumps of yellow iris that speared the silver water of the moat.

'Ned planted them last year,' Gertrude explained. 'Apart from managing the farms, he spends his days making the gardens more and more beautiful.' She linked her arm inside Anita's and led her back across the bridge. 'Jem will see to your luggage. Ned would be here but he was required urgently in Lucy's wing. Whenever things go awry for my small grandson he summons Ned, having no faith in mere women to mend his world! My dear, why don't you go and find them while I lure your uncle out of his studio? He *means* to remember when it's time to stop painting and be sociable, but there's never any relying on him.'

She pointed to the corridor leading into the other ranges of the house. 'I expect you can remember your way about. In any case, if Charles is unhappy there will be a certain amount of noise!' She smiled and went away up the broad

102

staircase, leaving her niece to realize how tactfully she had been left to meet Ned again.

In fact he was outside in the courtyard garden, with a mutinous-looking toddler and a smiling, red-haired girl in the dark skirt and frilled apron of an upper servant. Ned was busy explaining to his nephew that a cat whose tail was pulled would certainly try to scratch him. There was a moment to catch her breath, and stand and stare. Light-brown hair still fell untidily across his forehead, and the kindness in his expression hadn't changed. But she didn't remember the scar that ran down from hairline to temple, nor the lines etched into the thinness of his face. He was twenty-nine now, but looked older. She stood quite still, and it was the child who first noticed her.

'Who *she*?' he asked disapprovingly.

Ned swung round and saw a slender young woman in a blue knitted suit; her dark hair waved crisply against her temples and skimmed the nape of her neck. She looked elegant and self-possessed, and not in any way like the girl he remembered. It took him so long to find anything to say that she half-expected him to repeat his nephew's question . . . who she?

'It's Anita . . . yes, of course it is! Welcome back, cousin.'

He smiled a little, and over the pain stabbing into her very heart she managed to smile back. 'Don't tell me – you were expecting a girl in an Edwardian frilled blouse and skirt, and enormous cartwheel hat!'

'Sort of . . . though I don't know why. Lucy wouldn't wear such things, and even Mama eschews cartwheel hats!' He came towards her, holding out his hand. 'How lovely to see you again.'

'And I'm so happy to be back. Ned . . . I began to think it would never happen.' She didn't mind, suddenly, whether he knew or not how much it mattered to her to be there; but she must be careful not to weep, because tears embarrassed even the kindest of men.

He let go of her hand, and she had the feeling of a small but definite retreat . . . unless it was only that a shadow fell on them as a cloud wandered across the face of the sun.

'Anita, let me introduce Mary Haskell, who looks after Charlie for my sister Lucy. Mary, this is my cousin, Miss Wyndham, come to visit us from America.'

The introduction left her disconcerted and unable to decide whether the girl was more friend than servant. She smiled but didn't hold out her hand, and decided in the next moment that, though it was now too late, it was what Ned had wanted her to do.

'*This* little corker is Lucy's son, Charles,' he said quickly.

Determined to do better this time, Anita bent down with the intention of kissing the child; but he turned and hid his face in Mary Haskell's skirt, crying as if he'd been threatened. She saw Ned smile at the girl, and felt cruelly excluded. The three of them belonged there, the smile seemed to say, but she did not.

Mary scooped the child up in her arms, and looked apologetic.

'Don't mind him, Miss Wyndham. It's time for his tea, and he always gets irritable when he's hungry!'

She gave a little farewell smile and walked away; a servant, maybe, but one who didn't have to wait to be dismissed.

'Time for our tea, too, I expect,' Ned said. He politely offered Anita his arm and led her back across the garden. 'I hope Uncle James is well? I can *just* remember him, you know, and for me he'll always remain as he seemed then – a giant of a man with very bright eyes and a red-gold beard like a Viking king! What a sadness that people can't stay for ever as one remembers them.'

Yes, it was a sadness. Anita stared down at her elegant silk-stockinged legs and the blue knitted skirt she'd thought so pretty. She had not only come too late, but changed as well. She couldn't be sure which was the greater mistake.

Chapter Nine

Legend had it that the Wyndham ghost – a sixteenth-century lady wrongly accused of adultery and murdered by her husband – haunted the Library; if so, she was the shyest of shades, disturbing nobody. In the Chapel Room, it was the gentle spirit of William's mother, Hester Wyndham, that Gertrude always felt close to.

This morning she offered her prayers as usual to the Virgin Mary, whose simple wooden statue held the place of honour on the altar. Hubert Roberts sometimes teased her about this feminine preference, but she tried to explain that gender had nothing to do with it; it was simply that the Mother of Christ seemed more approachable than an Almighty God reigning over all things. She remained on her knees, considering her family – prayer and thought about them being for her almost the same thing. There was much to be thankful for – William content, Ned his old, happy self, even untroubled by Anita's visit, and Sybil, their problem girl, settled at last and awaiting Henri's child in Paris.

It only left Lucy to worry about. She'd been so little trouble when small, so loving, and so rock-like all the time Ned was away in France, but something was wrong now. Her simple selfless plan in marrying Frank had seemed justified because it was working so beautifully, but Gertrude couldn't believe that it was working now. Nor, clearly could Jane Thornley, although all she permitted herself to say was that Frank should have more sense than to neglect his wife by staying for weeks on end in America. Gertrude prayed for her daughter, but couldn't help wishing that there was something more she could think of to do for her as well.

She'd stayed longer in the Chapel Room than usual. When she went downstairs William, Ned, and Anita were halfway through breakfast, discussing the chances of a fine weekend. The coming Saturday, the first day of May, was important in the village calendar. The women would watch their daughters take part in the May Queen's procession; then would come the traditional dances round the maypole. For these the smaller boys were press-ganged into performing as well, although the benefit was doubtful when their clear intention was to get the coloured ribbons into as much confusion as possible. The men of the village would, of course, be absent, having carefully arranged for themselves the duty of supporting Haywood's End against Hockley – a traditional enemy in the cricket field, and the one always chosen to get a new season off to a spirited start.

While Ned explained these ritual mysteries to his cousin, Gertrude pondered the wisdom of the gathering she was committed to for Anita's sake. Perhaps it *had* been rash to hope that time would have mellowed Louise Trentham's reaction to Lucy's father-in-law. She would have to rely on Hubert Roberts to entertain Louise, and on Maud to muffle the worst of Arthur's wood notes wild.

'Ned, as you love me, *don't* stir coals this evening,' she begged him. 'The subjects of Free Trade, Mr Lloyd George, and the Irish Question are all equally banned; I want a peaceful dinner-table, not a battlefield.'

He pushed back his chair and went to leave a kiss on the top of his mother's head. 'Trust me. I shall lie low, like Brer Rabbit and "say nuffin"!' Then he smiled at Anita. 'Feel like a drive to Bromycham? It isn't quite London or New York, though Arthur Thornley would have you believe it's better than both! There's quite a good art gallery you could visit while I talk my vegetable whole-salers into increasing their orders.'

'I could come *with* you, if you thought my feminine wiles might help with the wholesalers.' Anita smiled as she said it but felt again his faint withdrawal, as if any step he made towards her was instantly regretted.

The morning was soft and overcast but Ned predicted a clear sky by the time they reached Birmingham. He was pleasantly talkative on the journey, a man with nothing on his mind except business and the casual entertainment of a guest. His weather forecast proved correct, and by the time he left her in the centre of the city she was regretting a fine morning that might have been better spent. One unlooked-for pleasure of her visit was a growing friendship with her shy uncle. William had examined the sketches she'd made in Paris and pronounced them remarkably good. Now, he seemed to enjoy instructing her in the technique of painting in oils.

But she was in Birmingham, not roaming the park at Providence with him, looking for 'subjects'. She made a dutiful visit to the Cathedral and confirmed that the baroque wasn't her favourite style; spent an hour in the City Art Gallery confirming that the Pre-Raphaelites weren't among her favourite painters; then it was time to meet Ned. She half-expected him to suggest that they might eat luncheon somewhere, but sat beside him disappointed and hungry as he turned the car in the direction of Haywood's End. They were free of the city and in open country again with the suddenness that still surprised her, when he veered off the road, bumped along a rutted lane, and stopped at the foot of a wooded hill.

'I cadged a picnic lunch off Emmy,' he explained with a smile, 'praying I was right about the weather! Do you mind a bit of a climb? This is Lark Hill, and there's a good vantage-point up above.'

She followed him up a path between beech trees caught in the very moment of breaking into brilliant green leaf. If she stood quite still she thought she might even hear the little sigh with which each tiny bud unfurled itself. Ned led her to a grassy space sheltered by the last upward spring of the hill. Anita stood and stared at the wide green kingdom spread out below them, while he shook out a rug and then delved into Emmy's wicker basket. Perfect peace was all about them, and such privacy that they might have been alone in the world. A hope was strengthening in her heart that he had brought her here deliberately, and it seemed safe to rely on it. He knew, after all, that what had been begun between them was not yet completed. She made a faint clutch at amusement to calm her thudding pulse, and decided that they would eat the picnic first. Ned was nothing if not English through and through . . . even if passion should stir, it would be indecent not to see his companion fed first!

He was about to ask her why she smiled, but the reedy call that floated up from the woodland below them interrupted him.

'A cuckoo today, instead of lark song,' he said. 'What do you make of it? One school of thought here insists that he begins on D sharp, another that it's C natural. This being funny old England, our feelings are liable to run high on the subject!'

'*Dear* funny old England,' she amended quietly, and wondered at the expression that touched his face for a moment. He sat squatting back on his heels, apparently intent on spreading out food. The scar on his temple was a white line against the brownness of his skin, and his mouth was firm and self-controlled . . . a man's mouth now. He'd been a boy still, the only time he'd ever kissed her. It was pain to look at him now, and long for him to kiss her again.

'Throw yourself at him' Lucy had advised; she hadn't said *how*, with a man whose attention seemed to be evenly divided between chicken patties and the notes a cuckoo sang.

'The dispute will have to go on for all I can do about it,' she murmured with difficulty. 'I'm no musician.'

'No? Well, my father says you have the makings of a good artist instead.'

Anita smiled faintly. At any other time the compliment would secretly have pleased her very much, but not now. 'I enjoy painting . . . it isn't enough to prove that I'd ever be any good.'

'A *natural* artist, he says,' Ned insisted, 'not just one who can be taught the right techniques. He's untaught himself, so he should know.' He crumbled pastry on the plate in front of him, then stared out across the bright landscape. 'We haven't talked about the past, and perhaps it's time we did. It's so long ago that you may not even remember what . . . hopeful idiots we were.'

'Oh, I can *just* remember! I was to go home to New York while you were to grow a little older and a little less poor.' She marvelled at the deceptions women were capable of – her voice sounded as level as his, and even faintly amused.

The view apparently absorbed her attention, and it was safe for him to look at *her*. He was still trying to rediscover the shy, diffident girl who'd arrived one golden summer and taken Providence, England, and Ned Wyndham to her heart. He hadn't even noticed, then, that she was the daughter of a rich man; now it couldn't be ignored – hand-made brogues, slender legs covered in pure silk stockings, ivory-coloured blazer and skirt, and a blue silk scarf fastened at her throat by an antique cameo. She was the frighteningly finished product that only taste and wealth could achieve. She was dear, but different, and quite completely beyond his touch.

'Time and war took care of the ageing process,' Ned said carefully. 'In fact the war nearly did for me altogether. I think I'm all right again now, except for one thing so worrying that I try never to think about it. "Dear" England you said a moment ago, and so it always will be – above price. But the terrible truth is that if there were to be another war, I shouldn't be able to fight for it. Think of *that*, Anita: I couldn't go to war again, even for England.'

The confession seemed so shameful that he waited to see her face grow cold with disgust, but all she did was smile. 'Dear Ned, no-one's going to have to fight, ever again. There's a thing called the League of Nations now . . . remember?'

'So there is! Still, it remains a bit of a worry, like my poor old head.' He poured out cider for them both while he considered the other fence that reared, high and impassable, above him.

'There's another worry nearer home. The Wyndhams haven't got noticeably richer since you were last here. Agriculture boomed during the war because merchant ships were being sunk and we needed home-grown food. A lot of land changed hands when owners died and their sons didn't come back from France, and tenants borrowed money to buy their farms, believing the boom would last for ever. It never does, of course. Foreign food is coming in again, and the Government's subsidies have been withdrawn; so the poor men are caught with dwindling incomes and mortgages to repay.'

'Does that affect you?'

'The income from the land we farm ourselves isn't too badly hit because we've switched to producing the stuff we've a market for on our doorstep; but we still have tenants, and we're affected by the rents *they* can afford to pay. Countrymen are powerfully set in their ways, and a chap who's spent his life growing wheat isn't easily persuaded to try dairying or pig-farming instead. In any case, whatever we do, farming as a way of life means a lot of hard work and a poor return for all concerned.'

She wondered with a wry, tender amusement who else but Ned would choose *this* moment to drag pig-farming into the conversation. Still, no doubt he would get round to *them*, eventually.

'All the same, you don't see yourself doing anything else,' she said gently. 'Why should you? You've got the lovely land that belongs to the Wyndhams, and Providence itself . . . that's more than enough, without rolling in vulgar wealth!'

She knew instantly that something had changed. Instead of being companionable, the silence between them was charged now, and ominous. It was broken by the cuckoo's persistent call and she could have sworn that the unseen bird was mocking her for some unforgivable piece of stupidity.

'I *wondered* if you knew,' Ned murmured at last. 'It didn't seem possible that Uncle James hadn't told you, and yet . . .' His voice trailed away, forcing her to prompt him.

110

'Yet . . . what?'

'We no longer own Providence. The house was mort-gaged years ago, almost as soon as my father inherited it. The bank foreclosed during the war, when we hadn't a hope of buying it back. It belongs to Frank now, and we live there as his guests.'

It made a lot of things clear, and she marvelled at her blindness in needing to be told. 'That's why Lucy married Frank.' She said it as a fact but saw Ned frown.

'It was *part* of why she married him,' he amended with a touch of stiffness. 'She'd grown very fond of him . . . grown used to relying on him in all sorts of ways while I was away. But it's true that she wanted us all to be able to stay at Providence – me especially because, though I was half-cracked at the time, I was more sane *there* than anywhere else.' His eyes fixed themselves on his cousin's face, steady and sad. 'The war did terrible things, Anita. There are families at Haywood's End cut to pieces by it, never to be the same again, and God knows *they're* no different from a thousand other villages up and down the land. But the great thing, they would tell you even now, is not to flinch, whatever happens.'

She stared down at her hands and found that her fingers didn't tremble. Her blood was mixed, but she had *some* claim to Haywood's End. Perhaps without knowing it *she'd* been handed down through countless generations the stubborn knowledge that whatever had to be borne *could* be borne. Even so, she had to make a try for happiness.

'Wars change circumstances . . . they don't necessarily change us. Can't *we* remain the people we were?'

While he made up his mind she listened to her heartbeats and the voice of that damned cuckoo, still harping on the note of D sharp, or perhaps C natural. At last he lifted his head and looked at her.

'We *haven't* remained the people we were, Anita,' he said simply. It was a statement of fact, as unarguable as death itself.

She might have argued all the same; trampled in the dust the long habit of self-concealment and shouted that she cared nothing for learning to paint, for wealth, for which of them owned Providence, if only she might stay with him. But she'd lost the knack, possessed once upon a time, of stepping into his mind. She could offer herself, be accepted or rejected, and never know for sure the reason for what it turned out to be . . . suppose he didn't want her at all, but took her out of pity because she'd been waiting for him . . . ?

She brushed crumbs from her lap, and arranged her lips in a smile that she feared might become permanent, like the grotesque faces of childhood their nurse had often warned them about.

'It's time we went . . . there may be something I can do to help Aunt Gertrude.'

Ned nodded, and began to repack the basket. Then he held out his hands to pull her to her feet. His mouth lightly brushed her cheek and she turned her head so that his lips met hers instead. The grip on her hands tightened unbearably, then suddenly she was released again.

'I'd forgotten the family gathering,' he said unsteadily, 'but in any case it's certainly time we went.'

They walked down the hill in silence and found nothing to say until Providence was almost in sight.

'Was the visit to the art gallery a waste of time?'

'Not at all. It put an idea in my mind,' she lied bravely. 'I must go home first and settle things with my father, but I'd like to come back to London in the autumn and enrol for painting classes at the Slade.'

Ned turned his head to stare at her calm profile – thin Wyndham nose, pretty mouth, and firmly moulded chin. 'The makings of a natural artist', and one who would never need to come near starving while she learned to paint. *That* was what he must remember. The car swerved a little, forcing him to concentrate on the road again.

Anita didn't permit herself to rush away from Providence. She was almost certain her aunt guessed why the picnic had taken place; nothing was said, but Gertrude treated her with even more loving kindness than before, and made it easy for her to escape with William on expeditions that kept her away from Ned. She was aware of being greatly privileged in her tutor and gradually, from seeming ridiculous, the idea she'd aired to Ned on the spur of the moment became not ridiculous at all – became, in fact, the thing she knew she was going to do.

It was heartbreaking to leave when the time came, but a little less so for knowing that she needn't relinquish all that Providence contained. The faint hope of being loved by Ned had finally been slain, but the rest would always be there, waiting for her, whenever she returned. She travelled back to London, said an affectionate goodbye to Charlotte, and found amidst her sadness a trace of amusement in the fact that Harry was glad enough to see her go to offer to drive her all the way to the boat.

'I'm afraid you must think I'm going for good,' she pointed out solemnly. 'Hasn't Charlotte mentioned that I mean to come back?'

His face broke into a smile of such whole-hearted enjoyment that she caught a last, late glimpse of the young man Harry Trentham had been. 'A viper's tongue hath my sweet coz! Never mind, I shall return good for evil and still repeat my offer.'

'Well, the offer's truly appreciated, but the Labour Party's need is much greater than mine when all I have to do is take a taxi to the boat-train.' She smiled so charmingly that he was aware of sudden regret. It might have been worth the trouble of getting to know her, after all; but his habit was to fill every unforgiving minute of each day, and there was nothing more important than the work he was trying to do.

'When you arrive next time I *shall* be there to meet you,' he heard himself promise, and on that amiable note they said goodbye.

Anita would have been surprised to know how much she was missed at Providence. After two boring days spent dutifully with Charlie while Mary Haskell took a short holiday, Lucy seized on the excuse of an aching tooth to return to London. She attended the surgery of Mr Cuthbert Hickson in Wimpole Street and, having promised herself that it was her only reason for coming to London, forbore to get in touch with any of her friends. There was a perverse kind of pleasure in being alone in a huge, impersonal city that cared no more for her than the ocean cared for the fate of its composite drops of water. She spent a blamelessly dull evening by herself in St James's Place, warned Mrs Knightly, the housekeeper, that she would be leaving the following morning, and took herself off to a cold and lonely bed. Even Frank's body beside her would have been a welcome reminder that one other human being was aware of her existence. But he'd gone away not hearing the plea she'd made to him. She could die in the night and no-one would even notice the infinitesimal gap left by Lucy Thornley. It was a thought so lonely that she fell asleep weeping a little.

In the morning the sun was shining. London on such a day in May was so beautiful and exciting that she would shop a little, stroll a little, and *then* go home. Burlington Arcade was a mysteriously dim and enticing tunnel compared with the brightness outside. She stopped in front of a jeweller's window and stared at beautiful useless tiaras and necklaces glittering with a thousand different points of light behind the glass.

'Tempted, my dear Lucy?'

She spun round at the sound of Harry's voice, and found him smiling at her . . . smiling as if he *saw* her and the sight gave him pleasure, just as he'd done a long time ago on the night of Charlotte's birthday party. She remembered the night for other reasons, but for that reason as well.

'I thought you'd gone back to Providence . . . I'm sure that's what Lottie said.'

'I had, while Frank is in America; but an aching tooth needed seeing to.'

'The tooth must be better – you look the very spirit of a May morning!'

She thought it might be true, because that was how she

114

suddenly felt . . . beautiful, carefree, and irresistibly happy. Even in the subdued light of the Arcade she could see the shine of his bright hair, and count the small lines that fanned out from the corners of his eyes. She wasn't little Lucy Wyndham now, waiting for him to look away from Emily long enough to notice her; he *was* noticing her. Enlightenment sounded like a trumpet-blast, and at last she could have told Anita what was the thing she lacked . . .

She blinked, and heard him say, 'I didn't intend walking this way, but Fate clearly meant me to. I *think* what it's prompting me to do next is run mad and celebrate a lovely unexpected meeting.'

'My dear Harry, it sounds much too frivolous! Surely there are people you must address. Some good that must be done?'

'You jest, and poke the finger of fun, but as it happens *I* was serious. It suddenly occurs to me that I've got very dull. What shall it be? A visit to the Zoo, the Tower, Hampstead Heath? Consider London yours!'

Even now she was afraid to believe that she was being offered this richness. 'I was going home . . . just c. . . came here for a moment . . . Harry, I think I should t. . .take the train . . .'

His finger across her lips stopped the rest of what she was stammering to say; for a moment he *did* look serious.

'I've got very dull and you, sweet Lucy, have got very dutiful. Shall we declare today a holiday?'

A joyous smile lifted the droop of her mouth. 'Oh, Harry . . . I'd *love* a little holiday.'

'Well, then, off we go . . . Regent's Park first, then we'll see how we feel after that.'

The man behind the jeweller's window sighed as they walked away; for a moment or two he'd felt quite sure of a sale. They hadn't even noticed him watching them, and that was a sure sign. There was nothing like being in love to make people forget that the rest of the world existed.

Chapter Ten

It was like being a child again. The actual moment in which she lived was filled with joy, and for as long as it could be made to last neither past nor future existed. In Harry's company Regent's Park, the Zoo, and even the strange assortment of people there, were sprinkled with the golden dust of happiness – she could see it glinting in the sunlight wherever she looked.

Beyond explaining why Frank was away in America, she didn't refer to him again. He was part of real life, and for the moment she was in the middle of a fairy-tale, shining and harmless and all too brief. The setting didn't matter at all; it was simply the colourful, noisy background against which the two of them walked, talked, laughed, and drew together in a companionship that finally excluded the rest of the world. It wasn't until the sun's lengthening shadows reminded them of time rushing past that Harry thought to glance at his watch.

'Great God . . . do you realize the time? My dear girl, *you* must go home and I must stop sky-larking. There's a meeting tonight at which I'm supposed to look as if I've spent the day intelligently studying the social implications of mass unemployment.'

The lovely day was coming to an end but her mouth still curved easily into a smile. 'Kindness, as well as devotion to the Cause, might earn you a place in Heaven! Explain that you felt obliged to take pity on a poor country cousin instead.'

'It will do as an excuse as long as my friends don't catch sight of you . . . you're nobody's idea of a needy country mouse!'

He smiled at her while they waitied for a taxi, but

already she could see the thought of the evening ahead drawing him away from her. The day's simple pleasures had released in him a spring of carefree gaiety blocked up since Emily's death, but now it was time to put away childish things. He flagged down a passing cab and helped her into it, then stood bare-headed on the pavement, looking at her.

'Thank you for a happy day, my dear . . . the best I can remember for ages past.'

It had been the best she could remember *ever*. She didn't say so, but smiled at him with unconscious wistfulness from the dimness inside the cab. 'Is the meeting so very imminent that you can't come back with me and drink a cup of tea . . . dear Harry, not just *one* cup?'

She waited for him to refuse – thus, almost certainly, would the gods punish her for being greedy; but after a moment's hesitation he climbed in beside her. 'Why not? I can consider myself a free man for an hour or two yet.'

She felt his shoulder brush against hers; happiness could be made to last a little longer after all, like the final, incandescent flush of colour in the evening sky before darkness fell. In the musty warmth that now enclosed them he was more conscious of her than in the open spaces of the park . . . could smell the fragrance of her skin and, because her head was tilted back a little to look out of the window, see the delicately chiselled line of cheek-bone, chin, and throat. He surprised himself by thinking that it was pure enough to have graced an antique coin. She was his little cousin, the quiet girl who'd grown up in the shadow of a more vibrant sister, and married a rich man he particularly disliked.

Lucy's voice broke into his jumbled thoughts. 'Did you see Anita again before she left for New York?'

'Yes, briefly. I understand she's coming back, to study art or some such thing.'

'Some such *useless* thing!' she gently mocked him. She hadn't any real wish to talk about Anita, but inconsequential conversation seemed suddenly necessary because,

117

minute by minute, she was becoming more and more aware of him. Even the sight of his hand resting on the seat between them shook her with the longing to put her own into it and feel it held. 'You think a woman shouldn't trouble her head with anything but safe domestic matters?' she suggested breathlessly.

Harry smiled at the question. 'It doesn't matter what I think of *anything* Anita chooses to trouble her head with; she can do as she likes. But since you ask me I'm bound to say it seems a waste of time. You won't thank me for pointing it out, but all the world's great creative artists have been men.'

'If only I could produce just *one* woman's name to confound you with! Still, it's my father's opinion that she should study. My *own* opinion is that she's the last person on earth to take herself very seriously . . . she just needs something to concentrate on, since she isn't going to be concentrating on Ned.'

'Was that ever more than a brief boy-and-girl thing?' Harry sounded genuinely surprised. 'Even if it was, she's become much too citified and expensive-looking now for a simple chap like Ned.'

'It doesn't do to judge us by appearances,' Lucy said severely. 'In a man's world we need protective colouring.'

He might have denied any such need for privileged women in the class his cousins belonged to, but the memory of Frank Thornley rose in his mind – charmless, taciturn, and authoritarian. It wasn't surprising if Lucy felt the need of protective colouring against *him*. It was thoroughly wrong that *this* girl should be married to such a man, and he'd been blindly insensitive not to realize it before. Over the sense of protest growing inside him he tried to concentrate on the girl they were supposed to be discussing.

'Anita left it too late. If she'd wanted Ned, she should have come back sooner.'

It was exactly what Lucy had said herself, but now it made her angry. 'Life is a good deal less easy for women than you make it sound. Anita was waiting to be asked . . . hoping to be told that Ned still wanted her.'

'And you think he's forgotten that he *did* want her?'

'Not forgotten,' she said slowly. 'I think something got in the way – Providence, probably.'

'Well, she could have come back during the war. No invitation was needed for that.'

'How could she have come when Patrick didn't? It would have made *his* shirking seem even worse. I think it broke her heart not to come.'

Harry couldn't disagree about Patrick, but his opinion of his American cousin wasn't for putting into words suitable for Lucy. Instead, he touched her hand. 'Well said, little one! Most of the women I know prefer to sink their claws in one another.'

She was suddenly made aware of how little she knew about his life, but it was certain to contain women queueing up to try to take the place of Emily Trentham. They wouldn't succeed . . . *no-one* would, she thought desolately.

When they got to the house in St James's Place, Harry took a considering look round. 'I didn't realize you lived so close to me in London, or in such style! I suppose I prefer to forget that you have a disgustingly successful husband.'

She gave a little shrug which seemed to dispose of her husband as well as the house. 'It's convenient enough. Frank spent a lot of time here during the war, but when he's away I'm meant to bury myself at Providence. He left angry with me because I insisted on staying in London with Anita.'

She had no right to sound forlorn; Harry told himself she was a beautiful, spoiled child much given to self-pity. 'Most people wouldn't see it as a hardship to be "buried" at Providence,' he pointed out brusquely. 'Families living two or three to a hovel that ought in any case to be condemned might wonder what was so unbearable about the life you lead.'

'So they might,' she agreed with a strange, sad smile. 'But what do you expect? I'm the selfish, pampered wife of a rich man . . . part of the feverish, post-war age that has no standards, no grace, and no faith! It's not how I *wanted* to be. Harry, do you remember our grandmother Hester at Providence? I meant to grow up like her – gentle and sweet and strong. Doesn't that strike you as being extremely f. . .funny?'

She turned away so that he shouldn't see her trembling mouth, but she could do nothing about the tears that brimmed over her eyelids and trickled down her face.

'I don't find it funny,' he said behind her. 'It occurs to me now, rather late in the day, that you didn't have much choice in what you became because Frank was the only hope of keeping Providence for your family. As things turned out, Sybil didn't need it, but the rest of them did. I was still away in France, so it wasn't very clear to me at the time. I should have learned better since then, but I was content to accept the idea that marrying wealth rather appealed to you. I'm sorry, Lucy.'

The rare humility in his voice completed her undoing. She turned round blindly and found his arms waiting for her. The instinct to accept them could no more have been resisted than the tide could have failed to respond to the tug of the moon. Her mouth offered itself in a gesture that was equally inevitable. His lips accepted it gently at first, grew urgent, and finally demanded surrender. She was pulled closer and closer against him while his lips explored the pulse beating in her throat and then returned to her mouth again.

'Lucy, my sweet . . . my little love . . .' The murmured words scarcely reached her above the clamour of senses demanding to be satisfied. She couldn't bear it when he lifted his mouth away from hers. 'No . . . don't stop loving me, please, Harry.' Her body seemed to want to melt into his, but he managed to hold her away from him.

'My darling love, this is madness,' he said unsteadily. 'All *my* fault, but it has to stop while I still can.'

'Not your fault at all, and I'm glad you know the truth. Everybody else always knew that I loved you . . . with quite hopeless faithfulness!' She almost managed to smile at him. 'I thought I'd got over it – *pretended* I'd got over it so that I wouldn't have to admit what was wrong with me. Even for Ned I couldn't have married Frank if you hadn't already married Emily.'

'She was dead by then,' Harry said harshly.

'I know, but it made no difference. There still wasn't any room in your heart for me.'

'It's true that I go on loving the memory of her.' The confession was hard to make because the habit of putting feelings into words was something else that had died with his wife. 'Until I touched you I hadn't held another woman – didn't expect to even want to. They've offered themselves, but I almost enjoyed proving I could do without them. Self-sufficiency, I called it; loneliness was for weaklings. It's taken my "little cousin Lucy" to upset *that* stupid apple-cart!'

'It will be something to remember,' she said softly. 'Harry . . . we forgot all about tea, and now it's time you went to that wretched meeting.'

'God, yes . . . the meeting! Dearest girl, I simply *must* go to Great Smith Street. Will you be all right?'

For the moment she felt brave and strong enough for anything. 'Cross my heart and hope to die.'

'What will you do . . . go home tomorrow?'

'Yes; I shall spend tonight convincing myself that I'm a natural mother after all, who longs to see her son.'

His hand stretched out to touch her cheek. 'Funny . . . I must have known you almost since you were born, without knowing you at all. Good night, my dear, sweet girl. I doubt if our grandmother would have been so *very* disappointed in you.'

She let him go to the door alone, and didn't look out of the window to watch for the moment when he rounded the corner of the street. But the room's emptiness without him slowly became a tangible thing, a presence in the air that might end by suffocating her. She ran down the stairs to find the comfort of another human being; even the frigid politeness of the housekeeper in the kitchen would be better than nothing at all.

'I . . . I decided not to go home today, Mrs Knightly,' she murmured. 'I shall be in to dinner.'

If she forced herself to smile, for once the woman might smile back . . . but no! Mrs Knightly knew that she owed her job to Frank, it was he who'd chosen her and provided a home for her and Alice, her daughter. They looked after *him* with devoted care, and reserved their cool, respectful hostility for his wife. Now, hovering uncomfortably at the kitchen door, Lucy found it insufferable to stay in the house with them. 'No . . . I've changed my mind . . . forget about dinner,' she stammered.

Mrs Knightly's face didn't even express relief or satisfaction; her nod communicated nothing at all. Lucy turned and fled full-pelt up the stairs to her own room. The idea that had suddenly blossomed in her mind was now blotting out everything but the need for haste. To be too late would be the only thing in the world she couldn't bear. For the first time in her life she was going to a political meeting.

She was among the last to arrive, squeezed in at the back of the packed hall – faceless to the people on the platform, simply one more dot in a crowd brought there by anger at the way things were, or by reforming zeal, or the burning desire to be a revolutionary. The men around her seemed to belong to the last category. They interrupted the proceedings as a matter of course, and cheered loudly any other heckling from the floor, but only grew really restive with the unimpassioned performance of the evening's chief speaker.

'Not a bleeding spark of fire in *his* belly,' the man beside Lucy muttered resentfully. 'It's a bloody Sunday school meeting we've come to.'

'What d'you expect . . . calls himself a Fabian,' said the man in front.'

'. . . no violence, my friends,' the speaker was suggesting hopefully. 'We must achieve a just society by peaceful, gradual means . . .'

It was as far as he got before the rumbling volcano beside her finally erupted. The man was on his chair now, egged on by the others around him. 'Action . . . violence . . . we don't care what you call it. We *want* it now . . . not bloody sweet reasons why we're supposed to go on waiting for justice till Kingdom come.'

'Yes . . . *now!*' The cry was taken up; they were all on their feet, shouting and gesticulating, and she was among them – dangerously isolated because she wasn't sharing their fervour. Even as the thought occurred to her, she was jerked to her feet, and a livid face thrust itself up against hers. 'What d'you think *you're* 'ere for, stuck-up bitch? Come to stare at the animals in the Zoo? Go on – *shout*, like the rest of us!'

His grip on her arm was cruel, but it had the saving grace of making her angry enough to shout at *him*. 'Let go of me . . . I'll shout when *I* feel inclined.'

Excitement lit his face at the prospect of *one* fight he could win, but it was too late . . . the hubbub all around them was beginning to die down. A tall, bright-haired man had sauntered to the edge of the platform and stood there, waiting to be heard. He made no attempt to control the audience, but Lucy thought it was like watching one of the new vacuum-cleaners at work, sucking up dust . . . he simply absorbed the violence of the mob at the back of the hall. She didn't consciously listen to what Harry said, but she was aware of the moment when the atmosphere had changed enough for him to make them laugh. Then he promised them a better future than the present they knew if they would only help people like himself work for it. They were sent out into the night at last, pacified for the time being – no revolution *yet*, at least. She understood, now, the strength of his belief that the old order must change; the men around her had allowed themselves to be persuaded because they didn't doubt *his* conviction.

When they surged towards the exit she was carried along with them, faced by the new problem of how to get home. The chances of a cab seemed slight, she was in a part of London she didn't know, and it was even difficult to decide in which direction to start walking. The crush around her eased a little and a hand suddenly held her shoulder from behind. She recognized it at once for what it was – 'a little touch of Harry in the night'! But he was frowning when she turned round, and sounded not much less angry than the man who'd bruised her arm.

'What in the name of God do you think *you*'re doing here . . . of all the bloody stupid things . . .'

'I came out of curiosity.'

'So that all your prejudices about the lower orders could be confirmed? Well, now you know. They're hungry, angry, and tired of being told that the meek shall inherit the Kingdom of Heaven. They want slightly more reward *now*.'

'And are entitled to it, I'm sure,' she agreed steadily. 'But violence won't get it for them. That's what my father would say, and I think he'd be right.'

Harry's taut face relaxed a little. 'I hope you didn't air that philosophy inside . . . you couldn't have found a more militant bunch to sit with if you'd tried. I didn't spot you until I was waiting for them to be quiet, and then damned nearly died of fright.' He put an arm round her shoulders and steered her through the crowd. 'Come on . . . home, little one.'

They walked in silence until they found a cab, and climbed inside. Harry was untalkative, she supposed because he was tired. Her own tiredness wasn't physical . . . she'd never felt less like sleeping, although she was wrapped in the delicious lassitude that follows excitement and the stimulus of fear. She didn't care what happened to her as long as Harry seemed not to notice that his hand still held hers.

'Has this been an eventful enough evening for you, or will you round it off by having supper with me?' he asked abruptly.

'Well, yes . . . of course; but I'm not dressed for anywhere grand.'

The light from a street-lamp shone on his face and she saw him smile. 'And *I'm* not a plutocrat, Lucy . . . I was thinking of a whelk-stall along the Embankment! No, perhaps I've got a better idea.' Five minutes later he

124

stopped the driver outside his flat in Arlington Street. 'Service flats haven't much to commend them, but at least they provide service when it's required.'

She followed him into a small, neat sitting-room, which became less impersonal when he drew curtains and lit lamps. The eventful day couldn't be said to be harmless now. She knew that she shouldn't be there, even with a man who was her cousin; but guilt and the knowledge that present joy would have to be paid for could make no difference now. She was well and truly abroad in the strange new country she'd crossed into on the night of Charlotte's birthday. Harry ordered food to be brought up to them, and poured wine while they waited for it to arrive.

'I didn't go to the meeting just in order to despise your supporters,' she said suddenly. 'The man next to me called me a stuck-up bitch – is that your impression too?'

'No, it isn't. I'm sorry I swore at you . . . I was angry because you'd given me a fright.'

'I went because I wanted to be where *you* were.' The simple confession went unanswered and she was forced to go on. 'Will you let me stay here tonight?'

The silence in the room was broken only by the rattle of traffic in Piccadilly, and a clock somewhere chiming the hour. At last Harry dragged himself out of the paralysis that gripped him and moved across the room to kneel by her chair.

'My dearest girl, for pity's sake think what you're saying. You're a . . .'

'. . . married woman who ought to be ashamed of herself. I know, but it doesn't matter as long as *you*'re not ashamed of me. I've wanted you to love me for as long as I can remember, and now is my only chance.' Her eyes met his with perfect candour. 'Frank won't be away for long; I can't go on being a nuisance to you.'

'A *nuisance*! Oh, my God . . . if you knew the trouble I had tonight keeping my mind on that infernal meeting instead of you.'

She smiled with such delight that he had to smile too. 'Harry, please don't send me away.'

He leaned forward to kiss her mouth. 'How can I? But I'm an out-of-practice lover, my sweet. You'll have to forgive me if I'm clumsy.'

When the waiter arrived ten minutes later there was no reply to his knock. The door was locked and he went away leaving his tray on the floor outside. People were barmy, in his considered view – not that Mr Trentham made a habit of ordering food and then forgetting about it.

That first night, far from being clumsy, Harry taught her what it should mean for a woman to be made love to with tenderness and passion. He led her expertly to such fulfilment for them both that it couldn't be thought of as the same physical act she sometimes had to share with Frank. In the morning when she woke he came towards her, smiling and fully dressed. 'No shame, I hope, sweetheart . . . and no regrets?'

'None at all, but now it's *your* turn to ask!'

He bent down to kiss her smiling mouth. 'I fully intended to! Mr Trentham presents his *warmest* compliments and hopes to have the pleasure of his lady's company tonight.'

'She thinks she *might* manage to be here . . . darling Harry, nothing will stop her being here.'

When he'd left she dressed and walked home, still wrapped in the incredulous delight of the night just past. She had sufficient regard for appearances to explain to Mrs Knightly that she would be sleeping in Thurloe Square while her cousin, Miss Trentham, was poorly. She wasn't in a condition to notice that, for once, the housekeeper's expression did briefly register a change.

She made no attempt to go to any of the haunts where friends might be found; the following days were spent quietly waiting for the nights . . . and Harry. Each morning he left her to plunge back into the political fray that was his working life; she never asked to be allowed to go with him, nor did he suggest that their first carefree day together could be repeated. He was the perfect companion of her nights, and the certainty only grew slowly and sadly in her that he didn't wait for them as she did. His body enjoyed hers, but his mind and heart still belonged for the moment to that damnably righteous, all-devouring Cause.

'For the moment' . . . that was how it seemed to her. New-found devotion to his Socialist friends kept him occupied while he waited for the life mapped out for him to unfold itself. The discovery that she was wrong came accidentally one morning. She broke her own rule and mentioned Frank, because the days left to her in London were dwindling to a terrible few that needed counting . . . it was important to know that Harry was counting them, too.

'Frank's ship docks in three days' time,' she said abruptly. 'I got a letter forwarded from Providence yesterday . . . it was posted before he left New York.'

Now, if she prayed to God and the Virgin Mary and all the company of Heaven at once, he would say that she must stay for ever, beacuse he couldn't live without her any more than she could live without him. His eyes and mouth were kind, and he managed not to look at his watch as he came to sit beside her on the bed, but he didn't say what she needed him to say.

'Sweetheart . . . three whole days yet. Don't let's spoil them by thinking about what happens after that.'

'I can't *help* thinking about it,' she cried. 'I know I made a bargain, and bargains are meant to be kept, but to go back to Frank after *this* . . .'

Harry took hold of her hands, kissed them, and kept them imprisoned in his own. 'Dearest, listen to me. I'm sure I'm not wrong about Thornley . . . he's the last man in the world to agree to a divorce. Even if he did, and we could marry years from now, other awkward facts remain. I have a tiny income which just enables me to live without getting paid for what I do. It wouldn't begin to provide the kind of life *you*'re used to. I can't change, even for you. The people you saw at the meeting that night are my friends . . . sooner or later I shall represent them in Parliament.'

'Until you inherit from Uncle Alec,' she pointed out with a faint smile.

'No, for the rest of my working life. I shall give up Somerton . . . renounce the title when my father dies.'

'You're not serious.' His face *was* serious but she persisted nevertheless. 'Harry, you *can't* mean it. Somerton's belonged to the Trenthams for a dozen generations.'

'For much too long, in my opinion. Charlotte can stop her harmless play-acting and take it on if she chooses to; but I shan't. A tiny percentage of the citizens of this country enjoys its privileges and owns its wealth; the rest slave for a pittance to keep *them* rich, or live on the edge of starvation and hopelessness. The system's rotten, Lucy, and it's got to be swept away.'

She wanted to shout that she cared nothing for systems. Happiness, and fulfilling passion between a man and a woman in the only life they would ever know, were all that mattered. But despair was seeping into her bones, and her only weapon against the humiliation of begging him not to let her go, was a pitiful saving attempt at anger.

'The "tiny" income you live on – is that inherited from the same tainted system we're supposed to sweep away?'

He flushed because the jibe had found its mark. 'It is, but I don't mind accepting it. I *enjoy* using it for people who can't afford to pay me for the work I do. Is that so hard to understand?'

'Not if your friends are the only ones who count. But what about the others, who are going to be destroyed along with the system . . . your parents and mine, and people like them? Ruin *them* and you ruin rural England. Isn't there something of value in that, or is it only your violent, unwashed agitators who matter? What did you *fight* for, Harry?'

His face was cold and expressionless now. 'Just like any other woman, you argue with your emotions. What I fight for *now* are the principles that will build a decent society.'

A memory came back to her of the moment when she'd flung at Frank the accusation that he didn't argue, simply laid down Thornley's law. Harry saw white where her husband saw black and vice versa, but he saw it with the same arrogant conviction that only he was right. There was a difference of theory between them, but no difference at all in their ability to put her aside whenever they felt inclined; even her opinions weren't worth listening to.

'We can't help being women,' she pointed out quietly. 'Charlotte must be allowed to play-act until it suits you to have her take Somerton off your hands. Anita can fill her days studying art but it will be a waste of time because great artists are bound to be men. And I, dear Harry, must stop arguing and remember that you have vital masculine affairs to attend to!'

He stared at her, suspecting mockery, but her pale mouth that had received and given back passion, was smiling again. She was beautiful and desirable, and he'd miss her atrociously when she went away.

'Sweetheart . . . we're mad! Three precious days left and we're wasting them arguing about politics!' His mouth brushed hers, lingered because desire leapt easily whenever he touched her, then reluctantly moved away. 'I *must* go . . . until tonight.'

She got up and dressed as usual, and returned to St James's Place. Two hours later, with a telegram despatched to Providence, and her cool goodbyes said to Mrs Knightly and Alice, she was on her way to the railway terminus.

The train journey passed unnoticed; she registered nothing, felt nothing. Her body was quite empty, and if someone had touched her accidentally she thought it would have given off the hollow sound made by a child's drum. Only the sight of Jem Martin waiting on the platform as the train steamed into the station reminded her to alight. Half an hour later she walked across the bridge at Providence and, obedient to the habit of a lifetime, stopped to stare at the tranquil water. She was home again.

Ned found her in the courtyard garden next morning, after Charles had been carried away screaming by Mary Haskell.

'Lucy . . . we'd no idea you were back. I thought I'd better come because it sounded as if murder was being done.'

'It was,' she agreed tonelessly. 'My son was amusing himself stamping on a butterfly he'd managed to catch. I slapped him for it, but the butterfly remains very . . . dead!' Her voice broke on the word . . . everything seemed dead, herself included. The sun was warm in the sheltered garden but she shivered with the terrible coldness locked up inside her.

'Sweetheart, don't take it to heart so. Charlie's only two. He's got a lot to learn, and it takes time. Don't you remember *me* doing awful things like pinching birds' eggs . . . and getting flayed by Gramps for them?'

She tried to smile, and say that she did remember, but burst into tears instead. Ned's arms enfolded her and she turned her face into the soft warmth of his pullover.

'Better now?' He offered the childhood phrase so hopefully that she was obliged to lift her head and nod. She *was* better, because the most terrible of her fears had suddenly been removed. There'd never been the slightest chance, after all, that she could learn to hate Ned for trapping her at Providence, and none of the other spectres that gibbered at her seemed half so dreadful.

'Come with me for the ride to Blake's Farm?' he suggested. 'It would be just like old times.' He bent over to leave a shy kiss on her cheek. 'I have the feeling that we're *both* getting over something. Isn't that what Mama used to say when we were small?'

Lucy stared at him, realizing for the first time that his thin face was no longer allowed to reveal whatever he happened to be feeling.

'Why did you send Anita away? There was no need, if you still wanted her.'

'I'm afraid there was *every* need; otherwise she would have stayed out of loyalty to a vision, ten years old and based on fantasy. Alas, the splendid vision faded. She isn't the shy dreamer who fell in love with Providence and all it contained, any more than I'm the same young hero who

130

was going to wrest success and fortune out of failure!'

After a moment or two he gave a little shrug that said the subject was to be put aside. 'What about you? Is it the mistake of marrying Frank that you have to recover from?'

Lucy took a long time to answer; when she did, she spoke as if each word had to be forced past her lips. 'That *wasn't* my mistake; my error was in believing that I'd been so generous in accepting him that it was all the effort I needed to make.'

'You're whipping yourself for no reason; it takes two to make a happy marriage.'

'I *could* have made ours happy, and didn't, because I preferred to play with a childish dream of my own instead. It collapsed yesterday, when Harry made it brutally clear that dreams were enjoyable, but not to be confused with reality.'

'Is that where you've been – in London, with Harry?'

'Yes . . . it wasn't his fault; he could scarcely refuse when I threw myself at him. Our little interlude is now over, and I shan't hear from him again.' Lucy's mouth twisted in a wry, painful grimace. 'The Cause can't be put aside, you see!'

'What happens now, love?'

'Nothing, except that perhaps I shan't be fool enough to confuse substance and shadow again.' She tucked her arm in his and managed to smile at him. 'Give me a few minutes to change, and then I'll race you to Blake's Farm.'

Frank reached Providence three days later, and the moment she'd dreaded took her unawares because he arrived several hours earlier than expected. There was a commotion outside, and excited yells from Charlie as he caught sight of his father. It was imperative that she should move – run outside, smile, and kiss her husband; but her legs were paralysed, and her face felt stiff with fear. She had got as far as the bridge when Frank put down his son and walked towards *her*.

'Frank . . . how tired you look . . . welcome back to Providence.' The words spoke themselves after all, and she discovered that she even meant what she said enough for it to sound sincere.

He smiled the rare sweet smile that usually only Jane Thornley saw. 'I was like a child waiting for Christmas to come, counting off the days! Has everything been all right here?'

'I think so – I. . .I stayed in London for a while, but in the end *I* wanted to come home, too. I've been riding with Ned a lot, and Charlie has allowed himself to be put up in front without objecting!'

'I hope you told my father.' They walked back across the bridge together, and she didn't flinch away from his arm around her waist. Nor did she flinch that night when he took possession of her again. She had promised Ned that if he got over what ailed him, so would she. She *had* to; the bargain with Frank remained. Nothing had changed, except that a lesson had been painfully learned. If she didn't find happiness at Providence, she would find it nowhere else.

The year hadn't quite reached high summer when Henri telegraphed the news from Paris that Sybil had given birth to a daughter – but Josephine Hester Blanchard wasn't to be the only enlargement to the family. Soon afterwards the doctor confirmed what the village already thought it knew – Mrs Frank was pregnant again, and about time too in the opinion of Haywood's End.

1925

Chapter Eleven

Twins were not something a Thornley was accustomed to, but having had time to get over the shock of a family innovation he hadn't been responsible for, Arthur gradually grew to adore his new grandchildren. It didn't even matter that, unlike Charlie, they looked so much more like their mother than Frank.

At nearly four, Victoria was the mixture of sugar and spice that all little girls were supposed to be made of and Thomas, younger by half an hour, was already a true chip off the Thornley block – energetic and pugnacious. Almost best of all, Arthur reckoned, after the twins' birth his dear little Lucy had settled down again. Far from always wanting to be in London, she scarcely went there nowadays; the gardens at Providence had become as much hers as Ned's, and the pair of them were always out there together, changing designs, and endlessly replanting. Arthur didn't properly understand it himself; growing things was all very well, but nothing to make a song and dance about. Still, like Janey pottering in her conservatory, Lucy seemed to be happy working outside with Ned, and more than most other things in life Arthur wanted his daughter-in-law to be happy. The only shadow on the sun of his contentment was Charlie's refusal to enjoy having a sister and brother younger than himself. Jane kept explaining that the age-gap was bound to be awkward till the children grew up; but Arthur couldn't wait for that – he wanted them close *now*, aware that they were Thornleys together, and glad of it.

'They're half-Wyndham, too,' she was stung into pointing out one day. 'You've got to allow William and Gertrude a look-in.'

'I know that, Janey, but there's Ned and Sybil to give *them* more grandchildren. *We've* only got Frank, and there's nothing wrong in reckoning on a three-quarters share in *his* nursery.' He grinned at the expression on his wife's face and prudently changed the conversation. ''Spect you've heard from Gertrude that George Hoskins is poorly again.'

'Yes, she told me they're worried about him; Ned's cancelled a visit to Paris to see Sybil because of it.'

'Wouldn't hurt for her to come over here once in a while. Beats me why she doesn't. William still misses her, and so does old George. He told me once that he loved her specially because she always made him laugh. Well, where he's concerned, she'll find she's left it too late one of these days.'

Arthur was never surprised to be proved right, but matters didn't always arrange themselves immediately according to his forecast. In the case of Gertrude's father, confirmation came quickly. Within a week George's bronchitis had developed into pneumonia and, at the age of seventy-nine, his condition was known throughout Haywood's End to be very grave. Instead of Ned travelling to Paris, William took the unprecedented step of summoning his daughter to England after an absence of eight years.

She was delayed in Calais by the first thick fog of the autumn and reached London twenty-four hours later than expected. Harry Trentham collected her from the station, but waited until she was installed in Thurloe Square for the night to break the news that she was too late to see her grandfather; George Hoskins had died the previous evening.

'It's not *fair*,' she said with sudden fury. 'I *wanted* to see Gramps – he should have waited for me a bit longer.' She stopped abruptly and buried her face in her hands. Then, when she looked at Harry again, his expression made her speak more quietly. 'Go on . . . say it. It's *my* fault for not coming years ago, and it's also about time I learned that life doesn't arrange itself just to suit *me*.'

She was given the gentle smile that only a few people were privileged to receive from Harry Trentham. 'No need for me to say what you already know perfectly well, and no point in asking *why* you've never come. In my experience, if people can't work out the whys for themselves, no amount of explanation will make them understand.'

Sybil stared at him thoughtfully. He was now thirty-nine to her thirty-two, but looked much older than that. Boyish high spirits had long since disappeared; responsibilities and the habit of hard work had set his features in an unrevealing and disciplined tautness that made a stranger of him. It wasn't until he smiled that she glimpsed the young man who'd been more like brother than cousin throughout the years when she, Ned, and Lucy were growing up.

'I half-expected you to seem very different . . . to *be* different, even . . . but I don't think you are after all.'

'What were you expecting, for God's sake – a cloth cap, or the red flag sticking out of my button-hole? My dear girl, you're years out of date. The Labour Party's respectable now. It's already held office once, and will certainly do so again.'

'Sorry, I'm sure! So, you're no longer shunned at dinner-parties or pointed out by the Conservative gentry at home as a wild man! But what about Aunt Louise and Uncle Alec? Are *they* any nearer working out for themselves the things you can't make them understand?'

'Oddly enough, I think Father *does* understand. My invincible mama remains convinced that I'm touched in the head, and blames it on the war. It's the most charitable explanation she can think of!'

'She's a relic of Victoria's Empire – tough but splendid,' Sybil said thoughtfully. 'I should like to see her again.'

'You will. Dear coz, I'm sorry to remind you of the fact, but there will be a funeral to attend now at Providence. My mother will certainly be there; she accepts unpleasant duties as a hermit dons his hair-shirt.'

'She may not understand you, but I don't think it stops you feeling proud of her.'

'I'm immensely proud of her, as it happens.'

Sybil smiled at the brief statement, then grew serious again. 'Gramps' funeral, of course . . . I hadn't got as far as thinking about that. Old Biddle, Hodges, and the rest of the servants will all be there, got up in their decent black. The farmers will be wearing suits that come out for an airing once or twice a year, stiff as boards and reeking of camphor; and Hubert Roberts will try to convince us with archaic, beautiful, meaningless words that throwing a gentle old man into a hole in the ground and heaping earth on top of him isn't unbearably barbaric after all.'

In the extreme pallor of her face her eyes were dark with the horror of an indignity she could picture vividly but not prevent. Harry had almost forgotten her habit of feeling everything in life, good or bad, happy or sad, with an extravagant intensity that other people were spared. There'd never been any half-measures for Syb, and he remembered something else about her – grief had always made her angry, as she was now.

'Hear what comfortable words your cousin sayeth,' he suggested, half-smiling at her. 'If you believe in Heaven, your grandfather's certainly there, sitting not far below God's right hand; if not, the fact remains that whatever's done to him now can't hurt him, my dear.'

It sounded true either way, but she preferred the first of Harry's alternatives. She was about to say so when the door opened and Charlotte walked in.

'Syb dear . . . here at last! It's lovely to see you, and they'll be so thankful to have you back at Providence . . . especially now.'

'The return of the prodigal daughter? I hope you're right, Lottie dear. Do you realize it's five years since we bumped into each other in Bond Street? Why haven't *you* ever come to Paris? Even if you weren't anxious to see *me*, you might at least have been curious about life on the other side of the Channel.'

'I'm *very* curious, but also unalterably queasy . . . seasick before the boat's even steamed out of Dover

138

Harbour! Harry maintains that we shall be able to fly before very long: *then* I'll come.'

When supper was over and Harry had left for Westminster, Sybil fitted a cigarette into an amber holder and took a long time about lighting it. 'Lottie . . . I'm nervous,' she confessed unexpectedly. 'Without really thinking about it, I suppose I took it for granted that Providence was under some enchanted spell that would protect it from ever changing. But Gramps is dead, and I can't help wondering what other gaping holes there are for me to fall into.'

'None as permanent as that . . . in fact, probably none at all,' Charlotte answered after a moment or two. 'It seems to me that Haywood's End scarcely changes, and Providence doesn't change at all, except for the different miracles of beauty that Ned and Lucy keep working in the gardens.'

'Provided you can overlook one small inconvenient fact that outweighs all the rest – the Wyndhams now live there by kind permission of Frank Thornley! I suppose you didn't know that Lucy's delightful father-in-law lusted after Providence long before he bought Bicton. No doubt he drops in on Frank and saunters about my mother's courtyard garden whenever he feels like it, just to underline the fact that he now *can*. The mere thought of it makes me angry, and Grandfather Wyndham must be turning in his grave!'

'I doubt if he has much right to,' Charlotte pointed out impartially. 'Less money spent on hunters and lavish entertaining in *his* lifetime would have made Providence easier to hold on to.' She stared meditatively at her cousin. 'It hadn't really struck me before how much like Harry you are. A lot of things seem to make you both angry, and in you jump, boots and all, on one side or the other. I'm so busy seeing everybody's side that I never jump at all.'

Sybil's strained face relaxed into a smile at the truth of the simple statement. She thought it likely that people overlooked her quiet cousin because she never insisted on being noticed; everyone else clamoured to make themselves heard, but Lottie didn't care whether they listened to her or not.

'Is that why you've taken to hiding behind spectacles, and the sort of clothes that a middle-aged suburban housewife might *just* be forgiven for wearing?'

Charlotte didn't look offended, but a tinge of colour came into her long, thin face. 'As bad as that? Someone else accused me of hiding the other day. Intending no compliment, he said that I had a talent for self-effacement amounting to a kind of suicide! Perhaps he was right. I'm quite competent at getting things done – like Mama! – but hopeless at claiming anyone's attention for myself. *Not* like you! I can remember the impact you were making at the age of five, and I dare say you'll still be doing it when you're ninety-five.'

'I should hope so; otherwise I'd rather be dead.' Sybil was tempted to enquire who it was that had tried to shock her out of concealment, but the sight of Charlotte's shapeless fawn cardigan distracted her. 'I'll have to take you in hand . . . forbid you, for a start, ever to wear a garment like *that* one again. We can't all be raving beauties like Lucy, but that doesn't mean that we need give up and allow ourselves to fade into the wallpaper.'

No-one, Charlotte had to admit, looked less like giving up than the girl sitting opposite her. The redness of Sybil's mouth and the briefness of her skirt would probably both be moderated for her grandfather's funeral, but whatever deep suspicions Haywood's End cherished about Paris and the French would certainly remain intact when they caught sight of Sybil Blanchard. The strange thing was, though, that for all her bright, quick glance and dazzling sophistication, she left Charlotte with an impression of some haunting inner sadness. The Wyndham legend concerning her was of a girl who'd known clearly what she wanted from life, and flouted family, home, and convention in order to obtain it; the truth might be different, Charlotte decided now; perhaps Sybil had done no better than Anita, Lucy, or herself in putting salt on the tail of the elusive bird of happiness.

Before leaving for Providence the following morning, Sybil offered what she thought was accurate news of Anita: after two years in London and Paris she'd been travelling around Europe; when last heard from, having spent the spring in Rome, she seemed settled in Florence.

'It's the spiritual home of those few Americans bold enough to follow Hannibal's elephants across the Alps,' Sybil said definitely. 'I think she'll decide to stay there for good.'

For once Madame Blanchard had fallen behind the course of events. Anita was already in Paris, with no intention of staying there or going back to Florence. She took the train out to Pont-sur-Seine, as she'd done many times in the past, found Henri there alone with Josephine, and discovered why her cousin had finally returned to England.

'Poor Syb . . . heartbreaking for her to go home at last, only to find everyone plunged in the sadness of a funeral,' Anita said regretfully. 'What a grief for Ned, too – I remember that he and his grandfather were the closest of friends.'

Henri nodded, surprised to find how vividly he could call to mind the old man whom he'd been taken to visit when he was last at Providence. Then he smiled at his unexpected guest. 'My dear Anita, I'm enchanted to see you. My daughter is an entrancing companion but, alas, she retires to bed early, which means that I have to dine alone! She won't have forgotten you from last year, by the way. Among her many gifts is the sort of memory an elephant would be proud of. It's only inconvenient when she's asked to recall someone to whom she took a strong dislike; *you*, I'm happy to say, are remembered with pleasure!'

To prove it, Anita was appropriated by a leggy, dark-eyed child who announced that Tante 'Nita must share their morning promenade. She was a plain little girl who might one day surprise her friends by growing into a beauty. She was given to solemn silences and sudden sweet smiles, and chattered in a mixture of English and French as baffling as a newly invented language.

When she had finally been persuaded to say good night and go to bed, Henri remembered to ask his guest over dinner what had brought her back to Paris so unexpectedly.

'Well, like Saul on the road to Damascus, I was struck by a great light!'

'You were in Florence at the time of this *coup de foudre*?'

'No, I was in the half-empty dining-room of a pension in Montreux two nights ago, to be precise!'

He gave a rare shout of laughter. 'My poor girl, say no more; I can see it all – Lake Leman wreathed in autumn mist, and a Swiss pension wrapped in out-of-season gloom . . . suicide would seem preferable!'

'I think it was the other women there who decided me,' Anita said ruefully. 'They were all trying not to look as if they minded dining alone, and eating with immense care so that their knives and forks shouldn't clatter in the echoing emptiness of the room. I could see a sad procession of them drifting around Europe, getting a little more grey and a little more desperate with each passing season!'

Henri's amused stare took in the self-possessed and elegant woman sitting opposite him. 'You're far from being one of them, if I may say so, but you made a decision then about the future?'

Anita took a sip of the wine he'd poured for her before answering. 'I made several, in fact. The first was that it was time to give up the dream of making myself into a decent painter.' Violet-blue eyes, her only claim to beauty, challenged him and he was obliged to be honest with her.

'I think so, too, Anita. You're a more competent artist than most; it would be easy enough to imitate one of today's lunatic trends – but I don't think that's what you want.'

'I was born much too late for what I want, and with far

142

too little genius. Given the choice, I'd have plumped for being a seventeenth-century Dutch master, creating beauty out of ordered interiors full of peace and cool northern light!'

'I think I might have guessed,' Henri commented thoughtfully. 'Was your decision the result of a year spent in Italy? Sybil always calls you a true Wyndham. What did a lot of hot-blooded Latins make of you, I wonder?'

'To begin with, as little as I made of them! But mutual tolerance gradually led to friendship; I found them kind and charming people.'

'I agree with you, but it doesn't sound as if you've decided to live in Italy permanently. Perhaps you feel obliged to return to New York?'

'I might have done, but for the discovery that my father is finally planning to leave America himself. Homesickness is like certain kinds of disease – dormant for years, then suddenly springing to life with overwhelming strength. I think that's *his* condition now; he suddenly realizes that he *must* return to England before it's too late. Patrick and his family are already living permanently in Ireland, so there's no reason at all for me to go back to New York.'

'My impression is that you aren't going to stay here, either. Why should you? Paris in this year of grace is a far cry from the ordered loveliness of your Dutch paintings. Sybil still enjoys it, but I find it disillusioning and sad . . . full of cynical men, brittle women, and artists ready to dabble in any perversion, sexual or philosophical, that will shock our worthy bourgeoisie!'

She couldn't help smiling, even though his weary distaste for a city he had once loved was saddening. 'Well, I *have* decided on London,' she confessed, 'but for the simplest of reasons. I'm tired of being a foreigner . . . struggling with other languages, other traditions and instincts. In London I shall be among people who laugh at the things I find funny, and who get angry – though they rarely do – at the things I find myself objecting to. But I shall come often to visit you if I'm allowed to . . . for one

143

thing, I must watch my delightful god-daughter grow up.'

Henri's tired face broke into a transforming smile. 'I was remembering a moment ago a visit to Providence when Sybil's grandfather took me to task – with the most exquisitely gentle firmness! – for regretting the past. The *future*, said Monsieur Hoskins, was what should concern me. I doubted him at the time, but now find that he was right . . . Josephine is my future.'

His eyes were still brilliantly alive in a face that had aged in the year Anita had been away from Paris. It was easier now to remember that a whole generation separated him from Sybil, and painful to suspect that it might be more difficult for him to deal with *that* than the two generations between himself and his daughter.

'Sybil spends most of her time in Paris now,' he said suddenly. 'Fired by the example of a certain Mademoiselle Chanel, she is the co-owner of a very select establishment in the Rue de Rivoli. Her friend, Comtesse Colbert, manages the venture, and Sybil gathers together clothes which I am assured are the very pith and marrow of female elegance! Since Josephine and I ask nothing better than to live here for ever in perfect harmony, and Sybil is happy to return to us at weekends, the arrangement suits everybody!'

Anita found herself with nothing to say about an arrangement which couldn't have been accommodated within most marriages, and was grateful when Henri himself continued the conversation. 'Had we come to the end of *your* decisions?'

'Not quite . . . although I'm afraid you'll be horrified when you hear what I'm going to do. During the past few years of discovering that I wasn't going to make a painter of myself I've haunted just about every picture gallery in Europe – in company with the tourists who are beginning to flock here from America. They're the most earnest of sightseers, and probably the most ill-informed! I've seen them again and again setting out for home tired, bemused, and irritably aware that they aren't any more informed than when they arrived, simply because no-one had given

144

them the right help. *Eccomi*, as my Italian friends would say! My introductions will neither blind them with technicalities nor bore them to death with history. I shall lead them gently to the waiting feast of beauty with simple, accurate explanations of what they're going to see.' She looked doubtfully at Henri's expression. 'I knew it would strike a serious scholar as an unbearably irreverent approach to art . . . almost as bad as whistling in front of the High Altar in Notre Dame!'

'Not nearly as bad,' he corrected her, smiling broadly. 'In any case, if art can't survive a little irreverence, it doesn't deserve to survive at all. I'm rather sorry I didn't think of the idea myself, but perhaps you'll need my help when you arrive at the nineteenth century! You'll enjoy *writing* your introductions, but they must also be printed, published and sold. Have you considered all that?'

'Not yet; the first thing is to find myself a home in London before I can start work.'

Henri lifted the decanter again and refilled their glasses. 'There speaks today's woman . . . assured, competent, and thoroughly emancipated! I wonder if any of you remember that the great Queen died little more than twenty years ago. She would scarcely believe the rate of your progress, and it's only just gathering momentum like an avalanche beginning its rush down a mountainside. Mere men will be swept out of its path, grateful to be allowed to hide in little nooks and crannies where they can do no more harm! Dear Anita, I shall drink a toast to conquering Modern Woman!'

He drank, and then smiled at her, but she knew that she'd been misled a few moments ago. He understood with his mind Sybil's need of a career, but heart and soul were affronted and hurt by her independence. Whether his wife remembered it or not, he *was* a Victorian, born into a world where a woman, according to her circumstances, was protected, ignored, or abused. Her natural place was still in the frame provided by a man, and her natural satisfaction was to look after him and the children he gave her.

Anita lifted her own glass. 'I shall drink a toast of my own, Henri. To the kind and understanding husband that a modern woman needs – supposing she's lucky enough to have one at all!'

Chapter Twelve

Sybil saw the house waiting for her at the end of the drive. In the silver-grey light of a November afternoon it looked insubstantial and vaporous, like the bubbles blown in childhood with clay pipes and soapy water – a little puff of wind and the whole thing might float away.

'Jem, stop for a moment, please. I'll get out and walk the rest of the way.'

He remembered even though it was years ago that the French gentleman had once made him stop in just that spot; seeing that she was closely married to him, it was something she'd caught, like measles, Jem supposed. He drove on alone, and explained to Sir William that his daughter was finishing the journey on foot.

Sybil walked slowly, forgetful of Paris shoes not intended for scuffling through the damp stream of brown, gold and crimson leaves that flowed along the edge of the drive. She was lost in memories of the past, recalling the antics of children who'd done that very same thing each autumn, infuriating Biddle when they jumped into the huge heaps of fallen leaves that he laboriously raked together. She half-expected him to be waiting for her now to inspect her tell-tale shoes. But the old man she'd wanted to see *wouldn't* be there, with patient explanations for all the things that had baffled her then and still baffled her. Grandfather Hoskins was the one person she'd had no dread of meeting again, because *he* would have welcomed her as if she'd never been away. She was aware of having disappointed or hurt everyone else, and now couldn't be sure whether she wanted to fling herself at them demanding forgiveness, or simply turn and run away.

Another twist in the drive showed her the house much

closer now, and brought her as well to a little group scuffling through the leaves as she had done. There were two small fair-haired children and a tall girl who, not being Lucy, was presumably their nurse. All three of them turned to look at her, and she was examined with the same measuring stare that her own daughter used to disconcert strangers.

'Good afternoon,' she said to the girl. 'I think these two must be my niece and nephew; I'm Madame Blanchard.'

'Yes . . . Ned said you'd be coming today. I'm Mary Haskell. Victoria, Tom – this lady is your aunt Sybil.'

She was sensible . . . didn't try to make the children say hello and risk having them ignore an aunt they'd never seen, but Sybil was too irritated to feel grateful. Here, right at the start, was one of the gaping holes Charlotte had failed to warn her about. Mary Haskell was clearly a servant, but 'Ned', she'd said, not 'Mr Wyndham'. Irritation strengthened into anger: home, family, old friends left behind, were supposed to have remained unchanged, like flies eternally preserved in amber, but she was suddenly aware of having stayed away too long. The rest of them as surely as her grandfather, though in different ways, had *not* waited for her to catch up with them. She should never have come back at all to a place that no longer wanted her. Angry tears pricked her eyes but she was saved by the touch of a small warm hand wiggling its way into her own cold one.

'Uncle Ned's coming to tea . . . *you* come too. It's cake with icing and candles cos of being Charlie's birthday.' Victoria's enchanting face frowned in sudden concentration. 'I spect you know he's th . . . theven – bigger than us.'

'I *didn't* know,' Sybil confessed. 'You see, I haven't been here for a long, long time.'

'Doesn't mind,' her niece said kindly, 'you're here now.'

Sybil smiled and, because the child smiled back, felt ridiculously comforted.

'I'd like to come to tea,' she'd heard herself agree when Thomas suddenly took over the conversation.

'Tor . . . race you to the bridge, starting . . . *now!*'

His sister hesitated, torn between deserting her new friend and not wanting to let him win; then she pulled her hand away from Sybil's and tore after him.

'It's a daily game,' Mary Haskell explained. 'They're not allowed to challenge each other until we're past a different tree each time – it was Ned's idea, to get them to learn to count!'

There it was again – that casual, unselfconscious reference to her brother. Sybil stared at the girl who walked unconcernedly beside her. She was tall and graceful, but there was nothing striking about her looks except a mane of red-gold hair wound in old-fashioned plaits about her head. Her voice was soft, and its Midlands accent almost too faint to be noticeable.

'Have you been working here very long?' Sybil enquired coolly.

'Since before the twins were born. Charlie was two when I came.'

'You must think yourself fortunate to be living at Providence.'

'I *don't* live there . . . not in the house, I mean. When Ned brought us away from Birmingham Sir William offered my mother one of the Home Farm cottages. I still live there with her and my young brother and sister.' She offered the brief summary politely, untroubled by the faintly hostile air of the woman beside her.

Her composure was unnatural and Sybil was nettled by it. 'A little inconvenient for my sister, surely, such an arrangement?'

'Oh, Mrs Thornley doesn't mind. She knew when she took me on that I wouldn't be able to sleep in. My mother was ill . . . I was needed at the cottage. There's a nursery-maid living in at Providence.'

So *she* wasn't the nursery-maid. Then what the devil *was* she . . . a friend of the family?

'I suppose Charles will be going away to school soon, and the twins as well in four or five years' time. What happens then?'

'I shall have to find another post,' Mary said quietly. 'It's what always happens to someone who looks after other people's children.'

If she resented having the admission that she was a servant forced out of her, there was no way of knowing; status, she seemed to say, wasn't something she bothered her head about. Her mouth smiled readily, but perhaps no-one had explained to her that eyes revealed more than their owners might want known. Sybil caught a glimpse of sadness that was meant to be kept hidden, and felt a twinge of shame and pity.

'The twins will need you for a long time yet,' she pointed out more gently. 'You might even find that *you're* ready to leave them before they go off to school.'

'So I might,' Mary agreed politely, and a moment later they emerged from the drive on to the gravelled forecourt, with Providence directly in front of them. Below the battlement that made tooth-marks in the November sky, Sybil could see the huge mullioned window of the Great Parlour, but her father wasn't there painting as usual; he was outside on the bridge, watching with the same wrapt concentration as his grandchildren the fish that rippled the still surface of the water.

'Papa . . .' She was unaware of having murmured the word until Mary spoke beside her.

'If you'll give me a moment to grab the twins I'll take them away . . . otherwise they'll be wanting to chatter nineteen to the dozen with Sir William while you try to talk to him.'

She walked across the gravel, scooped up a child under each arm, and disappeared with them in the direction of the stableyard – kind, competent, and surely more nearly one of the family than any normal servant had the expectation of being. Sybil was intensely curious about Mary Haskell, but there was no time to think about her now; the bridge was empty except for the man who stood waiting for her. She stopped a little way short of him, wanting to weep because the beard she'd once said made him look like a Roman emperor had turned to silver, like his thin fine hair; she could have laughed as well because the handkerchief dangling from his jacket pocket was splotched with paint, as it always had been ever since she could remember.

'Dear Papa . . . how distinguished you look! More like M . . . Marcus Aurelius than ever.'

'But instead of feeling augustly stoical, I'm more inclined to burst into tears! Dearest child . . . we'd begun to fear you'd never come. I can't tell you how lovely it is to see you here.'

Their eyes were wet as they smiled at each other; then she reached up to kiss his cheek. 'Am I forgiven, or have I caused too much shame and pain?'

'Never that . . . once we knew you were safe and happy with Henri, that was all that mattered. Come along in . . . your mother's waiting, and we've got half an hour's peace before we must go and eat indigestible birthday cake with Lucy and the children.'

'I know . . . Charlie's theven!'

'You must have met Victoria on the way in – a missing tooth is causing a little difficulty. Jane and Arthur are invited too, of course, but Frank's in London . . . yet another Royal Commission to report to the Government yet again on the condition of the mining industry. Sir Herbert Samuel required two industrialists, and Frank was bound to be one of them, poor fellow.'

He led Sybil into the house, but released her hand as they stepped into the Great Hall where Gertrude was waiting. His wife and daughter confronted each other after a gap of eight years – Gertrude must surely be seeing mirrored in their vivid elegant daughter the girl *she'd* once been, and Sybil looking at the serenely beautiful woman she might one day hope to become. It seemed a long time to him before either of them moved or spoke, but finally Gertrude leaned forward to kiss her daughter's cheek.

'Welcome home, my dear.'

Then Sybil also found something to say. 'Mama . . . I'm sorry I came too late to see Gramps; you must miss him very much.'

'Yes, but he was so tired that we couldn't want him to stay. He was happy to know that you were coming . . . wanted a little opal ring that was my mother's kept for Josephine.' Gertrude's thin face was suddenly lit by its transforming smile. 'We're longing to see *her* as well, you know. Is she like you?'

'Probably like I was, I think . . . therefore not pretty, as Lucy's daughter was bound to be! I've just met *her* in the drive, with her brother and a girl I couldn't place at all.'

'Mary . . . Mary Haskell, the daughter of a man who fought with Ned in the war. Tom Haskell was killed, and his family was left in great distress. Ned traced them eventually and brought them here so that he could keep an eye on them. Mary has had the *most* beneficial effect on Charlie, so everybody is happy.'

Sybil remembered the expression in Mary Haskell's eyes, and doubted that she, at least, was entirely happy, but there seemed no point in saying so. 'Henri insists that Josephine makes up in character what she lacks in beauty. If that's another way of saying that she's stubborn and impossible to deal with on occasion, then I'm bound to say he's right!'

'*Just* like you were,' Gertrude agreed, 'but look how beautifully that turned out!'

It was Sybil's turn to smile, and William was aware of a change in the room. For reasons he didn't fully understand, the meeting had been difficult for both of them and something dangerously close to hostility had glinted in the air. Now, resistance was melting into acceptance again.

'I've been invited to the tea-party, though not by Thomas, who seems no more talkative than I remember his father to have been,' Sybil reported to her mother. 'Still, Papa says Arthur Thornley will be present, so we shan't run short of conversation.'

Three days later the church was crowded for George Hoskins' funeral. The farmers and the village people would have come in any case, because anything that

152

happened to the Wyndhams, happened to them. The fortunes of Haywood's End and the family at Providence had been bound up together for so long that the arrival of Frank Thornley among them had been no more than a nine-day wonder – talked about over washing-lines and the ale-house counter and then forgotten. In any case, he was never there, it seemed to them, and nothing in their lives had changed because of him. Squire still fiddled with his bits of colouring, same as he always had; Ned saw to it that anything they needed done, got done; and her ladyship was there to go to in times of trouble.

But the villagers also came to church because the man they were burying had lived among them for nearly fifty years – serving Squire as he was bound to do, but never unfairly, and never to the harm of Haywood's End. It was a rule of country life that tenant-farmers, labourers, and their wives, hated land-agents as a race of men; but none of them had hated Gertrude's father.

She listened to Hubert Roberts talking about him, and only wept when Ned stood up at the end of the service to offer his own quiet goodbye, with words borrowed from a favourite poet:

'. . . of this bad world the loveliest and the best,
Has smiled, and said "goodnight",
And gone to rest.'

After the interment ceremony in the churchyard Gertrude hurried back to Providence with William, unaware that among the various members of the family beginning to straggle behind them along the lane was someone she would never have dreamed of seeing there. She was in the dining-room checking the cold buffet luncheon set out for returning guests when Ned's hand touched her shoulder. He looked unfamiliar in formal clothes when she turned to smile at him, but his brown hair was untidily ruffled as usual, and his face gentle with concern.

'You all right, Mama? I think we put Gramps to sleep quite fittingly, don't you?'

'Yes, dear Ned.' His choice of words was typical, and she knew what the words meant. Just as his precious flowers sprang to life again after their winter sleep, he reckoned that his grandfather's goodness and gentle strength hadn't died with him; some of it was bound to reappear and blossom in anyone who'd been lucky enough to know him.

'You'll never guess who's here, by the way,' said Ned, as an afterthought. 'Patrick Wyndham was in London for some reason and bumped into Harry. I don't know who suggested it – Charlotte probably – but he drove down with them this morning.'

'*Patrick!* Good Heavens . . . no, what am I saying,' Gertrude muttered distractedly. 'Of course it's good of him to take the trouble, but I wish he hadn't come *now* when there are so many other people to look after. Dearest, avoid the subject of Ireland, and keep him away from Arthur, if you can . . . better still, keep him away from your Aunt Louise *and* Arthur!'

'Don't fret – I'm going to ask Syb to keep him occupied. Do you remember how they used to measure up to one another like a couple of terriers spoiling for a fight?'

It didn't seem an ideal solution to the problem of what to do with Patrick Wyndham, but before she could say so the sound of voices outside in the courtyard garden signalled the arrival of the first people back from the church. A tall man was among them whom she recognized at once, not because much remained of the youth he'd been thirteen years before but because, in the way he held himself and walked towards her, she was suddenly reminded of James Wyndham.

'Aunt Gertrude . . . I thought my father would like me to be here. Does that excuse me for imposing?'

She was disarmed by his unexpected gentleness, and by a diffidence that hadn't belonged to him on his first visit to them. 'My dear Patrick, how could a Wyndham be unwelcome at Providence? I'm very glad you came. Now that you're here, can you stay for a little while, or must you rush off again?'

He seemed to hesitate about how to answer. 'I wasn't planning to hurry home – I had the idea of going across country by easy stages to Liverpool.' His gaze wandered round the room, and lingered on the motto cut in the stone lintel above the huge fireplace – 'it is required of a steward that he be found faithful' – then returned to his aunt's face again. 'I think I'd like very much to stay, just for a day or two.'

The invitation had been impulsive but she was surprised to find that she didn't regret it. There wasn't time now to stop and consider why not, but neither the coolly measuring young man who'd arrived with Anita before the war, nor the revolutionary firebrand disowning England to become a republican, seemed to have much in common with *this* hesitant visitor, who looked around the room as if he searched for something that he might find there.

'That's settled, then.' She smiled as Sybil, despatched by Ned, came up to them. 'Dearest, look after Patrick while I help your father with all these people. I'm glad to say he's not going to rush away.'

She left them inspecting one another – Patrick remembering the provocative girl whose face and body had deliberately tormented him, Sybil angry that he should be there at all, but aware amid her anger that there were more differences in him to be considered than simply age and added experience. While she still stared, he was allowed to make the opening gambit. He did so knowing that in the past her opponents had never been allowed a second chance to get the upper hand.

'Congratulations, my dear Sybil. Looking at you, I think I now understand what is meant by Parisian chic.' His pale eyes, fringed by dark lashes inherited from an Irish mother, glinted with what she took to be malice. 'We've heard the phrase even in our sleepy Dublin backwater, but I never expected to see it made so dazzlingly manifest!'

'I dare say you've been too busy destroying each other. Anita says you spend your time now reconstructing damaged buildings . . . it seems a thankless task, given that if your delightful friends don't blow them up again, they'll probably burn them down.'

'The destruction isn't quite as wholesale as you seem to think, although I have to admit that it's bad enough.'

She was considering a reference to the war he *hadn't* taken part in when he forestalled her, guessing what was in her mind. 'Shall we agree to avoid contentious subjects, or simply admit that the safest thing to do would be to rejoin the rest of the gathering? Then I can admire your elegant appearance from afar, and you can raise the heartbeat of some other captive male!'

'We have just attended my grandfather's funeral, not a Paris cocktail-party,' she reminded him in a swift, furious undertone.

'I know . . . I was there. Still, I doubt if he'd expect you to try to be other than you are, and *as* you are you can't help throwing out challenges! I shouldn't allow you to live so dangerously if I were your husband.'

An expression he couldn't understand touched her face for an instant and was gone again, leaving it faintly smiling. 'Henri allows me to live in any way I choose. He's lost the taste for cities himself, and prefers to stay at our country home writing his life's work – a history of the French Impressionists. My own small talent is in providing clothes for women who haven't any taste of their own; I spend most of my time in Paris.'

His eyes flicked over her black jacket and skirt, starkly simple except for the froth of white silk at her throat.

'I seem to remember that you have a daughter. What happens to her while you are both busy exercising your individual talents?'

'She's with Henri at the mill – happy and well looked-after. I spend the weekends with them and almost manage to convince myself that they miss me a little when I'm not there!'

She couldn't stare at him much longer and go on smiling brightly: his eyes were too intelligent for safety, and she thought he would enjoy discovering what she kept hidden from the rest of the world. 'What about your own life,

Patrick? If we charitably stretch a point and allow that Ireland can be thought of as part of a civilized continent, have you regretted coming to Europe and abandoning America?'

It was like rattling a stick along the bars of a lion's cage – exhilarating, because it was faintly dangerous. She had the feeling that, like the lion, he would have been glad to swallow her whole.

'You're very free with your gibes, but I shall remind you that Christianity might have perished in these benighted islands during the Dark Ages had it not been for *Irish* monks. I could insist that Ireland's troubles are by no means entirely of her own making, but I'm sure you'd prefer *not* to be troubled by a few awkward historical facts. Instead, I'll suggest again that we part company, cousin; *you* can return to your more civilized friends, and *I* shall summon up all the courage I possess and go and talk to Aunt Louise!'

She was startled by the sudden charm of his smile, but before she could think of anything else to say he nodded and walked away, leaving her with the unpleasant feeling that she had been dismissed. It was certain that she didn't like Patrick Wyndham any more than she had done a dozen years ago but, unlike most of the men she met, at least he wasn't negligible. Walking across the room to greet her godmother, she realized something else: his brief lecture on Ireland had neatly diverted attention from the fact that he hadn't answered her question. If he *did* regret his decision to leave America, he wasn't inclined to say so; but she had an impression all the same of a man who could hide himself successfully from the rest of the world simply because he'd had much practice in doing so.

157

Chapter Thirteen

The morning after his grandfather's funeral Ned got up earlier than usual and let himself out of the sleeping house. Even without things on his mind that needed thinking about, the early-morning world would have beckoned him out of doors. The day-time hours were filled with the claims that other human beings made on his attention, but he need only share the soft darkness with small nocturnal creatures who were indifferent to whether he was there or not. A brown owl returning from a night's hunting hooted unconcernedly from a roof-top in the stable yard, and he could hear the rooks assembling above his head for their morning patrol; it wasn't light enough yet to make them out, but their chatter and the swift rush of wings sounded through the still air. The temperature had dropped sharply overnight and the path to the churchyard was suddenly soft underfoot with fallen sprays of ash – there was never time to see them change colour before the first frost brought them down while they were still green.

He stood for a while by his grandfather's grave, and only discovered as he turned away that the world wasn't exclusively his after all. What was worse, the man who stood waiting by the churhyard gate was the one he'd least have chosen to share the quiet dawn with.

'Morning,' he grunted, but it sounded so impossibly surly that he felt obliged to try again. 'I always used to start the day with a visit to my grandfather – suppose I haven't got out of the habit yet.'

Patrick fell into step beside him. 'I haven't that excuse for being here, and you probably think I haven't any right to be at Providence at all.'

It was so nearly what Ned *did* think that he was left

floundering for an answer. 'Kind of you to have come and represented Uncle James,' he mumbled finally, 'but I didn't expect you to want to stay. Our quiet life here can't be anything like the one you're used to.'

'Sybil puts it less delicately – she seems to think that all we do in Dublin is blow each other up. She just managed not to refer to a different war in which I chose to take no part, but *not* mentioning it probably puts even *more* of a strain on someone like you.'

Ned felt an even sharper prick of irritation. Courtesy to his mother's guest ruled out what he would have liked to say, but it was hard to hold his tongue when Patrick seemed to be deliberately needling him into bluntness.

'I imagine you to be an American citizen,' he muttered uncomfortably at last. 'It wasn't your fight until . . .'

'. . . until it was almost over – quite so! Harry managed not to say *that*, but he was so damned polite that I could see what an effort it was for him.'

Ned abandoned courtesy and took candour by the horns. 'Look, you chose Ireland a long time ago. It can't matter a tinker's cuss to you now *what* we think.'

Patrick smiled at him in the faintly strengthening light. 'The odd thing is that I've discovered it *does* matter.'

They walked on in silence until the path led them out of woodland into the open meadows of the Home Farm. A pale-gold rim of light was beginning to run along the eastern sky-line, but in the west the last faint stars still pricked the darkness over Highfold and Goose Hill. There was no sound at all until a thrush hidden in the trees behind them decided to announce that the day had begun by practising its winter song.

'What is there for you to do this morning?' Patrick asked suddenly. He turned to see Ned looking puzzled and asked again, 'I mean what's required of you in the next few hours because you happen to be Ned Wyndham?'

Ned considered the question extraordinary but did his best with it. 'First off, I've to see Sid Moffat about clearing ten acres of mangolds so that we can start winter-ploughing; then there are cottage roofs at Little Hay to be inspected in case they need re-thatching; and half a dozen saplings to be lifted from the spinney and replanted along our northern boundary – that's ticklish work, because oaks won't take if their long tap roots get damaged. Look, I could go on and on, but I can't believe you're really interested.'

'I'm interested in discovering England,' Patrick said unexpectedly. 'Try to understand, Ned: for years I was taught by my wife's family and friends to believe that this country was the enemy . . . the heavy-handed bully determined to oppress people fired with a simple, natural longing to rule themselves. After I'd visited Ireland I was just as keen as Ishbel to leave America for good and settle there; by then I hated the high buildings that were beginning to change the face of New York, and the scale of Dublin seemed beautifully human by comparison. I thought I could easily learn to belong there.'

'As a matter of fact, we thought you *did* belong . . . had swallowed the republican creed hook, line, and sinker,' Ned pointed out stiffly.

'I had, even to the extent of shouldering a gun against your Black and Tans. But I wasn't entirely blind, and *their* atrocities were more than equalled by what was done on our side in the name of Irish freedom. When the treaty with Britain was signed I waited for the dawn of peace and tolerance. Instead, the violence went on – Irishman against Irishman now – until finally a man I venerated, Michael Collins, was murdered while he struggled to re-establish law and order in a country that was tearing itself to pieces. It was the basest treachery, because Michael never in his life refused to face the enemy, but he was shot through the back of the head. After that I threw away my gun and went back to architecture.'

There was a little silence before Ned spoke again. 'You could have gone back to America.'

'No . . . Ireland is our home; we can't chop and change for ever. But now I know that I was being shown a picture of this country painted in the lurid colours that are the only ones fanatics use.' He gestured to the quiet landscape around them. 'There's nothing lurid about it at all, and I doubt if there's anything fanatical about its people.'

Ned grinned suddenly. 'That's true of most of them, but you can't have heard Aunt Louise on the subject of some of Harry's friends! She's still getting over the shock of a Labour Government last year. It only lasted six months, but a Prime Minister who was a war-time pacifist, and cabinet members who didn't possess one court dress between them in which to be presented to King George seemed to signal the beginning of the end of England.'

Patrick smiled as the memory of their aunt came to mind. 'She's still formidable, but I suppose she has reason to be. Is Harry really going to turn his back on Somerton for good?'

'I think so, which makes life seem pretty rum. There's Harry determined to give away an inheritance he doesn't want, and me unable to prevent Providence going to the son of a man who sees England only in terms of factories belching smoke. According to Frank, they don't smoke nearly enough . . . we need more of them, more trade, more industrial effort. The land doesn't matter; I think I heard him telling you so last night.'

'He told me about the changes he wants to make at Haywood's End; I gather you don't approve.'

'That's right; I don't.' It was said with such brevity that Patrick abandoned a subject his cousin would clearly refuse to go on discussing. After a moment or two he tried another one, even though it would almost certainly receive the same treatment. 'It's years since I've seen you all and perhaps the day of a funeral isn't the best time to judge, but I got the impression yesterday that I'm not the only one of us who's had a shot at happiness and missed.'

It was a long time before he got an answer. Ned was listening to Patrick's confession about himself, but hearing also an uncanny echo of what was in his own mind. 'I think we might *all* have aimed and missed,' he admitted finally. 'At least, I'm not sure about Charlotte, and I can't answer for Anita, but Harry, Syb, Lucy, and I have certainly missed. Perhaps it's something to do with the generation we belong to; but whether our parents and grandparents had an easier time of it, or simply coped better than we've managed to do, I'm blowed if I know.'

He shrugged the problem aside, reluctant to share it with a cousin who might have improved a little but was still an unknown quantity. 'Shall we get a move on? It must be nearly breakfast time.'

At the Rectory breakfast-table Hubert Roberts laid aside the volume in front of him as Maud came into the room.

'Trollope, by the thickness of it,' she observed, kissing the top of her brother's head. 'Do you suppose his publisher paid him by weight?'

'I was considering a less commercial question – wondering whether he ever met a bishop's wife as odious as Mrs Proudie, or simply invented her.'

Maud poured coffee while she passed under mental review certain of the ladies encountered in the course of Hubert's ecclesiastical career. 'Feeling charitable this morning, I'm prepared to settle for three-parts invention.'

'What would Trollope have made of yesterday's gathering, do you think? Plenty of material there for present-day chronicles of England.'

'Yes, although I think some of the material would have puzzled him as much as it puzzles me. Hubert, what is to become of a generation that believes in motor-cars and wireless and American cocktails, but *not* in God, and goodness, and the civilized traditions we were reared in?'

'I don't know any more than you do, but my guess is that it will soon learn to take its extraordinary inventions for granted, and then find that it must either accept our old-fashioned certainties after all, or discover some new ones of its own.'

'I think *that*'s what troubles me,' she said sadly. 'I have no faith in what it will discover – although perhaps that's only another way of admitting that I'm growing old.'

She saw a smile spread over her brother's tranquil face. 'My dear, when has one generation *not* believed that the next was like the Gadarene swine, rushing to disaster? I can only offer you the comfort of the Reverend Sidney Smith's sensible advice – "take short views, hope for the best, and trust in God"!'

'What a good parish priest he must have been . . . almost as good as you! On which more cheerful note I shall go and bustle about in the store-room, instead of giving way to despair.'

She was still engaged on the humdrum task of counting jars when Gertrude Wyndham called to interrupt her.

'Dear Maud, you're busy . . . shall I murmur soft words of encouragement and tactfully disappear?'

'I hope you'll stay and insist on asking my advice about something . . . *anything* . . . rather than leave me here. What does it matter to know whether I have twenty pounds of strawberry jam in the larder and ten of green tomato chutney, or the other way round? It's *this* ridiculously slavish attention to domestic duty that absorbs our time and prevents us from producing works of art or becoming great philosophers.'

'My elder daughter would agree with you but insist that it's a male plot to make sure that we *don't* toss off the occasional masterpiece!'

'Yes, that sounds like Sybil,' Maud agreed with pleasure, leading the way into her little book-lined sanctum. 'Now that she's here, I hope she's going to stay for a while?'

Gertrude's face looked tired and preoccupied. 'I don't know; I'm not sure that she knows herself, but she doesn't confide in me. All I'm certain of is that she's restless and unhappy beneath the bright façade, and that age hasn't made her any more tolerant. She still treats Frank like a duchess condescending to the peasantry, and doesn't even notice that instead of being angered by her, he now has the wisdom and humour to be amused. Patrick receives much the same treatment, but *he's* more liable to explode. It's much too late now, but I *wish* I'd remembered how antagonistic they were before I pressed him to stay.'

'Gertrude dear, however misguided we think his sympathies may be, he remains your nephew and William's.

What else in decency could you do *but* invite him?'

'Well, yes . . . but kinship isn't the reason I did. I had the strangest certainty that he *needed* Providence, and that it would have been a kind of betrayal of the house to send him away.' She stared pensively at the fire Maud was trying to poke into life; it seemed as reluctant to burn as the jumbled thoughts in her head agreed to be marshalled into a coherent argument.

'Have you noticed how a column of ants march along a chosen path so determinedly that you can't imagine them swerving to right or left . . . and then suddenly some communal instinct seems to suggest to them that it's time for a change, and they *all* switch direction together? That's how it seems to be with us at the moment. The Wyndhams have been marching along peacefully for the past few years – *we* finally recovered from the dreadful stresses and strains left by the war; James and *his* family fixed and separate from us in the places they'd chosen for themselves. There seemed no reason why anything should ever change.'

Her beautiful grey eyes stared mournfully at her friend. Maud didn't dare smile, and tried not to sound too bracing; there was nothing more objectionable than a would-be bracer to someone who didn't wish to be braced. 'Dear girl, you're tired after yesterday and getting things a little out of proportion. Patrick's visit was awkward, I grant you, but it scarcely signals the beginning of a family upheaval.'

'The upheaval *has* begun,' Gertrude said bleakly. 'You haven't heard the rest of it yet. Sybil has already been inspired by the example of Anita's independent life to get involved in a dress-shop in Paris. Her husband and child now see her when she can be bothered to remember them, although that isn't, of course, how *she* describes it. But that won't be the end of Anita's influence; according to Charlotte she's going to find a home for herself in London. She unsettled Lucy disastrously the last time she was here, and will probably do so again. Lucy's been so much better since the twins were born . . . I shall find myself hating Anita if she upsets her again.'

'Are you also afraid that she can still upset Ned, after all these years?'

'No, I don't think I am, but he's got problems of his own which *Patrick* is complicating. Frank's been hinting for a couple of years that he wants to build new houses at Haywood's End for some of his Birmingham work people. He claims that it will not only help *them* but prevent the village dying. Ned's view is that Frank's remedy for a declining population will kill it anyway with an influx of townees from the city who know little about rural life and care less.'

'What has that got to do with Patrick?'

'He's an architect, and Frank was having a long talk with him last night. I could see my son-in-law wondering whether he'd found someone not only to share his enthusiasm but also to design his wretched houses for him.'

Maud smiled ruefully at her friend. 'I see why you'd have preferred James's ants to stay away from yours!'

'You haven't heard the worst thing of all . . . William received a letter from James himself this morning. After nearly forty years in America he's decided it's time to come home. It's really too much, coming on top of everything else.'

It was hard not to smile, even though Maud knew that the reason for her agitation was not to be laughed at.

'One of your own skeletons rattling in its cupboard, my dear?'

'No, I dealt very firmly with *them* a long time ago. It's William I'm concerned about.'

'Now *why*, I wonder? I should have said that in between deciding whether or not a touch more burnt sienna on the palette would produce a warmer shade of madder, he would have expressed the view that his brother, having been unpredictable for sixty years, couldn't be expected to change now!'

Amusement touched Gertrude's face fleetingly, then faded again. 'It was roughly what he *did* say, but William never enlarges on what he's feeling. Fine painter though he is, it wouldn't occur to him to measure *that* against the wealth and worldly success James has achieved; he'll fall over backwards to see himself through his brother's eyes, as the Wyndham who failed to keep his inheritance. *That's* how James will see things unless he's changed more than I can believe possible.'

She gave a little sigh, then straightened her shoulders and smiled resolutely. 'What a tale of woe, Maud dear . . . forgive me. I miss my father, who always pointed out to me that fretting over things I could do nothing about was a senseless waste of time. I shall go home instead and make myself useful as a buffer between Sybil and Patrick. Left to themselves, they are liable to fight the Easter Rebellion all over again!'

She walked back through the wood, stopped to talk to Biddle in the kitchen-gardens, and then met Ned, who reported that Patrick and his sister had just ridden off through the park together.

'Cantering amicably, would you say?' she enquired with faint hope, 'or making a tussle of it?'

'Well, Syb was in front, but Patrick had the air of a man who didn't intend that she should remain so!' He grinned at his mother's anxious face. 'I'm teasing, love. On the pair that Artie saddled for them, they're hardly going to go thundering about the countryside, breaking their necks! Sybil will do well to get more than a swift trot out of Polly, and Patrick will soon discover that *his* horse prefers to walk!'

It seemed to Gertrude that she laughed for the first time for days. 'Dear daft *clever* Artie . . . they can sink their differences by venting their spleen on him! By the time they get back they might even be friends.'

'I'd really rather Patrick went off in a huff, if you don't mind,' he said, smiling ruefully. 'If he and Frank see much more of each other, they'll have an estate of houses planned at Haywood's End before I can put the evil eye on either of them!'

'Dearest . . . I know you hate the idea, but isn't there

just a *little* truth in what Frank says?'

'I don't think so, Mama. To my way of thinking, the village has to stay what it is . . . the home of generations of people attached to the land; otherwise it will lose itself entirely. Shove a bunch of arty-crafty William Morris Socialists in the middle of it, drifting around in homespun smocks and spouting about the simple life, and not much harm is done; they eventually get discouraged by rain and muck and derision and go away again; what Frank is suggesting is something that will change Haywood's End for good. For as long as I can, I shall resist it.'

His brown face smiled at her but she detected tiredness and discouragement in his eyes. He didn't relish a battle now, as he might have done years ago, but he wouldn't avoid it. Gertrude didn't relish it either, but even though it meant fighting Lucy's husband and the owner of the house they lived in, she would range herself on Ned's side, now and for always.

'You work too hard, my dear one. Can't you play a little more? The Maynards were saying only yesterday that they never see you.'

'You're being tactful; they probably hinted that I neglect their rather boring daughters.'

'Being neighbourly doesn't take much effort, Ned.'

'I know, but all the Maynard sweetness and charm went into Emily. Her younger sisters are a frightful pair . . . I'd rather talk to Mary across the courtyard any day – she doesn't giggle like a lunatic at everything I say, or leap about tennis courts with quite unfeminine vigour!'

'She doesn't get the chance,' Gertrude pointed out quite sharply. 'Ned dear, you're being deliberately obtuse.'

'No, I realize what you're saying – Mary Haskell is bound to be different from Gwen and Georgina Maynard. *I'm* only pointing out that I know what I like, and it isn't Mrs Maynard's "fillies", as I'm afraid Grandfather Wyndham would certainly have called them!' He smiled at his mother with engaging sweetness and then strolled away to discuss autumn sowing with Biddle – a much more profitable subject, in his view.

She watched him go, and then went on towards the house. Ned's apparent determination to lead a single life was a worry that she never aired even to William. It might have been easier to deal with if she were sure of the reason for it – Anita, perhaps, or some lingering concern about his own mental health; but, more likely, it was a general anxiety about the future. She looked at the grey stone flank of Providence reflected in the still water of the moat, but for the first time that she could remember it brought no comfort – her life, Lucy's, and now Ned's, seemed swallowed up by its constant demands for care, repair, and love. The terrible idea invaded her mind that instead of loving Providence, she might one day come to hate it. The burden of preserving it was only bearable if the next generation *also* believed that it was too precious to be allowed to die.

She reached the courtyard garden and found Lucy there, balanced on a ladder and absorbed in the task of pruning the Albertine rose that clothed the walls in summertime in a mass of copper-pink bloom.

'Dearest, I hope you have Biddle's blessing,' she called up to her daughter.

'Well, his grudging permission, at least. He allows that the job needs doing, and he's not as sprightly as he was at shinning up ladders.' Lucy descended to earth and stared at her mother. 'Speaking of which, you looked sad and tired just now. Are you still getting over Gramps and the funeral yesterday?'

'Perhaps that's it . . .' She stared round the little garden that was always sheltered and still, and beautiful at every season of the year. 'No, that *isn't* it . . . I was having a day-time nightmare a moment ago, wondering whether Providence, lovely and dear as it is, has cost too much. . . .' Her voice trailed away with the sentence not completed, but Lucy understood and rescued her.

'If you think it's cost more than it's worth, you're wrong,' she said with gentle certainty. 'There was a time when I thought it had, but I'm quite sure now that it mustn't ever be lost.'

She inspected her mother's face, then added severely, 'You'd better tell me what else is worrying you; otherwise I shall have to winkle it out of you, bit by bit.'

Gertrude smiled suddenly. 'Like that oriental gentleman in *The Mikado*, I have a "little list" of anxieties! Sybil is unhappy and I don't know why; Ned is lonely and I'm afraid I do know why; Frank doesn't understand about Haywood's End, so I suppose I can't help wondering whether he understands about Providence, either. And even if he does, will *Charlie* understand when the time comes?'

Lucy felt grateful that she'd asked herself the same question and arrived at an answer.

'No-one who's born and bred here can fail to grow up loving it. Charlie already begins to realize that it will be his to take care of one day.'

'Then I shall stop worrying, my dearest, and go and make Emmy happy. She's been fidgeting for days to know when she can start making Christmas puddings!'

Gertrude kissed her daughter and went into the house. The anxieties that beset her remained, and Emmy's rich concoctions that no-one much enjoyed would also have to be faced; but the important thing was surely to accept afflictions – anxieties and indigestible puddings alike – with what fortitude and grace they could manage.

Chapter Fourteen

Out of sight of Ned and the stables, Sybil gave the mare her head – with results that would have dumbfounded Artie. Not only did they cover the ground at full gallop, but their female exhibitionism provoked Polly's stablemate so unbearably that he was roused to making a race of it. Patrick urged him on, aware that the whole point and purpose of his life was suddenly concentrated for the moment in not letting Sybil win. Polly was gradually overhauled, and on the verge of being beaten when two things occurred to save her – a gate ahead of them, and leading up to it a particularly green and succulent stretch of clover. Polly didn't mind gates, and consented to lift her rider over this one without any fuss, but behind them Patrick had less luck. Sybil heard sounds which made her rein in immediately – an anguished shout and a heavy thud, followed by silence. She turned round to see Patrick sitting on the ground and rubbing his shoulder; he was apparently not much hurt but looking murderously angry. When Polly had been tied up to a tree, she climbed the gate and walked back to him.

'You *seem* to be all right . . . are you?'

His scowl strained her to the utmost but she did her best to look decently concerned.

'It's no thanks to that knock-kneed, broken-down apology for a horse if I am.'

'But perhaps just a *little* ruffled in temper?' she suggested sweetly.

'Enough to administer a beating if provoked any more, so be warned.' From his seat on the ground, he glared at her hoping that what she said next would give him an excuse to touch her.

She gripped a quivering lip firmly between her teeth, but the sight of Patrick's horse with clover dangling from its mouth and an expression of ineffable self-congratulation in its eye undid her.

'I remember now . . . Artie did say try to . . . to avoid c . . . clover!'

'You remember *now*,' Patrick said with disgusted emphasis.

It was no good – laughter was welling up inside her, irresistible as the need to sneeze, and she would have to give way to it or burst. By the time he'd struggled to his feet she was doubled up beside him, helpless because she'd now remembered something else as well.

'Artie c . . . *calls* him The J . . . Jumper! Oh, Patrick, please admit it's f . . . funny.'

He was enraged with Artie, the horse and – for some reason that didn't seem unfair – with *her* most of all; he was damned if he'd laugh. But in the end he couldn't help himself. She was too captivating to resist, and she was right – it *was* funny, and merriment that he hadn't experienced for years was exploding inside him.

They were nearly sober again, wiping streaming eyes, before he managed to sound severe. 'You still deserve a beating . . . I'll swear you made straight for that blasted gate.'

She shook her head, afraid to trust her voice, but amusement still lingered in her eyes and in the curve of her red mouth, enticing him to a different punishment.

She was pulled hard against him and his mouth came down on hers. It wasn't meant to be serious, but it became so. She fought against his strength, broke free, and was immediately dragged close again. His hands slid across her back, this time gently compelling surrender, and under the persuasion of his lips her mouth had to open under his. The attraction of years ago was now desire that leapt between them, as mutual and complete as their laughter had been a few moments before. With their lips still clinging, she allowed herself to be pushed gently to the ground, and his body straddled hers as if it had always belonged there.

'We can't stop now . . . can't possibly,' he murmured. The smile that curved her mouth again answered him; no, they couldn't stop now. She closed her eyes, felt his hands undoing her jacket and breeches, and yearned for the moment when his body took possession of her. But the moment didn't come.

Instead, his weight rolled off her, and she was left feeling cold and desperately cheated. He made a sound, half-laugh, half-sob, that she heard above another persistent noise. She opened her eyes and saw The Jumper's nose almost beside her head; a clover patch just there offered the greenest, sweetest mouthfuls of all.

'I'm afraid lust can't compete with that,' Patrick said unsteadily. 'It's the second time he's brought me low, but perhaps I ought to thank God he did – shall I apologize?'

'No need,' she muttered, trying to fasten her clothes again with trembling fingers. 'But you *could* offer me a cigarette.'

Instead of doing as she asked at once, his hand first touched her cheek in a fleeting gesture of tenderness. 'You look different now . . . bright, sparkling Sybil has suddenly disappeared and in her place there's another woman altogether – someone soft and vulnerable and very appealing. Does anybody but me know she exists?'

'Probably not, now. Sparkling Syb is what they all expect, and I don't like to disappoint them.' She took the cigarette he gave her and smoked it in silence for a while. The fever in her blood had died, leaving her cold and sad, and humiliated by the fear that her own need a moment ago had been stronger than his, and her disappointment greater. 'I asked you once whether you regretted choosing Ireland – you didn't give me an answer,' she said abruptly.

'All I regret is the gulf between me and my father. He's never forgiven me, and won't do now, even though he's coming back to England. In fact I suppose *that* accentuates the different choices we've made. But I'm certain of something now that only nibbled at my conscience

172

before . . . my son Christopher isn't going to be allowed to grow up not knowing his grandfather and the rest of his English relations. Ishbel will protest, but he must have some of his schooling over here.' Patrick frowned over another thought in his mind. 'I'm not sure I'm right now, but I had the impression you didn't concern yourself much with Josephine. It seemed very terrible to me. *We* had a daughter, Teresa, but she was born severely handicapped and died when she was three.'

His quiet voice spoke the words without stress or emotion, but she was left with the awareness of a hurt that hadn't mended.

'I'm sorry . . . I didn't know, Patrick,' she whispered. 'None of us knew.' If there was comfort to give she didn't know what it was, except to say, 'There's time to try again.'

He ground out his cigarette and carefully buried it under a stone before answering her. 'There's no time at all, because the doctors couldn't guarantee that the same deformities wouldn't occur again. Ishbel has refused ever since to take the risk, and I can't force her. She's a devout Catholic, which is not only a comfort to her but an absolute bar to abortion or birth-control. I'm not nearly devout enough for it to be of any comfort to me.'

The confession died on the quiet air, while she searched for something to say. She was desperately sorry for him, but it was a hurt of her own that was expressed, because it was more easily put into words.

'*That*'s why you thought you'd make love to me, I suppose . . . for a moment or two I imagined that you really wanted *me*!'

He tried to tell himself that the Sybil he knew was back again – spoiled, petulant, and vain. Then she turned to look at him and he saw her desolate need for reassurance.

'If you're thinking that I needed a woman – any woman – you're about as wrong as you can be,' he said deliberately. 'I wanted *you*, and the longing is nothing new. You had the same shattering effect on me years ago, only then you didn't need me to tell you so.'

A smile lit her face, wiping away sadness. There was no provocation in it – only genuine amusement mixed with sweetness. 'If you aren't completely unnerved by The Jumper's desire for our company, would it help to . . . to finish what he interrupted?'

She'd thought Patrick's pale eyes intelligent but malicious; now they seemed as full of tenderness as his mouth, that touched hers in a brief, gentle kiss. 'Thank you for that, but I'm afraid it wouldn't help at all, only make matters a good deal worse! For probably the only time in my life I shall behave like the English gentleman my father no doubt hoped I'd be. I shall take you home, and find some reasonable excuse to offer my aunt for cutting short my visit.' He pulled Sybil to her feet, but didn't immediately let go of her hands. 'Get on Polly's back before I weaken, and for God's sake prevent her from inflaming my horse all the way home.'

They rode back close together, but almost in silence.

William was in the hall at Providence emptying the mail-bag that Jem had collected from the post office in the village. It contained exactly the 'reasonable' excuse that Patrick needed – a letter from Charlotte giving him the news that Anita was expected in London. His aunt made it easy for him – smiled with the warmth of her relief at detaching him from Frank and his building schemes, and insisted that of course he must want to see his sister in London rather than stay on at Providence.

Sybil volunteered to drive Patrick to the station the following morning, and refused her brother's offer to go with them.

'Making sure that you see him off the premises, Syb?' Ned asked. 'I've rather changed my mind about him, as a matter of fact.'

'So have I, but I'm glad he's leaving,' she said briefly.

The train was late in arriving and the time had to be filled with things that could safely be talked about. A bright flow of speculation about Anita's future life in London kept them going, but Patrick suddenly interrupted it.

'It's odd to think I might never have seen you again – I had no intention of coming to Providence until I bumped into Harry.' His eyes fixed themselves on her pale face, lingered on her mouth because he remembered how it had felt beneath his own. 'Are you happy in France?'

'Sometimes . . . and when I'm not it's my own fault. Nothing new about that – Ned would tell you it's how I've always been. I think I miss *him* most of all.'

Patrick nodded, then gave a faint smile. 'We can't wish another funeral on the family to bring us back to Providence together, so this is where we go our separate ways; but I shall always be glad I came.'

'Me too . . . I'm quite often disastrously wrong but my only saving grace, if I have one, is not to mind admitting it. I was wrong about you, and I'm sorry for all those stupid gibes about the Irish.'

'Your saving graces are legion and most of the gibes are deserved! There's nothing to be wished for ourselves, but I'd like to think Christopher and Josephine might meet one day . . . meet and be friends.'

She had to strain to hear what he said, because the train was finally puffing into the station, isolating them in a cloud of steamy vapour. His mouth touched hers, then doors banged, a whistle blew, and she was left standing there alone. For a moment or two the rear of the guard's van was still visible; she could see the lamp on the back of it swaying to and fro. Then even that disappeared round a bend in the track. It was time to go home.

Ned disliked seeing her getting ready to leave for Paris – making a round of farewell visits among neighbours and village friends; like them, he had the impression that for as long as she was there life was touched with a little more colour and gaiety than usual.

'Any good hoping that you'll come back more often now?' he suggested as they walked home from church together on her last morning. 'We'd prefer to see you on happy occasions as well.'

She shivered, not only because winter had set in early

175

and every branch and twig along the lane carried a frail glittering carapace of frost. 'No more funerals because I can't spare *anybody*; the Grim Reaper must take his wretched scythe elsewhere.' She glanced at her brother's face. 'I'd come like a shot for *your* wedding, dear Ned!'

He grinned, recognizing a leading question when he heard one. 'If you're about to extol the charms of Georgina Maynard, don't bother . . . Mama is working hard on her behalf!'

'Very well. I'll try a different question. Where does Lucy stand in your battle with Frank?'

'Uncomfortably straddled, I should think, poor girl. She's bound to be loyal to him, but I'm almost sure she shares my feeling about the village. It would be a great deal easier for all concerned if we just agreed to sell Frank the land he wants. *We'd* get our hands on more money than we're ever likely to see otherwise, and *he*'d be happy – he hates having any of his pet schemes thwarted.'

'But you won't let Father agree, all the same?'

'I *can't*, Syb. Frank doesn't understand. His raw materials are quite different from ours, and his work-people put down their tools and go home when the bell rings. For *us* the land is our life, as well as the job we do. You can't mix his sort of people and ours and expect them to understand each other. God knows agriculture's in a poor enough way as it is, but what remains of rural England won't survive at all if men like Frank are allowed to take it over.'

'Forget England for a moment and think of the Wyndhams . . . what's going to happen to *them*?'

She saw a rueful smile touch her brother's mouth. 'I'm afraid they are in for a bad time! Captains of industry, like Frank, see us as a collection of antiquated relics of the past, hanging on to land that could be mined for coal or covered with factories and workmen's tenements; Harry and his revolutionary hot-heads reckon we're dyed-in-the-wool conservatives hanging on to privilege, the trappings of feudalism and, if we're lucky, inherited wealth we've done nothing to deserve. Either way, we irritatingly resist extinction instead of allowing the juggernaut of progress to roll over us!'

'I worry about *one* of the Wyndhams – you!' Sybil said slowly. 'Papa will go on working in the Great Parlour, and die happy with a paint-brush in his hand, Mama will spend what remains of her life contentedly looking after him and everybody else. But what happens after that, Ned?'

'Frank will do nothing to hurt *them* – it's one of the nicest things I know about him that he loves them both in his own way. If you're asking what happens after *him*, I can't answer you. Unlike his father, Charlie's known no other home but Providence; he may grow up preferring to be a country gentleman instead of an industrialist, in which case nothing will change here at all.'

'Fat chance – he's Arthur Thornley all over again. My guess is that he can't wait to have a factory of his own, and all the fun of browbeating his slaves and counting his ill-gotten gains!'

'My dear girl, he's not eight years old yet. Arthur doted on him from the moment he was born, but I'm bound to say he wasn't a very engaging small boy. Still, Mary's doing wonders with him, and she and Jane between them will see that he grows up all right.'

'You don't think Lucy might take a hand in it?'

'I have the feeling she prefers the twins,' Ned said briefly.

'Mary Haskell might not be here long enough to see Charles grow up. She's got her own life to think of . . . For all you know some lusty lad from the village might already be wanting to marry her.'

'Rubbish, Syb . . . she's not for coupling with someone like Willy Moffat or Matt Parsons; they're nice enough chaps, but good God – can't you see she deserves better than that?'

'She's a children's nurse,' Sybil pointed out sharply, 'a servant, even though she may have been encouraged to feel that she's almost one of the family, because you respected her father. What happens when Lucy doesn't need her any more and she's missed the chance of marriage? Even at the terrible risk of having Charlie grow up like Grandfather Thornley, I think she should be encouraged to leave Providence if she gets the chance.'

They walked in a silence broken only by the sound of their feet on the frozen ground, aware that for the first time since childhood they had suddenly come close to quarrelling.

'Now that I think about it, you're right, of course,' Ned muttered finally. 'It's just that I've got in the way of feeling she belongs here. I traced the family after I came back from Craiglockhart and found them in great distress – Mrs Haskell hadn't been able to cope with Tom's death, and Mary at the age of fifteen was trying to be bread-winner, and mother to the two younger children as well. She still is the lynch-pin of the family, but somehow I must make sure that she can get away if she wants to.'

Sybil remembered the expression in Mary's eyes when-ever she spoke Ned's name. He was the best of brothers and the dearest of men, but he didn't know very much about women.

'Let Mama deal with the problem,' she suggested gently. 'She's got rather more experience than you have.'

He nodded and by mutual consent the subject of Mary Haskell was abandoned.

It wasn't until after Sybil's final goodbyes had been said and William had decided to make one of his rare visits to London so that he could travel with her, that Ned thought of something he *might* have said to soothe the anxieties she'd hinted at. When he was getting old and going grey, and an unloving nephew finally evicted him from Providence, he could move into the cottage adjoining Mrs Haskell's. Mary or her sister would then feel obliged to take care of him, and the captains of industry and the political reformers could look at the last of the Wyndhams finally become a dinosaur! He grinned with pleasure at the ridiculousness of the idea, regretting that it was too late to share it with Sybil. For the moment, though, there were more pressing things to think about. The hard weather meant that animals were already having to be fed, and they were behind-hand with the normal tasks of early winter. Uncleared ditches and leaking barns must all be seen to this side of Christmas, and the December days were very short. He thought of Patrick Wyndham's question about how he filled his time – the real answer was in doing what farming required, season by season, year by year. Patrick wouldn't have understood any more than Frank Thornley did. But Ned wasn't minded to become a dinosaur yet, and for as long as he lived he would abide by his grandfather's philosophy about the land.

Chapter Fifteen

Anita was back in London well before Christmas. She went to stay with Charlotte in Thurloe Square, and Harry allowed that *this* was reasonable. It was *not* reasonable to find her still there, filling the flat with her arty friends, by the time winter was giving way to spring. He accepted that it was his sister's fate in life to be battened on, but her readiness to be trampled over to *this* extent was becoming absurd and infuriating. He could never find her alone nowadays, and he was beginning to think that she was less ready than before to share in whatever burning issue occupied his own mind. Anita's effect on her was deplorable, and one March evening when he did manage to find Charlotte by herself, he told her so.

She listened to the lecture patiently, not daring to smile, because she knew his affection for *her* was as real as his hostility towards Anita. It was odd and saddening that what she liked most about their cousin – her keen eye for the absurd – was the thing that Harry seemed to enjoy least. It didn't occur to her that he suspected Anita of laughing at *him*; she merely assumed that life for her once-carefree brother had become too serious to be laughed at. The war and politics had had a permanently solemnizing effect on him; but the war had been over for nearly a decade, and surely even the most ardent reformer could find something to smile about if he tried?

'You've had a bad day, I expect,' she risked saying now. 'It always makes you irritable.'

'And *that* infuriating female trick is something else you've caught from Anita – turning a rational comment into a personal attack. Irrespective of the sort of day I've had, the fact remains that if you make her too welcome, she'll be here for good, and her ramshackle crowd of friends will be here with her.'

Charlotte loved her brother and was prepared to forgive him everything except downright injustice.

'Anita didn't ask to come . . . I invited her, and I'd be very happy if she *did* stay. Her friends visit us because I also invite *them*. They're intelligent and interesting, and I've suddenly discovered that there's more to life than earnest Socialism – I *enjoy* mixing with artists and literary people.'

'Freaks and phonies, all of them – especially that long-haired creature from the north, who seems to haunt the place.'

The contempt in his voice for a man he hadn't bothered to get to know stung her into rare anger. 'My dear Harry, you're being ridiculous! The "freaks and phonies" are established artists and writers, even if *you* don't happen to have heard of them. Men like John and Paul Nash, Wadsworth, and Nevinson *are* the modern movement. Roger Fry is an acknowledged authority, and Clive Bell writes brilliantly, but because their subject is modern art and not labour relations you haven't heard of *them*, either.'

'Have you finished?'

'Not quite. The long-haired creature has a name, Ian Nicholson, and I'd rather you used it in future. He works for the Unicorn Press and is going to publish Anita's art essays. That's why he comes here, to talk to *her*. I can guess your next sneer and am happy to forestall it; no, he didn't fight in the war because he was a conscientious objector. Instead, he spent four years carrying wounded men out of the front line; does *that* entitle you to despise him?'

Anger brightened her eyes and made her nearly beautiful; Harry noticed the fact, and it seemed to be an additional good reason for resenting Ian Nicholson.

'I can scarcely be expected to know the details of your visitors' private lives,' he said furiously.

'You know nothing, except soldiering and politics,' she pointed out. 'You're like a tree that only grows branches

181

on one side, because the prevailing winds shrivel every shoot it puts out anywhere else.' He was shocked into silence, not so much by the onslaught itself as by the fear that what she said was true. She saw his expression change and immediately her anger melted into sadness for him. 'Dear Harry, there *is* more to life than constituency meetings and the division bell in the House of Commons but you do nothing but work. If you can't bear Somerton, why not spend a weekend with Ned at Providence occasionally?'

'Because I can't bear Thornley, either. Uncle William's probably forgotten by now who owns the place, but how Ned puts up with it God only knows.'

He knew as well as she did that Ned put up with what he could do nothing about, but it didn't lessen the rancour that sounded in his voice whenever he spoke of Frank. Charlotte remembered explaining once to Anita that they couldn't be expected to approve of a successful capitalist, but she'd since been forced to admit to herself the logic of her cousin's argument that a capitalist's first obligation *was* to be successful. Harry himself despised failure and, although his philosophy was different from Frank's, they were both men who loved England in their own way and spent their lives working for it. It should have been possible for them to tolerate each other, but apparently it wasn't.

'I suppose the Samuel Commission's report has been published and you're blaming Frank for his share in it,' she commented quietly. 'Does it go against the miners?'

'It does exactly what you and they would expect – suggests throwing them small concessions in the future to bribe them into keeping quiet now; it also piously regrets that, given the lamentable state of the coal market, the owners' demands for wage reductions must be accepted as reasonable. Having delivered themselves of this conclusion, the worthy Commissioners retire to their rich estates and leave the miners to explain to their wives that what is already a bare subsistence wage must fall still further in future.'

182

'Will the concessions be enough to quieten them?'

'Certainly not, and *this* time the TUC is committed to giving its support. A General Strike's been threatened for years and avoided at the last minute, but it can't be avoided now, for all Stanley Baldwin's "honest" platitudes and air of sweet reason.'

Charlotte stared at her brother's face and fully registered its tiredness and dejection. 'I don't understand . . . I'd have expected you to be triumphant, but you're not.'

'It's too late,' he explained sombrely. 'Last summer was the time to strike, when the Government was totally unprepared for an embargo on the movement of coal. Then, it *must* have given in, but the nine-months subsidy it granted has bought it time to prepare. Now, it can not only ride out a general stoppage but come out of it with increased public popularity. The miners will lose again, as they always do, because the men in other unions won't go on supporting them for long enough.'

Charlotte accepted that what he said was true; he was often wrong about things that didn't touch his heart, but never about what mattered to him deeply. 'I chose a bad time to rip up at you . . . I'm sorry,' she said after a moment or two.

The corners of his mouth twitched in a sudden smile. 'Rip you certainly did, but I'm sure I deserved it. Where *is* our troublesome cousin, by the way?'

'Measuring and making lists in the house she's found for herself and Uncle James,' Charlotte said demurely.

'And you're going to be kind enough *not* to point out that, apart from interfering in your affairs, I was flogging a horse that wouldn't even run! Am I allowed to say that I hope the house she's found is nowhere near Arlington Street?'

'It's in Walton Place, conveniently halfway between you and me,' Charlotte said, smiling broadly. 'At the moment it looks rather sad and shabby, but Anita will make something elegant of it.'

'Of course! According to you, there's *no* miracle she can't work. You're besotted with a cool, opinionated, over-independent wench who's been cushioned by wealth and comfort from the day she was born. That's a purely factual assessment, by the way, so you needn't feel obliged to slay me again!'

'I grant you the wealth, *made* by Uncle James, not inherited,' Charlotte said thoughtfully, 'and I accept the fact that Anita has a proper respect for it. But has the rest of her life been so easy? No mother since she was a tiny child, the sadness of her father's separation from his only son, and her own disappointment over Ned. She's self-contained because life has made her so, and "opinionated" because she's intelligent enough to hold views of her own; that's the worst I can find to say about her. The worst *you* can find is that her views don't coincide with yours!'

Harry held up his hands in the gesture of a boxer accepting defeat. 'Pax, Lottie . . . I'll provoke you no more on the subject of Anita, and confess instead to a burning curiosity to meet Uncle James. He came here once after his wife died, but I was away at school and you were still in India with Father, so we didn't meet him.'

'It's strange the way family genes get shared out,' Charlotte remarked thoughtfully. 'He and Uncle William sound about as different as *any* two men could be, much less two who are brothers; and I can't think of anything Sybil and Lucy have in common except courage, and most women have that, so it isn't remarkable.'

Harry gave a non-committal nod that left Charlotte free to assume he agreed with her. He never allowed himself nowadays to think about Lucy Thornley, but still felt an uncomfortable constriction about his heart whenever her name was mentioned. They met only at the rare intervals dictated by family gatherings, but when these occurred there was opportunity enough to discover that her golden beauty was now probably at its peak, and that she seemed serenely indifferent to a man called Harry Trentham. He refused to examine what he felt about *her*, but he knew that he hated Frank Thornley.

'I must go,' he said abruptly to Charlotte. 'I've work to do before I speak in the debate tomorrow.' He kissed her good night and set out to walk through the damp lamp-lit dusk to his own flat. There was time to think, among other things, about his sister's remarkable outburst; he might have expected her to stand up for Anita, but she'd rushed to the defence of the man called Ian Nicholson as well. Harry remembered the becoming flush of rage in her cheeks and thought that it would be just like his dear, dim Lottie to fall in love with someone who was not only thoroughly unsuitable, but already attracted to Anita by her clear signs of wealth. He was ashamed of the thought even as it formed itself in his mind, because it was unfair to his cousin, as well as Nicholson. There was more to Anita's attraction than money. Her spare elegance and grace were obvious for any but a blind man to see, and her friends weren't blind. Harry was startled by the strength of his objection to having her living permanently in London, throwing out her amused challenges to *him*, and completely overshadowing his impressionable sister. If Fate hadn't made a mess of things as usual she'd be safely anchored in New York or Paris by now, or anywhere else where they need never feel obliged to think about her. He trudged along Knightsbridge, tempted to hail a cab and ride the rest of the way. Tiredness wasn't something he normally allowed himself to feel, but tonight it dragged at his legs as heavily as unusual dejection had settled on his heart. He was depressed by the hopelessness of the general situation, of course . . . the mistakes that his friends and colleagues continually made, as well as the guile and heartless self-interest of his opponents. No, damn it, it was more than that; just at this moment, if he was honest with himself, he'd admit that he wasn't thinking about the general situation at all – it was his own muddled life that was the trouble. He stood on the kerb, waiting for the traffic to allow him to cross into Piccadilly, but stayed there fixed to the spot long after he might have safely stepped into the road. Charlotte had been right – he'd become an automaton, sucking in facts and figures and case-histories, spewing them out again in opposition speeches and political tracts. He was scarcely a *man* at all.

The following weekend, for the first time since George Hoskins' funeral, he went down to Providence to see his friend Ned.

Anita moved into her new home but, for the time being, moved into it alone; her father's departure from New York was delayed by several months while he made a final visit to the west coast. Without her, Charlotte's life in Thurloe Square reverted to the quietness Harry approved of, but she was surprised to find that one of her cousin's friends still persisted in calling on her. Ian Nicholson occasionally appeared on the doorstep, looking faintly embarrassed to be there but determined not to be daunted since he *was* there. Charlotte wondered why he came, and assumed that he needed a friendly listener while he talked about Anita. One evening he brought a piece of news she hadn't heard.

'It seems that your uncle's certain to be elected to the Royal Academy this summer . . . did you know?'

Her face lit with pleasure at the idea, although she smiled as well. 'Uncle William would almost certainly forget to mention it! He paints because it's the only thing he wants to do, not to get money or fame. But my aunt will be happy for him to be properly recognized at last.'

'He was too far ahead of the rest of the Academy men, and out of sight altogether of the general population. What can you expect of people who stared at El Greco's "Crucifixion" at the National Gallery and "excused" it by saying that he must have been insane?'

Charlotte smiled at the disgust in Nicholson's voice. 'All right, but admit, at least, that it's stunningly different from the Victorian paintings they were used to. I suppose Impressionists like Uncle William were, too, but my cousin's husband, Henri Blanchard, always insisted that it was only a matter of time before public taste became educated.'

'There's more to frighten them now than the things William Wyndham produces . . . and such lovely things they are,' he said quietly, with his eyes fixed on the only canvas of her uncle's that Charlotte possessed.

'It's a picture of Providence, where he lives,' she explained. 'I can imagine I'm there, just by looking at it. My own home at Somerton isn't nearly so beautiful – municipal-classical, my uncle calls it!'

'Well, at that, it has to be roomier than a Victorian terraced cottage in Leeds, which is what I was brought up in. My father's an apothecary and, instead of being the lady of the manor, my mother gives lessons on the pianoforte. I won a scholarship to Oxford . . . it isn't where Nicholsons are normally educated, but no doubt you guessed that.'

He flung the facts at her like the pebbles a small urchin might use as ammunition against his tormentors. She simply turned them aside with a smile in which he could find no trace of condescension, however hard he tried.

'I envy you if your mother taught *you* music as well; *my* dear mama's a marvel, but she'd be the first to admit that she can hear no difference at all between Johann Sebastian Bach and Claude Debussy!'

Ian Nicholson stared at her – she was probably the most tranquil woman he'd ever met, and certainly the nicest.

'You were meant to raise an eyebrow, or curl your lip a little, not find something tactful to say.'

'I wasn't being tactful. I don't blame you for an accident of birth that put you in a cottage in Leeds. You should try not to hold Somerton against *me*,' Charlotte said gently.

His frown gave way to a reluctant grin. 'Inverted snobbery – the curse of the lower classes!' With his gaze lingering on William's canvas again, he muttered something else. 'Providence did you say it was called? Funny name! It looks like the sort of house a child imagines – all the lovely bits it can think of, jumbled up together. They shouldn't fit at all, but then again somehow they *do*.'

'You could come with me and see it for yourself one day, if you'd like to,' she heard herself say. She couldn't read the expression on his face, but felt sure that disgust at such forwardness must be there. The embarrassed colour deepening in her cheeks made her look young and vulnerable, and just for a moment he was almost sure the

187

terrace in Leeds didn't matter after all. A mother who sounded formidable and an overbearing brother had left her short of the personal vanity that gave confidence to women and conceit to men. She was a shy, kind woman who thought she was plain and didn't expect a man to notice her. He liked her very much and although he foresaw that he'd be patronized by her grand relations, it didn't occur to him to snub her by refusing.

'I'd like to come if you think your aunt and uncle wouldn't mind,' he said after a hesitation she misread.

'They don't mind anything at all, except malice and unkindness.'

'It makes Providence sound like paradise.'

She rewarded him with a charming smile. 'I think that's almost what it is.'

Chapter Sixteen

The General Strike took place, as Harry had said it would, almost as soon as the term of the Government subsidy to the mining industry expired. He was proved right, too, in his prediction that little would come out of it except further suffering for men who already lived on the edge of despair. The Government hadn't wasted the nine months since the last crisis; their emergency measures had been well-organized, and a large proportion of the population agreed with them that a national stoppage of *this* kind wasn't playing the game. It was political . . . perhaps the first step along the road to anarchy. Unionized labour couldn't be allowed to get the upper hand, and for once the Government had shown the right amount of firmness. The troops and police who kept essential food, materials, and transport moving were probably hindered rather than helped by volunteers; but their most useful contribution was to convince the other unions that the miners couldn't win.

The strike collapsed nine days after it began. What had been dreaded ever since the end of the war had finally come to pass, and nothing very catastrophic had happened after all. It was true that the miners were being stubborn as usual – holding out by themselves when it was as plain as a pikestaff they'd have to give way in the end; but for most people normality was back again. Summer and the cricket season had begun and, after a few nerve-racking days that had the smell of danger about them, a Bolshevik revolution in England looked more impossible than ever.

The summer of 1926 didn't seem much different from any other but, looking back on it afterwards at Providence, Gertrude decided that it had been a turning-point in more ways than one.

To begin with, there was William's election to the Academy, and the rare necessity of a stay in London. Without putting it into words to herself, much less to anyone else, she regretted that James hadn't arrived in time to see his brother's moment of public glory. Nor could she persuade Ned to share in it by going with them to London. It was haysel-time, and the weather looked set for exactly the fine dry spell farmers prayed for in early June.

'I'd be a terrible liability to you among all the arty nobs, Mama,' he pointed out truthfully. 'Much better not trust me among a crowd of elegant swells all trying to prove to each other how much they know about art! In any case, someone ought to stay here to keep an eye on the children.'

'There's no truth in you,' she said, trying not to smile. 'Admit that you hate London, and wouldn't dream of letting the men bring in the hay harvest without you.'

'There is that, too,' he was forced to admit.

His parents drove off with Frank and Lucy the following morning and he was left alone, guiltily aware that while *he* would enjoy the next few days, his father almost certainly would not. For as long as daylight lasted he worked out of doors with the other men. The smell of cut grass hung sweetly on the air, growing stronger as it dried. Just as the smack of ball on willow was the *sound* of summer, to Ned the scent of drying hay held the essence of the season. The flower-strewn swathes patterning the meadows were haunted by butterflies – meadow-browns, brimstones, and blues – and the sun shone as if it had never been known to abandon them in the past to a sodden, ruined harvest.

It was useless to expect the children to stay in the schoolroom, and Mary Haskell knew better than to try to keep them there. Charlie, at the responsible age of eight, was allowed to ride on a tractor that bore the name of Thornley painted on it, while Ned tactfully offered Thomas the important job of helping him to rake the fallen grass. Victoria began the day with them outside but had to be carried indoors weeping with rage at the sight of the first dead rabbit that hadn't been fast enough to escape the machines. By lunchtime she was persuaded to join the picnic party in the orchard, and had recovered sufficiently to accept Ned's peace-offering of a small animal whittled for her out of a piece of apple-wood.

When the children had eaten and got bored with sitting still they wandered away, leaving Ned stretched out on the grass, and Mary quietly making the daisy-chain requested by Victoria. She was restful to be with, he thought, unlike the other girls of his acquaintance, who always found it necessary to talk for the sake of talking. Yes, quietness was one of the things he specially liked about her. He liked her hair, too – the redness of it now given a patina of gold by the sun – and the freckles on her nose. She'd been almost sixteen when he'd found her, uncomplainingly working in a draper's shop in Birmingham. Six years later it seemed as if she'd always been at Providence, and he couldn't imagine her anywhere else; but Sybil had put into his head the idea that she might want to go away, and now he often found himself thinking about it.

'Do you wish you were with the others in London?' he asked suddenly. 'I try to remember sometimes that you might miss city life.'

She looked up to find him watching her, and for the moment in which their eyes met he had the strange impression that, in everything but years, she was much older than he . . . knew things he *didn't* know. Then she went back to the delicate flower chain growing under her fingers.

'I don't miss Birmingham, and I'm not in any hurry to see London. I'll go one day, though. Tom wants to see the soldiers changing guard at Buckingham Palace, and so do I!' She smiled as she said it, copying Tom's version of a guardsman presenting arms. He wasn't a chatterer like his sister, but being stumped for a word, as he often was, didn't worry him; he simply sketched his meaning in the air. His grandfathers were easily distinguished – a hand stroking his chin clearly indicated William's beard, while something removed from an imaginary waistcoat pocket was the heavy gold watch that Grandpa Thornley frequently consulted.

'I might find myself living in London one day,' Mary added calmly. She stared round the sunlit orchard, as if committing it to memory. 'That's why I have to taste all this as often as I can.'

'Taste?' Ned queried. She nodded but didn't offer to explain, and he realized that there wasn't any need because he knew what she meant. Why not taste as well as see and smell new-cut grass, and summer evening rain after a day's heat, and the misty sweetness of autumn mornings? She hadn't been born to the English land as he had been, but she'd grown to understand and love it just as well.

'You couldn't possibly live in London,' he blurted out. 'That's for people who don't know any better.'

Mary didn't look at him again. 'I'm not thinking of going just yet. The twins will be wanting me still for a while. But by the time Tom's ready to follow Charlie to school, I shan't be needed at home. My mother can manage now, and the future's taken care of . . . Mr Thornley's going to take Leslie as an apprentice as soon as he leaves the village school, and Nell's set on becoming a nurse. Lady Wyndham's going to get her enrolled in a hospital in Warwick . . . she's a clever girl.'

Nobody had bothered to enquire what Mary was set on becoming, Ned thought compassionately; she'd just had to get on with the job of holding her small family together after her father was killed. He had no idea what she thought of a world that shared out its rewards so unequally; she was too intelligent not to see that merit and prize frequently didn't match, but too sane to waste herself in anger or bitterness . . . the world was arranged thus, and always had been. She "tasted" the joys that came her way, and refused to spoil them by envy for what she didn't have.

Her bare arm moved gently beside his own brown one as she worked; he could see its fine reddish-gold down in the sunlight, found himself wanting to touch its softness. It was nonsense, this talk of going to live in London – he'd have to tell her so; and if she insisted, he must command her to understand where she belonged.

'Mary . . . don't leave Providence.' It wasn't a command, but a hoarse plea that startled her into looking at him again. 'This is your home . . . promise me you won't want to go.'

Tension grew, filling the gap between them; it was an electric spark that leapt and linked them together, annihilating everything but their awareness of each other. He *must* touch her, taste her sweetness. But the spell holding them together was abruptly broken.

'Mary . . . M. . .Mary . . .' Victoria's distress call invaded their small enchanted circle even before she arrived to fling herself down full tilt among the daisies.

'Charlie . . . Charlie says . . .' Angry tears overflowed and had to be wiped away before she could report the monstrous thing her brother had just said, and by then her audience had had time to jerk themselves back to the world of everyday. 'The hen-lens and the rabbits and the dear little ducklings are *his* . . . he says *Black Beauty*'s his . . .' She could get no further than this mention of her dearest favourite of all – a black sow of immense proportions and ugliness in whom *her* eye of love detected perfect beauty when no-one else's could. She stared at Ned, unwilling to believe that for once he was going to fail her. 'You said *I* could have Black Beauty, but Charlie says she . . . she b'longs to him.' She stumbled over the unfamiliar word engraved on her memory by grief, but had no doubt about its meaning.

Ned sat her on his knees, shook hay dust out of his handkerchief and gently mopped her cheeks. 'Sweetheart . . . no need to cry. Charlie doesn't understand, that's all. Black Beauty belonged to me, but I gave her to you . . . she's yours now.'

An entrancing smile broke across Victoria's tragic face – all was right with the world after all. 'She's *mine*,' she informed Mary, in case her friend hadn't heard.

'Yes, but Uncle Ned will explain it to Charlie . . . no

need for *you* to go and tell him so. Now, put your daisy chain on. Then you can show it to Emmy and the girls in the kitchen and tell them it was a lovely picnic they brought us.'

Happy again, Victoria trotted away; Emmy and the girls first by all means, but then she'd call at the sty and make sure Black Beauty knew who she belonged to. She left behind her a silence quite different from the one she'd interrupted. Electric tension had given way to something on Ned's part that felt like a smothering blanket of despair.

'What a good thing the pig was mine to give away,' he said after a while. 'Victoria rightly reckons that she may have everything I own, so it's God's mercy that she didn't ask me for Providence itself.'

Mary heard no bitterness in his voice, but only the bleak acceptance of a fact he'd almost been tempted to overlook.

'A child of five can't be expected to understand,' she pointed out quietly, 'and even Charlie's still got a lot to learn. Victoria and Thomas irritate him because they're younger and not so clever. He's neat with his fingers and never breaks things as *they* do . . . that's why he's always saying that things are *his*, because he wants to take care of them.'

'He's my nephew . . . you don't have to explain him to me.'

She ignored the sudden harshness in his voice. 'I sometimes think I do have to explain – not to his father, but to other people. He's different from the twins – they just reach out and help themselves to everybody's love, but Charlie can't do that, and the more he wants people to like him, the more difficult he makes it for them to get near him . . . even his—' She bit off what she'd been going to say, but Ned thought it was 'even his mother can't'.

Before the silence could become awkward he filled it himself. 'I ought to be grateful to Charlie for reminding me that Providence is never going to belong to me. I forget sometimes – did so a moment ago when I was pretending that I had the right to ask you to stay.' He got to his feet, and stood looking down at her, unsmiling, almost hostile. 'You must do whatever *you* want, of course. As for me, it's about time *I* got on with raking hay.'

He nodded and walked away, and she carefully put together the spilled flowers in her lap, wondering how much longer she could bear to stay at Providence. There had been one miracle in her life – the day Ned arrived at their Birmingham tenement after the war and explained that he'd fought with her father. She'd always understood her mother's grief but not the anger that seemed to be slowly destroying their lives. Edith Haskell had begun by refusing Ned's proposal that they should move to the country; she didn't want anybody's help or charity, it was good of him to call but they'd manage somehow . . . he'd been on the verge of giving up when he saw Mary's eyes fixed on him, imploring the salvation her mother was rejecting. They had gone to the cottage at Haywood's End, and finding Providence after the draper's shop had seemed like stumbling on the Holy Grail.

Mary knelt in Mr Roberts' church each Sunday, gave her thanks to God, and prayed to be forgiven for wanting one more miracle. But no amount of kneeling, and gratitude, and prayer, lessened the hunger in her heart, and the fever in her blood whenever Ned Wyndham was near. One day soon she would have to leave Providence.

It was agreed by the family assembled in London that the most enjoyable of the functions they attended was the reception given by Anita in her new home. The house in Walton Place had briefly been submerged under a shroud of scaffolding and tarpaulins, and risen from it like Venus from the waves, pristine and beautiful. Inside, it was a revelation to anyone born in Victoria's age and used to being suffocated by a plethora of drapery and overstuffed furniture. Ivory-coloured walls and pale, silk-covered upholstery offered comfort and simplicity, and against this cool background Anita's individual taste was displayed with startling originality. A Shaker rocking-chair wasn't the obvious companion for a long-case clock made in London in the eighteenth century, but neither seemed to object to the other, nor to the embroidered Russian altar-cloth beside them that made a pool of colour against the pale wall.

Harry looked round the rooms, aware that he liked them without knowing why. He tried to credit wealth with the achievement and knew in his heart that he was being unfair. Wealth alone wasn't enough to produce this restful perfection; the skill behind it was Anita's, just as she was behind the success of an oddly matched party that shouldn't have succeeded at all. They'd been invited to bring friends and the resulting haphazard collection of guests broke all the normal rules of entertaining. Even more odd was the fact that the unlikeliest people chose to congregate together. William Wyndham, most reticently aristocratic of men, was deep in conversation with the flamboyant leader of the Labour Party, brought by Harry himself; Frank Thornley was enjoying against all probability a spirited argument on the subject of design with the man who had been Anita's teacher at the Slade School of Art, Professor Tonks; and at the other end of the room Harry could see Aunt Gertrude calmly handing over the President of the Royal Academy to the tender mercies of Arthur Thornley. But the sight of his mother locked in a cut and thrust debate with Beatrice Webb sent him hot-foot to Charlotte.

'For God's sake go and rescue your heroine, or else rescue Mama,' he muttered in his sister's ear, 'otherwise we shall have blood flowing all over Anita's expensive white carpet.'

Charlotte seemed unperturbed. 'Nonsense . . . they're enjoying themselves. Anita must be brilliant at this sort of thing, because everyone looks happy.'

'I dare say the ability to provide the *very* best champagne helps a little, too!'

'Ungenerous, Harry,' Charlotte said, and he knew that it was true.

196

'All right – I grant you her talent, and her taste. It's entirely *my* fault that she irritates me so much!' He tried to make amends by greeting very civilly the man called Ian Nicholson who had come in search of Charlotte. His sister's delighted smile might have given him food for thought at any other time, but for the moment he was struggling with a difficulty of his own: the uneasy combination of emotions his cousin always aroused in him. He couldn't help admiring her competence, because any kind of bungling irritated him; he took pleasure in her understated elegance, which he thought highly desirable in women; but he deeply resented the fact that she was so clearly self-sufficient. Harry didn't object to women who could do things, but he preferred their competence to be discreetly veiled. Surely it wasn't too much to ask, the impression that men were indispensable to their lives? His cousin Anita saw no need for this essential piece of feminine tact.

He had to wait until late in the evening before he managed to catch her alone.

'Congratulations, coz . . . quite a feather in your cap! Even Uncle William is enjoying himself, and he normally hides in corners, waiting for the moment when he can go home. I hope you feel properly pleased with yourself.'

Her darkly-blue eyes, fringed with black lashes, surveyed him with the cool amused stare that always made him feel that he was being measured; if she got to the point of making up her mind about him, he suspected that it would only be to find him wanting.

'I don't seem to have succeeded with *you*,' she said thoughtfully. 'You still have the air about you of a man whose time could be better spent elsewhere . . . it's *very* hurtful to your hostess, my dear Harry!'

'I expect I'm unnerved by the company I'm keeping. Charlotte seems to have quite got into the habit of mixing with artists and the literati, but she'd be the first to tell you what she tells me . . . I'm out of my depth, rude soldiery and nasty rough politicians being more in my line.' His eyes, of a much paler blue than her own, flicked over her face and the pleated column of sea-green chiffon that she wore. She was as close as she would ever be to beauty and the startling idea came into his mind that he would have liked to tell her so. 'I like your rig,' he said abruptly and saw her smile because she appreciated a compliment that had been dragged out of him.

'Thank you! We can't compete with Lucy, but I hope you've noticed how well Charlotte's looking?'

Harry turned to stare at his sister, now happily introducing her friend to Aunt Gertrude. Then he looked at Anita again. 'It might not work out, you know. If Nicholson gets frightened off by my formidable mother, Charlotte's last state will be much worse than her first.'

'We can't take the risks for her. She's a grown woman coming properly alive for the first time – the process is bound to be a mixture of joy and pain.'

Harry was irritated by the calm statement and tempted to ask what Anita herself knew of a process she was happy to wish on someone else, but she was looking across the room at Gertrude Wyndham, deep in conversation with Nicholson.

'Shall I tell you which of the ladies present my old friend, the Professor, would choose to paint?' she asked suddenly. 'Aunt Gertrude! Not because she's beautiful – although she is; but because of the lovely spirit that shines out of her.'

Harry nodded unsmilingly, struck by the novelty of the idea that had just taken possession of his mind. Anita watched his stern face and wondered whether there was the slightest hope of success in her next campaign – that of saving Harry Trentham! It was family history that he'd been a brave and brilliant soldier. Now, he was steadily climbing the rungs of the political ladder, and if there were to be another Labour Government, he would certainly be in it. Whatever he did would be done with all his heart and mind and body. He was only a failure in one respect; somewhere along the way since Emily's death he'd lost the knack of being humanly happy.

'Is *this* to be your new career – society hostess par excellence?' he enquired suddenly.

'No, because I'm only intermittently sociable. In any case, I've got work to do – my art essays have been commissioned by Ian's company.'

'Would an occasional visitor be a nuisance?'

'Not at all – I'm thinking of being at home every alternate Thursday.'

'Then I shall make a point of calling on Wednesdays or Fridays. You don't have to admit me, of course.'

His pale eyes gleamed for a moment with their old challenging gaiety. Anita didn't look away from him, but she was aware of having to make a great effort not to do so.

'I may not admit you,' she said at last. 'It will depend on how I feel.'

Chapter Seventeen

Gertrude thought it safe to suppose that, once they were back home again from London, life would return to its normal peaceful pattern – painting in the Great Parlour for William, and for herself the constant daily round of duties that Providence and the people of Haywood's End still required. There was only one departure from the norm that she was prepared to admit to in her mind: while Lucy went to stay with Sybil at Pont-sur-Seine and Frank paid a business visit to Paris, she must spend more time than usual in the other wing of the house with the children. She would *not*, though, dread the imminent arrival from America of a man they hadn't seen for thirty years. James would pay them a brief duty visit, find that he disliked staying in a house the Wyndhams no longer owned, and go hot-foot back to Anita and the metropolis. There was no need to worry about meeting James again. Instead, she would worry about Ned. He looked thin and tired from working too hard, and must be made to take a holiday as soon as the summer work of harvesting was over.

It wasn't exactly a holiday that he suddenly proposed himself, but something even more surprising.

'I thought of taking the children to London to see Lucy and Frank off to France,' he said one morning.

'To . . . to *London*, Ned?'

He grinned at the astonishment on his mother's face. 'The hub of Empire, Mama – not Outer Mongolia, or Timbuctoo, as you seem to imagine! According to Mary, the children are at an impressionable age now, so we'll do all the things that country bumpkins do – admire the Household Cavalry, visit the Zoo, ride on top of a motor-bus, even go in an underground train if we feel really intrepid!'

200

'It sounds very strenuous, dearest,' she objected.

'We shan't do all that in one day; Lucy says we can put up in St James's Place.'

A *stay* in London for Ned seemed even more surprising, but Gertrude was long resigned to the occasional oddities of her children's behaviour.

The expedition was arranged and, at Ned's insistence, it finally included Mary Haskell as well.

'Mrs Knightly and her daughter can look after the children,' Lucy had suggested. 'Why not give Mary a rest from them?'

'She wants to watch the changing of the guard at Buckingham Palace,' Ned explained gravely.

When they drove away, Mary's grey flannel suit was exactly what she might have been expected to wear, but the white straw boater perched over her coil of burnished hair unknowingly ruined much of the decorous effect she was striving for. Gertrude registered the fact in passing, but had more to think about than Mary's hat – she'd been assigned a number of extra duties while the twins were away, the most essential of which was a frequent visit to Victoria's sow, to assure her that she was still loved, and would be sorely missed in London.

They went first of all to Victoria Station to wave the boat-train on its way. The melancholy attaching to all platform farewells infected the children for a moment or two, but didn't survive Ned's suggestion that the Zoo should be their next port of call. From then on the next three days were crowded with more excitements than any other comparable number of hours in their lives would ever be able to hold again. They managed to fit in calls on their cousins as well – civility where civility was due, said Ned – and also went to the Houses of Parliament with Uncle Harry. Joy of joys, *they* were saluted by the policemen at the gate, and *he* was mysteriously wrapped in some air of authority they never noticed when he came to Providence.

Ned liked Lucy's little house – it was unexpectedly peaceful in the heart of London – but he found her housekeeper stony-faced and unwelcoming. Mary, more observant where a fellow-servant was concerned, noticed that Mrs Knightly ignored the twins and reserved what little warmth she seemed to possess for Charlie. It was the reverse of what usually happened and she was inclined to think kindly of the housekeeper because of it.

On their last evening, after the children were in bed and Mrs Knightly's daughter had been appointed to keep an eye on them, Ned suggested a final stroll in the soft London dusk. They loitered outside St James's Palace to watch the sentries being changed, and then crossed the Mall into the evening peacefulness of the park.

'Lighting-up time in half an hour,' Mary said, looking at the little fob-watch pinned to the lapel of her jacket. It was a recent birthday present from the Thornleys, and she never lost an opportunity to consult it. 'The notice says we must be out by then, or get locked in.'

'I don't think I'd mind,' said Ned. 'Rather nice to spend the night sleeping here.'

She didn't answer and they walked in the silent awareness of each other that was suddenly all about them because, for once, they were without the children.

'Well, what do you think of London?' Ned asked quietly. She always treated questions seriously, even the ones the twins put to her all day long, and took her time now about answering this one. 'It isn't as bad as I feared,' she admitted at last.

Her careful honesty was something he liked, but he couldn't help teasing her a little. 'I was hoping you might say you'd enjoyed yourself!'

'That isn't what you asked me,' she pointed out.

'True, oh wise one! What I *wanted* you to say was that you'd had a lovely time but were now happy to go home.' He used the word deliberately, and noticed that she changed it when she answered him.

'I'm wanting to go back, but I shan't ever forget these three days. Now that I've seen London for myself, I think I could get used to it. Miss Trentham and Miss Wyndham both said to get in touch with them if I needed to. Wasn't that kind of them?'

'Very kind, but I wish my dearly-beloved cousins wouldn't interfere. There'll be no need for you to get in touch with them.' The sudden vehemence was so unlike him that she stopped to stare, startled by the knowledge that this wasn't just any evening stroll after all; the easy companionship of the past few days had suddenly disappeared, and moment by moment the time they remained alone together grew more dangerous.

'I wanted you to enjoy this visit because you were with *me*,' Ned said, 'and I wanted you to discover that you'd *hate* London if *you* were here and I was back at Providence. Couldn't you have managed something on *those* lines, my very dear Miss Haskell?'

For once she wasn't sure of understanding him. His voice tried to sound lightly amused as if she needn't take him seriously; but something quite different was in his face – urgency and a desperate longing that she recognized. She wasn't ignorant, knew about the physical needs that women weren't supposed to have and men *were*, because they couldn't help being more coarse and brutish. Ned wasn't a careless village youth and even great need wouldn't stampede him into hurting her . . . But there were her own needs too, rising like a fever in her blood, and those she *was* afraid of. The touch of his hand on her arm set fear alight; she pulled away from him and began to run, desperate as a wild creature escaping capture. She could run like the wind with the children across the park at home, but not hampered by city shoes and constricting skirt. He caught her without difficulty, and pulled her against him in order to steady her. Only to steady her he thought, but her mouth was suddenly too near his own, and couldn't be resisted.

When he lifted his head again they were both breathing hard; nothing had changed, London went about its evening rituals all around them; and yet *everything* had changed.

'You needn't have run . . . I wasn't going to hurt you . . . wouldn't ever hurt you,' he murmured.

'I know . . . I was j. . .just being d. . .daft as poor

Artie!' She tried to smile, to show that she was still capable of joking, but Ned's grave scrutiny of her face didn't alter. The moment of truth had arrived and must be confronted.

'I don't know how much longer Providence will be my home, but will you share it with me – share *whatever* I have to offer?'

His arms still held her and she could feel his heart thudding against her own. He was Ned . . . he'd asked nothing of her ever, and now when he did she'd tried to run away.

'Are you wanting me to sleep with you, Ned? I will, if that's what you want,' she said simply.

'God damn it, *no*!' He shouted the words, disturbing a flock of sparrows investigating a near-by rubbish basket. 'I want you to *marry* me.'

Her taut body almost gave way under his hands, and she ducked her head against his chest for a moment, fighting dizziness. Then she looked up and faintly smiled. 'I wasn't expecting you to say that . . . there's no need.'

'Of *course* there's a need, you wee daft girl.' Another evening stroller walking past turned round to stare at them and Ned tried to lower his voice. 'Mary . . . I haven't got much to give you, but what I have is yours. I want to love you and sleep with you and take care of you when you're sick, and have you take care of me, for as long as we both shall live. On *those* terms, will you come with me?'

She stared at him through the gathering dusk. He'd always treated her as an equal, and so had Sir William in his own gentle way, but every other man she knew made a smaller or larger distinction that she noticed and expected.

'I'm the nursery-governess, Ned – not nearly good enough to be your wife. That's what everyone would say, and I'd feel bound to agree with them.'

She saw pure amusement mingle with the tenderness in his face, but didn't understand why.

'*Now* I've got you, sweetheart! Don't you know that Mama first went to Providence to work for my grandmother? If anyone said *she* wasn't fit to become Lady Wyndham, they've had plenty of time since to discover that they were wrong. I don't think we'll bother with what the world says, any more than my father did.'

'That's the difference between us,' Mary explained with a faint smile. 'Wyndhams don't *have* to bother; Haskells do!'

Joy was almost under her hand, shining so brightly that if she stared at it she would be blinded to everything else. But she was obliged *not* to reach out and grab it, because more than anything else in the whole wide world she wanted happiness for Ned.

'I'm not Gertrude Wyndham – "lovely and pleasant in her life" – that's what the Bible would say of *her*.'

'You remind me of the girl she must have been,' he said simply.

Mary risked a tiny glance at the treasure under her hand. 'Ned . . . are you *sure?*'

'Quite sure, provided we get something clear. I want to marry you because I love you, not because I feel sorry for you. You must only marry me because you love me, not because you've got some daft idea of feeling grateful.'

She stared at him and solemnly told the only lie of her life. 'I don't feel a bit grateful.' Then happiness glimmered in her pale face, like the first star in an evening sky. 'Dear Ned, I'll be such a *very* good wife to you!'

It could only be answered with a kiss, and he was about to oblige when a discreet cough sounded behind him.

'Park'll be closing in five minutes, sir. Might I suggest . . .'

'Suggest anything you like,' Ned agreed lavishly. 'This lady has just agreed to marry me.'

'Has she, now? That's very nice, I'm sure, but I'm afraid it don't stop the gates closing.' The park-keeper's face, jowled and mournful as a bloodhound's, rearranged itself into something approaching a smile. 'I was goin' to suggest a bit of a sprint, if you could manage it.'

'We can manage anything in the world. Good night, and thank you.'

He took Mary's hand and sprint they did, arriving breathless and laughing as the gates were being swung together. Out in the Mall the lamps were already making pools of golden light among the trees. At the far end the Royal Standard, cunningly illuminated, floated above the Palace, making its simple, silent appeal to national pride.

'London's rather beautiful, after all,' said Ned. 'Still, I'm glad we're going home tomorrow.'

They walked back hand in hand, finding no need to talk about the wondrous thing that had happened, safe in the happiness of being together. Mrs Knightly opened the door to them and Ned smiled his thanks, but it didn't occur to him to share his joy with her, as he had with the man in the park. She registered the expression on their faces, murmured good night, and retired to her own room. It wasn't difficult to guess what had happened. She could detect easily enough in other people the happiness she'd never found herself – remembered clearly, even though it was years ago, the look on the face of Frank Thornley's wife when she'd come back from spending nights with a sick cousin, so she'd said. Mrs Knightly hated liars almost as much as she hated people who were happy when they had no right to be.

The news of Ned's engagement was brought back to London by Charlotte after a visit to Providence. She was curious to see what Harry's reaction would be. He was a committed Socialist, but he hadn't quite been able to believe that all men and women were equal; the strong should feel privileged to take care of the weak, but the weak must understand that they were different. Harry did his best, nowadays, to treat Ian Nicholson on level terms, but the effort was visible to Charlotte and probably, she thought, to Ian as well.

'Ned is going to marry Mary Haskell,' she said, when her brother asked for news of Providence. 'I'm very glad – what about you?'

Harry's silence lasted only a fraction too long. 'Yes . . . yes, of course. It's time Ned found himself a wife.'

'But not *this* wife?'

He heard the faintly belligerent note in his gentle sister's voice and picked up the challenge she offered him.

'Lottie – don't let's pretend. I'm sure she's a pleasant enough girl, but Ned could have done better for himself than the nursery-governess daughter of a man who was shot for cowardice during the war. I don't quite see Mary Hoskins as the next Lady Wyndham.'

'She'll be a farmer's wife, not the châtelaine of Providence, and she's more than intelligent, loyal and kind enough for *that*. You're wrong about her father, too. A man who fought gallantly in the trenches for two years can scarcely be called a coward. At the end . . . well, how many times have I heard *you* say that some of the orders sent down to the Front Line *should* have been ignored, because they were insane?'

'Saying it here is one thing, refusing to obey in the thick of battle was quite another,' Harry explained uncomfortably. He was about to add that, be she never so kind and loyal, Mary lacked education, but he remembered in time what Charlotte would undoubtedly remind him of – Gertrude Wyndham had managed well enough with the village school at Haywood's End.

'I won't argue with you,' he said instead, 'I always seem to lose nowadays. Either your cause is just, or Ian has filled you with confidence!' He smiled suddenly, with his old sweetness. 'It's *that*, isn't it? With him beside you, you're capable of slaying any number of dragons, our darling mother included!'

'I'm certainly capable of marrying him if he asks me,' she said quietly.

'Oh, he'll ask, if I read the signs correctly. Don't be put off this time, Lottie; grab happiness when it's offered to you.'

'That's what Ned is doing at last, and what *you* must do, if the chance comes again. It doesn't mean forgetting Emily.'

'I know, but the chance *won't* come again; I'm certain of that now.' He shrugged the subject aside, and talked of other things until it was time to leave. He walked home, more aware than usual that his flat would seem empty and unwelcoming when he got there. It was no different from what it had been for the past eight years; the change was in *him*, that he should notice it.

He trudged along Knightsbridge, trying not to think of a charming house that was as enticing as a mirage compared with his own cold, impersonal quarters. It was becoming too much like a habit to call there, to drink the glass of wine Anita offered him, and air some opinion or other just for the pleasure of having her argue with him. Unlike the other women he knew, she could defend her point of view stubbornly without getting emotional; occasionally it occurred to him that he wished she *would* get angry; it would be interesting to see her less than self-controlled.

He crossed the entrance to Walton Place, and remembered that he had an *excuse* for calling this evening – news to impart.

'We're to have a wedding in the family,' he told his hostess when he was settled in her lovely, restful room.

'I know – Lottie telephoned me.'

Anita's almost curt reply reminded him of a fact as uncomfortable as a pebble in his shoe.

'Sorry . . . I wouldn't have blurted it out if I'd remembered in time.'

He sounded so contrite that she smiled at him more warmly than usual.

'No harm done, as it happens. Perhaps no-one else believes it either, but youthful passions fade "into the light of common day"! I simply love Ned in the way that we all do. Charlotte said that he looked *very* happy.'

Harry nodded and sipped his wine without saying anything. He looked tired, as usual, and Anita thought she wouldn't have recognized him for the conventionally good-looking, carefree, young man who'd partnered his sister at her twenty-first birthday ball in those uncomplicated days before the war. It was another world they lived in now, and they had all become different people. The years since then had tightened the skin over his cheekbones and jaw, making his face look stern. His eyes were sunk further back in his head these days, and it was rare to see them smile.

'It can't be the thought of Ned's marriage making you look grim,' she observed calmly. 'Is something else troubling you . . . the failure of the General Strike . . . the state of the Party, the country, the world . . . some worrying little thing like that?'

'All those little things, as a matter of fact – the state of the Party most of all, probably, because that's the only thing I ought to be able to do something about. However, I won't bore you with it – the health, or otherwise, of the Labour Party is not something *you're* likely to care about.'

'Wrong, dear Harry! I don't have to be a Socialist to believe that an effective Opposition to His Majesty's Government is a good thing,' Anita said with the air of sweet reason that was a continual irritation to him. She poured sherry into antique glasses brought back from her wanderings through Italy and set one down beside him. Her face was serious, and he realized that for once she hadn't intended to provoke him. 'You think highly of Ramsay MacDonald . . . can't he do whatever has to be done?'

'He can't work miracles, brilliant though he is,' Harry said tiredly. 'The Labour Party is a mess . . . a hopelessly disorganized hotch-potch of men and women who distrust or misunderstand one another – highbrow intellectuals like the Webbs theorize about what will make a new Utopia; stubborn, hard-headed trade unionists like Ernest Bevin don't give a damn for political theory and fight only for what *their* particular membership wants; and the lumpen mass of working men think only of the wage they get, the hours they work, or the job that may be taken away from them tomorrow. So few people care about the *general* good, that I sometimes think we're trying to achieve the impossible.'

'You're too impatient, that's all,' Anita said with unusual gentleness. 'It takes generations to build up party unity and party machinery. The Labour Party will achieve

209

it in the end, and meanwhile *every* Government from now on will put *some* Socialist legislation on the Statute book, because it *has* to. The general good can't come with the wave of a fairy's wand, but it *is* coming, in spite of all the terrible problems left by the war.'

Harry stared at her serious face. She spoke as if the general good mattered and she'd bothered to find out about problems that were indeed terrible. It was odd, unnatural almost, that a woman adept at the grace notes of life, should be able to think so logically, and talk so lucidly.

'I agree with you, up to a point – which must be today's small miracle!' He smiled, because agreement between them was such a novelty. 'But since we're on the subject I'll confess what sometimes brings me to the edge of despair. It isn't the fact that we can't have Utopia now; it's the near certainty that we shall *never* have it, because men are incorrigibly selfish and stupid. Strikes are often unsuccessful and always wasteful, but sometimes unavoidable against a harsh or unfair opponent. You might suppose they would be unnecessary with a Labour Government in power. When the moment we'd toiled for for years actually arrived, what happened? Strikes *still* went on. The transport workers even struck while their own union president was the Minister of Transport in a Labour administration! That's the sort of thing to make a man wonder whether he's touched in the head to go on trying.'

'There's still Somerton as an alternative,' Anita ventured after a glance at Harry's sombre face.

'Not for me; I'm committed to politics, whatever happens. I thought Charlotte might want to take it on, because she only dabbled in Fabianism not knowing what else to do; but if I'm not wrong, she'll marry Ian Nicholson, and with the best will in the world I can't see *him* running Somerton.'

'I think you're right about Lottie,' Anita said slowly. 'She loves him, and as soon as she's convinced him that the daughter of a lord would actually be glad to marry him, he'll carry her off in the teeth of everybody, including darling Aunt Louise!'

Anita stopped speaking, and a faint colour disturbed the pallor of her face. Harry observed this change with interest but didn't imagine that it had anything to do with him. She took a sip of wine from her glass, and he didn't know, either, that it was to give her Dutch courage for the venture she was embarking on. 'I'm glad you're determined to go on living in London. As far as your inheritance is concerned, I suppose that for as long as Uncle Alec is alive you *could* change your mind; but there's another matter on which you do have to decide quite quickly.'

'There is?' Harry asked the question, conscious of a sudden tension in the air. Their interesting but impersonal discussion of the state of the Party was over; they were now involved in something so different that it had put a tremor in his cousin's voice, and made her fingers shake when she replaced her glass on the table.

'I'd like you to decide whether or not to . . . to become my lover,' she said, with a marvellous pretence at calm. The silence that followed was only shattered by the chiming of the clock in the hall; the interruption reminded Harry that it was necessary to resume breathing, and he took a gulp of air into his protesting lungs.

'Your . . . *what*?'

She smiled brilliantly with the relief of having said what she'd been nerving herself to say; nothing in her life had been so difficult, but now she could smile at the dumbfounded astonishment in his face. 'Lover was the word I used, but we could find some other way of . . .'

'We could do nothing of the sort!' Harry roared. 'My dear Anita, have you gone completely out of your mind? We fight all the time, we have never given each other an improper thought . . .' He was compelled to stop because, apart from the fact that it wasn't even true, her head was suddenly buried in her hands and she was helpless with laughter.

'Anita, you're impossible, hysterical . . . for God's sake *stop* laughing!'

She pulled herself together with a tremendous effort, wiped the tears from her face, and tried to speak seriously. 'Forgive me . . . I wasn't laughing at you – only at this ridiculous conversation. I didn't mean to hurl it at you so baldly but the more I tried to think of a tactful way of saying it, the more impossible it became.'

'If you were trying to say that you've ever wanted *me*, I don't believe you. Tell me the *truth*, and if you can't do it without breaking into riotous mirth this time I'll put you across my knee and beat some sense into you.'

'It *was* hysteria,' she admitted. 'I wasn't sure I'd actually be able to get the suggestion out at all! Now that I'm rational again I'll try to explain. I have everything I thought I needed – family, friends, a home, work I enjoy, and sufficient wealth to live on. It's much more than a great many women have, but most of them have the one thing I *don't* have – the knowledge of what it means to be a woman. At *that*, I'm a failure. I don't know what it means to be possessed by a man, to bear his child, to have a stake in the future. I'm thirty-seven, and I haven't much time.'

Harry found his voice, but it sounded strange and hoarse in his own ears. 'You've roamed around the Continent by yourself for years . . . don't tell me men didn't offer themselves.'

'They did, but unfortunately none of them would do.'

'You said "possessed" a moment ago; don't you want to be loved?'

'I can't expect to be loved to order,' she said gravely. 'In any case, I don't want a husband; don't you think *temporary* possession should be enough to create a child.'

She was fully serious now and it was the strangest conversation he'd ever taken part in.

'Why me?' he asked bluntly. 'In God's name, Anita, why *me*?'

'Because as well as being arrogant and stubborn and opinionated, you're also a brave, upright man. More important, you don't love anyone else, or *want* a wife and children. I wouldn't be hurting any other woman, or damaging your chance of a normal married life.'

He was aware of a sudden strange urge to deny what she said, but clung, instead, to practicalities with the desperation of a drowning man clutching at a raft.

'There's no guarantee that sleeping with me would produce a child; if it did, there is the little matter of explaining it to the rest of the family.'

'I shouldn't explain anything at all; the child would be mine, father unknown. Your name wouldn't come into it and your career wouldn't suffer.'

The expression on his face, a strange compound of hostility, bewilderment, and sadness, prompted her suddenly to move across to him and hold out her hand. 'Harry, it probably sounds an outrageous idea to you, but this is 1926, not the Victorian era. It no longer seems impossible to me because I've been thinking of almost nothing else; and the *more* I think about it, the more sensible it seems. Will you go away and consider it? You must make up your mind soon, though . . . before my father gets here.'

His grip tightened for a moment on her hand, then he released it so that he shouldn't be touching her when he delivered the ultimatum that was suddenly clear in his mind. 'It's *you* who must decide, Anita. I'll possess you with pleasure, do my utmost to give you a child . . . but I'm still a Victorian at heart; if you become pregnant I shall claim the child as *ours* and you will have to agree to marry me. Promise me that or find yourself another partner.'

'But . . . you don't *want* a wife,' she cried out. 'Haven't ever wanted one since Emily.'

'I still don't; but it seems only fair that we should *both* have to take the risk of getting something we don't want.'

Amusement touched his face for a moment, because it had been his turn to astonish *her*, and he wasn't above wanting the last word. 'It's been a delightful visit, my dear – I can scarcely wait to call again!'

A moment later she was alone in the room, uncertain whether to laugh or cry, or to know whether she'd succeeded or failed in her campaign to save Harry Trentham from himself.

Chapter Eighteen

Ned's engagement to Mary was to be kept a secret while Lucy and Frank were still in Paris. It required, as William said, heroic discretion because Ethel, their parlour-maid, was not only related to half the inhabitants of Haywood's End, but was also the nerve-centre of an information network covering the servants' quarters of most of the big houses in the county.

'The thwarting of Ethel,' he said to his wife, 'is quite a challenge in its way!'

She smiled but so briefly that he braved the obvious question. 'Are you as happy about Ned as you seemed to be downstairs?'

When she smiled this time the gladness in her face left him in no doubt. 'I'm delighted, and so very thankful to see *him* happy. The girls we might have expected him to choose wouldn't have done at all – I see that now. I was only wondering what Lucy and Frank will make of losing Mary to Ned. How do you suppose the news will be received at Bicton.'

'*That* I can tell you,' William said promptly. 'Jane will be as delighted as you are, Arthur will be seriously torn. As a self-made success himself, he's bound to applaud a working girl who betters herself, as the obnoxious phrase goes; on the other hand, there's no fun in hoisting *himself* into the gentry if everyone else is doing it too!'

'So you think he won't be kind to Mary?'

'My dearest, of *course* he will, because his generous heart will get the better of him. He'll provide a wedding present a great deal more lavish than anyone else's, and I shall suggest to Mary that she thanks him for it by asking *him* to give her away.'

'Perfect tact,' she agreed, smiling again. 'I should never have thought of it.'

He hadn't referred to Lucy's likely reaction to the news that her children's governess was going to become her sister-in-law, but Gertrude decided that the question was better not asked again.

Three days later the answer seemed to be that Lucy was delighted. She was delighted with everything – their Paris visit, with being back at home, and with the children's excited report of their trip to London. Her own impression was that the smile pinned to her mouth might become so permanent that it would remain in place even when she was asleep. The need to find a hiding-place where she could finally abandon it drove her one afternoon along the woodland path to Hubert's church. She now went regularly to Evensong again, but without conviction and without hope. The responses and the hymns had been learned by rote years ago, and were now as irrelevant to her life as all the other lessons learned in childhood had become.

After the midsummer glare outside, the church was blessedly cool, and very dim except for the shafts of light slanting down through the beautiful windows of the Lady Chapel. The flowers there were sure to have come from Maud's garden – sweet-scented white paeonies, and delphiniums as blue as the Virgin's robe that she held wrapped tenderly about the infant Christ in the stained-glass above the altar.

'I know that my Redeemer liveth . . .' The remembered words beat against the barriers in her mind, promising a salvation she no longer believed in and had almost persuaded herself she didn't want. Without the angry sadness permanently locked up inside her she would be nothing at all – empty as a snail-shell in the garden cleaned out by a blackbird's beak.

'Lucy, my dear . . . how nice to have you back.'

Hubert Roberts' voice sounded behind her, quiet and unsurprised to find her there alone. She must pin on her bright smile again after all, say that Maud's flowers were beautiful, and walk back into the blinding heat outside. *That* was what she certainly ought to do . . . but her feet refused to move, and tears unshed for years chose *this* unlooked-for moment to well up out of the secret places of her heart and trickle down her cheeks.

'I only came here looking for my spectacles, because I leave them in church more often than anywhere else.' The Vicar's calm explanation assumed that a weeping woman in the chapel was a perfectly natural thing to find. 'Shall we choose a shady seat outside? I usually favour Amos Moffat myself – he's just the right height, I find!'

The suggestion was gently made, but her legs consented to move again, as if understanding that the invitation was not one to be refused. She followed him outside and sat down on the stone that had sheltered the bones of Sid Moffat's great-great-grandfather for a hundred years. Hubert gave a little sigh of relief. 'I've got to the stage when it's always a pleasure to sit down! My dear, you came back to some splendid news. The village bush-telegraph is working overtime.'

'And the village women are even now blowing the dust off their wedding hats, I expect,' Lucy mumbled, scrubbing at her wet cheeks.

'Something for them to rejoice about at last . . . there hasn't been much in recent years.'

She didn't agree or disagree and, after a glance at her face, the Vicar went on as if there'd been no pause. 'Maud will want to know how you found Sybil.'

'Tell her Sybil was well . . . very busy now that her dress-shop in Paris has become fashionable. Rich women flock there, apparently, and Syb's in her element telling them what they ought to wear. Ned always used to say she was a bossy piece!'

She tried to smile but her mouth refused to be obedient. If her legs could have been relied upon she would have got up and run away, but her body seemed to be operating now independently of her will; it remained as heavy and immovable as Amos Moffat's stone.

'My dear . . . could you tell me what's wrong?'

The quiet direct question slipped through her guard – the most obvious and simple of thrusts, and the most impossible to avoid.

'Everything is wrong,' she found herself answering slowly. 'Wrong with *me*, most of all.' She stared down at her fingers, examining them as though she'd never seen them before. 'It's a blessed relief to admit that I'm *not* delighted about Ned's engagement, and I could hate Mary Haskell for the happiness that shines out of her.' Lucy stared at Hubert Roberts with huge desperate eyes. 'I've depended on Ned, you see . . . come to think of him as being *my* prop and stay; now there's someone who matters to him more than I do.'

'Why think of it as some sort of race? But if you must, there's someone else with whom you *do* come first.'

'Frank? I don't think so,' she said with the calmness of despair. 'Perhaps I did once, but no longer. That's why I needed Ned so much.' The Vicar didn't seem to look appalled, but even if he had, *she* couldn't stop now. 'Frank doesn't trust me, you see. He's courteous and considerate . . . and convinced that my only reason for marrying him was to keep Providence. If I begged him to believe that now I also wanted him to be happy, he would offer me an incredulous smile, and a lecture on the Government's stupidity in returning to the Gold Standard.'

There was silence for a while, broken only by the crickets whirring in the long grass and the chiming of the church clock. She listened for the hesitation that always preceded the last chime, as if it was never quite certain what the time really was. Three . . . er, four o'clock . . . time for the children's tea; she could use it as an excuse to escape. But Hubert had one more question to ask.

'Why do you only come to Evensong nowadays?'

'Because I can't come to Communion,' she answered baldly. 'Because I'm a shameful mess of sadness and spleen. I expect you can guess which of the Commandments I broke. I shan't ever do so again, but how can I ask forgiveness for something that I haven't been able to repent of doing?'

'Frank knows?'

'No, he just believes I'm unfaithful to him in my heart; so if there's a side to be on, he expects me *not* to be on his. He doesn't even tell me about the houses he wants to build in the village because he's certain I must agree with Ned. I'm not sure that I do, as it happens, but he wouldn't believe me if I said so.'

'Why were you in the Lady Chapel a little while ago?'

Lucy gave a little shrug. 'I think I was hoping some of its peacefulness might rub off on me.'

'It didn't occur to you to ask for some of its strength, I suppose?' Vehemence amounting almost to anger was in the Vicar's voice, but he swept on without noticing her startled glance. 'My dear girl, the church isn't simply a beautiful museum-piece, quiet as the grave, and just about as useful to those still living. Don't you understand? It's a power-house, fuelled by centuries of prayer. You don't have to struggle on your own . . . all the strength you'll ever need is there for the asking.'

Perfect faith in the God he served illuminated his face; it was a faith she could see no way of sharing, but she found herself wanting to pray after all – that he would be right, and she wrong.

'Make a start,' Hubert suggested. 'Come to Communion on Sunday, and talk to Frank about the new houses; say you can't make up your mind whether they would be good for the village or not.'

An odd smile touched her mouth for a moment. 'I thought you were going to tell me to make my confession to *him*.'

'And ease your conscience at the price of passing on pain? No, my dear, I should never tell you to do that.'

It wasn't the answer she'd expected, but amusement glimmered in her face for a moment. 'Do you remember what you used to tell us when we were children? "Pretend you're St George and the horrible great fat dragon is the Devil. Ride a great wallop at him and you're bound to win"! Syb used to enjoy that as much as Ned did; I rather prided myself on having a soft spot for the dragon, but probably it was only because I wasn't valiant enough. I haven't changed, I'm afraid.'

'"Be valiant, but not too venturous,"' Hubert quoted with a smile.

'The golden mean, in fact! Well, I'll try.' She confirmed the promise by kissing his cheek, eased herself off the stone, and a moment later walked out of the churchyard. He watched her go, then returned to his power-house. 'Whatsoever thou asketh in My name . . .' The people in need of praying for were many, but today he thought it wouldn't hurt to make a start with Lucy Thornley.

She walked slowly home, thinking about the confession she'd just made. Sometimes the need to make it to Frank had been well-nigh unbearable, but she saw now that it would only have been to punish him for *his* share of the failure they were entangled in. The more she tried with him, the less he believed that she was sincere; the less he helped her to succeed, the more completely she failed.

She stopped in front of Ned's new herbaceous border that now stretched a glorious ribbon of colour beside the kitchen-garden wall. The sound of the children's voices came from the stable yard, but Providence itself slept in the afternoon heat, content like any ancient thing to feel warmth seeping into its bones. She used the rear bridge over the moat and the entrance into the kitchens, where Emmy smiled at her, placidly drinking tea. The west wing of the house was peaceful without the children. She never thought of it as hers or Frank's – it was simply Providence, where the Wyndhams had always lived.

Petals had fallen from a bowl of crimson roses on to the polished surface of an old oak chest. She stopped to collect them and became aware of the sound of voices coming from the drawing-room round a bend in the corridor. The sounds were growing louder, invading the quietness of the house, and making no attempt to pretend that they were part of a pleasant chat between friends.

'You could have *told* me,' Ned suddenly shouted in a voice shaking with anger. 'Instead of that I'm left to hear from the village gossip that you've bribed Andrews into parting with his land.'

'The village gossip is ahead of events, as usual. Andrews has only just been here to accept my offer, and it's a fair price, *not* a bribe.'

'And I suppose you were surprised to find that he couldn't say no! Soon you'll get the cottage and the land next door. Old Gideon would die rather than let it go to you, but his widow will sell, when the time comes.'

'Why not? She doesn't have to ask permission from the Squire,' Frank sounded as cold as Ned was hot, and it seemed to Lucy that it gave him an advantage in the battle. 'Time was when she might have thought twice about vexing the Wyndhams, but things are different now.'

'And a Thornley owns Providence . . . stupid of me to need reminding of the fact. Well, you won't build on *our* land for as long as I'm alive to prevent it.'

'I realize that, but you can't stop me buying freehold land at Haywood's End. What I'm going to do is right, but you're a pig-headed Wyndham and won't admit it.'

'And you're happy to rub in the fact that we don't rule the roost any longer. What you want to do is right for *you*, and your Birmingham friends who are looking for a painless taste of "country" life. You don't give a damn what happens to Haywood's End.'

Lucy had got as far as the half-open door. The time to be valiant had arrived sooner than she'd anticipated, but it had arrived *now* if she was to stop them reaching the point where friendship could never be recovered.

She pushed the door open, then closed it behind her with a snap that made them both spin round. 'You can be heard outside . . . is that what you want – to let the children and the servants know you're quarrelling?'

'I'm sorry; we'll finish the discussion in whispers,' Frank said grimly. 'There's no need to stay – we're not about to murder each other.'

'I'd rather you finished it with me here; I have an interest in the subject as well as you.'

She saw colour come into his pale face, and knew with a

feeling of despair that she'd gone wrong already. 'Tell him,' the Vicar had said, but how was a man to be told who was convinced of what he thought he already knew? She was still searching for words when Ned spoke to her from across the room.

'There's nothing more to discuss. Frank wants to flood Haywood's End with townees from Birmingham, and has rightly pointed out that I can't stop him. I would if I could.' He touched Lucy's arm as he walked past her, but shook his head when she tried to stop him. 'Let's leave it at that, my dear.'

The door was firmly shut, and the silence left behind billowed about the room like smoke – acrid as smoke, too, because her eyes were stinging.

'Frank, can't you and Ned discuss the building thing *without* quarrelling? How can you listen to each other if all you do is shout?'

'Your brother *won't* listen. He wants to believe that the world – his world – can be made to stand still. It *can't*, not for all the Wyndhams in Christendom. He knows that labourers and their families are leaving the land, but he doesn't want to admit it. The only way to keep Haywood's End alive – not as it *was*, but alive – is to bring in people who want to live here because they can't find a decent home elsewhere.' Frank's set face offered her a brief, sardonic smile. 'Of course, they won't understand feudal ways, and touch their caps to the Squire . . .'

'That's where *you* go wrong,' Lucy cried. 'You spoil a perfectly reasonable argument by harping on the past all the time. Ned doesn't care what people think of him or the Wyndhams, only of what they feel for the land, and that's something Grandpa Hoskins taught him. He's afraid the people you bring here won't understand what is important about places like Haywood's End.'

She stood there, hands outstretched, passionately wanting to make *him* understand. Frank stared at her beautiful face and body, and was filled with the familiar aching sense of inadequacy that only she could arouse in him. With the rest of the world he knew that he could win; with

222

this one woman on earth he would never do anything but lose, because she loved everyone but him. He could abandon the village scheme, even though he knew it to be right, and she would smile and thank him sweetly enough, but he would still be the man she'd married for the sake of Providence and her family.

'I can't turn urban families into country people over-night,' he said harshly. 'They and Haywood's End must learn to live with each other – it's what we all have to do.'

Her hands fell to her sides. 'Yes, it's what we *all* have to do,' she agreed.

He heard the catch in her voice, but never for one moment dreamed that her sadness might be for him, as well as for Ned or for herself.

'I promised to take Charlie over to Bicton . . . we shan't be late back,' he said curtly.

He didn't suggest that she might go with them, nor did she ask to be taken; Charlie preferred to have his father to himself.

She found Ned where she expected him to be – digging furiously in the kitchen-garden. Anguish could usually be dealt with by being siphoned into care for the soil and the plants that grew in it. He looked up and smiled as she went to stand beside him, but carried on with his digging.

'Sorry about the shouting-match, Lu dear . . . bloody silly, really; it never achieves anything and all we do is make fools of ourselves. Still, I think I'm certain of one thing: it's time I moved out of Providence. I shall set my Mary up in a cottage . . . she won't mind a bit, bless her!'

'And leave Mama and Papa rattling around in a half-empty house, and everybody else wondering whose side they ought to take? Dear Ned, promise me you'll do nothing of the kind.' She stared at his set face, and suddenly took hold of his arm so that he had to stop and look at her. 'Can't you *try* to consider the possibility that Frank genuinely wants to save the village, not help it to a sudden death? It may not be the way you'd prefer it to be helped, but as things are, there isn't any choice. Ned, country people are a stubborn lot . . . can you see the likes

223

of Queenie Briggs and Annie Moffat being tamely swamped by newcomers? I think it's much more likely the townees will have to come to terms with *them*!'

He fidgeted with his spade but she knew he was listening. Then he straightened his back and grinned at her. 'All right . . . I hear you, missus.' It was what the village men always said when offered some unpalatable truth by their wives.

She smiled at the thought, then grew serious again. 'You won't think any more about moving out? Promise me, please.'

'I'll promise not to think about it *yet*, at any rate. I can't help feeling, all the same, that Frank's glad of something we can disagree openly about. If he'd like to see one less Wyndham at Providence, I could scarcely blame him – it's his house.'

Here, at least, Lucy felt herself to be on firm ground. 'I don't believe he does think that. He's not a small-minded man, and the ownership of things doesn't bother him.'

'Well, then, let's say I sometimes have the feeling that it would make things easier for *you* with Frank . . . as it is, you're being torn in two, poor girl – old loyalties against new. I don't know why it took *this* row to make me realize it properly.'

She stopped to tug a piece of groundsel out of the newly turned soil. By the time she'd shaken soil off it and deposited it in his wheel-barrow she had her answer ready.

'You know something about our problems, and they aren't of your making . . . I've contrived them all by myself! I wonder if the youngest child of a family always takes longest to grow up? I certainly have. Hubert Roberts chided me this afternoon for ignoring Heavenly help in life's little battles. For a moment or two he almost managed to convince me that I might learn to win after all. I shall try, anyway.'

He smiled at her with huge affection. 'That's the spirit, love – dogged as does it!'

Chapter Nineteen

Everyone at Haywood's End agreed that a September day of more than usually golden perfection was exactly what they were due for Ned Wyndham's wedding. Recent years had offered them precious little to celebrate, and there hadn't been a flag flying over the battlemented roof of Providence since the Armistice was declared; but it was flying now, and with the harvest safely in – trust Ned to wait for that! – the day could be declared a rare and glorious holiday.

Crammed into the church in good time so as to be sure of not missing anything, the ladies of the village first inspected each other's wedding finery, and then settled down to the even richer pleasure of watching the family and neighbouring gentry arrive. There was a communal watery sniff when Ned, flanked by Harry Trentham, took his place at the chancel rail. Hadn't they known him all his life – child, youth, and war-shattered man – and loved him all that time? Now, at last, he was to be paired right and tight with a girl of whom they thoroughly approved. Edith Haskell was a queer one, but there was nothing wrong with her daughter; she'd do all right for Ned. True, she did seem to be late arriving, but they weren't in any hurry, and the longer the day could be made to last, the better. Only Victoria, dressed in Kate Greenaway dress and bonnet, got bored with the delay. Convinced that everyone had come to see how beautiful she looked, she set off up the aisle without waiting for the bride and had to be hauled back by Lucy. Mary finally arrived on the arm of a resplendent Arthur Thornley, the postmistress and honorary organist abandoned 'Where Sheep May Safely Graze' and launched into

225

a triumphant attack on 'The voice that breathed o'er Eden'; the service had begun.

Louise Trentham, majestic in pale mauve, didn't skimp her duty. Old neighbourhood and village friends were greeted, checked up on and, where necessary, advised, before she allowed herself the pleasure of a quiet chat with her sister-in-law. She watched Mary walking hand in hand with Ned among the guests, and gave a nod of reluctant approval. The girl looked charming but, more important to Lady Trentham, behaved with a shy and unexpected grace.

'I like that rig.' She nodded at Mary's simple voile dress and wide-brimmed straw hat. 'Your choice?'

'No, hers,' Gertrude answered with a smile. 'All I contributed were the white roses on her hat – a last-minute inspiration! Ned thinks she's beautiful, and so she is.'

Louise nodded, then made a sudden pounce in a different direction. 'I was hoping Sybil might have been here. Another bridesmaid wouldn't have come amiss, and Josephine Blanchard would have done nicely – she's about the same age as the twins, isn't she?'

'Almost exactly. We thought she'd have done nicely too, and Sybil fully intended to come but she had to abandon the idea – Henri has been unwell lately; rather worryingly so.'

'At this rate *your* grand-daughter will be grown up before you even meet her, and *we* shall have no grand-children at all. Heaven knows I don't hanker after huge Victorian families and women worn out with constant child-bearing, but now we seem to be going to the opposite extreme. Lucy has done *her* duty, but that's of no benefit to the Wyndhams – it just enables Arthur Thornley to look more disgustingly complacent than ever.'

She swallowed what she was about to say next and contorted her face into a grim smile as the man himself bounced towards them. Gertrude solemnly excused herself and left them together, knowing the procedure well by now. After the barest preliminaries that decency allowed, their swords would be out, cutting and slashing. The battle was bloody, but so much enjoyed by both that it would have been cruel to deprive them of it.

Always a kind hostess, she noticed Georgina Maynard looking wistfully at Ned, and offered her the consolation of one of Harry's Trentham cousins instead; then, walking on, she met Harry himself, balancing a complicated arrangement of plates and glasses.

'Dear Harry, the best man's work is never done,' she said with sympathy.

'Not when the bridesmaid has Victoria's capacity for ice cream! Tom has already confessed himself beaten but this is her third lot. Never mind – my reward will be a strawberry-flavoured kiss and the assurance whispered into my neck that I'm a werry nice man!'

'That's Victoria's beautifully simple world; people are either werry nice or werry nasty – there are no degrees in between and no indecision about who is which.'

'*Blessedly* simple! Dear Aunt, is the best man allowed to say that the mother of the bridegroom is looking very lovely?'

Her grey eyes smiled at him from beneath the brim of her pink straw hat. 'He certainly is . . . the older we get the more precious compliments become!'

'Pity about Syb. She must be disappointed not to be vetting Ned's bride. Still, I'm sure she'd have decided that he's done well for himself.' It was Charlotte's view, but Harry had had time to come to the conclusion that she was right.

Gertrude felt pleased with him, and faintly surprised; but almost in the same moment it occurred to her that she was only surprised because she'd missed an important change in her nephew. There'd been a time not so long since when Harry Trentham had been turning into an arrogant, humourless man with no time to spare for anyone who didn't share his views. She had no idea what had happened to alter this state of things, but humility and humour were seeping back, and even some of the sweetness that had been missing since Emily was killed.

She was tempted to say so, thought better of it, and

227

murmured instead, 'I'm glad you like Mary. I always imagined I'd think that *no-one* deserved Ned, but this girl does.'

Harry's mouth suddenly twitched into a smile. 'Most tactful of aunts! Not even the merest suggestion that I'd be much more bearable if I followed Ned into matrimony again? Hints have been falling like confetti all afternoon, but it was left to Arthur Thornley to smite me with his bludgeon. It's the duty of every able-bodied man, apparently, to reduce the surplus of single women left by the war!'

Gertrude's glance strayed round the lawn and came to rest on two such women – her nieces, talking together. What a waste it would be if neither of *them* got married.

'I don't make a habit of agreeing with Arthur,' she admitted, 'but, less often than he thinks, he *is* sometimes right! Contented wives always fall into the trap of thinking that every woman ought to marry, but in Charlotte's case I'm sure matrimony would be a blessing. Without it, in a few more years she'll be left with elderly relatives to care for, other people's offspring as godchildren, and a string of worthy causes. She deserves much more than a life of small public duties and large private sacrifices.'

Harry nodded but his own gaze lingered on the elegant cream-suited figure of the woman standing beside his sister. 'I notice you don't say what Anita deserves.'

'We were talking about needs, not merits. Anita is so complete in herself that she's one of the few women who doesn't need a husband.'

'Quite right, Aunt. She's just like the clothes she wears – clear-cut, expensive, and sure! None of the muddles of lesser mortals, and none of their mistakes, either.'

He spoke with a sudden harsh vehemence that startled Gertrude into realizing they were not talking about Anita's clothes at all. But the conversation had to be hauled back to a trivial wedding level, and she must pretend that they were.

'The result is beautiful, you must allow. I'm afraid poor Alicia Browning was perfectly happy with her frills and draperies until she came up against Anita's simple elegance.'

Harry didn't smile or reply, and his expression when she glanced at him was so strangely compounded of anger, sadness and pride that she was jolted into blurting out the extraordinary idea that had just formed itself in her mind.

'You and Anita have disagreed about a lot of things in the past . . . is one of them the question of whether or not *she* needs a husband?'

Harry's disciplined mouth suddenly relaxed and twitched with rueful amusement. 'Not *any* husband, dear Aunt . . . only whether or not she needs *me*!' His smile broadened at the astonishment in her face, but he took pity on her before she need find something appropriate to say.

'Time I attended to my duties, I think. Victoria's refill has turned to liquid now, so I'd better start again.'

He nodded and walked away, leaving her still standing there.

'Either, like Lot's poor wife, you've been turned to salt, or your shoes are adhering to something sticky . . . which is it, love?'

She twisted round to see Ned smiling at her. 'Neither, as it happens. I was deep in thought!'

'It's being a happy day, isn't it?'

'Almost perfect, I'd say,' she agreed with the same simple conviction as his own.

James Wyndham didn't sail directly for London, even when his American affairs were eventually settled. Expecting to hear that he would arrive to spend Christmas with her for the first time in five years, Anita received instead a letter that left her full of anxiety.

She wasted half a morning thinking about it – fruitlessly, because James was already on board the ship bringing him to Europe; sat down at her desk determined to concentrate on a description of the treasures awaiting the visitor to Amsterdam's Rijsmuseum; and for the tenth time found her mind straying to her father's probable reception in Dublin. She finally admitted defeat, and spent the rest of the afternoon trying to decide whether a letter to Patrick would do more harm than good. She still hadn't made up her mind when a ring at the doorbell was followed by Harry's brisk stride into her drawing-room. She hadn't seen him since the day of Ned's wedding at Providence. His visits to Walton Place had ceased even before that – from the moment she refused the terms on which he was prepared to sleep with her. She had missed his calls, missed *him* more than she was ever likely to tell him.

'I thought you'd taken too much umbrage ever to darken my door again,' she said, smiling faintly.

'I had, but I suddenly remembered how much more comfortable your home is than mine! You were looking very forlorn when I walked in – are you going to tell me why?'

'Of course – visitors are for making use of! I want you to convince me with good masculine logic that I'm worrying needlessly. My father has finally sailed from New York, but he's decided to go first to Dublin, to spend Christmas there.'

'Unexpected,' Harry agreed, 'but need it cause you anxiety? I should have thought you'd be pleased.'

'I should be delighted, except for one thing. My father's only intention in going there must be to make his peace before he settles down in London. He's hated being at odds with Patrick and there's been the added grief of losing touch with his grandson, Christopher.'

'I still can't see anything wrong with trying to mend that situation.'

Anita's slender shoulders lifted in a small gesture of despair. 'You don't understand. My brother *might* accept the olive branch, even though he's quite as stubborn as the rest of the Wyndhams. But Ishbel *won't*. She's an O'Neil, and they're implacable haters of the English – bigoted, fanatical people who look upon the smallest compromise as a sign of weakness. When Patrick fell in love with her – most understandably because she was as beautiful as the morning – he had to commit himself heart and soul to the Irish cause before he was allowed to marry her.'

'So now you're afraid that James will turn up full of the Christmas spirit of forgiveness only to find the door slammed in his face?'

'Something like that,' Anita mumbled. For once her short dark hair was ruffled where she'd driven her fingers through it, and her eyes were darkly blue in the pallor of her face. Harry thought of her as being fiercely independent – the last woman on earth to invite a man to believe that she needed him on any terms but her own; now, she looked vulnerable, and he would have given a great deal for the right to hold and comfort her.

'I'm being ridiculous,' she said with an effort at brightness. 'Father will have written to say he's coming, and even if Ishbel and her frightful blood-hungry relations won't meet him, that's the worst they can do. I'm fairly sure that Patrick, at least, will see him, because I got the impression when he was in London that *his* viewpoint had shifted a little.'

She tried to sound calm, to sound convinced, even, that the people in the drama were capable of seeing reason; but her eyes were full of fear. Harry chose the only way open to him of helping her – he could at least make her angry.

'I hope James realizes that *his* viewpoint has to shift a little, too, although I get the impression that he's not a man exactly accustomed to giving way. I guess that in *his* philosophy the subject races, like the working class, are expected to know their place and be content to be told what's good for them.'

Anita's drooping dark head lifted like a plant being given rain and sunlight. 'If you mean that because my father believes in successful capitalism and a free economy he must also be a bullying oppressor of the poor and downtrodden, you couldn't be more wrong, my dear Harry.'

'I'm *not* your dear Harry, so don't be so bloody patronizing,' he shouted, suddenly enraged on his own account. He didn't much care *what* James Wyndham was, but the man made a convenient excuse for venting some of his own pent-up frustrations. 'I suppose your father's just like you – entrenched in his own opinions, protected from reality by wealth, and convinced that everybody must change except *him*.'

'*You* don't have to change – for him or for me,' Anita flung at him. 'Stay as you are – entrenched in your own kind of bigotry. Go on believing, if you can, that anarchists with guns and bombs in their hands have the right to decide the future of Ireland; go on bellowing to your mobs of working men that only *they* are holy, and that wicked land-owners and employers should be put down. I don't care *what* you believe . . .' Her voice trembled on the edge of breaking under the weight of emotion long kept hidden. Cool and calmly controlled Anita Wyndham was on the verge of demolishing her reputation, and screaming like a fishwife in a fight that hadn't existed a few moments ago. She took a deep breath and completed her ruin by shouting at him. 'Go away, and don't ever come here again. I must have been mad to think that a child of yours would have been better than no child at all.'

She saw the flame that leapt in his eyes, and the sudden whiteness around his mouth. If there'd been time she might have retracted the last and worst of what she'd said, but there wasn't any time. She was caught and held, hurt by the grip of his arms and helpless to prevent his mouth crushing hers. She was to be punished – that was Harry's only conscious thought. For the first time in her life Anita Wyndham must be made to learn that she wasn't in control of every situation.

But with her mouth soft as velvet under his, and her slight body trembling in his arms, he wasn't in charge either; sheer need was taking over. He lifted her off her feet and carried her to the huge white chesterfield that mutely offered all the space they needed for making love. She didn't fight to save herself, only stared up at him, trying to defy the possibility that she could be forced. If she'd wept or cried out, he might have heard, but she made no sound. His hands were not tender when he undressed her, and his body wasn't gentle in its possession. Afterwards, when he lifted himself away from her, content and yet appalled, he was already fumbling in his chaotic thoughts for something that he could possibily find to say.

She opened her eyes and looked at him. 'I was very frightened . . . ashamed of not knowing what to do.' Against every possibility that might have occurred to him, she smiled, leaving him speechless. The tenderness that had been completely missing a few moments ago washed over him now, and his hand touched her face with infinite gentleness.

'I was going to try to apologize,' he murmured hoarsely. 'Instead, I shall ask if you'll feel frightened *next* time?' He waited for her to say that there would never be a next time, but her dark head moved slowly against the white silk cushions of the chesterfield. 'No, I shan't feel frightened.' She lay there content to remain where she was, faintly surprised to find that she felt no shame and no embarrassment. Perhaps the life of a courtesan had been more agreeable than she'd always supposed. When Harry asked why she was smiling, she told him and heard him shout with laughter. It seemed to complete the extraordinary circle of emotion they'd travelled round since he arrived.

'You've avoided me for weeks and weeks. What made you change your mind and come today?' she asked suddenly.

He looked shame-faced for a moment, because it was difficult to remember the reason for his visit. 'I'd just left Charlotte with Ian Nicholson . . . My dear, they're engaged to be married. I thought I'd break the news to you myself, because it's always seemed to me that you were . . . were rather fond of him.' She didn't answer, and he was forced to enquire, with a gentleness she hadn't thought him capable of, '*Are* you very upset?'

It would have been simple to say the truth. That she wasn't upset at all; but the time hadn't yet come to be completely honest with him. 'I'm glad for Charlotte,' she said instead. 'I'm delighted for *her*.' She felt a twinge of shame that Harry should look so approvingly at her, but duplicity – like a courtesan's lot – was also easier than she'd supposed.

'Are you going to complete this extraordinary evening by offering to take me out to dinner?' she asked next.

'No . . . difficult though it may be, I shall go home and pore over the complexities of Empire tariff legislation.' His hand under her chin forced her to look at him. 'May I come again . . . say, tomorrow night?'

'Let us say tomorrow.' She smiled as she said it, and knowledge shone suddenly in his mind like a blinding light that he loved her, in *all* the ways that a man should love a woman. Not quite yet, but very soon, he would have to tell her so.

'In a few weeks' time your father will be here,' he said abruptly.

'I know . . . but we *did* say temporary possession, didn't we?'

For the first time in his life he knew the meaning of fear. Emily's death had left him bereft and angry, but now he was afraid – he loved and needed a woman who didn't need him, except for some brief purpose of her own. He made a huge effort at self-control and managed not to shout at her.

'*You* said temporary,' he pointed out. 'Suppose we wait and see?'

Anita appeared to consider the matter, then smilingly agreed.

When he walked out into the December night five minutes later Empire tariffs were far from his mind; before long he was going to give her a child, and then he would drag her to Haywood's End so that Hubert Roberts could make them man and wife. If he achieved nothing else in life, he was going to achieve *this*.

Chapter Twenty

The memories of a Christmas in which the Three Wise Men fought a pitched battle in the middle of the Nativity play, and Thomas Thornley brought shame on his family by refusing to walk on to the stage at all, were growing mercifully dim by the time James Wyndham finally returned to Providence. He'd been back in London for weeks, been introduced to Harry, Charlotte and her fiancé, but still seemed in no hurry to make the short journey to Warwickshire. William hid disappointment and explained to Gertrude that his brother was bound to have lost interest in a house the Wyndhams no longer owned; Gertrude hid agitation and explained to William that James was probably waiting for the season to change – after a gap of more than thirty years he could delay a week or two more in order to see Providence in all its spring-time beauty.

It seemed for a while as if the season were going to refuse to change at all. A wind blew steadily from the north, blanketing the sky with a sullen mass of grey and sulphur-coloured cloud. By the edge of the lake the hazels defied the cold by hanging out a few brave golden tassels, but there was no encouragement for anything to blossom. Then the miracle, doubted every year until it happened, occurred again. The wind backed and settled in a different quarter, the earth observed the change and burst into life, and nesting birds raced about the sky singing to each other that there was much time to be made up. *Now*, if at all, it seemed to Gertrude, James would come to Providence.

He arrived with Anita on a morning in late March when the sun was shining. At Ned's insistence, the flag was flying again to welcome him, and Biddle had talked the courtyard garden into coming into bloom. Blue and white hyacinths and golden daffodils still proclaimed the Wyndham colours and, with the rightful owner tactfully in London when the arrival ceremony took place, there was no discordant reminder that much had changed in thirty years.

James stepped out of the car, and gave a long look round that became a smile when he saw the throng of people waiting for him – old Hodges, leaning on a stick, Biddle sporting the new tie Gertrude had given him for his last birthday, Emmy and Ethel – small, new scullery maids when James had left to go to America – and the entire Moffat family, some of whom hadn't even been born in 1884. Everyone who belonged to Providence was there. They would have found reasons to be outside in any case, but Gertrude had invited them, for her own sake as much as theirs.

She watched William greet his brother, but hid herself behind Maud Roberts, waiting for the moment when it would be her turn to smile and find something to say. Then suddenly James was in front of her, staring at the woman he'd had to do without for forty years because William had been clever enough to marry her while his back was turned.

'My dear girl . . . I'm afraid *I've* got rather fat, and you've grown elegantly thin, but I think we can still recognize each other.'

There was no difficulty about that although, by one of the tricks time liked to play, it wasn't the dashing young James Wyndham she was remembering. It was his father who came to mind – old Sir Edward, squire when she was still little Gertrude Hoskins in her pinafore and dreadful boots. He'd looked down from his horse with bright, kind eyes, just as James was looking at her now. Suddenly she could see the whole pattern of her days at Providence unrolling in her mind's eye – the span of her own life there merging backwards with all the Wyndhams who'd preceded Edward, and forward to the lifetime of her children, to Charlie and the twins, and a future beyond them that she wouldn't live to see. The pattern was seamless, generation running into generation – a procession in which only continuity mattered, not any of their individual lives. The certainty that this was so brought her such comfort that it was a pleasure, after all, to reach up to kiss her brother-in-law and murmur, 'Welcome home, dear James.'

Much later that night only the men were left sitting round the hearth in the Great Hall – William, James, Ned, and Frank back from London in time to join them. The conversation didn't flag for want of subjects to talk about, but there were some that no-one seemed inclined to touch upon. They had dealt with Germany's inability to pay her war-reparations, argued the rights and wrongs of the French occupation of the Ruhr, and even considered the astonishing rumour that a man was going to make a solo flight across the Atlantic; but something that was in everybody's mind wasn't mentioned until William deliberately chose to put it into words.

'James, you'll be wanting to take a good look round tomorrow, and the village will certainly be expecting to take a look at *you*. Haywood's End probably appears much as you remember it, except for the garage tacked on to Matthew Harris's forge, and a war-memorial which manages to be hideous and infinitely moving at the same time. But there *are* other changes, which you'll soon discover. We can't make up our minds, I'm afraid, whether to rejoice in progress or deplore it!'

James smiled at the characteristic indecision. William, at least, hadn't changed . . . bloody war, tragedy, the loss of his home to the clever, tired-faced man who carefully didn't remind them of his ownership – none of these things had altered the gentle spirit of a man who'd managed to puzzle and infuriate him ever since they were children. It had always been easy to win against William; but since he didn't ever fight, in the end he never seemed to lose.

'There's nothing to be done with progress but accept it

with gratitude, especially *here*,' James said definitely. 'Providence was falling to pieces when I went away, and there was a woeful air of discouragement about most of the farms. Times may be difficult, but from what I've seen so far all that seems to have changed.'

William gave a little shrug. 'Frank can tell you about today's discouragements – cities where the old traditional industries are dying and thousands of men are out of work. Here, we're more fortunate than we deserve – no, I'm more fortunate than *I* deserve. The land is in good heart, thanks to Ned; and Providence is devotedly preserved by Frank and – I think he would allow me to say – by Gertrude. I can take no credit for it at all.'

'Your paintings are your contribution,' Ned said swiftly. 'Without them we shouldn't have been able to buy back Wyndham land. It would have been sold and built on by now.'

In the silence that fell on them James was aware of tension seeping into the room, as tangible as the draught that stirred the curtains.

'Land built on by men like me, Ned means but is too polite to say,' Frank explained to their visitor. 'It's one of the changes you'll discover in the village. I've already made a start there – repairing some of the cottages, rebuilding others that are beyond repair.'

'We use more machinery than before the war, and employ fewer men,' Ned was obliged to admit. 'That's inevitable if our prices are to have a chance of competing with the cost of cheap, imported food; but it means that families whose roots have always been here drift away to lead miserable lives in cities. I should like to try to keep them at Haywood's End, but Frank's solution to a shrinking village population is to bring in outsiders who want to *escape* from city life. Lucy clings to the hope that they'll learn country ways and no harm will be done. If she and Frank are right, I shall have to eat a large helping of humble pie!'

James saw Frank look curiously at his brother-in-law, as if something Ned had just said had taken him by surprise.

When he spoke again himself it was in a slow, reflective way unlike his usual briskness in disposing of any conversation. 'I've spent a lot of time at Haywood's End recently. The village people are enjoying themselves – pointing out to the builders I brought from Birmingham all the mistakes they're making, and reckoning among themselves how long it will be before townees get tired of mud and muck and rush back to the palaces they're supposed to come from in the city!'

'Whereas *you* will choose the townees with care, and make sure that they're as tough and humorous and awkward as the tribe they have to settle among,' James suggested calmly.

'I shall do my best,' Frank agreed with a rare and charming smile. Then he turned to Ned. 'We've come near to quarrelling on the subject of the village and I'm sorry about that. I still think I'm right, but there's something else to be said. The people at Haywood's End are happy to see me spend my money there, and they deal with me very courteously. I'm allowed to touch their magic circle because I married Lucy, but I shall never be accepted inside it. Between them and the Wyndhams there's a different relationship which I didn't understand or properly value before. It probably breaks the hearts of men like Harry Trentham, vainly trying to teach them that they're all equal, but the fact remains that the people here know what binds them to Providence as clearly as Ned knows what binds the Wyndhams to *them*. I don't want it to be my townees who destroy that.'

It was a long speech for Frank to have made but William was certain that he'd deliberately chosen *that* moment to make it . . . partly for Ned's sake, and partly to reassure James about Providence itself. It had been generously done, thought William.

After that first day Anita left her father at Providence and returned to London alone. Always uncertain about Harry's Westminster and constituency duties, she never knew whether to expect him or not. If he came, she welcomed

239

him; if not, she had no right to complain. James had accepted her tranquil explanation that she was conducting an experiment in free living, and she was unaware that he'd also been given Harry's version of a relationship that would sooner or later change.

The evening of her return to Walton Place seemed long and lonely after the family gathering at Providence. She tried to busy herself with writing, sighed because what she wrote seemed intolerably wooden, and abandoned it for the even more depressing task of thinking about the future. It was no-one's fault but her own that she'd got caught in a trap of her own making. Harry had asked her to marry him and she'd refused; he wasn't the man to ask her a second time. She had talked blithely of wanting experience and a child; it was late in the day to know beyond any doubt that what she had wanted most of all was Harry. All the gods above must be laughing themselves sick that she, who was going to make Harry Trentham human again, had succeeded brilliantly with him and failed completely for herself.

She'd got thus far in her thoughts when his knock, firm and familiar, sounded at the front door. The future looked no less bleak than it had a moment before, but the present was bright again until he explained that he'd merely called in to hear about James's visit to Providence.

'You're not intending to stay?' She kept disappointment out of her voice because free living demanded it, but it would have been easier to burst into tears. Then she saw him smile.

'Sweetheart, since you ask, I was certainly hoping to stay. I was just trying to pretend that I wasn't desperate to rush off to bed with you!'

She smiled but did her best to sound severe. 'The *visit*, Harry . . . well, I think it's going rather well, even though Uncle William and my father still mystify one another. I imagined that James was dreading going because he'd lived for years with a dream that might not match reality. I was right about *that*, but all wrong about the dream itself. What he yearned for was not Providence itself, but his brother's wife.' She saw the disbelief in Harry's face and shook her head at him. 'It's true . . . Passion may be long since spent, but he still loves Gertrude; even his voice takes on a different note when he speaks her name. It makes clear a lot of things I didn't understand before.' Anita remembered again with aching sadness the long, empty years of her father's life in America . . . youth and energy and the capacity for love driven into a single outlet – the cold, successful pursuit of money. Harry tried to imagine how *he* would have survived the discovery of loving Anita if she had already been married to Ned.

'I gather there was a visitation from Somerton,' he said abruptly. 'How was my dear Mama?'

'Distinctly cool to begin with, because of course I enthused about Lottie's engagement, but I'm afraid I became devious! Aunt Louise pretends to disapprove of James, but she can't help being impressed by his success . . . So I asked *him* to mention, en passant, how highly he thinks of Ian. *That* made her look thoughtful, but then a neighbour of Aunt Gertrude's completed the good work by congratulating herself out loud at the dinner-table on being spared a war-shirking Socialist intellectual as a son-in-law!'

A gleam of pure amusement lifted tiredness from Harry's face. 'I can imagine the rest . . . my mother demolished her!'

'Hook, line, and sinker. She not only repeated all the things Father and I had said about Ian, but threw in several virtues it hadn't occurred to us to mention as well!'

'"And even the ranks of Warwickshire could scarce forbear to cheer"! . . . Marvellous, my dear. Should I enquire whether your deviousness also included priming the unfortunate neighbour?'

'Certainly not . . . she was quite silly enough to need no help from me.'

He gave a shout of laughter, not even noticing now how easy it had become to laugh when he was with Anita. They were both sober again when he decided to take her completely by surprise. 'I have to confess to a little deviousness of my own. Neither of us belongs to the parish of Haywood's End, so I wrote to Hubert Roberts to ask whether he could officiate for us at St Stephens, Westminster. I shouldn't feel properly married without his help.'

'Married?' Anita queried faintly. 'You didn't think to mention it to me first?'

'The element of surprise, my dear – every soldier is taught to make use of it when he can. I wanted to make it impossible for you to refuse this time.' He said it confidently, so that she shouldn't know how desperately he still feared losing her. 'You haven't got the child you wanted . . . we might do better if we nailed our colours to the mast of matrimony.'

'The child I want may not be worth a wife you *don't* want,' she said slowly.

'True, but it happens that I *do* want you.' His hands suddenly gripped her shoulders, forcing her to look at him. 'Have you still not guessed how completely I love you? Everybody else has; including your father. I want you for my wife more than I want anything else in the world. It's marriage or nothing now, Anita – I can't go on with this damnable charade any longer.' He stopped speaking, the better to observe the extraordinary thing that was happening. 'Love of my heart . . . you're smiling and weeping at the same time . . . does that mean you're going to let Hubert marry us?'

'Yes, if you think Aunt Louise can withstand another shock! Dearest Harry, I've been so mortally afraid you wouldn't ever ask me again . . . without stealing Lottie's thunder, could it be soon?'

His arms scooped her up. 'As soon as Hubert can arrange it, but meanwhile don't you think we can now more or less decently retire to bed?'

Two marriages, Charlotte's to Ian Nicholson at Somerton and Harry's to Anita in London, brought the summer of 1927 to an end in a flurry of family celebrations. James used one of them, Anita's wedding, as an excuse to lure her brother back to England. Patrick came without Ishbel, as expected, but brought with him a fair-haired boy of nine, who stared measuringly at a cluster of strange English relations.

'He makes me nervous,' Arthur Thornley confided to his wife. 'I get the feeling that he's counting the years till he can bring a gun and shoot the lot of us.'

'He makes *me* want to weep,' said Jane. 'He's the same age as Charlie and they haven't exchanged a word because he's been taught to think of us as an enemy. What sort of upbringing is that for a Christian woman to give her son?' She stopped, blushing vividly, because indignation had made her speak more loudly than usual and James Wyndham had turned round to stare at her.

Jane smiled apologetically. 'I'm sorry . . . this isn't the time to talk of unhappy things, but I can't bear the vicious circle we seem to be trapped in – their hatred breeds hatred in us; it's never-ending.'

'Perhaps not in Christopher's case, Mrs Thornley. At least I shall see to it that he grows up knowing *both* sides of the argument. He'll have to make up his own mind after that.' James didn't explain that his terms were already well-known to Ishbel's family in Dublin: Christopher would be named as his heir on condition that he was allowed to visit England occasionally. The O'Neils banked on his affection for the people he'd grown up among; James banked on his intelligence. Patrick did what he could to shield his son from an emotional tug-of-war, and prayed that Christopher would have the strength of mind to resist taking sides at all.

James smiled at Jane, who still stood watching him. 'I have a trump card up my sleeve, of course. Gertrude will welcome my grandson at Providence . . . I don't see how he can resist *her*, do you?'

'Nobody can resist her,' Jane agreed simply. 'She and Providence together put a spell on people.'

James looked with warm approval on this small, neat woman who looked so kind and seemed so sensible. He still deeply resented the fact that anyone but a Wyndham should own Providence; but an innate sense of what was just obliged him to see that Frank Thornley was a good deal more capable of taking care of it than William. He bowed to Jane and moved away because he could see his sister bearing down on him.

'Well, James . . . we didn't expect *this*, did we?' Given time, he might have said that it was exactly what he *had* expected, but Louise had more to say. 'Do you suppose it's all right? I don't care for marriages between first cousins as a rule.'

'My dear girl, our stock's as tough as old boots, and so is Alec's. Even allowing for some unfortunate Irish blood in Anita, I don't think you need worry.'

Louise rewarded him with a rare smile. 'I'm too thankful to worry. To see Harry happy at last makes up for everything else.'

'Even for having him give up Somerton when the time comes? Anita won't try to persuade him, you know. I tried to persuade *her* and got nowhere. Pity – she'd follow very well in your footsteps.'

'Well, I intend to plod on for a while yet,' Louise pointed out firmly. 'After that, if Harry's delightful friends get their way, the aristocracy will be abolished in any case. A distant cousin will get Somerton, if he wants it, and I shall spend my old age in the Dower House, terrorizing him and his unfortunate wife!'

'I don't doubt it,' James said truthfully. He was thankful to have lived for years at a safe distance from his sister, and intended to go on doing so, but he was immensely proud of her; when she and the order she represented had passed away, the strength and savour of Victorian England would finally have disappeared.

He lifted his champagne glass and saluted her. 'We'll drink to your eccentric old age, my dear . . . God bless you.'

Louise smiled and drank, and then looked round the crowded room. 'It's a pity the family isn't quite complete . . . we always seem to be missing Sybil. I hope you'll meet her *one* of these days; you'll find she's not quite like any other woman you know.'

James had to wait some months more to meet the niece he'd never seen. As summer gave way to autumn, Sybil's letters began to report that Henri's health, after seeming to improve for a time, was declining again. She wrote of plans to spend the winter with him in Egypt so that he could escape the cold Paris weather, then for some while she didn't write at all. Gertrude was anxiously aware that news was overdue, but still trod warily where her daughter was concerned; it was Sybil who set the terms of their connection, just as she always had. Then, at the breakfast-table one morning, William handed her a letter that was postmarked Paris. She read it in silence, offered it to her husband, and walked out of the room.

Henri was dead. The man who had seemed more vividly alive than anyone she'd ever known was lost to them for ever, and Sybil had chosen not to let them know until he was already in his grave. Gertrude balanced one pain against the other, unable to decide in that first agonizing moment which hurt the more.

Sybil's letters after that always refused help and politely refused visitors. Whatever had to be done, she could do, because Henri had taught her. The mill was to be sold, and eventually she would return to England with Josephine.

She came back six months later, bringing the seven-year-old daughter William and Gertrude had never seen. Josephine spoke politely if speaking was unavoidable, but was silent otherwise; she seemed to have decided with almost adult determination to stand aloof from a world that no longer contained her father. The twins did their best, primed by Lucy; Josephine defeated them by speaking French if she said anything at all. She looked at the toys they offered her, then handed them back, and sat silently through the lessons that Mary still gave them in the schoolroom. Gertrude wept in private over an unhappiness that seemed too great for a child to bear.

'What can we *do* for her, William . . . tell me, please.'

'My dearest, no more than we *are* doing – love her, take care of her, and wait.'

'Sybil is talking of setting herself up in London . . . with the sort of dress-shop she had in Paris. I can understand that she desperately needs something to do, but what is to become of Josephine? Every time I look at her shut-in face I want to hug her into believing that there *are* people left in the world to love her, but it wouldn't do a particle of good . . . she only wants Henri.'

'Dear heart, she's seven . . . eventually she'll learn to make do with us instead.'

Gertrude nodded, keeping to herself the other grief that couldn't be mentioned at all. If Josephine kept them at arm's length, it was only what Sybil was doing. Her thin, elegant body roamed about the house and grounds, and she talked composedly to friends who called, but heart and spirit wandered in some cold region where she rejected the company of her family. It seemed to Gertrude that between her daughter and *herself*, especially, there was a barrier as cold and hard and unimpressionable as glass. On her own account she was prepared to take the risk of shattering it, but she was afraid of destroying Sybil's frozen calm.

Then, one morning, Sybil herself drew down the inevitable storm about their heads. She went into the room where her mother was occupied in writing letters; aimless and bored, she picked up a small leather-bound volume of poetry and dropped it again without sufficient care. It fell to the floor with its cover awkwardly turned back, but before she could stoop to pick it up a cry from Gertrude rooted her to the spot.

'Leave it, please . . . don't touch it again . . . you had no right to touch it at all.'

Sybil stared at the anguish in her mother's face; it seemed so out of proportion to her offence that she spoke curtly, barely apologetic for what had been an accident, after all.

'I'm sorry . . . if it's damaged, I'll have it repaired. I didn't *mean* to drop it, and it's nothing but a small book of verse.'

'It happens to be the book I value most.' Gertrude had

picked it up herself now, and held it cradled against her heart.

'Then I dare say Henri gave it to you.' The cold, calm words dropped into a well of silence in the room. Gertrude could hear them echoing in her mind, little hammer-strokes of pain – hers and Sybil's, so intermingled now that she couldn't tell which was which.

'It was just . . . just a little gift. He brought it when he came to give us the news of your marriage.'

'A consolation prize, Mama?' Sybil offered the cruel taunt in the hope of easing her own hurt, and saw her mother's face go ashen-white where it had been flushed a moment before.

'A *gift*,' Gertrude insisted with difficulty. 'A gift from a dear friend.'

'Let's admit the truth now. Henri *loved* you. I knew it even before I went to find him in Paris, but I was stupid enough to think I could win. I was young and attract-ive . . . couldn't fail to please . . . but I did fail in the end. I've spent the past nine years torn between hating you for it and trying not to feel intensely proud that he chose *you* to love out of all the women in the world.' Her eyes shone with tears that gathered, brimmed over, and trickled unheeded down her cheeks. It was too late for conceal-ment now; the glass barrier lay in shattered fragments about her feet and she would never be able to piece them together again.

'There isn't any more truth to admit to,' Gertrude said slowly. 'We were never lovers . . . just two people who met and recognized each other out of all the unnumbered millions in the world. I think your father knew, but he didn't allow it to harm *our* marriage; I imagined yours was safe because you didn't know. No wonder you stayed away, and how stupid of me never to have guessed the reason.'

Without knowing that she did so, Sybil scrubbed at her cheeks in exactly the same gesture Victoria used to wipe away grief. 'Henri did his best at the beginning to send me away, but I was determined to stay and *make* him love me.

247

I got the punishment such arrogance deserved and knew that every time he made love to me he pretended that it was *you* he held in his arms. That's why I opened the shop in Paris – I had to have something that was truly mine, not yours.'

'Josephine is yours,' Gertrude reminded her quietly. 'A priceless gift Henri gave you that he never gave to me.'

'Yes, I know. It doesn't help very much, though, because she only wants what she can't have – her father. I make a lot of mistakes but not the same one twice, so I shan't try to force *her* affection. May I leave her here while I open my shop in London?'

'Yes, if you think Providence might help to heal her.'

'It will if anything can, but . . .' Sybil stopped speaking, and stared at her mother, trying to put into words the conviction that had just taken control of her. It was unbelievable that it should be there, but in it she caught a glimmer of hope of her salvation. 'I want her here for another reason as well, because I've just realized what I need to do – I must share Henri's gift with *you*.'

Gertrude's eyes filled with tears, but a smile lit her pale face, wiping away tiredness and pain. 'Dearest, it would be the most precious gift of all. I'll accept it if you promise not to stay away yourself in future. *You* must come and be healed as well.'

Sybil nodded, smiling faintly. 'We'll heal each other, shall we? God knows it's time we did.'

1935

Chapter Twenty-One

Josephine had been at Providence for seven years by the time the King's Silver Jubilee celebrations interrupted the quietness of village life. Forewarned by Ned of a ritual that only bloody revolution could have disturbed – tea and coconut-shies in the gardens, and fireworks after dark – she escaped from the house in good time and hid herself in the May-time greenness of the Home Wood. She was lonely from choice, knowing that only by keeping aloof from the people around her could she keep clear in her mind the image of her father and the life they'd shared at Pont-sur-Seine. It had been hard at times to close her heart to Providence, but she had always understood that if she once gave in, she would forget where she truly belonged.

'Tea and coconut-shies make no appeal, cousin?'

She recognized Christopher Wyndham's voice even before she turned round. He was different from her Thornley cousins – tall and fine-drawn . . . more interesting, in her opinion. She suspected him of being in the same boat as herself – a reluctant visitor; when the time came to make his own choice, he probably wouldn't come at all.

'I don't like crowds,' she explained briefly, 'and in any case the celebration's nothing to do with me. I expect Victoria's enjoying herself . . . she knows all the village people. I prefer being here.'

She waited for him to nod and walk on, but he squatted down beside her on the fallen trunk of a tree brought down by a winter gale. The spring-time beauty of the woodland was suddenly the better for being shared, and she was filled with the strange certainty that he *was* sharing it – seeing the vivid greenness of each tiny frond and leaf above a bluebell lake that rippled in the breeze. Near at hand chaffinches and robins whistled duets and, softened by distance, the sound of the visiting brass band drifted on the air, faint and enticing as the horns of elfland.

'It's lovely,' she said in the low, husky voice that always took him by surprise. There was no French inflection in it now, but she still *looked* out-of-place among the fair-haired Wyndhams and Thornleys. Like a blackbird, he thought, among a flock of doves.

'Lovely enough to make you want to stay?' he asked. 'I always thought you were marking time here . . . waiting to grow old enough to get away.'

'I am. I'm going home to France as soon as I can.' Her dark eyes fixed themselves on his face – set under slender black brows, they were her only claim to beauty at the moment. 'You don't belong here either, do you? Are you going to live in Ireland when you're free to choose?'

'I'm *not* free,' he said with sudden sharpness, forgetting that at the age of fourteen she might not be able to understand. 'I'm supposed to hate one side or the other, but I won't be talked or badgered or bribed into such stupidity. In two years' time when I leave the University in Dublin, I shall find a medical school in America where no-one's even heard of the Easter Rising, or the Black and Tans.'

She heard the vehemence in his voice, and nodded gravely, liking the fact that he ignored the five years between his age and her own. All the same, it was hard to imagine him becoming a doctor. She thought of Dr James at Haywood's End – slow-talking, kind and gentle; not a bit like the impatient, fierce young man by her side.

'What are *you* going to do in France when the time comes? Share your mother's interest in women's clothes?'

From the expression on her face he guessed the answer even before it came. 'I shall be like Papa, of course, and learn all there is to know about paintings.' Her mouth quivered with the pain of remembering that her father would never know and be glad of what she was doing. 'Victoria thinks I'm mad because I don't want to help her groom horses or watch Uncle Ned's prize cows drop their calves into the world. It's a horrible, messy business, if you ask me.'

'Or me!' He grinned at the note of *hauteur* in her voice; however much she longed to be 'like Papa', there were times when she strongly resembled her mother. 'There's nothing very pretty about nature in the raw,' he agreed; 'much safer to concern yourself with gentle works of art.'

'Some of them aren't gentle at all. If you don't know *that*, you don't know anything about paintings.'

He'd felt sorry for her a moment ago, but remembered with a spurt of resentment that she'd always been opinionated and self-sufficient, even when small. Victoria had once explained with just the irritation he was feeling now that there was no getting on terms of friendship with their French cousin – the toys they offered her she politely handed back, and the life they would have made her free of at Providence was measured against a picture in her mind and rejected. He didn't blame the twins for having given her up.

'I'm a half-Irish barbarian, don't forget . . . you mustn't expect me to know much!'

He was laughing at her, confident that he knew more than she did. Anger tinged her cheeks with colour and flashed an answer at him. 'I don't expect *anything* here; that's why I'm going to live in Paris, where people know about important things.'

She was tiresome, absurd, and pathetic all at the same time. He wrestled with the temptation to tell her so, but she didn't wait to hear what he would say. She sprang to her feet and plunged into the greenness of the wood, leaving him still sitting there, irritated with her and, uncomfortably, with himself.

Mid-way through the long afternoon of the garden-party William Wyndham coaxed his wife into the courtyard garden for a brief rest. She gave a little sigh of relief as they sat down, and then smiled at him.

'Does it seem nearly fifty years ago that we were

celebrating Victoria's jubilee? We're all wearing more comfortable clothes, but nothing much else has changed at all. No wonder Frank insists that we're obsessed with the past!'

'I'm afraid he's concerned with something more important than the time-honoured pattern of village entertainment! He'd say that we cling to outworn industries instead of starting new ones, and still believe that we're rich enough and powerful enough to keep the rest of the world in order. He's right that it's no longer true, but you can do almost *anything* except get an average Englishman to change his ideas!'

She smiled because the man beside her would be the very last of the breed to change at all. He still hated playing the rôle of country squire. Hated it even more now that it meant welcoming people to a house that wasn't his; but Frank left this one burden to him, and to accept it cheerfully was the only repayment he could make his son-in-law.

'Some things certainly haven't changed,' Gertrude observed after a while. 'We can now be sure that Haywood's End still enjoys garden-parties; and the entire population seems determined to find the King's jubilee worth celebrating.'

'And thereby some among us are confounded! Ned's fears about the newcomers to the village were groundless, after all – they're all out there heaving coconuts with just as much gusto as the rest; more important, their children are helping to keep the village school alive.'

'Ned's glad to have been proved wrong. It doesn't worry him to admit that Frank was right; the survival of Haywood's End was all that mattered, and I'm bound to say it does seem very stubbornly alive.'

'No doubt our Marxist intellectuals are less happy about acknowledging error than Ned. For years they've been predicting the end of the monarchy, and now find their theories drowned under a tidal wave of royal fervour!'

'I'm glad,' Gertrude said firmly. 'So may *all* traitors perish.'

254

'Not quite traitors, my dear . . . well-meaning but misguided men.'

'*Stupid* men! The people of Haywood's End could tell them easily enough what *their* clever minds can't comprehend. The past twenty-five years have been terrible, but the country and the King have come through them together and learned to trust each other.'

'And the worst of the Depression years are behind us, thank God, so that a little grateful rejoicing is in order.' William spoke cheerfully for Gertrude's benefit, trying to ignore the fears that waited on the margin of his mind. For the moment the shadows thrown by ranting Fascist leaders on the Continent were no bigger than a man's clenched hand, but even if they were to darken and spread their stain, he must cling to the knowledge that they weren't England's responsibility. It was the job of the League of Nations to keep the world at peace. From the expression of frowning concentration on his wife's face he thought she guessed what was in his mind, but she suddenly broached a different subject.

'*One* thing has changed, William. I used to believe that no-one could resist this house. Even Arthur Thornley, devoted to the idea that everything should be shining and new, only had to see it once to fall under its spell. But Providence has failed with Josephine, and so have we.'

He heard the aching regret in her voice and understood, more completely than she realized, that with Henri's daughter she would have wanted to fail least of all.

'You're unhappy that she goes off alone so much, but some people need solitude more than others, my dear.'

'I realize that, but it isn't natural in a child of fourteen. She doesn't accept us, even now – takes a fierce pride in *not* doing so, and waits for the moment when she can go back to France.'

'The choice is hers, however sad it makes us,' William pointed out quietly. 'She's intelligent, and much more nearly adult than the twins. We can't force her to accept doses of affection three times a day, like conditioning powders!'

Gertrude's tired smile admitted that what he said was true. 'I know . . . just as I know that we can't force Christopher to accept us, either. He's absent as well this afternoon.'

'To show his republican sympathies, of course, poor boy! Wouldn't you expect him to feel bound to exclude himself from anything that smacks of kow-towing to the monarchy?'

Her thin veined hand patted his gratefully. 'I can see that you're determined to cheer me up by pointing out that I take them too seriously. Maud Roberts would have told me the same thing. I know it isn't reasonable to expect clergymen never to retire, but I did warn her that I shouldn't be able to manage without her. We shall get used to the new Vicar's wife in time, but she's such a deedy little woman that anyone who needs to talk to her must first lassoo her to the Rectory gate-post.'

'I doubt if she would be told, in any case, that you worry about more than Christopher and your grand-daughter – that you agonize over Mary's miscarriages, and Sybil's feverish search for excitement, and the sad, empty travesty of Lucy's marriage. You wouldn't share *these* anxieties with the Vicar's wife any more than you share them with me.'

His quiet voice held no complaint, and his face was full of tenderness when he looked at his wife. 'I know *why* you keep them to yourself. I'm to be left undisturbed in my little ivory tower, free to daub paint while you struggle with the real problems of our life. I lead a very selfish existence, my love.'

'All artists are required to be a little selfish,' she said firmly. 'It's a duty they owe the rest of us!' She smiled at the thought, then grew serious again. 'I can't do more than pray for adults who are in charge of their own lives; but I agonize about the children, William. The twins are all right, but Charlie is almost as unapproachable as Josephine, and Christopher still endures his visits here with the stoic indifference of a saint among a crowd of heretics. Why are we so inadequate that we can't just *love* them into being happy?'

'My dearest, if love alone could do it, you'd have them wrapped in contentment by now. But not even you can make up to Josephine for the loss of her father, or persuade Christopher to forget that all his young life he's been taught to distrust the English.'

'And what is the thing I can't do for Charlie?' she asked painfully.

'Convince him that Lucy truly loves him or his father. He can't help but know the difference, because she *does* love the twins.'

In the long pause that followed Gertrude stared at the shadow thrown across her mind by fear. It was a dark and monstrous bird whose wings she could hear beating, more and more clearly. She got to her feet stiffly, then stooped to leave a kiss on William's thin silver hair.

'Don't trouble to come with me . . . I'm only going to make sure that I'm not needed to help in the marquee. I *shan't* be, because darling Mary will have everything running as perfectly as one of Frank's machines.'

'No hiccup in the supply of tea, no shortage of the cakes the children favour most, and no jostling in the queue!' William agreed. 'She only has to smile for gentleness to descend upon them.'

'And Heaven refuses her children of her own, while women who don't want them at all are blessed with half a dozen.' Gertrude swallowed the taste of bitterness in her throat, and pinned cheerfulness to her face again; then she crossed the moat and walked back into the crowded gardens.

The King's jubilee rejoicing was followed in less than a year by the shock of his death. Sadness was real, but tempered by hope. The Prince of Wales was just what the country and the times needed – he was young, intelligent, and informal – a *modern* King, welcome after the rigidity of his mother's Court. It was what almost everybody thought – everybody except Arthur Thornley.

'Not *my* idea of the King of England,' he growled to Jane. 'Not enough weight in the metal, if you ask me. Mark my words, Janey . . . he won't be the man his father was.'

She was to remember the prediction months afterwards, and weep over it, because by then Arthur couldn't know that events had proved him right. Long before Edward abandoned the throne at the end of the year to marry Wallis Simpson, Arthur himself was dead, the victim of a spring influenza epidemic. Jane had lived with him for sixty years and, given the option, would have chosen to die with him as well.

Gertrude went to see her after the funeral and found her in the conservatory, repotting begonia cuttings with her usual care.

'I thought I'd find you in here . . . are you all right, my dear?'

'Yes, as long as I keep busy. I can't bear the rest of this huge house – I rattle about in it like one pea in a pod; but I'm not lonely in here. I can pretend that Arthur's going to come in any minute and grumble at me for doing Fitton's work!' She brushed away sudden tears and smiled resolutely at her friend. 'In any case, I seem to think better with my hands in a flower-pot.'

'What are you thinking about?' Gertrude enquired gently. 'I know Frank's anxious for you to sell Bicton and move to Providence. You don't need telling how dearly welcome you'd be, but it's what *you* want to do that matters.'

The affection in her voice brought a tinge of colour into Jane's pale face, and she leaned forward to kiss Gertrude's cheek. 'I keep wanting to weep for the family and friends I'm blessed with. All the same, love, I'm not selling Bicton. I'm afraid Frank will say I'm mad, but you must help me convince him that what I'm going to do is something that would have made Arthur happy.'

'Tell me and I'll help.'

Jane brushed earth off her hands and removed her gardening apron. 'Better sit down . . . it'll take some explaining.' They settled themselves in wicker chairs under a canopy of sweet-scented stephanotis and her story was begun.

'Do you remember Ned bringing his Austrian friend, Peter Hoffer, here one day – the doctor he met at Craiglockhart?'

Gertrude nodded, remembering the occasion very well. He'd come to visit them at Providence, and convinced that he should see the worst as well as the best the valley could offer, Ned had insisted on taking him to inspect Arthur's yellow-brick monstrosity.

'Bicton made him shout with laughter, and I liked him from then on,' Jane confessed, 'because it was exactly what *you* told me to do, the first time you came here.'

'What's that got to do with Bicton now?' Gertrude asked, smiling at her.

'Ned put the idea into my head by mentioning the other day that Dr Hoffer has come back to this country for good.' She broke off, distracted for a moment from her own affairs. 'Gertrude, terrible things are beginning to happen in Europe. Can you believe that there's no place in Germany or Austria for good men who happen to have Jewish blood in their veins? According to Dr Hoffer, we're only at the start of dreadful persecution and suffering. I asked Frank what *he* thought, and he had to agree – Germany's on the war-path again. Hitler's reoccupation of the Rhineland is just the first step; he isn't going to be satisfied with *that*.'

Gertrude nodded, reluctant to add William's pessimism to Frank's. He did his best not to frighten her but she couldn't help but know that he was seriously perturbed. Whatever a lackadaisical Government might pretend, a conspiracy of evil was gaining ground. Italian designs on Abyssinia were sinister, and German ambitions on the Continent even worse. Even a peace-loving man like William was forced to see re-armament as vital and another war with Germany as almost inevitable.

Gertrude closed her mind against such horror and dragged the conversation back to Bicton. 'Peter has had to come to England, but I still don't know what that has to do with you.'

'I'm going to offer him the house,' Jane said simply. 'Ned says he's been doing marvellous work in Austria, pioneering a way of treating disturbed children. He doesn't need complicated equipment – just space and peacefulness to work in. Nobody can say Bicton hasn't got plenty of both, and Arthur has left me more money than I shall ever want. If Dr Hoffer accepts, I shall run the house and pay the bills, and he can do the rest.'

She stared at her friend's face. 'You're not saying anything. I shall be bitterly disappointed if you're against the idea.'

Gertrude struggled against the deadening weight of reluctance she felt inside. Somehow she must push it aside and answer Jane with the enthusiasm she deserved.

'Of course it's a glorious way of using Bicton,' she said eventually. 'Arthur *would* have loved it, and I can't imagine Peter Hoffer possibly refusing the offer.'

Sharing the news with William afterwards, she wasn't prepared for him to ask why she disliked the idea of sick children being cured at Bicton.

'Was it so obvious? Put like that, it sounds downright wicked, not just unreasonable,' she confessed slowly. 'And why don't I rejoice that Ned will have his dear friend, Peter, within reach?'

'Because you're worrying about Frank. He makes a habit of distrusting foreigners, and he expects Jane to sell Bicton. The news that she intends to make a gift of *these* proportions to an Austrian Jew she scarcely knows will strike him as the extremity of madness.' William stared at his wife's troubled face. 'Isn't *that* what's worrying you?'

'Yes, but there's something worse still. He'll blame Ned for having introduced Peter to Jane at all. After their village quarrel Frank and Ned patched up a sort of friendship, but it can't stand more than the strains of every day. It certainly won't be able to survive *this* new burden, and Lucy will have to choose between them again. It's what she's had to do all her married life – make intolerable choices between what her mind and her heart prompt her to.'

Gertrude was right to anticipate that Frank would disapprove bitterly of his mother's scheme, but she went ahead with it, trusting in the blind conviction that Arthur would have approved of the Thornley-Hoffer Institute for Children. Once Peter understood the richness of what she was offering him, he accepted it with the stunned delight of a man who had been shown a vision of the Kingdom of Heaven. He had left his homeland heart-sick, and fearful of what was about to happen to it. There was no choice; he must come to England. But the best he looked forward to was a routine hospital post, and the traditional methods of treatment that overworked doctors could only apply indiscriminately to all the children under their care. He knew with absolute certainty that he could do better than that, but accepted that short of a miracle he would never have the chance of proving it. The miracle had happened, and led him with Ned's help to a small, courageous, and extraordinary woman called Jane Thornley.

In the course of dinner at Providence one evening he described their progress in getting the Institute ready for its first patients.

'The dream is about to come true,' Ned said, smiling affectionately at him. 'You're deeply content in a way, but I expected you to be brimming over with excitement. Why aren't you?'

'Because your brother-in-law's no nearer accepting the Institute now than he was six months ago when we started the alterations to the house. His mother pretends not to mind, but I know that it is making her unhappy. We can't possibly give up now, but I have a struggle not to hate Frank Thornley . . . and *there*'s an admission from a man who is supposed to know how to sublimate anger!'

'You're a man, not a saint,' Mary pointed out gently. 'Frank won't hold out in the end. He's a hard opponent to win over, but he can always be persuaded by success. When the Institute is working – curing children, or

261

making their lives at least bearable and useful – *then* he'll come round.'

Ned smiled at his friend. 'You might as well accept what my beloved says. She's occasionally wrong about the finer points of good farming principles, but never about people!'

'Then I shall wait patiently for Thornley to admit to Frau Jane that he was mistaken,' Peter said quietly. 'I suspect that he will never admit it to me, but that doesn't matter.'

The Institute received its first batch of violent, troubled children, some of them victims of the violent, troubled world Peter himself had escaped from. He began the slow, patient work of mending them, and gradually it became known outside the valley that remarkable things were being achieved at Bicton. Still, Frank withdrew his hostility so reluctantly that even Jane almost ran out of excuses for him. She tried to explain to Gertrude that he was bound to ignore what Peter was doing. The world was sliding towards disaster, and Frank was burdened with more knowledge and more responsibility than any one man could fairly endure. The Thornley factories were being turned over to the production of armaments again. The outbreak of civil war in Spain was just one more proof in the summer of 1936 that madness was running riot.

'Frank is scarcely ever here,' Jane admitted, 'but I can't blame him for that when his life is taken over by work for the Government. Lucy tries to make up for him, though. Bless her, she's often here, but she doesn't only come out of kindness. It seems to me that she's deeply interested in what Peter is doing . . . even to the point of wanting to learn how to help, no matter how heartbreaking the work is at times.'

Gertrude stared at her friend and, almost without hesitation, put into words the truth they both knew. 'She's deeply in need of *something* worthwhile to do. When happiness can't be found anywhere else, there's comfort in just loving the children, but being taught how to help them is even better.'

'Frank's fault . . . all the unhappiness?' Jane asked slowly.

'I don't think Lucy would say so. But helping to put shattered children together again must seem to her a wonderfully positive thing to do, especially in the world we live in now.' She remembered suddenly a piece of news that had been wildly rumoured for several days and finally confirmed. 'Nothing is safe from upheaval even here. William heard the King speaking over the wireless, Jane. In order that he can be free to marry Mrs Simpson, he *is* going to abdicate. The Duke of York will be crowned King instead.'

She expected Jane, a devoted royalist, to look devastated by the news, but saw a proud smile touch her friend's face instead.

'Arthur was right, after all. He *said* Edward wouldn't make a proper king, my dear.'

Chapter Twenty-Two

Josephine only went to London for small ordeals that couldn't be avoided. Routine visits to the dentist, which she didn't mind at all, entailed staying for at least one night at her mother's flat in Pont Street, above the elegant premises of Blanchard et Cie. She hated the deliberately French-sounding name, the rich women who went there to buy Sybil's clothes, and the ultra-modern setting that her mother had chosen to live in. The décor of the flat might have struck a country-bred adolescent as novel and exciting, but Josephine was accustomed to the shabby beauty of Providence, which her grandmother still patiently repaired and cherished. It wasn't the mill at Pont-sur-Seine, but it didn't clash with memories of what had been her home. Black glass, silver chrome, and huge armchairs covered in white leather offended her. She saw that such things matched the cool, modern style Sybil Blanchard had made her own, but she rejected them for herself and grew out of childhood believing that her mother was a beautiful puzzle she would never understand.

There were only two things to be said for London: it held treasures that Henri Blanchard's daughter meant to learn about; and it was the home of her only real friend – her godmother, Anita Trentham. At the house in Walton Place, especially if cousin Harry wasn't there, she could talk in French to someone who remembered Pont-sur-Seine; better still, Anita understood her determination to learn all that her father had known.

One morning when she called there she was disappointed to find none of the family at home; even Anita's small daughter, Katherine, was out, playing in the park with her governess. The only person the drawing-room contained was a tall young man she hadn't seen for more than a year. She hadn't forgotten him, nor the conversation that had ended so abruptly when she ran away from him into the wood at Providence. It had been something to regret afterwards, and the memory of it now made her greet him stiffly.

Christopher Wyndham observed that she was no more friendly than before, but a year had made a startling difference to her physically. She'd grown tall and slender, and now held herself with a free grace different from the maidenly aim instilled by English mothers in their daughters, of concealing bosom and hips. Beside Victoria at Providence, she'd always seemed not only foreign but sullen and rather plain; now, she'd become an interesting, olive-skinned oddity, beautifully dressed in the clothes her mother chose for her.

He put aside the magazine he'd been flicking through and got up to shake hands. 'Good morning, Josephine. Is this a holiday, or have you escaped from the schoolroom to come jaunting about town?'

'I haven't jaunted very far – only from Pont Street. Maman is busy, of course, but I hoped my godmother might be here.'

'She's with Harry at Westminster, for a rehearsal of the Coronation ceremony. My grandfather's there too, of course – he can never bear to miss anything!'

Josephine's face was suddenly bright with mischief. 'You were looking very glum when I walked in – like one of those problem pictures my grandfather says the Royal Academy used to be so fond of. "Portrait of a young man about to make a confession to his guardian" might have done as a title! I should have known you were just disapproving of the royal goings-on, like a good Irishman.'

Christopher stared at her, not sure whether to be irked or amused. He had never seen her before with laughter lighting her dark eyes and tilting the corners of her mouth. It was a startling change from the morose expression she always seemed to wear at Providence. On the other hand, she was still a schoolgirl and ought to behave like one; she wasn't supposed to laugh at someone who'd outgrown the stage of being an undergraduate, and was conscious of his dignity.

'I'm *never* glum, and I'm an American citizen – though of pro-Irish sympathies,' he said distinctly, to make matters clear. 'You still haven't said why you are here instead of in sleepy Warwickshire.'

She heard the frosty note in his voice and felt disappointed in him. 'Grandpa William is on the Hanging Committee at Burlington House. I came to keep an eye on him for Grandma.' She said it without a smile, and went on to correct an error of his own. 'By the way, Victoria isn't quite past doing lessons, but I *am*. If girls still wore long hair nowadays, mine would be *up* by now.'

'I'm sorry . . . Stupid of me not to realize,' he apologized, amused himself this time, 'but it's been quite a long while since my last visit to Providence.' Then his mouth relaxed into a smile, and Josephine observed the effect with interest. When his thin face was laughing, it was a good deal more attractive than the conventional, fair good looks of her Thornley cousins. She noticed that his eyes were deeply blue, just like her godmother's; but better than anything else he looked intelligent – as if he might easily understand the things that Charles Thornley *never* did. She knew about his parents' separation from the rest of the family, and that, too, made him interesting.

'You don't come to Providence very often,' she said consideringly. 'When you *do*, I suppose it's only to please your grandfather.'

'Something like that. I come occasionally because I have to, but I don't intend to make a habit of it.'

She nodded, pleased that they had in common the feeling of being separate from the people who lived at Providence. *He* had chosen not to fall under its ancient spell, either, and the knowledge made her feel less lonely. She was a Blanchard, not a Wyndham at all, and she *wanted* to be different; but there were times when she badly wanted a home to belong to as well.

266

The sudden sweetness of her smile took him by surprise. He knew as much about *her* story as she knew about his, but it had taken him until now to realize that she'd used surliness to conceal grief. Her mother had chosen London; Josephine, with no choice at all, had been left to make what she could of relations she didn't know, and Providence.

'So schooldays are over. What comes next . . . the art studies you once told me about?' He managed to sound genuinely interested, and she discovered for the first time that it was pleasurable to talk about herself.

'My mother wants to send me to the finishing-school in Switzerland that *she* went to, but I've made up my mind that it's not what I'm going to do. I shall start studying here on my own until I'm old enough to enrol at the Courtauld Institute of Art.'

'That will mean living in London . . . won't you hate that?'

She gave a little shrug, reminding him that she was more adult and more foreign than he kept remembering. 'I can bear London for as long as I have to . . . It's only until I can go back to France.'

'Do you still have a home there?'

'No . . . the mill had to be sold, Maman said.' Her expression was tragic for a moment, then changed with a speed that bewildered him. 'Perhaps I shall find myself a *very* rich husband so that he can buy it back for me!'

Christopher thought she might very well succeed. Her eyes and mouth were still too large for the rest of her face, but wouldn't be so much longer. Her body was already beautifully put together, and once the awkwardness of being sixteen was left behind, he doubted if she would have much difficulty in attracting men.

'The rich husband, by all means,' he agreed. 'But while you're waiting for him to materialize, why not stay at Providence and be taught by your grandfather?'

'I don't wish to study how to *make* paintings, you understand. I want to learn how to tell good from bad, how to look after them, and clean them without hurting them.'

'So that we see what Titian and Rembrandt actually painted, instead of a blanket of grime?'

She nodded, happy to be proved right. He *did* understand. Out of sheer loneliness, she'd once made the mistake of confiding her ambition to Tom. All he could suggest was that it would be easier to throw old paintings away and start again.

'One day I shall work at the Louvre – that's where Papa's collection of modern paintings now hangs. Who should look after them but me?'

'Your mother would like *that*, I imagine.'

Josephine shook her head, and her face was suddenly full of haunting sadness. She looked too adult to be sixteen. 'I think my mother would rather I did anything but that. She doesn't like me to remember my father.'

Christopher had seen Sybil Blanchard in the company of his aunt and grandfather in London. She was successful, amusing, sophisticated by any standards – dazzlingly so to a young man used to Dublin society; but he wasn't convinced that Josephine was right about her mother. He wondered how to say so, but hesitated too long. She had already changed the conversation.

'You said one day that you refused to choose between England and Ireland. I think you're wrong . . . people have to choose in the end, one way or the other.'

He stared at her grave face, unaware again of the age gap between them, and of the strangeness of taking her understanding for granted. 'If I'd been old enough years ago, I'd have made the choice my father made, and fought for Irish freedom. Now, I shall choose neither Dublin nor London. My plan was to go to study in America, but Medical School must wait . . . there's something else I have to do first.' A charming smile softened the sharp lines of his face. 'What you said when you came in was uncomfortably near the mark . . . I did come here to make a sort of confession! My grandfather won't like it, but I rely on Aunt Anita; she's rather good at keeping him in order.'

Josephine wished very much that he would ask her to

stay and hear his confession, too. After that first moment of stiffness she'd felt so at ease with him that she'd forgotten the gap between sixteen and twenty-one. There was nothing she couldn't say to him, nothing he wouldn't understand. But she felt obliged to suggest that she could come another time to see her godmother, and he merely led the way out of the room to see her to the front door. Disappointment made her face expressionless again, but he was beginning to know that it was merely a façade she often chose to hide behind. He was surprised to discover that he wanted to help her if he could.

'Don't let anyone stop you doing what *you* think is right,' he said abruptly. 'They'll put all sorts of obstacles in your way, with the very best intentions, but you must keep your eyes fixed on the target *you've* seen in front of you.' His face looked so grave, that she realized his advice was for himself as well as for her. The need for it was something else they had in common. She stood still, because the moment and the conversation were too important not to be committed to memory, and he leaned forward on an impulse he didn't properly understand, to kiss her cheek. She turned her head and his mouth touched her lips instead. For a second or two they trembled under his, then she broke away from him and fled down the steps to the pavement. The moment had become more important still, and there was no chance that she would ever forget it now.

Before she went back to Providence she heard from her mother what his confession had been. He was going to Spain, to enlist in the International Brigade fighting for the Republicans against Franco's Nationalist Army. It didn't occur to her that he might not come back at all; he was simply making a choice and going to fight for a cause, as his father had done. She thought instead of the unimaginable spaces of America that would swallow him up afterwards. It didn't *matter*, of course, because her own future was mapped out, but she was more lonely than before, and even her shining vision of Paris lost a little of its lustre when she remembered the feel of his mouth against her own.

Victoria was more well-disposed towards her cousin than usual. She didn't underestimate the will-power needed to withstand Aunt Sybil when her mind was made up, but Josephine had finally won the battle over the Swiss finishing-school. The victory was important because, if she'd failed, Victoria herself would have been packed off there as well. It was a terrible prospect to a girl whose only ambition in life was to become a veterinary surgeon. She explained to Tom, home from Rugby for the summer holiday, how close the shave had been.

'Stupid . . . all you had to do was tell Father that you didn't want to go . . . he wouldn't have minded a scrap,' Tom pointed out. 'You know as well as I do that he's not a bit keen on foreigners.'

Victoria sighed and shook her head. She loved Tom dearly – he was the best of brothers, kind and calm and sensible; just like Grandma Thornley; but he *wasn't* sharply intellectual, and the finer points of life that she knew needed thinking about often passed him by.

'I know Father wouldn't have minded, but Mama seemed so set on it that I couldn't bear to say it was the last thing I wanted to do.'

After working outside with his uncle all day, Tom's face was burned to an unsightly pink that clashed with his fair hair. It wore an expression, affectionate but critical, that she was used to.

'You're too soft, Tor, that's your trouble. How are you going to tell some hulking great yokel that he's ill-treating his animals if you can't manage to stand up for yourself here?'

'It's not size that daunts me,' she said truthfully, 'only hurting people, and having to take sides.'

'Between our parents, I suppose you mean?' he muttered after a long pause.

Victoria nodded, caught his eye, and saw there the same anxiety that troubled her. 'There's something wrong,' she said with sadness. 'It's such a lovely life we live here that you'd think *anybody* could be happy, but they aren't. Uncle Ned and Mary seem almost like two halves of the same person. I know marriage isn't always as perfect as that, but our parents are *polite* to one another, like strangers.'

Tom examined a graze on his hand as if he'd just discovered it, and finally delivered himself of the worry that had burdened him for several days.

'Do you realize that Father hates Peter Hoffer. I only discovered it when I told him that I'd joined the OTC at school. What do you think he said? "I suppose your mother isn't the only one who listens to that damned Austrian at Bicton. Oblige me by having nothing to do with him in future."'

'What on earth did you say?' Victoria breathed, distracted for a moment from her main worry.

His expression hardened into the mulish obstinacy that occasionally reminded her of Charlie. 'I told Father that Peter was my *friend*, of course. It didn't go down very well, but I can't help that.' His troubled eyes met Victoria's again. 'It's odd all round because, apart from the fact that Peter is a marvellous chap and a doctor besides, I thought Father would be pleased about the OTC. He knows better than anyone that we shall have to stop Hitler one day.'

Victoria nodded but didn't look surprised. Grown-ups quite often expected of them behaviour they didn't produce themselves – like common-sense and consistency.

Tom suddenly remembered how the conversation had begun. 'What's Josephine going to do now?'

'Live in London with Aunt Sybil for a bit, so that she can study art. It'll seem funny not having her here, even though she never makes much noise. I used to think I hated her for not seeing how lovely Providence is, but it was only pretend . . . I couldn't manage to hate her at all.'

'I don't envy her London, *or* Aunt Sybil – good fun, but too much to cope with except in small doses! Do you remember how old Hodges used to run on about everything that happened years ago? "Reg'lar little tartar" he'd say, and I never knew who he meant – Aunt Sybil or Great-Aunt Louise. When I asked him one day he said proudly, "Both of 'em . . . like as two peas in a pod, they were"!'

Victoria's peal of laughter floated over the wall into the stable yard; anxiety was forgotten for a moment, or made bearable by the security of Providence wrapped about them like a warm, familiar cloak. Nothing too dreadful could happen, because they were all there, enclosed by it and kept from harm.

Lucy wavered on the verge of telling Artie to unsaddle the mare again; by the sound of it, the children were back, and when she was with them she could forget for a while her driving need to be at Bicton. The moment of hesitation came and went without her saying anything. Artie stood waiting for her to ride away, and in the end she did. It would be for the last time . . . knowing *that* was what had stopped her from going for days past.

In the beginning she'd gone to the Institute simply to lessen Jane's embarrassment; if Frank refused to show the slightest interest in it then she *must*. It had been only a short step from that to finding herself concerned with the children who arrived filthy, violent, or silently locked in memories of an ugly world that some adult had inflicted on them. She had been concerned, but afraid, until Peter Hoffer had begun to teach her how *not* to be afraid; she had learned to love the children, and love had made her confident in helping them. It was an unlooked-for path to happiness, and the quiet Austrian was the last man she would have expected to find it for her; unlike anyone else she'd ever known, he'd begun by being simply Ned's clever, foreign friend, whose ugly face and gentle hands seemed capable of instilling peace in even the most seriously disturbed child.

She reined in the mare on the slope looking down over the gardens at Bicton. Even softened by the greenery all round it, the house remained comic in its riot of turrets and curlicues, but although she might not see it again after today she would always remember it. There were children playing outside on the ingenious toys Peter and his helpers had constructed for them, but he wasn't with them; inside, she found only an assistant in the music room, where rage and grief and hurt could be eased by the frantic banging of drums and cymbals. She had watched these expressions of anger being gradually transmuted into the happiness of learning to make not only noise but music; and she had never known any of the children fail to listen when Peter played to them.

She found him at last in the small room that had become his study. He stopped writing when she went in, got up from his desk, and smiled. She must be used to that, he thought; there surely wasn't a man living who failed to smile a welcome at Lucy Thornley. Ned had told him something about her; the rest, having met her husband, he guessed. Finding quiet fulfilment at Bicton had become a necessity for her. Hiding what he felt about her had become a necessity for *him*.

Lucy stared at the dressing on his hand; blood was seeping through the bandage, and for a moment it made her forget what she had come to say.

'Nothing to worry about . . . it looks worse than it is,' he said lightly.

'An accident with your razor?'

'No, I was careless in a different way.' He put the subject aside, and she had to persist because she had to know.

'Trouble with a new patient, perhaps?'

'A little . . . I didn't allow sufficiently for Irish ingenuity! Danny O'Hara arrived with a pen-knife hidden in his shoe, and I was clumsy in persuading him to part with it. Thank God he vented his anger on *me*. Forget it, please, and tell me why we haven't seen you for several days.'

Lucy still stared at his hand, wondering how she would find the strength to stay away from Bicton and never know what was happening to him there, and to the children.

'I came to say goodbye,' she said jerkily. 'This is my last visit.'

The room felt cold and quiet, and his face looked cold, too . . . and more stern than she had ever seen it.

'Why? I thought you were happy here.'

She forced her lips to smile, and even managed a shrug that almost convinced him. 'It's been interesting, but the . . . the novelty wears off after a while. Frank said it would, and I should know by now that my husband is *always* right!'

The voice that offered these inane lies must belong to her; she could hear it echoing in her head, bright and intolerably flippant. She couldn't look at his face now, stared at the floor instead, expecting to see it strewn with the broken fragments of her heart.

'I'm glad that we kept you interested for a while!' He spoke very quietly, while a voice shouted inside his head that *this* woman above all others should have known that damaged children were *not* sent by God to amuse a bored wife whose husband ignored her. He would, *must*, tell her so; but when he looked at her, rage faltered and died. Her mouth tried to smile, but she could do nothing about the desolation in her eyes.

He came to stand in front of her, so that she couldn't move away from him. 'Shall we have the truth now? I think the real reason is your husband. He has never approved of the Institute; never approved of *me*, I suppose I mean, because I didn't refuse his mother's generosity. I accept that he can ask you not to come, but I will not allow you to pretend that you've grown bored with the children. Why did you?'

'So as *not* to have to tell the truth,' she confessed in a low voice. 'Frank resents my visits, but he wouldn't demean himself – that's how he would see it – by asking me not to come. I couldn't come and conceal the fact, even if I wanted to, because Mrs Knightly would keep him informed. She's the housekeeper he brought down from London when our house there was sold. For some reason that I don't understand, she hates me as much as she loves him.' Lucy stopped to gather courage together and then went on speaking. 'I was unfaithful to him years ago in London. I didn't tell Frank, but I'm sure *she* knew . . . perhaps that's why she watches me now.'

'Is that why your marriage now is . . . as it is?'

'It's never been other than as it is . . . a total failure,' she said steadily, 'my fault, mostly, not his. The London interlude wasn't important, although I thought it was at the time. Now I know what is important . . . that's why I can't come here again.' She felt, with a vague sense of pride, that she had done rather well. The truth had been told without putting any burden at all on a man who needn't even acknowledge that he knew what the truth was.

Peter walked away from her over to the window, and stood staring out at the sunlit gardens. 'I thought Frank hated me because I was an Austrian, a Jew, a sponger – as he saw it – on his mother's matchless generosity. Now, I doubt if it was that at all. He knew, in the way that a man does know, that I should fall irretrievably in love with his wife.'

Lucy heard the quiet, calm voice that might just have been mentioning that it was very warm for July. She ducked her head against sudden faintness, because unless she was going mad, she *had* heard what he'd said. Then he walked towards her, and she felt his arms holding her with more tenderness than she'd known existed in the world.

She lifted her head to smile, wanted to sing and dance and weep for the joy that was flooding over her, but his own face was full of anguish. 'Heart of my heart, don't look like that. Even if I could ignore the fact that your husband loves you to the point of pain . . .'

'. . . you can't ignore the fact that it's Jane who makes the Institute possible,' she interrupted him. 'I know there's nothing we can do to change that. I shall learn to live without you because I must – it's one of the few advantages there are to growing older . . . growing up, at last. Heaven won't grant me what I want, but I finally discovered who and what it was I loved.' She bent her head to touch his bandaged hand gently with her mouth, and then she smiled. '"Kiss it and make it better." That's what our nurse used to say when we were children. Will you promise faithfully to inspect the shoes of all your new patients in future?'

Her smile went awry, and not even for the debt he owed Jane Thornley could he stop himself from holding her close against his heart. His mouth came down on hers, and the world swung off its axis for a moment or two of time and went wheeling out into space.

Finally, with a voice hammering in his brain that he must stop before it was too late, he lifted his head and held her away from him.

'You must go, my dearest, and not come back, but I *must* say it once in my own language . . . *Ich liebe dich, mein herz.*'

'And I shall love you for as long as I live, and try my hardest not to worry about you.'

'Am I not to worry about you?'

'There's no need. I shall find something else to do. Aunt Louise has been telling me for years that I should bestir myself . . . become a Justice of the Peace, get myself elected to the County Council, to Parliament even, so that the Woman's Voice can be heard. I shall become what Mama says the new Vicar's wife is – *very* deedy!'

He smiled because she required him to, and didn't move when she turned and fled from the room, out of his life.

Chapter Twenty-Three

London at the beginning of 1938 was an edgy, nervously excited place. Neville Chamberlain – Prime Minister, after Stanley Baldwin, of a Government that was 'National' in name only – continued to believe what no-one else believed: that he alone could sit down with wolves and not get eaten. On the day in March when Hitler ended the farce of Austria's so-called independence by ordering his army to invade, Harry went home from Westminster to tell his wife that war, sooner or later, was now inevitable.

'It's not just Germany, is it?' she asked, looking at his face. 'There's more worrying you even than that.'

'It's the whole infamous Axis plot. The Japanese, hell-bent on expansion, pin us down in the Far East, that bombastic Italian swine's doing the same thing in the Mediterranean. Hitler is left with a free hand in Central Europe to carve out *his* mad dream of a Greater Germany.'

'What about our allies?' Anita asked hopefully. 'We must *have* some, even if the League of Nations will do nothing but wring its collective hands.'

'Our allies must be making Hitler weep for joy. Look at them – Russia on our side for as long as it suits *her*, the Americans safely invisible on the far side of a nice wide ocean, and the French broken reeds. And our leader is an arrogant Victorian civil-servant who believes he can tame the devil by talking to him.'

'Even my father agrees with you about Chamberlain,' Anita had to confess. 'Can't Attlee take some kind of lead on behalf of the Labour Party?'

'He is on the record as voting in the House against re-armament,' Harry said in a voice of near-despair. 'I *know* we pinned our hopes on the collective security of the

League after the carnage of the war, but to refuse to accept re-armament *now* is national suicide.'

'My dear, we *are* re-arming. Frank isn't free with his confidences, but it's perfectly clear that the Thornley factories and many more besides are being turned over to munitions again, as fast as possible. We shall start from behind, of course, but remember the tortoise and the hare!'

Harry smiled at last. 'The small quiet voice of reason!' To his way of thinking, if his wife changed at all with age it was only to grow more serenely lovely. Marriage and motherhood had added the one attraction she had ever lacked – the warmth of manner that made an instant gift of her loving heart to other people. When he remembered that he'd once imagined he disliked her, he could only conclude that he'd been certifiably insane at the time.

There was someone else he'd been wrong about, too, and he chose this moment to admit his error. 'I used to loathe Frank Thornley . . . took it for granted that he stood for everything I disapproved of. Now, if we're to survive the next few years, it will be because men like him are working themselves into early graves, and digging into their own pockets to pay for the industrial research that ought to be a Government responsibility.'

She knew that it was a generous confession for Harry to have made. He probably didn't like Lucy's husband any more now than before, and in truth Frank seemed to go out of his way to make it difficult for people to like him; but they shared a patriotism that, if not discredited, had certainly become unfashionable. Harry had persisted in seeing him as a cowardly war-time profiteer, but he saw him more clearly now. She suspected that he had also hated Frank for having bought Lucy, but even that no longer mattered. He was too content with his own wife and daughter to begrudge the chance of happiness to anyone else, and more likely to feel sorry for a man who clearly hadn't won the elusive prize. Relationships were inexplicable, private things, but Anita knew her cousin's marriage had failed. Whenever she was with Lucy she felt oppressed by sadness, and guilty to have received herself such an unequal share of joy.

'Charles is doing brilliantly at Cambridge – mopping up all the chemistry prizes,' she said, determined to find something to sound cheerful about. 'Arthur Thornley was a trial in some ways, but I can't help wishing he were still alive to see his grandson overtaking all the swells at King's!'

'My love, he wouldn't have had the slightest doubt that a Thornley was bound to do just that. Sublime self-confidence wasn't the least of Arthur's qualities, and Charlie's inherited it.'

'Only on the surface, I think. Rugby and Cambridge, and his father's wealth, have given him the gloss of outward assurance.' She smiled at Harry's expression and conceded a little more. 'All right, he comes close to being unpleasantly cocksure at times! But I think it proves my point . . . he's hopelessly *unsure* when it comes to dealing with people.'

'You didn't mention what Providence has done for him,' Harry pointed out thoughtfully. 'Hasn't that made a difference to Arthur Thornley's grandson?'

'It's confused him, that's all; he can't make up his mind whether to hate or love it. The poor lad will have to decide, since it will be his one day.' Amusement glimmered in her face as she smiled at Harry. 'I feel like Madame Arcati peering into my crystal ball! What else shall I tell you about our joint family?'

'You could have a shot at telling me that all is well with it, but I doubt if I should believe you.'

'Well, Ned's all right with Mary. Aunt Gertrude grieves over their lack of children, and probably Mary does too; but I think Ned accepts it in a curious way, as part of a predetermined pattern . . . the end of the Wyndhams at Providence.'

Harry nodded; it *was* exactly what his cousin might think. 'Are you going to tell me Sybil is all right, too?'

'She's happier than she was, at least,' Anita said slowly, 'because she and Josephine are gradually coming to terms, after years of not knowing one another at all. With her daughter living in the flat, Sybil has to be rather more decorous, and I wouldn't be surprised if she'd discovered that life is delightfully restful without lovers!'

Harry's shout of laughter disturbed Anita's beautiful Siamese cat, who stared inimically at him and then stalked out of the room. Still laughing, he stooped over Anita to kiss her mouth. 'I hope you're not about to tell me that you'd find it more restful without a husband?'

'More restful perhaps, but *much* less enjoyable!'

'Truth and tact combined . . . what more could a man ask!' He smiled lovingly at her, but returned to the subject of Sybil's daughter. 'It seems to me that Josephine is the one who's changed. She was having tea with Charlotte when I called in last, and I scarcely recognized her. Not only has she become rather attractive in some unusual way of her own, but she was actually laughing.'

'She's growing up, and leaving some of the agonizing uncertainties of adolescence behind her. Knowing what she wants to do, and being confident that her father would have approved, makes her happy, but there's a little more to it than that. For the first time she's beginning to appreciate her mother as well. One day she may even understand that Sybil is not only clever and hard-working, but a brave, loyal woman who might have loved her daughter more if she'd loved her husband less. *That*'s what Josephine has always held against her . . . the mistaken feeling that Sybil didn't love either of them enough.'

Anita gave a little sigh, then made haste to smile at her tired husband. 'It's late, my love. Go and kiss Kate good night, and let us thank God that we have a ten-year-old daughter instead of a son old enough to go to war.'

She watched him walk out of the room, and knew that in talking about the family she'd wanted to avoid having to discuss Lucy. That once-tranquil, gentle girl was forever smiling, and constantly busy in order to keep God alone knew *what* sadness at bay. Anita loved her enough to want to hate Frank Thornley, but how was it possible to hate a man whose haggard face proclaimed his own unhappiness?

The uneasy spring gave way to a summer overshadowed by the worry of events on the Continent. By no means content with Austria, Hitler's demands grew increasingly strident. The Treaty of Versailles had condemned millions of Sudeten Germans to be separated from the Fatherland. They must be allowed to secede from the new state of Czechoslovakia and return to the fold. The Governments of France and England, paralysed by the Führer's rhetoric, seemed to agree that *he* was being less unreasonable to the Czechs than the Treaty of Versailles had been to Germany. Harry, raging from the back benches of the House, found himself for the first time in his political life ranged alongside a maverick firebrand called Winston Churchill. A groundswell of anger that something shameful was being connived at by England and France made no difference to their Governments' conduct of affairs. A small country would have to be coerced into allowing itself to be dismembered; if it refused, it faced the hopeless prospect of withstanding Hitler's armies alone.

At Providence one day Harry found himself giving vent to rage in the quietness of the Great Hall. 'It's treachery . . . so cynical and dishonest that I'm ashamed to call myself an Englishman.'

'*Quite* as bad as that, do you think, dear boy?' William queried doubtfully. 'Our hearts may bleed for the poor Czechs, but we have no treaty obligation towards them.'

'No, but France *has*, and *we* are bound by treaty to support France. It's betrayal all along the line, and something else as well – utter folly, which is being sold to us as the only sensible way of dealing with a madman. Hitler is convinced that we shall never do anything to stop him. He only has to decide what he would like to swallow next – Poland, probably.'

'We have little to stop him *with*, at the moment,' Ned pointed out quietly. 'Frank is convinced that if we pushed Hitler into war now, we should lose. Czechoslovakia's fate is the price of buying the rest of us time; no consolation to them, but it might be vital in the long run.'

Harry snorted with disgust, but couldn't disagree. 'Yes, and *that*'s what years of inertia and complacency have brought us to.'

The rest of what he had been going to say was omitted in deference to Gertrude Wyndham's arrival in the room. He knew the views of a Victorian like William – men were obliged to protect women from the horrors men had to confront. Harry's view was that Gertrude and his own mother were more capable of surviving horrors than most men, and that the events of the past twenty-five years had proved it.

She smiled at him with the beautiful kindness that had been his earliest memory of her. 'Harry dear, your presence is required outside. Victoria thinks the first lesson has lasted long enough, but Kate particularly wishes you to see before you leave how well she sits her pony.'

He knew that his aunt's gentle insistence was deliberate. Whatever international terrors consumed his peace of mind, a father was not excused from putting them aside to watch his daughter astride a pony for the first time. It was Gertrude Wyndham's way of reminding him of the small, important things of life. He got up and walked to the door, leaving an unexpected kiss on her cheek as he went out. He admired the performance in the stable yard, congratulated Kate and her smiling teacher, and kissed them both goodbye. A gap of six years in their age made no difference to their friendship, and he was well aware that a fortnight at Providence with Victoria wouldn't be nearly long enough to persuade Kate that she would rather be back in London with her parents.

He drove home framing a suggestion in his mind that he should take his wife on a brief visit to Paris. The invitation must be worded cunningly, or she would guess the frightful fear that was in his mind. If they didn't go soon to a place she loved, they might never go again at all.

But when Anita met him at the door the expression on her face wiped all thought of holiday invitations from his mind. 'My dearest . . . something's wrong. Is it James?'

She shook her head, trying to smile. 'Nothing is ever wrong with my father! Patrick telephoned from Dublin this morning. Christopher's been wounded in the fighting around Madrid . . . he's being brought back to London for surgery.'

'What sort of wound?'

'A bullet lodged in his head. He's blind . . . may remain so permanently.' She said the monstrous thing with such calm that someone who knew her less well than Harry did might have supposed her unfeeling, but it was her own way of coping with disaster . . . self-control mustn't be allowed to disintegrate into useless tears, and pride forbade a shameful whine against Fate. Every so often the Gods above had a way of cutting human beings down to size; it achieved nothing to whimper that they were being unfair.

'Sweetheart, is there anything we can do?'

'Not at the moment, except help Patrick when he arrives. He's going to leave Ishbel with her family . . . she's distraught, of course – not fit to travel.' Anita made the comment trying not to judge her sister-in-law, and went straight on to something else that set a frown of worry in her eyes. 'Josephine happened to be here when Patrick telephoned. There wasn't time to . . . to edit the news. I would have imagined that she scarcely knew Christopher, but she looked so stricken that I thought she was about to faint.'

'Why be surprised?' Harry asked unexpectedly. 'She's very like Sybil. Everything that happens, happens to *her*. The only difference between them is that Sybil never leaves you in any doubt about what she's feeling; Josephine says too little, and feels too much.' He stared at his wife's pale face and voiced another anxiety. 'How's James taking it? All his hopes are tied up in Christopher.'

'He's taking it as you might expect . . . making anxiety bearable by *doing* something. He's gone off to get advice. By the time Christopher arrives James will have waiting for him the best eye-surgeon that money, persuasion, or brute strength can supply.' She said it with a touch of pride, aware that even at the age of seventy-six her father was a force to be reckoned with. It had been a temptation some-times to think that *he* should have inherited Providence, instead of his gentle brother. He had a healthy respect for Lucy's husband, but even now he couldn't help feeling that no-one but a Wyndham had a true right there.

'Kate all right when you left her?' Anita asked. She knew the answer, but it was something else to concentrate on, rather than the thought of blind Christopher being carried back to London.

'My dear, I doubt if she even noticed me go! As long as she can get in the way of Ned and Victoria – "helping", she calls it – she asks very little more of life. Resign yourself to the fact that she's going to end up married to a man who owns a lot of land and loves a lot of animals. A city gent won't do for Kate at all!'

Two days later Christopher was in a hospital in London. By the end of a week he'd been operated on by the man James had been advised would save his grandson's sight if any surgeon living could. Now, he lay with bandaged eyes, forbidden to move or lift his head, while the agonizing weeks of waiting crawled by.

Anita left her father the task of distributing news around the family and chose for herself the more painful job of keeping Patrick company.

'Until these last few days I hadn't seen Sybil since I went to Providence for her grandfather's funeral,' he said suddenly one day. 'It's more than ten years ago, but I can't see any change in her at all.'

'Do you mean that she's still just as attractive, or just as provoking?' Anita suggested with a smile. 'I seem to remember that she had an infallible knack of rubbing you up the wrong way!'

Instead of answering her question, he asked one of his own. 'Why does her daughter behave as if they're compara-tive strangers who *might* manage to become friends?'

Anita frowned over the question, uncertain how much to say. 'I think they *have* been strangers to each other, and I can only make a guess at the reason because Sybil doesn't strew confidences about for the rest of us to pick up. My *impression* is that she felt a failure with Henri. Josephine walked straight into the innermost places of his heart, but Sybil always remained convinced that she was left outside. Josephine was too young to understand that her mother wasn't outside by choice. When they came back to England Sybil's life for a while was desperately hectic, full of so-called friends and admirers. They didn't make her happy, but they were necessary to prove that she wasn't always a failure. She's calmer now, I think, and resigned to whatever life has, or hasn't, given her.'

He abandoned the subject with a nod, and didn't return to it with his sister. For as long as he remained in London he made no conscious effort to avoid Sybil, but they never found themselves alone together until he was almost on the point of leaving for Dublin. They shook hands formally, like acquaintances, both knowing that, even after ten years, it would have been the most natural thing in the world to walk into each other's arms.

'I'm sorry Ishbel is so unwell,' Sybil said immediately. 'You must feel terribly torn, anxious about *her* but hating to leave before the result here is known.' The signs of strain were etched into his face, making him look older than his real age. She ached to kiss away his tiredness and share his anxiety. He was on the rack now about his son, but the truth was that much more than that ailed him. He'd chosen his life, and known that he must make the best of it since no other option was open to him. It wasn't much to say of a marriage, but it was all that could be said of his marriage to Ishbel O'Neil.

'I can only leave London at all knowing that Christopher is surrounded by the affection of a family I rejected for years,' Patrick said quietly.

'But reject no longer,' Sybil insisted. 'Isn't it something, at least, that Uncle James knows that he still has a son, after all? *Some* good has come out of evil, my dear, and even if it isn't of a kind to comfort Ishbel, *you* must accept it, as your father does.'

'I know . . . I do.' He wanted to say that his greatest

comfort came from being close to *her*, that his most terrible pain would be in walking away from her again. But these things couldn't be said, and he stood in silence beside her, aware with one level of his mind of her longing to comfort him, and with every nerve in his body of her nearness to him.

'Your father has been very kind to me in London, and takes a great interest in Josephine,' Sybil murmured when the silence between them seemed to have lasted too long. 'She isn't very approachable as a rule, but they've reached some kind of understanding. James even put up with her outburst over Christopher the other day when she was laying down the law – in a way quite worthy of *me*! – about the futility of getting involved in other people's battles. Christopher's job in life, according to my darling daughter, is to heal people, not get himself nearly killed because Spaniard insists on fighting Spaniard.'

'I come close to agreeing with her,' Patrick admitted. 'But years ago on that principle, I stayed out of a battle I now know I should have got into. Perhaps Christopher thought he was redressing the balance for me.' He smiled at her with the sweetness she still remembered from years ago. 'Go on – say it . . . maudlin self-indulgence! The fights my son chooses to get into are the ones he chooses for himself – nothing to do with me.'

'I'm not as sure as you are that our children don't feel obliged to do something about our mistakes.'

He stared at her as if it might be the last time he would ever see her and now he must forget nothing about her. Her face presumably owed something to clever make-up; but cosmetics, however skilfully applied, couldn't give it warmth and life and the quick intelligence that had always been hers. Nothing but the woman she *was* accounted for his longing to stay with her always.

'You have to go. Time and boat-trains wait for no man,' she murmured unsteadily.

His hands gripped her shoulders suddenly, starting a pulse beating in her throat. 'Will you take care of Christopher for me?'

'Of course. There was no need to ask.'

He tightened his hold, then deliberately found her mouth with his own. The kiss drew the heart out of her body. There was no passion in it, only a tender sweetness that admitted what couldn't be put into words.

'If we don't manage it before, shall we agree to meet in Heaven?'

She nodded, trying to smile. 'No misunderstandings there, I believe, and no goodbyes!'

Long after he had walked out of the room she still stood there. Heaven would be long in coming, but until it did she would have to manage without him.

Chapter Twenty-Four

Josephine was accustomed to being different from other people. She knew her fellow-students at the Courtauld Institute regarded her warily as an aloof, intense-looking foreigner whose family connections in the world of art were prestigious and unfair, but the idea didn't worry her. Easy friendships and petty quarrels and occasional love affairs were not for her; she was there to work, and she could do without people.

The theory had worked very well until Christopher came back to London from Spain. Ever since then she'd felt like a sea-wall battered by a flood tide. Emotions poured over her, and rather than struggle with those she couldn't understand, she took refuge in anger – the one that was easiest to cope with. Christopher had been a *fool* to go to Spain. What should it have mattered to him if civilized people decided to become barbarians? The world seemed slowly to be going insane, and her father would have said that the only thing for intelligent men to do was stand aside from it, as the monks had done in the Dark Ages. Civilization had survived, but only thanks to them.

In this confused and furious state of mind she watched her mother come back from the hospital each evening, tired and quiet after sitting with Christopher. Josephine was frightened of offering to go herself, and ashamed of *not* offering; it was terrible to be seventeen and not know how to deal with the emotions that assailed her.

Then, one evening she was trapped. 'Christopher needs help at the moment,' Sybil suggested. 'Why not forget your studies and come with me?'

'He doesn't seem to lack visitors . . . I doubt if he needs *me*.' Sickened by the peevishness of what she'd just said,

288

she muttered as well, 'I'll come if you like, though.'

She hadn't been inside a hospital since her father died. The memory of it had been carefully buried in her mind but that, too, was now exploding into remembered pain. The place she walked into was exactly the same – the smell, the whiteness, the sense of suffering contained within its walls. She followed her mother blindly along endless corridors, stopped when Sybil stopped, and finally stared at a closed door.

'Go in and talk to him while I speak to the Sister in charge. Just say who you are at once, and then try to chat normally.'

For the first time in her life Josephine was brought to the verge of begging her mother for help. Chat normally? Dear Lord, *how*, when her lips were stiff with fear and her heart thudded like a sledge-hammer? But Sybil had walked away, and Christopher was in the room in front of her, requiring help. She opened the door on to dimness, and a silence so complete that it seemed as if the man lying on the high, white bed must even have stopped breathing. He possessed the terrifying stillness of death, and all she could see of him was his bloodless mouth, cheek-bones protruding sharply from sunken flesh, and lank fair hair falling over the bandages round his head. His eyes would have made him familiar but they were hidden; she remembered their blueness, lit by cool amusement, or sometimes bright with anger. Imagination, running out of control, pictured their beauty shot into bloody pieces; in a vision of horror she saw what men could do to each other in the name of war.

'Who's there?' Christopher's murmured question scarcely made itself heard above the turmoil in her mind. 'Someone came in . . . who *is* it?' He'd grown adept at the game of guessing who his visitors were even before they spoke. The nurses were easy, bringing with them the starched rustle of authority. People from the outside world were more interesting to guess at – his grandfather's clothes smelled pleasantly of cigar tobacco, Anita's perfume was different from Sybil's, and even by the touch of their hands he could tell them apart. He was irritated now by the arrival of someone who gave him no clue.

'If you're not going to tell me who's there, you might as well go away.' Silence still, and it was suddenly intolerable at the end of a bad day. Despair had sat gibbering at him from the end of the bed – he could see *that* clearly enough through the darkness of his bandages. 'Damn it; go away in any case. I don't *feel* like being visited.'

He'd meant to be dignified, and knew that he'd sounded like a sulky child, but Josephine was beyond either telling the difference or answering him.

When her mother walked in a moment later she was in the grip of silent, uncontrollable weeping, and Christopher's hands on the white counterpane were clenched in helpless rage. Sybil simply pointed at the door, and moved towards the bed herself. Josephine registered even amid her own distress the loving warmth that now filled her mother's face and softened her voice.

'Nothing to get in a fuss about, darling. Josephine was going to talk to you but she's feeling a little faint because it's hot in here – she'll be all right outside. Now, I'm going to read to you. I hope you share my father's preference for Dickens – I've brought *Martin Chuzzlewit*, Papa's favourite.'

Her daughter's stupidity, and Christopher's spurt of anger, were both absorbed and rendered harmless as she put her hand into the one he automatically held out. He probably hadn't even taken in who it was that had been there irritating him; in any case, it didn't matter now. Josephine Blanchard could go and not be missed.

The evening air outside the hospital blew coolly against her skin, reminding her that her cheeks were wet with tears. She began to walk in the general direction of Pont Street, with only one thought beating in her brain – she must get away from that dreadful hospital. Nothing else penetrated the cloud of misery isolating her from the rest of the world. It even muffled sound, until a motorist's blaring horn jerked her out of the road she'd wandered into in front of him. She was shocked into awareness at least; she was very tired, and Knightsbridge and the road leading round the back of Harrod's to her godmother's house were just in front of her. Without conscious thought she found herself knocking at Anita's familiar black door, and saw it open in front of her before darkness closed in, annihilating everything else.

A moment or two later she found that it was Harry Trentham's hand pressing her head down between her knees. He released her and she sat up, wondering why it had been left to him to deal with her.

'Sorry,' she muttered. 'I'm all right now . . . I shouldn't have disturbed you, but it suddenly seemed rather a long walk home. I can carry on now.'

'You can stay where you are,' he insisted.

She was making an effort to seem composed, but in the sallowness of her face her eyes were dark with pain. He wished fervently for his wife, but she wasn't there and he knew that he must somehow manage on his own.

'Whatever's gone wrong, can you make do with me?' he asked gently. 'Anita's gone out to collect Kate from a birthday party.'

He was simply her godmother's busy and important husband, a cousin of sorts whom she scarcely knew, and the last person on earth she would ever think of talking to.

'I went to the hospital with my mother.' The words burst out of her, giving so much away that she had to go on. 'I was supposed to be helping Christopher, but all I did was upset *him*, and make a fool of myself as well.' She looked at Harry and her mouth trembled. 'I couldn't even tell him I was there.'

He had a sudden recollection of a conversation with Anita; everything involving Christopher Wyndham seemed to matter extravagantly to this strange, self-sufficient girl.

'It's nothing to get upset about,' he suggested calmly. 'Most people dislike hospitals, just as they dislike confronting someone else's pain and helplessness.'

It was a well-meant attempt at consolation and Josephine appreciated it as such, but she had to reject it all

291

the same. She would have liked to reject as well the memory of her mother's expression, and Christopher's hand searching for *her* hand. 'Maman wasn't unnerved; she . . . she seemed quite at home there.' Admitting that was bad enough; she couldn't mention the love that had transfigured her mother's face in the dimness of that dreadful room.

'Your mother spent years nursing injured soldiers in France during the war,' Harry pointed out gently. 'She had to get used to hospitals and suffering. Thank God you *haven't* had to share that experience.'

He moved across the room to a table set out with a tray of decanters, and came back with a glass in each hand.

'Sherry's my choice at this time of the evening, but I've given you brandy and water. It will stop you shivering.'

She sipped the drink, then sat staring at the glass in her hands. 'I've been trying to work out *why* I couldn't say anything to Christopher,' she said suddenly. 'It's because I wanted to shout at him, but couldn't because he looked so . . . dreadful.'

'Why shout? Why should you feel angry with him?'

'Because it was *stupid* of him to go and get hurt – he was going to become a doctor. It isn't his quarrel if the Spaniards want to kill each other.'

'True but the bullet taken out of his head was a German one, and it could just as easily have been Italian. The world is so much smaller than you think that other people's quarrels have to become our quarrels. Hitler and Mussolini may not greatly care who governs Spain, but *that* war gives them a training-ground for their own fighting men. *They* are involved, and so must we be.'

Josephine stared at him with huge perplexed eyes. 'You mean we're all *going* to be involved in fighting *them*?'

'I don't know when but, yes – this year, next year, *sometime* for certain; because unless we stop them, they will take over Europe.'

'Frenchmen won't allow the Germans into France,' she insisted with sudden fierceness. 'I know that terrible mistakes were made in the Great War, but they wouldn't happen again.'

Harry doubted if his wife would have thought he'd done very well in replacing Josephine's immediate worries by something much worse, but at least she had got her mind off the humiliation of the hospital visit. She handed him her empty glass and stood up to go.

'The walk was much longer than I realized, but now I can perfectly well manage the rest of the way,' she said firmly.

Harry accepted what he was meant to understand – tiredness was to be the excuse for her brief collapse on his doorstep, and there was no need to mention it to anyone else at all.

He smiled suddenly, liking her gallantry. The business of growing up was probably difficult enough for a girl at the best of times, but this one made things harder for herself by doing it on her own.

'There's one thing you overlooked about Christopher,' he pointed out when they stood on the doorstep together. 'He may yet recover to become a doctor – I think there's a good chance that he will.'

Josephine accepted the idea with a little nod and turned away; then came back and surprised herself by shyly kissing Harry goodbye.

She walked on towards Pont Street, thinking that her confession had been true as far as it went, but it hadn't been complete. What she hadn't admitted to was the grief of discovering that she'd been wrong about Christopher Wyndham. The comfort of thinking him her friend, the conviction that some special understanding existed between them, had grown strongly in her heart all the time he'd been away. He had told her what she must do, and kissed her when he said goodbye. How could he *not* have understood this evening that her heart was breaking at the sight of him, and chosen her mother instead? The disappointment was painful enough to overshadow everything else; she wasn't prepared to find Sybil already waiting for her at the flat, and didn't notice that her mother's face looked anxious.

'I walked home,' she said coolly, 'to recover from the heat in the hospital.'

'It was silly of me to ask you to come this evening; I won't suggest it again.'

The effect of Harry's brandy had worn off now and Josephine felt very tired, but pride demanded one more effort. 'I hope the reading went well. Excuse me if I go to bed now, Maman.'

Sybil watched her go, and tasted the bitterness of another defeat. It was the easiest thing in the world to handle Patrick's son, and the hardest thing of all to succeed with Henri's daughter.

By the end of September when his eyes were unbandaged Christopher was able to see a little. Day by day as the damaged tissues healed, he could see more and more, and gradually it seemed safe to rejoice in a miracle. He was released from hospital and thought he bore patiently with the tedium of convalescence in Walton Place. Anita explained to her god-daughter that he rarely bit her head off more than three times a day, and always apologized sweetly afterwards!

Josephine would have minded rudeness less than the treatment *she* received. A thin, pale stranger hidden behind dark glasses asked her polite questions about her work at Courtauld's, and she gave him polite, uninformative replies. She waited for him to describe Spain to her, to talk about life and death, and art, and healing . . . and instead they discussed the weather. She never referred to her shameful visit to the hospital, and nor did he; understanding had fled, and they had nothing of value to say to one another.

Unable to confess so much even to Anita, she said instead, 'Harry was right about Christopher recovering his sight. Do you believe he was right about something else – that we're all involved in what's happening, whether we like it or not?'

'Yes, he's right, my dear. John Donne used more noble

words to describe it three hundred years ago, but the meaning is the same – "each man's death diminishes *me* because I am involved in all mankind".'

'I've always pretended not to be,' Josephine confessed slowly. 'Life seemed less dangerous that way, less . . . agitating.'

Anita smiled at a word that only this odd, reflective girl would have used. 'I had much the same idea when I was your age. But in the end, like everybody else, I found that I had to get involved. Other people are much too interesting to be ignored, in any case!'

'"Characters", you mean, like Great-Aunt Louise?' A grin suddenly lit Josephine's face, wiping away gravity. 'Victoria dreads her visits to Providence and I'm not sure Grandpa William doesn't, too, but I used to rather enjoy them myself!'

Her outward likeness to Henri Blanchard lay only in her colouring, but every now and then she seemed so unmistakably his daughter that Anita was vividly reminded of him.

Josephine's next comment dragged her godmother back to the matter in hand. 'Harry said war was certain to come, but it looks as if he might be wrong, after all.'

'Well, yes, if the popular press and Mr Chamberlain are to be believed,' her godmother agreed. 'We're supposed to have been saved by his dramatic flights to Germany, and the Munich agreement.'

'What about poor little Czechoslovakia, though?'

'Jungle law says that the fate of the small and defenceless is to be eaten by the large and powerful,' Anita explained with sad, rare cynicism. 'We excuse ourselves for letting it happen by telling each other that many of the people involved aren't Czechs at all, and in any case almost anything is preferable to another European war.'

'Are you like Harry, and *don't* think so?'

'I remember young men like Christopher and Charlie and Tom, and no longer know *what* I think.'

She knew for certain, though, that Harry would speak against the Munich agreement when it was debated in the

House. Another vehement opponent was the Conservative member for Epping Forest, but no-one then foresaw that, after years of being in the political wilderness, he was destined before long to become the next Prime Minister.

Peace still reigned when they left London to spend the Christmas of 1938 at Providence. Anita was careful to extract various promises before they set off: Harry was not to mention the fact that the Royal Navy was being mobilized; James was not to interrogate Lucy's husband about the number of weapons his factories could turn out in a day. She was tempted to ask Christopher not to be unkind to Josephine, but abandoned this as being the sort of interference a mere aunt was not permitted to indulge in.

Long after the event, *that* Christmas remained for all of them a culminating memory of what life had been, and was never to be again. They walked to church through the cold, starlit darkness of Christmas Eve and awoke the next morning to a world touched by magic. 'Earth stood hard as iron, water like a stone,' but overnight every twig and leaf and stem had been veiled in the sparkling crystal lace of hoarfrost. Winter sunlight glowed on the stone walls of Providence, and its twisted chimneys flowered like roses in a wondrously pale-blue sky.

Within doors the house breathed warmth and welcome, and its indefinable grace seemed to promise that all individual sorrows could be made bearable. Gertrude sat at the foot of her long dinner-table, aware of the private unhappinesses her family brought with them. Neither she nor Providence could cure them, or prevent the disaster that was overtaking the world; but if they went away remembering that peace and affection and quiet loveliness *were* to be found, something precious would be gained.

When dinner was over William played the piano for them to sing carols to in the Great Hall. Lucy escaped to a shadowy window-seat but found herself followed by her sister.

'I never see you now,' Sybil murmured. 'Don't you ever

come to London? You must need to buy clothes, even if you don't buy mine.'

'At the risk of seeming hopelessly provincial, I shall admit to a dressmaker in Birmingham.' Lucy smiled suddenly at her sister. 'Don't tell me so, even if it shows!'

'There's nothing wrong with your dress – it's rather good as a matter of fact. The trouble is with *you*. I'm thought to be fashionably thin, but for a woman who used to be well-rounded, you're damned close to emaciation. Why?'

'Oh, I rush about a lot,' Lucy said vaguely. She stared at the pattern of the brocade curtain that almost hid them from the room. 'You all right, Syb – happy, I mean?'

'I manage, thanks. I was even beginning to do quite well with Josephine until Christopher complicated things.'

'Even if she's unhappy about him, why should that affect you?'

'I should have remembered from the war that damaged men fall in love easily with any woman who's kind to them. Being twenty years older, and a second cousin to boot, it didn't occur to me that he might react in the same way.'

'Awkward, I can see . . . but does it really bother Josephine?'

'I think it breaks her heart. The "parfit gentil knight" who rode off to war wasn't supposed to turn into a querulous invalid with a ridiculous fixation on her mother! She despises him now, and has gone back to hating me. There are no half-measures about my daughter.'

'Just like you,' Lucy pointed out gently. 'Why *have* you been as kind to him, by the way, as I gather you have?'

'It's the only thing I can do for Patrick while Ishbel is alive.' She smiled faintly in the dimness of the window-seat. 'To spite the English she will live for ever; I'd certainly try to if I were her!'

'I'm sorry, Syb . . . I didn't know,' was all her sister could find to say. She was still thinking that the two of them had shared a rare talent for loving the wrong men when Sybil spoke again.

'I know Frank doesn't approve of Peter Hoffer, but I expected to see him here with Jane. Mama doesn't usually play for safety, and it's her strong conviction that Providence is more than a match for people who aren't in love and charity with each other.'

'This time she knew better than to take the risk. Frank wouldn't have stayed if Peter had come; knowing that, Peter *wouldn't* have come in any case.'

'Because of you? Is that why you stopped going to Bicton?'

'My final mistake,' Lucy admitted. 'At the age of forty-three I discovered what I'd been looking for all my life.'

'Wouldn't Frank let you go now, if you asked him?'

'I *can't* ask him; *we* made a bargain about Providence, and Peter owes Bicton to Jane.'

'Yes, of course. We haven't been terribly successful between us, have we?' Sybil muttered after a while, 'And by and large we've meant so damned well, too!' She caught hold of Lucy's hand and gave it a loving squeeze. 'Time we crept out of our confessional, but I'll tell you one more thing before we go. Somehow I'm going to finish up as brave and beautiful as Mama still is, or die in the attempt!'

Lucy's disciplined face broke into a smile. 'Dear Syb, we'll die together attempting the impossible, if you like. But until then we'd better go and sing with the rest of them.'

Chapter Twenty-Five

Charlotte had always felt more warmly disposed towards Frank Thornley than the rest of his wife's relatives, but she didn't expect to receive informal calls from him without Lucy. It was so great a surprise to see him on her doorstep one bitter February afternoon that she stared blankly at him for a moment. They'd met briefly at Providence over Christmas and she'd thought that he looked mortally tired, but since then overwork or some other grinding stress had made a difference that suddenly alarmed her. The stocky, powerful frame inherited from his father now seemed held together by the minimum of flesh and the maximum of will-power, and his face held the greyish tinge of extreme exhaustion. But ill as he seemed, he was still alert enough to notice her slight hesitation.

'I was passing by, and took the chance of finding you at home. If I've chosen a bad moment, don't worry . . . I'll move on again.'

Staring at him through the wintry afternoon murk that drifted up like fog from the hallway below, Charlotte wasn't sure that he was capable of moving at all. He was propped against the door from need, not indolence, and she was seized by the shocking fear that, like a dog in terrible distress, he had found some familiar place in which to die.

'My dear Frank, come in at once . . . of course it isn't a bad moment. I was just thinking of making tea, and it's much nicer not to drink it alone.' She was talking too much, and fussing round him because she was afraid. Desperation of some kind had brought him – she was as certain of *that* as she was unsure of her ability to help him.

Still murmuring gently about the disagreeable weather and the general unpleasantness of things, she led him to the comfort of her sitting-room and offered him a chair by the fire.

'You're looking rather tired,' she said with magnificent understatement. 'Make yourself comfortable while I fetch tea.'

When she returned with a tray ten minutes later he'd followed her advice to the extent of removing his overcoat and gloves. The noise of traffic outside came too faintly to be disturbing, the room was warm and firelit, and he thought how peaceful it would be if he could be allowed to stay there for ever, with nothing more required of him than to sit watching the flames reflected in the shining brass of Charlotte's fender.

He roused himself to accept tea, and make conversation. 'Where was it you went with your parents after Christmas – Egypt?'

'The South of France. Both Ian and my father slept most of the time, while my darling mother disapproved of almost everything in sight – the drains, the food, and the unreasonableness of the French in clinging to their own language. She enjoyed making it clear that they'd have done better to let themselves be included in the British Empire!' She smiled gently at Frank. '*I* was rather glad to get home.'

'I seem to remember that your husband has left the Unicorn Press and gone to Gollancz.'

'Yes, he's very involved in the Left Book Club now. It's probably anathema to you, but it does good work and it's very successful.'

'I accept its success, but not its theories! There was a time when I'd have been willing to expend a lot of energy arguing with him about them; nowadays time and energy always seem to be consumed by other things.'

'In making weapons, I suppose?' She stared at his face and decided to risk the sort of personal comment that he was usually careful not to invite. 'You look as if you work all night as well as all day. I know how inevitable Harry thinks war is, but can't you rest a little more than you do? There must be other factories involved besides Thornley's.'

'There are, but not nearly enough. The navy's pretty well up to strength, and the Royal Air Force is catching up fast, but the army has been starved of money for twenty years. We can't make *that* good without the sort of effort that requires us to work night and day.'

'Is Charlie going to join you eventually?'

'As soon as he finishes at Cambridge this summer. I wanted him to stay on – he's been offered an almost certain research fellowship – but he's convinced that I need help. There's no shifting him when he makes up his mind – he's just like my father all over again.'

Charlotte remembered her aunt at Providence saying that the nicest thing she knew of her elder grandson was his devotion to Frank. The twins loved everyone, including their father, but he and Charles were as close as Gertrude was to Ned.

'We hear of his brilliant performance at Cambridge,' Charlotte said, sure of giving pleasure. 'All the Chemistry prizes, and the certainty of an Honours degree. You must feel very proud.'

'Let's say that he stops me from feeling a complete failure.' The sudden harshness in Frank's voice, and the unexpectedness of what he'd just said, left her fumbling for a suitable reply. She was about to try to say that his idea of failure would be most men's brilliant success when he forestalled her.

'I'm obliged to travel again . . . make a round of factories in France in the hope of bullying them into a sense of urgency. God knows the hope's forlorn, but Hore-Belisha insists that I try.'

She was caught out again. How was it possible to tell a man like Frank that he looked as if he needed rest, not still more exertion?

'Lucy will remain at Providence, I suppose,' she murmured at last for something to say.

'Yes, since we no longer have a house in London . . . although I remember that when I went away once before

301

to America, and you were unwell, she stayed with you here.'

Charlotte looked surprised, then shook her head. 'You're mistaken, Frank. She'd be most welcome if she wanted to come, but I can't recall that she has *ever* stayed here.'

He stared at her out of empty eyes, then examined his hands carefully, as if he'd never seen them before. 'Then I *was* mistaken, of course,' he agreed tonelessly.

'Will you stay and dine with us?' she asked after a pause that seemed full of awkwardness. 'Ian would be glad to see you.'

He looked up again and she saw faint, self-derisive amusement flicker around his mouth and disappear again. 'You're a very kind woman, Charlotte, but you mustn't be untruthful. Your husband is the genuine Marxist article, and I am the capitalist villain of the piece! I can remember embarrassing you a long time ago in front of that fool, Desmond Brastead. Your husband *isn't* a fool, but I won't inflict myself on him.'

She had the feeling now that sadness as well as exhaustion weighed him down, and was astonished by her longing to be able to release him from it. 'Dear Frank, we're *kin*, are we not? People who can believe different ideologies but still remain friends.' Her gentle, plain face was flushed with her desire to convince him.

She was good and lovable – he'd always been sure of it – and even marriage to a left-wing intellectual hadn't spoiled her. He was tempted to say so, but it was a long time since he'd spoken without thinking. It was *too* long, and the moment when he might have done so was already past. She didn't press him further to stay, and he shrugged himself into his overcoat again.

Five minutes later she was left alone to reflect on a visit that had seemed oddly significant. It was ridiculous to imagine there had been a reason for it which he hadn't explained, and she was glad to be told by Ian that evening that she was letting imagination run away with her.

'I expect he was at a loose end, love – just finished

302

seeing the President of the Board of Trade, and waiting for his next interview with the Prime Minister. He's an important chap, your relative by marriage; no stranger to the corridors of power!'

'I'm afraid he's also a very unhappy man,' she said slowly.

Soon after Frank's call in Thurloe Square events across the Channel took them another step downward towards chaos. The moment came that foretold beyond the last remnant of doubt the future Hitler had mapped out for Europe – it was to be *his* Europe. In mid-March German troops marched on Prague, turning what remained of Czechoslovakia into a 'protectorate' of the Reich. There was no longer any hope of denying the nature of Hitler's 'modest and reasonable' demands, and even *The Times* went so far as to produce a rumble of its one-time thunder and denounce a 'crude and brutal act of oppression'.

At Providence, the horror of it was suddenly over-shadowed by a more personal tragedy. Lucy was given the news in a telephone call from Downing Street. Such a call wasn't unusual, and she listened to the grave message carefully, as if it were something she must be able to recall verbatim for Frank afterwards. Then she sat staring at the telephone – no need to remember this time; he had gone beyond the reach of Government demands and emergencies. They had taken his strength and endurance for granted once too often, and he had died of a heart-attack on his way to Paris.

For twenty-two years she had tried hard to love him and failed; she thought he had tried *not* to love her for equally as long and had also failed. She seemed to be watching them with the calm detachment of a woman at a play – the characters were doomed, but not real enough to weep over. Still, she couldn't sit for ever staring at the tele-phone; she had assured the voice at the other end of the line that she had people enough at Providence to help her. The poor things didn't yet know that help was needed . . . she would have to go and tell them.

Her mother was outside, talking to the 'lad' who had now become the gardener. He didn't seem to mind when she forgot and called him Biddle. She was apologizing to him again when she saw Lucy step out into the courtyard garden.

'Dearest . . . good morning!' She pointed to a white cloud of early narcissi dancing in the wind. 'Come and sniff these paper-whites . . . don't you think they're what Heaven must smell of?' Lucy didn't reply and Gertrude looked up at her daughter's face. 'No, another time, my dear . . . let's go inside. The wind is sharper than I thought.'

Lucy followed her along the corridor to the Great Hall – full of quietness and peace, and the fragrance of white hyacinths in blue Delft bowls. It was her mother's room, where every childhood joy and woe had been brought to be shared or listened to.

She read the words carved in the stone lintel above the fireplace as if she hadn't seen them before, then turned round to face Gertrude. 'I don't know whether Frank entirely believed in Providence, but he believed in its motto.'

'Believed?' her mother queried carefully.

'He died of a heart-attack early this morning. They've just rung from Downing Street to tell me so. I don't really believe it, but it's what they *say*.' Her mouth uttered the words stiffly, as if an automaton were speaking; only her eyes seemed alive in the rigid pallor of her face. 'There are things to do but . . . oh, God . . . I can't remember *what* . . .'

'We'll get Ned, my darling . . . Ned will know. Stay there for a moment while I send someone to find him.' She fled from the room certain amid the shock that numbed her mind and set her body trembling that Ned was the person they needed. When he was there nothing was completely unbearable. She found her daughter-in-law in the corridor, gave her the news, and then hurried back to Lucy. 'Mary knows where he is, dearest . . . he'll be here soon.'

'I didn't ask Frank not to go. It wouldn't have made any difference if I had, but he looked so ill when he left that I *should* have asked, shouldn't I?' She didn't wait for her mother to reply; words began to gush out of her, exploding up from depths of misery and pain that couldn't be kept buried a moment longer. 'I should have done a lot of things I didn't do, Mama . . . errors of omission, Hubert Roberts used to call them. I was very much better at the errors of *commission* – I slept with Harry, fell in love with Peter, and allowed Frank to guess that I hated to have him touch me. Maud once told me to leave time to cure the mess I was in, Hubert recommended the power of God . . . but it's too late either way – Frank is dead.'

Gertrude's eyes were wet with tears but her voice was firm when Lucy finally ran out of words. 'Perhaps the things you didn't do were your responsibility, but some of the sins were ours, as well. We let you marry Frank knowing all the time that you didn't love him; we allowed you to believe that nothing mattered beside saving Providence from ruin and letting Ned and your father continue to live in it. Those were *our* errors, my darling, and I'm certain Frank was wise enough to realize it.'

'They said he died very quickly, without knowing what was happening. I hope so . . . he would have *hated* dying away from England.' The thought struck her with so much pain that she turned blindly to find the comfort of her mother's arms and burst into a storm of weeping.

When Ned came in, white-faced, she was calm again, able to talk sensibly to him, and to be persuaded by Gertrude that *she* must be the one to drive to Bicton and break the news to Jane Thornley. Charles was summoned back from Cambridge, and on the following day he and Ned left for France to bring Frank's body home.

Victoria and Tom wept for the loss of their father, accepted comfort, and gave comfort in return. Only Charles defeated every attempt Lucy made to get near to him. It was the one thing left that she could do for Frank and she bore patiently with their son's stubborn refusal to be helped. He rejected affection, even from his grand-mother at Bicton, and was hidden behind a barrier they couldn't penetrate. Lucy knew that Jane was hurt, and felt obliged to try to persuade him. She succeeded, at least, in breaking down the adult control he'd imposed on himself.

'Why do *I* need to go to Bicton? I expect you go often enough.' The words were thrown at her, sharp and painful as hailstones against her skin, but she told herself that she must be mistaken about their intention to hurt.

'Of course I go . . . your grandmother is old, and very sad. I should visit her even if I didn't love her so dearly.'

'Love her, Mama? You're forgetting – she's a Thornley!'

Lucy stared at him, stupefied. 'What does that have to do with it? We're all Thornleys – you, Victoria, Tom, and I by marriage. We're a *family*, Charlie.'

His young face was set in the expression of mulish obstinacy she was familiar with; just so had he always looked when determined not to have his opinion changed. Like Grandfather Thornley, he didn't ever allow for being wrong. She remembered Maud Roberts saying years ago that she might be glad of his resemblance to Arthur one day, but for once Maud had been mistaken.

'We've never been a family,' he said flatly. 'We shared the same house, but even *that* wasn't ours – it belonged to the Wyndhams.'

She had the nightmarish sense of looking at a world that was exactly as usual except that everything it contained was upside down. Nothing that she could say would change by any fraction of forgiveness or understanding the angle from which *he* saw a truth that belonged exclusively to him.

'Providence became your father's house,' she said at last. 'He bought it, as you well know.'

She saw the expression on his face and for a frozen moment of time waited to hear him say 'my father bought *you* as well'. Instead, he asked a question that seemed even more dreadful because it was flung at her so insolently. 'I suppose you're going to marry Peter Hoffer now?'

'What . . . what makes you think such a thing?'

'Mrs Knightly says it's what will happen.'

'She's a malicious busybody, but she's not infallible.' The words torn out of her were true, but even as Lucy spoke them she knew that they were not what she should have said. Her son had received from Mrs Knightly a devotion reserved otherwise only for Frank; she had served them both, and as far as possible ignored everyone else.

'She isn't usually wrong . . . Father doesn't . . . didn't find her so.' That seemed to dispose of the matter of Mrs Knightly's fallibility, and Lucy accepted defeat. His few swans would always be swans, and his geese would remain geese. There was no hope that he would change his mind about his mother, who had failed to understand him even as a child. Bleakly she accepted that he had a right to his attitude. There had been no joy in his conception or birth, and no amount of effort afterwards had been enough to make him feel secure with her.

'I can't tell you what will happen in the future,' she said quietly, 'and this isn't the moment to try to make you understand about the past. One day perhaps you *will* understand, and forgive me the mistakes I've made.' The temptation was great to stop there, but she knew that she must be completely honest with him now if he wasn't to despise her always in future. 'Dr Hoffer is a good, kind man who is overdue for a little personal happiness. He wouldn't consider asking me to marry him for a long time yet. He might never ask me at all, but if he did, I should want to accept him.'

'So Mrs Knightly was right!' That seemed to be what concerned him most, Lucy thought wretchedly. Then he suddenly recollected how the conversation had begun. 'Excuse me if I don't call at Bicton this morning . . . I'm sorry to neglect my grandmother, but there is an emergency Board Meeting at Thornley's; she will understand that I must attend that.'

He was scarcely twenty-one and already he sounded exactly like Frank. Thornley's would become the heart of his life, and if some unfortunate woman became his wife she would have to learn to be content with the crumbs of affection that fell from her husband's table. Lucy watched him turn and walk away, lonely but determinedly self-sufficient. She wanted to call him back and put her arms round him, but the truth was the same one that she had given her mother about Frank – it was too late with Charlie as well. Her voice just reached him, and he stopped and turned round.

'Charlie . . . try not to hate me, please.'

For a bare moment of time she thought he'd heard something more than the words themselves; his set expression almost crumpled into the muddle of grief and angry confusion that he struggled with inside, but Thornley obstinacy held. He recovered himself and shook his head as he walked away, leaving her to guess what it was he rejected – the plea itself, or the idea that he could hate his mother.

Among the members of the family converging on Providence for Frank's funeral, Sybil drove down in her own motor-car with Josephine. The need to concentrate relieved her of the necessity of finding something to say to her silent daughter. She had accepted defeat now – they shared the same flat, often spent the evening hours together, and always talked to each other with the careful politeness of strangers. Josephine never mentioned Christopher, or wavered in her attitude of courteous detachment from her mother's life.

They were almost at Providence when Sybil suddenly stopped the car mid-way along the drive. She didn't consciously decide what to do or say; instinct had taken charge and she simply followed its prompting.

'Uncle Ned always insists that the best vantage-point is on the other side of the lake, but *this* is the moment I look forward to – when I know I shall see the house round the next little bend in the drive.' She saw the surprised expression on her daughter's face and took another step forward. 'Your father agreed with *me*. Jem Martin told me that *he* once chose this selfsame spot to stop when he came here.'

Josephine scarcely registered the mention of Jem. Her mother rarely referred to Henri Blanchard, and had certainly never spoken before about his visits to Providence.

'It's not at all like the mill,' she objected. 'Did he enjoy coming here?'

She saw her mother's mouth twist in an odd smile. 'He said Providence was like the peace of God – passing all understanding. I didn't know what he meant then, but I do now. Your grandmother has always known . . . it was one of the bonds between them.'

Josephine wrestled with the unwelcome strangeness of the idea. For years at Providence she had brooded over her miser's hoard of memories, never knowing that her grandmother might have had memories of her own to share. The thought was so unsettling that she would have preferred not to know now; wished that her mother would just end this uncomfortable halt and let them drive on, but Sybil still didn't start the car. Instinct, given its head now, insisted that other things must finally be said.

'Your father came here first when I was four years old, and apparently I appropriated him even then! I began to *love* him from the time I was a schoolgirl, and eventually he was kind enough to marry me. I was less than half his age, and all the things he knew and cared about were a mystery to me. It didn't occur to me for a long time that I must have been the most inadequate of companions, and he tried very hard not to let me realize it!'

There was a note of such tender sadness in her voice that Josephine could neither mistake it nor pretend it wasn't there. Her own expression suddenly reflected a moment's pain, but Sybil shook her head. 'You were young but you *didn't* bore him. His view of you was always that you were the most perfect daughter a father ever had.'

She had her reward in the tremulous smile that lit Josephine's face. It was the slight encouragement she needed to go on, even though the ground ahead looked even more dangerous.

'When the time comes I hope you'll find a husband near your own age. I loved your father very much, and I think he loved me, but it's hard to close a gap of more than twenty years. Usually the effort doesn't have to be made because most girls have sense enough to understand the difficulties and be put off by them; but I was a Wyndham, too stubborn and self-willed to be thwarted.'

'Sometimes it's the other way round,' Josephine said in a small voice. 'The *man* ignores a gap of twenty years.'

Sybil understood that they were no longer talking about herself and Henri. 'Yes, but he doesn't ignore it for very long. He soon sees the absurdity of mistaking gratitude for love – which is why so many soldiers during the war didn't finish up married to the women who nursed them.'

Josephine considered this in silence for a while. 'If the man finally decides he's made a mistake, it's a little hard on the poor lady,' she suggested at last.

'Not really . . . she's twice his age, remember, with no excuse for mistaking anything at all!'

The see-saw on which Josephine balanced so un-comfortably swung again; without quite knowing why, she found herself liking her mother more, and Christopher Wyndham even less. She would have liked to say so, but with no words ready on her tongue, she could only smile again, making a shy, tentative gift of friendship.

'Shall we go on?' Sybil suggested gently. 'Tea will be waiting, and ladies of your grandmother's generation still believe that unpunctuality is a definite if minor sin!'

In the days immediately following Frank's death, Lucy had gone often to see Jane at Bicton but had caught no glimpse of Peter and didn't expect to. Beyond a brief, formal note offering his sympathy, she had had no contact with him by the time Frank was buried in the churchyard at Haywood's End. On the morning of the service the grass was covered with flowers – grandiose official tributes lying alongside small posies from women Frank had never known, but whose families he'd looked after in times of hardship. The village people attended, not only for the chance of rubbing shoulders with the high and mighty; Frank Thornley had become part of the Wyndham family and, in the end, part of Haywood's End too. Men from Thornley's who normally steered well clear of churches arrived looking out-of-place but determined to be there, and Charlotte's husband observed them with interest. His theorist friends would be glad to think they'd come to see their employer dead and safely buried, but Ian knew that, for once at least, the theorists would have been wrong.

Lucy said a composed goodbye to her husband amid the throng, and took an unexpected pride in the variety of people who were there. She prayed that Charlie did too, and saw thankfully that he was careful to stay beside Jane Thornley. Wyndhams and Trenthams greatly outnumbered the distant cousin or two who represented Frank's own family, but she was grateful to have them there, and too occupied to consider what her son's reaction might be to this spate of non-Thornley relatives. He greeted them all with the stiff courtesy learned from Frank, and she began to take heart. Her terrible interview with him had been the immediate result of loss and pain, and they would find a way back to friendship.

Louise Trentham observed the mourners and approved on the whole of the conduct of her family. Lucy was bearing up well, and she liked the way Sybil's daughter had thoughtfully ranged herself alongside poor little Victoria. There were some salvoes to be delivered with her usual gusto, but her family expected them. She pointed out that William had let himself get too frail, James too fat, and Ned's light-brown hair was turning grey before it should. Looking at Josephine, she kept to herself the recollection of Henri's olive skin and shining dark hair . . . The memories belonged to long ago; he was dead, and she had become a contented, opinionated old woman. Thank God, though, Charlotte had persuaded her husband to abandon his brown boots for something more suited to a funeral.

Chapter Twenty-Six

Josephine would have stayed beside Victoria anyway in the hope of giving comfort, but it helped her to avoid someone else who had driven down from London with his aunt and cousin Harry. Apart from the scar that slightly puckered Christopher's skin from hair-line to cheek-bone, there was little to remind her now of the condition in which he'd returned from Spain. He propped himself against anything that would save him the trouble of standing upright, and his blue eyes observed them all clearly again, unobscured by dark glasses. Beside Charlie's square frame suggesting an endless supply of strength and energy, his height, languid thinness, and dandified taste in clothes suggested the exact reverse of stamina. Josephine stared at him covertly, and decided that he'd become sickeningly precious, the last creature on earth to give himself the bother of dealing with the sick and dying. She intended to avoid him completely, but when the funeral ceremony was over and they were back at Providence, she found him standing next to her, calmly sipping sherry. He was part of the gathering, but aloof from it in spirit – just as he'd always been among his father's relatives.

'Hateful things, funerals, I always think,' he murmured. 'I shall try not to have one.'

A frigid nod would have been the best way of dealing with him, she realized, but then he might not understand that she despised him.

'You intend to live for ever?'

'Beyond me, I'm afraid. In any case, it's the business of disposal I find so distasteful, not shuffling off this mortal coil when the time comes; life's a rather wearying business.'

Spinelessness or affectation? She wasn't sure which, and was about to ask when the recollection came back to her of a time when they had seemed to understand one another. He'd spoken then of being torn in two – his loyalties painfully divided between Irish O'Neils and English Wyndhams. It might well be enough to make any man feel not only weary but heart-sick.

'You said you were going back to America,' she said eventually.

'*You* said you were going to France.'

'I am. I haven't got there yet, but I shall.' She repeated it again, the conviction that she had clung to for so long. France was where she belonged. But her eyes strayed round the room, now unfamiliarly full of people but unchanged in essence. Sunlight slanted through the stained glass of the windows, throwing down shafts of blue and golden light. She could see the huge tapestry that she'd stared at time and time again in childhood, determined to count every single flower and rabbit and mouse and bird that medieval artists had strewn so happily across the canvas. On the far side of the room her grandfather inclined his silver head courteously towards an awkward-looking Thornley engineer, and next to them a self-important ministerial visitor was impaled on the end of Great-Aunt Louise's measuring stare. This room, and these people . . . her father had known and loved them, but she had made up her mind that she belonged elsewhere.

'I've decided to stay in London after all,' Christopher said suddenly, 'among a crowd of rugger-mad, English medical students!'

She didn't smile, and he was faintly irritated to see that she didn't look pleased. In fact, he couldn't understand at all the expression in her large dark eyes. She was altogether too self-possessed for a girl of eighteen. Her beautiful Parisian clothes gave her more confidence than she should rightly have, and living in London had *not* improved her.

'I'm not going to change *my* mind . . . why did you?'

Her voice accused him of inconsistency or worse, and he found himself wanting to make *some* impression on her.

'We're heading towards a war even more frightful than the one that was supposed to end all wars. Doctors, even fledgling ones like me, are going to be needed on *this* side of the Atlantic. By the same token, if you don't get yourself to Paris soon, you may find that the Germans have got there before you do.'

'You're mad,' she said with extreme coldness. 'All Hitler has had to do so far is intimidate two small countries into giving way to him. Let him invade France and *then* we shall see what happens.'

'My sentiments exactly,' Christopher agreed sweetly. 'All the same, go soon if you're going. I know you don't want to stay here. Why should you? The days of Providence were numbered in any case . . . Frank Thornley's death only makes its future even more problematical.'

He *was* mad, but she was suddenly frightened. For years she had waited to escape from Providence; now the possibility that it might not be there for ever was something she couldn't bear. She wanted to rant at the languid pessimist who stood staring at her, wanted to shout with Shakespeare's Harry that if he had no stomach for a fight, he'd much better remember he was an American and run back to New York.

'Paris *won't* fall to the Germans, and Providence isn't threatened. You're wrong on both counts, I'm glad to say.' She decided these would be her last words to Christopher Wyndham, and delivered them with all the ferocious conviction of her heart. Then she turned on her heel and walked away.

He watched her go, no longer irritated, only sad. People who had known Henri Blanchard said that she much resembled him. It seemed to Christopher that she was more truly her mother's daughter – no half-measures, no compromises, and a valiant spirit that might be needed before long. It was a pity that what seemed so desirable in Sybil because it was combined with gaiety and kindness of heart, made this girl a tiresome, opinionated oddity. He shook the image of her face out of his mind and went in search of his grandfather. James was certain to have forgotten by now that for the good of his health he was required to eat a little less, and drink *much* less, than he always wanted to.

The reading of Frank's will took place the morning after the funeral. Its terms were tersely stated, its intentions brutally clear: Charles inherited his father's majority share-holding in the Thornley empire, and became the sole owner of Providence. For Lucy Thornley there was an ample allowance to support her during her lifetime. For Frank's other children there was nothing, except a dry reference to the fact that their mother's income would be more than sufficient to keep *them* for as long as she considered they needed help. If she decided to remarry her allowance came to an end.

There were numerous bequests to servants, to Thornley staff, and charities, but Lucy had ceased to listen. She was consumed by the fear of disgracing herself before the interminable reading came to an end. Nausea threatened to lurch uncontrollably from her stomach to her throat, and she waited for the moment when she would have to run from the room. The actual unkindness done to Victoria and Tom was terrible enough, but even that wasn't uppermost in her mind. They were excluded because she had loved them too well – the punishment was intended for *her*, not them. When she looked at them she found herself hating Frank for what he had done. Victoria's face was white as bone, but Tom managed the ghost of a grin. She thought he was capable of standing up there and then, and telling her not to mind, they could manage perfectly well on their own. Anger finally took over, quenching sickness, but her voice was steady when she finally spoke to the lawyer.

'You must have mentioned the date of my husband's will but I'm afraid I missed it.'

'There had been an earlier one, Mrs Thornley, which was replaced. This is very recent – dated the fifteenth day of February of this year. There is no doubt that it is his last will and testament, duly signed and legally witnessed in my office in Birmingham.'

'Are you permitted to say who the witnesses were?'

'Of course . . . my Chief Clerk, and a Mrs F. Knightly.'

'Thank you,' said Lucy, 'that is all I wished to know.'

As the laws of hospitality required, she forced herself to entertain the lawyer to lunch, and he smiled at her beautiful pale face not knowing that she thought only of the moment when she could free herself of the nearness of Freda Knightly. For the moment that one frantic desire was all that her mind seemed to contain. She scarcely remembered that the new owner of Providence had inherited it unconditionally – that the 'bargain' had finally come to an end.

Rather to her own surprise, Josephine accepted her grandmother's invitation to stay on at Providence after the funeral. The Easter vacation at the Institute had begun, and there was no need to go straight back to London, but that wouldn't have stopped her in the past. There was a difference now that she needed to understand, because it was in *her* – Providence didn't change.

The day after the funeral she walked across the courtyard garden and suggested to Victoria that they might take a walk together if she felt like it.

'I feel like *anything* that will get me out of this house,' her cousin agreed wearily.

'I don't suppose you slept much last night,' Josephine muttered after a glance at Victoria's strained face. 'You won't feel like believing me at the moment, but it *does* get better after a bit.'

They crossed the park in silence, and had stopped to get their breath halfway up Goose Hill before Victoria suddenly began to talk. 'Jo, we're in such a frightful mess. No reason not to tell you because you'll hear about it anyway, and if I don't talk now I'll burst!'

'Is it about . . . about Providence?'

'I suppose it's really about *us*. The house goes to

Charlie, of course, as well as all Father's share-holding in Thornley's. We expected *that*, but the rest of the will was rather a stinker – an allowance for Mama only for as long as she doesn't marry again, and nothing at all for me and Tom except what she, poor love, can spare.'

Josephine stared at her, almost inclined to believe that her cousin hadn't properly understood the strange language in which lawyers insisted on framing wills. 'You can't have got it right,' she insisted. '*You* are just as much your father's children as Charlie is.'

'As it happens, we *are*, but it seems that Father didn't think so.'

Josephine came to a sudden halt.

'Victoria, do come off it, please,' she begged. 'We're talking about your *parents*, not a melodrama by Mrs Radcliffe! Next you'll be telling me that Charlie's going to order you never to darken his door again.'

'Well, it feels a bit like that. Mama made Tom and me promise not to say anything, and we honestly didn't mean to. But our loathsome housekeeper – a witness to Father's will, by the way – was oozing so much pleasure that Tom muttered something about "thank God we can get rid of *her* now". Charlie overheard and the fat was in the fire. One thing led to another and at the end of it Thornley family life was in tatters!'

Victoria did her best to sound unconcerned, but her eyes looked feverishly bright in the whiteness of her face. 'You weren't in England at the time, but it seems that years and years ago my poor unhappy Mama had an affair with . . . with someone. It didn't amount to much, but that bitch Knightly has known about it all along. That's why she's always fawned over Charlie, and spat at Tom and me. In the end she managed to persuade my father that *we* were the result of the affair, and not *his* children at all. Charles blurted it out when he and Tom were shouting at each other. Mama heard, and insisted on telling us what really happened. There isn't the slightest doubt that we're Thornleys, unfortunately; I think I'd rather be *anything* else. I wanted to go and rail over my father's grave after first killing Mrs Knightly; but Tom pointed out that *that* would get us into worse trouble than we're in already.'

Josephine offered a rare demonstration of affection by suddenly hugging her cousin. 'He's right, I'm afraid. Tor dear, be comforted. Things are bound to get better. Now that Aunt Lucy's made Charlie understand, there'll be something he can do. It's no good agonizing about your father's unhappiness, and he brought most of it on himself in any case.'

'Very lucid . . . very French!' Victoria commented, wet-eyed but beginning to smile. 'You're right; things *will* get better. It won't be long before Tom's old enough to go into the army, and Uncle Ned's getting things arranged for me to start my veterinary training. There's really only Mama to worry about, but she'll be perfectly all right here with darling Grandma Gertrude.'

Her face was losing its unfamiliar expression of tragedy. With Josephine beside her, so Frenchly matter-of-fact and so unexpectedly kind, it was possible to see the afternoon's furore, terrible as it had been, as something they could get over. And there was always the added comfort that Mrs Knightly was mortal, and couldn't live for ever.

She walked home more cheerfully with her cousin, unaware that their conversation was not unlike the one Lucy was having with Gertrude.

'Listening to the will being read was bad enough this morning, but what came afterwards was even more dreadful . . . Charlie and Tom shouting at each other even while their father's body was still heaped with flowers in the churchyard.'

'Don't agonize over *that*,' said Gertrude, in the tone of voice that Josephine had used to Victoria. 'If Frank had *meant* his sons to quarrel, he could hardly have seen to it more certainly that they *would*.'

'That's the heartbreaking thing about it . . . They *are* both his sons. Tom and Victoria *are* Frank's children, and he truly loved them until that poisonous woman put doubt into his mind.'

Gertrude refused to put into words the thought that was

318

in *her* mind, but Lucy did it for her. 'You're trying not to say that I've always loved the twins more than Charlie . . It's true, but not because they weren't Frank's children. They seemed to be a reward for finally detaching myself from the idea of loving Harry. When they were conceived soon afterwards I thought that Frank and I had begun again – might become a real couple at last. It didn't happen, but I still adored the twins.'

'You once mentioned Peter Hoffer,' Gertrude reminded her gently.

'I haven't spoken to him for months; he might have forgotten me by now. In any case, even if he hasn't, what can we do about it? I can't forgo an allowance which the children need to share for several years at least, and Peter is entirely dependent on Thornley money – for himself, and the Institute. He might offer to find another job, but his life is at Bicton now.'

Gertrude said nothing for a while; it wasn't surprising that Lucy had sunk into despondency, but she couldn't be allowed to remain there.

'Dearest, you're being stupid now, but I forgive you because you've had a great deal to bear one way and another.' She almost smiled at the expression on her daughter's face – it looked more hurt than comforted by such briskness, but at least it was also startled out of despair.

'Peter isn't a boy of eighteen, and you're not an adolescent whose face happened to catch his fancy. His feelings are as unlikely to change as yours are.'

'Perhaps, but that leaves Bicton, and the children.'

'And *you*,' Gertrude said sharply, 'convinced that the sacrifice must always be yours. Tom might have to forgo Sandhurst. See if he cares! He'll go into the army anyway, and succeed. He's not a Thornley for nothing. Victoria's training fees we'll manage somehow, and her home can always be here. As to Peter and Bicton, you must put your trust in my friend, Jane. Her heart is no more likely to change than Peter's is; she loves you *and* the Institute. Neither will be allowed to suffer.'

Lucy's cheeks were suddenly wet with tears. 'Syb and I promised each other we'd learn to be a match for you – some hope, my darling Mama!'

Josephine continued to stay at Providence, even allowing herself to be taught to ride in her efforts to cheer up Victoria. In between painful sessions in the paddock spent trying to follow her cousin's commands, she still tried to understand why *this* visit to Providence should have become so different from any other. She had spent eight years there waiting to grow old enough to leave; now, she found herself each evening in the Great Hall, wrapped in the sort of contentment that remained her clearest memory of the house at Pont-sur-Seine.

One morning William Wyndham shyly suggested that she might like to call on him in the Great Parlour upstairs. No-one, except Gertrude, went there uninvited, and Josephine climbed the stairs aware of being privileged.

No canvas was propped against the easel, and she soon saw why. This time William was using the actual walls of the house as his material. The subject was, as so often before, Providence itself, fixed in his memory by the observation of a lifetime. Josephine stared at the two scenes he'd completed so far. What she looked at first was the season of high summer – the house wrapped in stillness and greenery, and beyond it the valley waiting to be harvested – golden and ripe and speckled with the scarlet and blue of poppies and cornflowers.

'It's . . . it's beautiful,' she muttered, 'but why did you start with summer.'

'So that I could finish hopefully – with spring!'

'I should have thought of that.' She grinned because it was typical of him, and suddenly he was reminded of his old friend, Henri. He had one delightfully pretty granddaughter, but this wasn't she. Josephine Blanchard wouldn't ever be pretty; her face was strong and intelligent instead, and he was very glad that she had wanted to stay with them.

She looked at autumn next, with its blaze of gold and

bronze and crimson reflected in the ancient stone of the house. The vantage-point this time was Uncle Ned's from the other side of the lake; no surprise now – he must have learned it from his father.

The third scene was only just begun – a charcoal outline of the design sketched on the prepared surface of the wall. There would be no lushness or rampant colour in this one; she could imagine the austere winter traceries of black on white and grey, the occasional richness of evergreens, and the flash of red from a robin's breast or a clump of berries. She was still staring at the picture clearly visible in her mind's eye when William handed her a brush with paint on it.

'Just *there*, my dear – do you see where I've sketched in the chimney? I shall know that it was Josephine's!'

'I'll spoil it,' she stammered. 'Grandpa, I can't paint a chimney from a horse . . . are you sure?'

He smiled and nodded, intrigued to see that there was no longer any hesitation when she took the brush. The chimney appeared swiftly under her hand, a glowing twist of colour against the winter sky. She stared at what she'd done – a particle of the entire, huge work, but he'd allowed her a share in it and it was hers.

'May I come back when you begin on spring?' she asked shyly.

'I shouldn't dream of completing it without you.' They smiled at each other over a promise, given and accepted.

Chapter Twenty-Seven

She didn't mark the actual moment when she was aware that something disturbed the serenity of the house, but the conviction grew in her of a trouble that she wasn't allowed to share. Her grandfather hid in his studio and didn't invite her to go there again, and she had a vague but unhappy feeling that her grandmother would be relieved to see her leave. She struggled not to feel hurt, and remembered to talk at dinner of an essay on the 'Tyranny of Perspective' that she had overlooked and must go home and write before the new term started. The excuse for a hurried return to London being clear, she was allowed to leave the following morning. Tom was going to Warwick with Jem Martin, and she could be left at the railway station at the same time. She took the precaution of warning her grandmother that she would be back to help with the painting of spring, and wondered why Gertrude's eyes should suddenly be bright with tears.

Even then she might have gone back to London with only a vague feeling of disquiet if it hadn't been for Jem's invariable habit of getting travellers to the station far sooner than was needed. Tom was obliged to wait with her, doing his best – he thought – to talk about anything but the subject that consumed his mind.

'For Heaven's sake tell me what's wrong, or go away and let me wait here alone,' she said abruptly.

His tight mouth relaxed for a moment into a grin – Jo might look grown-up these days with her expensive clothes and smart haircut, but she was still the forthright, uncompromising creature Aunt Sybil had dumped at Providence years ago.

'I thought you might know already, although Tor

doesn't – yet. It's Mama's idea to keep it quiet, but it seems pretty pointless to me.'

'Go on – *what* don't I know?'

'Charlie's feeling a bit uncomfortable about Father's will. He can't bring himself to *say* it's unfair, but he wants to be generous to the rest of us.'

'It's no more than he *ought* to feel, but there's nothing wrong with it, surely?'

'Only that he plans to get the money he intends giving us by selling Providence.'

She was standing on the platform of a busy, noisy station, unaware of the people and the bustle around her – she was isolated in a cold vacuum of fear which not even anger could help her break out of for the moment. She also felt very sick – a good start to a train journey.

'What about our grandparents, and Providence – doesn't he feel uncomfortable about *them*?' She murmured the words with care, because if she didn't speak very quietly she would find herself shouting at him.

'He doesn't *say*, but I think he reckons Uncle Ned can take care of Grandpa and Grandma, and that Providence doesn't matter. England doesn't *need* an old house that's always falling to pieces and useless people like the Wyndhams living in it. We need factories and trade and industrial research and clever chaps like him, instead.' Tom looked at Josephine's stony face and did what he could for his brother. 'Charlie's not *trying* to be a swine, Jo – he's even right in a way.'

'Don't work at making him sound reasonable to me,' she said bluntly. 'When I was nine and he was twelve he tried to tell me that only men like *his* father who ran great enterprises counted in the scheme of things; *my* father, who didn't even have the saving grace of being English, just sat and looked at other people's pictures. I threw a vase at him and cut his head. We haven't forgiven each other yet.'

'He misses Father . . . I suppose we *all* do, as a matter of fact; without him we're a bit like a wheel without an axle – spokes flying in all directions.'

She accepted this with a nod, realizing that it was true, but returned to the subject of his brother. 'Of course Charlie should share with you, but why does he have to sell Providence to do it?'

'Because Thornley's is more important . . . Father's money is needed for that, and there won't be the expense of keeping that lovely old house from falling to bits . . .' It was as far as he got before the up-train for London finally rumbled into the station, disgorging soot and steam. There was only time for a quick hug, and a glimpse of Tom trying to smile cheerfully at her from the platform.

She was left alone in the compartment, to try to understand why Tom's news, and the whole of her visit to Providence, should have been so shattering that she felt quite different from the girl who'd set out with her mother a mere ten days ago. Some, but not all, of it had to do with the fact that she'd expected to have to return to France to be reunited with her father, and she'd found him at Providence instead. A scowl of concentration and anger at her own stupidity drew her black brows together, unnerving the young man who sat opposite her. He'd been meaning to try an opening gambit or two. She looked interesting, and her legs were beautiful; but she stared at him without interest, not even seeing him, and he retired behind his copy of *The Times*. No joy *there*, either – only a rumour of conscription, and the usual moan about the slowness with which air-raid shelters were being distributed.

When she got back to Pont Street the flat was filled with Great-Uncle James. She thought in such terms of a man who seemed to take up all available space, whereas her grandfather William seemed to take up none at all. James also had the disadvantage of always bringing his grandson to mind. She was never anything but coolly polite to him, but wished with passion that she hadn't come home to find him with her mother *now*.

'Darling . . . I'm very glad you're back, but I thought you meant to stay longer. Was it too dull and quiet after Uncle Ned and Mary went away?'

'Not dull at all, but I think Grandma wanted me to go.'

'Unkind and untrue, Jo. She loves nothing more than to have you there. You know it as well as I do.' Sybil wanted to weep for the sharpness of her disappointment that nothing had changed after all. Josephine remained as she had always been. Only . . . Her polite, aloof daughter *wasn't* the same, because tears that she had rarely shed even in childhood were suddenly spilling over and trickling down her face.

'Mama . . . I *hate* Charles Thornley. I think I'd kill him if I got the chance.'

'May we know why?' James asked the mild question before his niece could say anything at all. He'd found Sybil's daughter a disappointment in the past. A man of getting on for eighty years of age had to be content as far as possible with merely observing the rest of the human race, and he suspected Josephine Blanchard of being well worth observation; but she'd always defeated him with a cool, reticent surface he could get no grip on at all. Whatever had happened now had shattered the barrier she hid behind.

Josephine had almost forgotten he was there. 'Grandpa William's painting something marvellous on the walls of the studio . . . Providence at each season of the year – even the smallest field animals and flowers are included: everything's there, complete and beautiful.'

'*Is* painting?' The question was put by James again, because Sybil's eyes were fixed on her daughter's face, discovering that love and pride and grief were all mixed up in it together.

'He's only about halfway through at the moment. He let me paint a chimney. There's winter and spring still to do. When I asked him why he'd chosen to do it in that order he smiled and said he wanted to finish hopefully.'

'It sounds like my father – ending where most people would begin,' Sybil said, entering the conversation at last.

'There won't *be* an ending.' Josephine almost shouted at her. 'Grandpa can only work slowly now, and Charles is going to *sell* Providence long before it's done.'

She *heard* the sudden silence in the room, as clearly as she would have heard noise.

'How . . . how do you know . . . did he tell you?' her mother murmured finally.

'No, and nor did my grandparents, but I knew something was wrong. Tom blurted it out on Warwick station.' She glared at her great-uncle as if he could be in some way to blame, and suddenly fled from the room.

'My dear but perverse daughter has left it rather late to fall in love with Providence,' Sybil said after a long pause. 'But then, I suppose, so did I. Oh, God . . . If Ned's away I don't suppose he even knows. What in the name of all that's merciful are we going to do? Suggest to my mother and father that they might like a little cottage somewhere from which they can watch Providence being pulled down? Persuade Ned that we need *another* factory turning out sewing-machines more than we need food, and the miracle of beauty he's toiled for twenty years to create?'

'Frank Thornley's argument would have been that at the moment we need another factory turning out fighting aeroplanes, for example; that we need *them* more than almost anything else you can think of,' James said quietly.

'Does that mean you agree with him?' Sybil's fierceness was suddenly like her daughter's. Anyone who wasn't with them, heart and soul, was against them. They didn't like tolerance, and would have no truck at all with compromise. James found nothing wrong in that; he'd lived his life by the same principles and had no intention of changing now.

'I was giving you the Thornley argument, not my own. God knows it's true that we need weapons, but not at the expense of *everything* else.'

'Well, how we look at it doesn't matter now . . . thinking what's to be done is all that counts. The proceeds from the sale of the mill were put into a trust for Josephine in case I should die before she was grown up, and the dress-shop does no more than provide us with a living. Father's paintings only keep his share of the house going, and Ned works from dawn to dusk in order to break-even on the farms.' Her mouth twisted wryly. 'A portrait of the privileged landed gentry in these modern times! The only commodity we have to sell is some jewellery of mine, and Wyndham land. *That* would break Ned's heart even if we could find a buyer, but I shall have to see what he says about it, all the same.'

'You haven't mentioned all the Wyndhams yet,' James reminded her. 'What am I expected to do – sit and watch the pair of you beggar yourselves in an attempt to buy off Charles?'

Sybil stared at him, reluctant to say what was in her mind.

'You're wondering why I didn't help before,' he said calmly. 'I didn't know about the bank mortgage years ago until it was too late, and in those days I was the last person on earth William would have gone to . . . My fault, not his, because I made it too plain that I thought he wasn't a fit steward of his inheritance. I was clever and hard-working and successful, and he was the failure he deserved to be. The real cause of the trouble wasn't that at all, of course. *He* had the sense to choose Gertrude as a wife and I could never persuade her to leave him for me.'

'That remains true,' Sybil said slowly, wondering why the explanation had never occurred to her before.

'I know, but I've had a good deal of time since then to realize that I had no right to despise William. All *I've* done with my life is make a lot of money, and waste years not even on speaking terms with my only son. I shall love Gertrude until I die, but covetousness would be ludicrous in old age – all I want now is to help her, and to preserve what must be preserved.'

'*You've* changed, but what about my father? Suppose he still refuses your help?'

'Then you and Ned will have to find some way of persuading him that it's better for Providence to go to Christopher than fall out of Wyndham hands again.'

'To *Christopher* . . . not Patrick, or even Ned?'

'It can't be either of them. The bargain was made years ago that Christopher would receive the bulk of my estate;

Patrick and Anita accepted that, and I can't alter it now.'

'Will Christopher even *want* it? He goes there, I know, but only on sufferance.'

'It will be safe and unspoiled for at least as long as your parents are alive, and by then *he* might have changed, too.'

Sybil smiled at her uncle, but great as her faith in him had become, there was still one anxiety left.

'Suppose Charles is so blinded by dislike of us that he refuses to sell to a Wyndham?'

Her uncle's faded blue eyes showed a flash of youthful brightness. 'Then I shall require your daughter's help to murder him! I jest, of course,' he added, seeing the gravity in Sybil's face. 'I also think you're worrying unnecessarily. Events may prove me wrong, but my guess is that young Charles Thornley has more on his mind than petty spite. He's his father's son all right.'

'I suppose we *all* have more to agonize about than one small family disaster,' she said slowly. 'Compared with what seems to be awaiting us, even the complete destruction of Providence could turn out to be nothing to weep about at all.'

'So it might, but that's no reason not to save anything we can from what William would call the barbarians.'

James made several visits to Providence, and matters were settled between himself, William, Ned, and Charles Thornley, without the difficulty Sybil had feared. The only thing to surprise him was his complete failure to dislike Frank's son.

'I tried to make my mother and the twins understand,' Charles explained stiffly. 'It isn't to *hurt* them, or my grandparents, that I'm doing what Father knew he should have done long ago. At least some good use is being made of *Bicton*, even though . . . well never mind about Bicton . . . but nowadays three-parts of Providence aren't used at all. Can't you see how *wasteful* it is? Not just for *us*, but for England? Instead of tackling today's problems, we'd rather stare at our reflection in the past . . . it's like Providence looking at itself in the moat.'

It was the longest speech Charles had ever made and he felt embarrassed at the end of it.

'Do you need the money for expansion at Thornley's?' James asked, unaware that he was treating on equal terms a young man who might have been himself fifty years ago – as intelligent, determined, and single-minded as the young James Wyndham had been.

'Capital always helps; research is expensive, but we must do it if we're to stay ahead of our competitors. The money isn't for what Thornley's needs, though.' The next bit was more difficult but Charles managed it. 'My father's will was not . . . not quite fair to the twins. It suddenly changed things that I thought were settled, like Tom going to Sandhurst, and my sister wanting a vet's training.'

James stared at his nephew's set face, which only resembled Lucy's in its straight thin nose; the rest of it, its cleverness and tenacity, came recognizably from his Thornley grandfather. How was he to be made to see that, true as his understanding about England was, it wasn't the whole truth.

'I'll grant you *your* argument if you'll try to see some value in mine,' James suggested. 'Thornley's and you are *as* you are now because of an inheritance from the past – from your father, grandfather, and whatever earlier Thornleys there were that you never even knew. The same goes for this and any other country . . . the past is built into its fabric; you can't just tear it out in order to make a bit more room for the present.'

Charles waited a long time before answering. 'I'm still selling Providence,' he muttered finally.

'And I'm still buying it,' said James.

He reported briefly to the family that Providence was to be in Wyndham hands again, but left unmentioned his only conversation with Gertrude on the subject.

He invited himself to tea in the Great Parlour, for the pleasure of telling her himself that Providence was safe. She didn't pour tears and gratitude all over him, but her hands trembled among the tea-cups and he wanted to weep himself at the sight of them. Then she smiled, and he saw that her transfigured face was still youthful, and still beautiful.

'I don't suppose you remember more than fifty years ago, asking me to take care of Providence for you? I'm afraid we failed, William and I, but now it seems right and proper that *you* should be the one to keep it safe after all.'

'I should have been the one years ago . . . it might have made a great deal of difference – to Lucy, especially.'

'You've made her happy *now* – she isn't torn any longer. She can understand Charlie's point of view without agonizing about us. I *told* her that I wouldn't permit the sale of Providence to kill William, but she didn't have quite enough faith in me!'

'My dearest girl . . .' He stopped because she was staring at him. 'Surely I can call you that again now that we're not as young as we were – do you understand why the house has to go to Christopher?'

'Yes, and Ned understands, too. He says it's time for a new line that will be able to fight for it if necessary.' She hesitated and then braved the question that seemed to matter most of all. 'Do you suppose *Christopher* would fight for it?'

'My dear, I have no idea, but it's a gamble we have to take.'

Charles eventually left Providence even before the change of ownership was complete. He had arranged to move into a house of his own in Birmingham – to save precious time, he said; more probably, his mother thought, to escape from his family. He explained the lawyer's suggestion as to how some of the money from the sale of Providence should be put into a trust for Victoria and Tom; the rest would be used to endow engineering scholarships, as a memorial to his father. Implored by Lucy to accept what had been done for them, the twins abandoned their intention to refuse the trust out-of-hand, and brothers and sister finally parted company with relief but without any more quarrelling.

Watching them together, Lucy realized more clearly than before why Frank had been so easily persuaded that the twins were not his children. They were four years younger than Charles, but could have belonged to a different generation; where they were open, friendly, and charming children, he was already a man whose life was given to Thornley's. Just as his father had been, he was difficult and inflexible, but in just the same way he was admirable as well. His aims weren't selfish ones, and there was something heroic as well as sad about his determination never to be side-tracked. She wondered whether he would ever waste time as other people did – listening to music or watching a sunset or even falling in love.

When the time came to say goodbye she was so close to tears that he reminded her severely of the nearness of Birmingham to Providence.

'I *know*, but will you ever take time off from your meetings and inspections to remember that we're here? Will you ever *consider* taking proper care of yourself, or allowing Mrs Knightly to see that you eat and sleep as ordinary human beings require?'

She didn't stop to consider why it should be so important *now*, when he was leaving, to make him understand that she had loved him after all. His young stern face didn't relax, and she couldn't be sure whether she wanted to weep or shout at him.

'There are highly competent men at Thornley's, Charlie – they *must* be that or your father wouldn't have chosen them. Let *them* run things for you.'

'I shall have to at first, Mama – they're much more experienced than I am. Father's rule was to be able to do anything he required the men to do, and I have a lot to learn still.'

'All right, my dear, learn it, but remember that people matter as well as pieces of machinery.'

'They go together,' Charlie agreed unexpectedly. 'Tom's going into the mechanized side of the army, so that he can drive a Thornley tank!'

She thought it was to be the extent of their leave-taking,

but then he took her by surprise. 'I can guess what my brother thinks about me keeping Mrs Knightly on in Birmingham, but do *you* mind very much?'

It didn't occur to her not to be honest with him. 'I couldn't share this house with her still, but the harm has been done; there isn't any more now, and she will look after you so well that I need scarcely worry about you at all.'

'Mama, she only did it out of loyalty to Father – do you *see* that?' he asked with sudden desperation.

'Yes, I see, and I realize that you're taking her with you because now you must be loyal to her.'

His mouth relaxed into a smile so shy and sweet that for a moment he looked his real age. She kissed him goodbye, and his arms enfolded her in an awkward, brief hug before he walked away. He knew that he'd been right to get rid of an ancient and irrelevant white elephant; his mind was quite clear on that point; but he wished he'd been able to say for once what his heart felt – that he was *glad* the Wyndhams were still at Providence.

Chapter Twenty-Eight

The spring of 1939 merged into early summer and Lucy reminded herself frequently that there was much to be thankful for. Above all, the war that might have been calamitous hadn't come: beside *that* immense blessing one woman's lack of what she needed couldn't be thought to matter, and she learned to accept that her mother had been wrong; Peter Hoffer *had* forgotten her. He was as self-sufficient as the other men whose lives had been entangled with her own, and equally as single-minded. She couldn't blame him for not needing her any more than her husband or Harry Trentham had done. She couldn't stop loving him either, but at the age of forty-four a woman wasn't allowed to die of love. She must make herself useful, and smile, and listen to other people telling her about the marvellous work that was being done at Bicton by a man called Dr Hoffer.

His name wasn't mentioned whenever she visited Jane Thornley, but it cropped up one day when she was least prepared for it. Staying overnight in London with Anita, she found that Harry was away.

'A sudden visit to the Continent,' Anita explained casually. 'As a matter of fact he's gone to Vienna with Peter Hoffer.' She saw the sudden stillness in her cousin's face, but went on as if she hadn't noticed it. 'Jane had the sensible idea of asking Harry to help get Peter's naturalization papers through so that he could travel on a British passport.'

'He's *mad*, Anita . . . he's a Jew who escaped from Austria; they'll never let him leave again.' Her low voice held more anguish than a scream of pain, but she forced her lips to smile. 'Has he got so bored with his life in

333

England that he wants to throw it away?' If she even remembered that Harry had gone as well, it didn't occur to her to ask why; her mind was consumed with a vision of one man being led away to captivity.

'There was something he felt obliged to try to do – bring his old professor out of Vienna before it was too late. Harry's gone too, so that they will look like a couple of officials travelling together.'

'And what happens at the frontier, supposing they get *that* far?'

Anita resolutely pushed to the margin of her mind yet again her *own* nightmare of Harry's car halted at a border post, with an eminent elderly Austrian hidden in the back of it. 'They had a scheme which they declined to share with me,' she said with all the cheerfulness she could muster. 'Apart from that, I'm trusting in the protection of His Britannic Majesty's passport, and Harry's disinclination to be worsted by foreigners!'

Lucy's eyes stared at her out of a sheet-white face. 'Harry shouldn't have been involved . . . I'm sorry, Anita.'

'Darling, nothing would have kept him out of an adventure, even at an age when you might think he'd know better. He finds it intolerable at the moment to sit at Westminster waiting for the Government to decide whether the frightfulness of fighting Germany again is less than the dishonour of *not* doing so.' She took Lucy's hands in her warm ones and held them for a moment. 'They're *both* British subjects now, and we're not at war with Germany. The worst that can happen is that they have to leave the professor behind.'

'No, that *isn't* the worst,' Lucy murmured. 'You don't know Peter Hoffer. He would feel obliged to stay and share the professor's punishment. That's the sort of quixotic gesture he's capable of.'

Anita got up suddenly, to fetch something from her desk. She brought back a small package and put it into Lucy's hands.

'I was to give you this if anything went wrong;

fortunately no promise was made to return it otherwise, so I'm free to give it to you now, and you're free to open it. It was perfectly plain what Peter felt, but I didn't know about you. Now that I do, I refuse to allow another quixotic gesture – men are much too prone to them, I find!' She glanced at her watch and found a heaven-sent reason to leave Lucy alone with the package she still held gripped in her hands. 'We're dining with Charlotte and Ian tonight, but right now Nanny's out and I must collect Katherine from a dancing lesson.' At the door, she turned round again. 'By the way, I don't know who told him, but Peter is aware of the terms of Frank's will.' Then she walked out of the room, leaving silence behind her.

The rustle of tissue paper seemed as unnaturally loud as the thudding of a heart beating at twice its normal rate. Lucy unwrapped a small, jeweller's box, and the sheet of paper folded round it. There were only a few words on it, written in the beautiful black script she hadn't seen for months.

This belonged to my mother. Now, I offer it to you, *mein herz*, as the only treasure I have to give you.

The little box held an antique gold ring set with one perfect sapphire. She replaced it without trying it on: if he didn't come back, she would wear it always. If he did, she must first convince him that in marrying him she wouldn't be poor at all.

That evening in Thurloe Square it was obvious that something had upset their host. Since his marriage to Charlotte, Ian Nicholson had surprised himself by learning to enjoy entertaining his wife's relatives, but he wasn't at ease now. Anita was the first to abandon the pretence that nothing was wrong.

'Ian, my dear, you're trying very hard to listen to our conversation, but I doubt if you could remember what we've been talking about!'

His frown lifted for a moment in a rueful smile, then reappeared again.

'Just before coming home this evening I heard some news. The USSR has signed a non-aggression pact with Germany. So much for the stately diplomatic dance we and the French have been engaged in for months with Russia. Sworn enemies have decided to sup together in a thieves' kitchen, and what they feed off first will be the carcase of Poland.'

It brought the war nearer, surely, if Hitler need no longer fear being attacked from the east, but for the moment Anita was more concerned with what the news had done to Ian. He was a man who had dreamed dreams and seen visions of a just and perfect society in the Marxist ideology; now its guardians had betrayed him. Lucy saw his sadness, but her mind was still filled with a few words written on a sheet of paper, and her memories of the man who had left them for her. There weren't very many words *or memories* to sustain her if she never saw him again.

'Is Hitler so certain to invade Poland now?' Charlotte asked desperately. 'After all he knows that we and the French are pledged to fight for the Poles.'

'He knows that we didn't fight for Czechoslovakia, and that the French are even more disinclined than we are to fight for anybody at all, pledged or not. Yes, my dear, I think he's certain to invade.'

'The Government must think so, too,' Anita murmured. 'I saw a placard on my way back with Katherine. They don't seem to have a great deal of faith in the air-raid shelters they've given us; plans are being drawn up to evacuate thousands of children from London.'

'Then send Katherine to Providence. Victoria and the animals will keep her happy,' Lucy suggested.

She got ready to return to Warwickshire herself the following morning without mentioning to Anita what had been inside the package.

'It ought to be impossible to look desperately worried and deeply happy at the same time, but you manage it,' Anita said, smiling at her, as they said goodbye.

'I won't keep bothering you for news if *you* promise to telephone me.' She kissed her cousin goodbye, then turned round from the pavement to call out, 'Pray *hard*, Anita.'

Back at Providence later in the day, she explained to Gertrude that her great-niece would be sent to Providence if Anita and Harry decided she must leave London.

'Then she'll probably have company,' Gertrude commented. 'People from the evacuation committee in Warwick were going round Haywood's End this morning. I told them we could take ten children, if necessary.'

'Darling . . . *ten*? I know there's room for them, but . . .' Her voice faded away as she considered the prospect in the light of the other news she had to give her mother. 'It's scarcely the moment to tell you but . . . but the truth is that I'm praying I can move to Bicton. That would mean the twins leaving too.'

'To be with Peter?'

Lucy nodded, and Gertrude's face was lit by a transfiguring smile. 'Something's happened – you look different, though not as joyful as you should. If you're worrying about *us*, I forbid you to; if you're worrying about Jane's reaction, I forbid that too. Go to Bicton, dearest, and be happy.'

'I can't yet; Peter's gone to Vienna with Harry to try to rescue a Jewish professor,' she explained, caught between a laugh and a sob. 'But if he gets back safely, I shall camp on his doorstep until he agrees to marry me!' She smiled tremulously at her mother. 'Is there still time to tone the evacuee offer down a bit – to half a dozen, say?'

'No need,' Gertrude said tranquilly. 'Apart from Christopher spending the weekend with Ned, Josephine's here as well, helping your father put the finishing touches to spring in the studio! She's already decided that if the evacuees come, she'll come too, to help look after them.'

'In which case you *won't* need me. With Mary to mother them, Jo to keep them in order, and Providence to exert its usual spell!'

Gertrude smiled lovingly at her daughter. 'You will be

missed, but we shall know that you are happy. Are you *very* anxious about Peter? Don't be, darling . . . Harry won't let him come to any harm.'

'Harry Trentham being, in your considered view, *almost* as indispensable as Ned when life gets difficult!'

Gertrude nodded, but reverted to something Lucy had just said. 'I used to think Providence had failed with Josephine . . . she was so determined for years to resist loving it, but it won in the end.'

It had failed with Charlie, but she didn't say that to Lucy, or put into words her fear that it would fail with Christopher Wyndham as well. He came to Providence now knowing that he would inherit it from James, but she could detect in him no gratitude, or joy in the prospect – only a deep resentment at a burden he didn't want.

Josephine would have agreed with her grandmother. She watched him later in the day come slouching into the library where she was working for William. By the look of him, the time Ned had spent showing him round the farms had been wasted. She could have hit him for his indifference, and wept over the fear that he *hadn't* grown out of loving a woman twenty years older than himself.

'If you feel as bored as you look, why bother to come?' she asked bluntly. 'Stay in London among your sophisti-cated friends; I doubt if anyone here would mind.'

'My friends would think *you* looked fairly sophisticated yourself,' he said with a cool stare. 'I take it that you've recanted, and now *don't* find the home of your maternal ancestors boring.'

'No,' she agreed, 'I finally outgrew such childishness. It seems to be taking *you* longer.'

She turned back to the bookshelves again, and the problem of how best to index a library that had, like Topsy, just growed over several hundred years.

Christopher stared at what he could see of her – black hair cut into a silken, shining bob that swung like a bell when she moved her head, slender body outlined beneath an emerald-green cotton dress, and lovely bare legs. She was an oddity no longer; she was rather beautiful, and she had no right to turn her back on him and forget that he was there. He strode across the uneven polished boards and dragged her round to face him at arm's length.

'We're cousins of a sort, and you're supposed to be civil, my dear Josephine; but perhaps these are *French* manners.'

She might have been warned by the flash of something in his face – anger or dangerous irritation – but it suddenly seemed necessary not to concede an inch of ground or admit, even to herself, that his hands through the thin stuff of her dress felt warm and exciting.

'I'm busy, *cousin* dear, indexing Grandfather's books, otherwise of course I should be happy to sit prattling away to you, *Irish*-fashion. As a race I believe they're *very* talkative!'

The grip of his hands tightened to the point of pain. She could be certain that it *was* anger in his face, but the battle was too exhilarating to stop now.

'I told you once before I'm an *American*, and I'm not bored here, just sick of being entangled with a museum-piece that should have been allowed to fall down years ago. It doesn't belong to this day and age; or if it does, I don't damn well belong in England.'

'Then go back to America!' she shouted. 'Go and leave us to be pathetically irrelevant, or useless, or whatever else it is you think we are.'

She had despised him for his affectations, and wondered how he would ever find the energy and stamina required for doctoring. Well, *that* at least had been a mistake; she was dragged against a hard male body that had no weakness in it, and his mouth was suddenly hurting hers in his determination to teach her a lesson. There was no tenderness in that kiss, but within it there sprang to life some leaping, pulsing excitement that he recognized as dangerous, even though she did not. It made him push her far enough away at last to see that her quivering lower lip bled a little.

'I'm . . . I'm sorry, Josephine . . .' Now his mouth touched hers again gently, in a mute gesture of apology,

339

and she was adrift in a storm of sensations she hadn't experienced or even known about before.

'My . . . my fault,' she muttered. 'I wanted to annoy you.'

'Other people make me angry, but I don't usually end up wanting to make violent love to them!' His voice managed to sound lightly, extravagantly rueful, and she understood that she was meant to be lightly, extravagantly amused in return – it was bound to be how the women he knew in London would behave, but she wasn't familiar with the rules of the games they played.

'We could blame it on the Library atmosphere,' she suggested unevenly. 'Three hundred years ago Sir Ralph Wyndham strangled his wife here because she was supposed to have been unfaithful to him. The poor lady was innocent, needless to say.'

Real amusement touched Christopher's face now, changing him back to the friend she had found one day in Anita's drawing-room and never rediscovered since.

'Sir Ralph's wife may have been as pure as the driven snow, but let me tell you that ladies are not *necessarily* blameless!'

'True – there was a shockingly immoral creature who came after her – she's the very beautiful one whose portrait was banished in Victorian times to the darkest corner of the dining-room. I'm trying to persuade Grandpa William to move her back into the light.'

'On the grounds that she was led astray?'

'No, just because she's languished unseen long enough.'

Christopher's eyes lingered on his cousin's face – *not* really beautiful, like the ancestor she talked about with such surprising pleasure, but compellingly attractive and intelligent.

'Everything that's happened here matters to you now,' he said with sudden gentleness. 'You and Providence seem to belong, after all. If I'd realized that earlier I wouldn't have sneered, even though I *don't* belong, and never will.'

Josephine hesitated for a moment, doubted that she had

340

the right to do what had just come into her mind, and knew that she was going to do it all the same.

'Come with me . . . I want to show you something.'

She led him round the winding corridors of the upper floor to her grandfather's studio. It would be necessary afterwards to confess that she'd taken Christopher there uninvited, but even more than she disliked the idea of William's displeasure, she needed to explain to the man in front of her something that couldn't be put into words.

The room was golden with the reflected light of a summer afternoon. Round three walls of the room flowed William's completed vision of the little world of the valley – no mythical fantasy, but a real place set among its green hills, filled with recognizable wild flowers and the animals that belonged there, and always at its heart the same ancient stone house, serenely lovely and indestructible. It was the tapestry in the Great Hall made manifest in paint, vivid as an heraldic banner, lovely as an illuminated medieval missal. Along the bottom of the painting a glowing border was inscribed with the words from the hearth-stone downstairs: 'It is required of a steward that he be found faithful.'

Josephine said nothing, leaving Christopher to stand and stare. She loved the paintings more each time she came to visit them, but now she stood beside someone who could share the magic with her if he would, and increase it simply by being there. Her senses were almost unbearably alive. She could *smell* the cut hay in the sunlit meadow, and *hear* the song of the blackbird perched on the top-most spray of a cherry tree. But the feeling of being inside the paintings was only part of it; she was equally aware of Christopher. Since that moment in the Library she seemed to have become part of him as well, and knew that he was still doing what he'd always done at Providence – refusing to accept that he and it might belong to one another. Elation died, leaving her cold and sad. She had been mistaken and they had nothing to share after all – never would have, because he would always refuse what *she* offered, as well.

'It's extraordinary,' he muttered at last. 'I thought your grandfather was supposed to be an Impressionist.'

'My grandfather is a *painter*,' she corrected him swiftly. 'Don't tie silly little labels on him.'

'Sorry! Medical men are given to such things in order to avoid error. We can't afford to be imprecise.'

Josephine saw his eyes linger on the wall in front of him; she might have pointed out with pride the tiny splash of red that was 'her' chimney, but not now, when he'd refused to understand what she'd brought him to see.

'We ought to go,' she said abruptly. 'This is my grandfather's room; I had no right to bring you here. *You* don't have to tell him we came – I shall do that.'

'Because you think I might be tactless with my labels.'

'No, because the mistake in bringing you was mine.'

She walked away from him out of the room without waiting to see whether he followed her. Christopher remained there after she had gone, aware that he had just fallen heavily at the fence she had led him to. The feeling was unpleasant, but worse than the knowledge that he'd been weighed and found wanting was another hard fact that had to be accepted: he had kissed her to teach her a lesson, and had punished himself instead.

Damn her, and damn this house that James Wyndham was determined to thrust on him. He fought down a mad longing to walk along the painted walls shouting to them that he didn't want Providence and would never fall into the trap of thinking that it mattered. Charles Thornley had been *right*; it was a useless hulk, stranded on the shores of time, an immense and costly drag on the wheels of progress. He would not come there again until the Wyndham generation that still clung to it was safely dead, and it could be sold once and for all to the highest bidder.

He strode out of the room, and slammed the door. There'd been a moment or two of danger – holding Josephine's trembling body in his arms, in the Library, and that first astonishing glimpse of his great-uncle's vision – but he was confident now that he'd won.

He smiled and talked his way through the remainder of the weekend, though not with Josephine, and returned to London unaware that William's pictures were fixed on the retina of his mind's eye – still, small images of tranquillity in a world that was on the very point of running insane.

A bare week after the signing of the Russo-German agreement there followed what Ian Nicholson had predicted, and Hitler's armies marched on Poland. To Anita, still waiting to hear from Harry, the news was terrible but completely overshadowed by her own anxieties; how could it not make things still more hazardous for foreigners loitering with unlawful intent on German-held territory? She explained cheerfully to her daughter that Papa was making an interesting journey on the Continent, insisted over the telephone to Lucy that no news was good news, and raged privately to Charlotte over grown men who indulged themselves in behaving like heroes of the *Boy's Own Paper*. A respected, middle-aged Member of Parliament ought to have had more sense, even if a respected Austrian doctor felt obliged to play the rôle of the Scarlet Pimpernel.

'But you wouldn't really have wanted Harry to let Peter Hoffer go alone,' Charlotte suggested gently.

Anita reflected for a moment, then shook her head. 'No, of course I want him always to do what he believes is right.' She frowned over her next thought before putting it into words. 'I think he had several reasons for going, but I hope one of them was to do something for Lucy – something to cancel out the past, by helping her towards happiness at last.'

She saw Charlotte smile at her with warm affection. 'You're a very nice woman, Anita,' her cousin said simply.

Hitler's invasion of Poland turned out to have been the only mistake he had made since coming to power. Two days after it began, the ultimatum he had never believed in arrived. It had to be ignored, *natürlich*, by a leader flushed with success and chosen by destiny to make his people masters of Europe; but on Sunday, 3 September, England and France declared war on Germany.

Anita listened to the Prime Minister's wireless-broadcast, and now even her anxiety for Harry and Peter was simply part of a much more immense dread. She knew her husband's views well enough – the French had no real heart for a fight, and his own people had too little to fight with; but if he'd been there he would have smiled at her, and given her courage. Without him . . . she blinked away tears because the alarming wail of the air-raid sirens sent her rushing to find Katherine. War had started already.

The alarm was false, and the single note of the all clear sounded almost immediately. She walked back into the house again and heard the telephone ringing. A voice came faintly along the line, so heavily distorted by interference that she besought it, screamed out at it, to confirm that it was Harry.

'I can't *hear* you . . . Harry, *shout*, please.'

'Sweetheart, I promise you I'm roaring into this damned antiquated instrument.'

'Where *are* you? You *must* get out of Austria . . . War has just been declared.'

'I know, but we *are* out – all three of us, safely in Switzerland. Nothing to worry about now; just a longish drive to the coast, and then the crossing. With luck and no hold-ups, we should be home three days from now.'

'I could wait a *little* longer, if you'd drive more slowly.' The crackle was becoming deafening. She heard a disconnected word or two, then the noise ceased abruptly and the line went dead. It didn't matter, any more than it mattered that he hadn't said what was to be done with the professor.

This time her telephone call to Lucy at Providence was pure pleasure, and at Bicton Jane Thornley disgraced herself by bursting into tears. Anita offered her the problem of where to house Peter's friend, knowing that she would be restored by having something practical to think about.

The travellers arrived within the time Harry had promised, all of them very tired, and two of them looking quietly triumphant. The professor, a small, frail, white-haired man, seemed so bemused that Anita doubted whether he understood that he was safe in England.

'He *will* recover, given time,' Peter told her. 'It's just that too many dreadful things have happened to him recently, but my friend Jane will restore him, I promise you.'

'I don't doubt it.' Anita saw him smile, remove the horn-rimmed glasses he wore, and rub a hand across his eyes. Without them he looked younger, and more vulnerable, but she found that she was suddenly nervous about what must now be said.

'Lucy was here while you were away. I gave her the package you left with me, although I know it wasn't what you intended. Forgive me if I shouldn't have interfered in your lives, but time is too precious to be wasted when there's no need for it to be.'

He had to take time over polishing his glasses because his hands were trembling. 'It *has* need to be, Frau Anita . . . I have nothing to offer her, and without me she remains a wealthy woman, with a beautiful home to live in.'

'Without you she watches happiness pass her by, always just out of reach. If you call that being rich, she doesn't.'

His hands replaced the spectacles slowly, but he made no comment at all and she was left to watch him leave with the professor the following morning wondering whether she'd done more harm than good.

'You're looking very pensive, sweet,' Harry commented as the taxi drove away and they went back into the house. 'I suppose you hate the thought of sending Kate away?'

'Well, yes . . . and so do *you*, although we know perfectly well that she loves being at Providence.' She glanced at his face, overcome as she sometimes was by the sheer unlikeliness of a marriage that had turned out to be so necessary and right for both of them.

'Try not to feel obliged to play knight-errant again,' she

345

suddenly beseeched him. 'It's very hard on the poor creatures you leave behind!'

He didn't smile, but stooped to kiss her mouth instead. 'I'll make you a promise if you like. But now I must go and report to my worthy colleagues on what is happening in Nazi-held Austria. May God help Poland, because there's precious little *we* can do to stop Hitler there, either.'

Chapter Twenty-Nine

On the train-journey to Warwickshire Peter Hoffer struggled with the task in hand – to keep hope alive in the fragile wreck of a man who had been his teacher and friend for thirty years. Jakob Lindermann had stayed in Austria because an ailing, selfish wife who was not a Jew had refused to believe that he was in any danger. She had refused to leave, and Jakob had remained as well because she needed him. She had died a year later knowing the magnitude of her mistake, but by then it had been almost too late.

He sat staring out of the train window now, lost in reflection or memory, while Peter tried to harness his own wildly bolting thoughts to the responsibilities he was obliged to deal with. He was *not* required to think about Lucy Thornley . . . although, if Anita Trentham should happen to be right, he *was*, and must.

After three days at Bicton Jakob began to understand that he was safe. His frail hands no longer shook, and he sat in Jane's conservatory, saying very little but content to watch this small, kind woman who had taken him into her home. Her plants flourished mightily and he wasn't surprised; they did it for love of her, he supposed. The sick children in the house were comfortable again because the Herr Doktor was back, and Peter could think of no reason, except cowardice, why he should not cycle over to Providence. If he needed the childish help of looking for omens, it was something to clutch at that Gertrude Wyndham should be out in the courtyard garden, dead-heading roses. She smiled at him with her usual lovely kindness, as if she'd never even noticed that his visits in recent months had been only when he was certain Lucy wouldn't be there.

'Peter, my dear, we're so very glad to see you safely back with your old friend. I'd pelt you with questions now but William will want to hear about the journey too. He's in Warwick at the moment, sitting on the Bench – a duty he dislikes so much that he makes himself perform it with unfailing regularity!'

He smiled and bowed over her outstretched hand – one of his few remaining gestures to remind her that he was a foreigner. Nor had he ever addressed her with anything but the gentle formality he believed was due to the mother of his friend, Ned.

'You are looking a little tired, Lady Wyndham . . . should you be out here, working?'

'We have an English saying – "a change is as good as a rest"! Our evacuee children are due to arrive from London tomorrow, and my daughter and grand-daughter believe that snipping roses would be good for me after making up beds! They are still hard at work in Lucy's wing.'

'Shall I insist that a comfortable armchair indoors would give you *more* rest, or leave you in peace with your flowers?'

'Oh, leave me, I think . . . but it would be a kindness if you would go and persuade *them* to stop working.' She was almost certain that the beds were made, and Josephine already on her way to the village to shop with Mary, but there were times when the truth should be stretched a little if good could be wrung from it.

'Then *auf wiedersehen, gnädige Frau.*' He relapsed into his native tongue only when in the grip of strong emotion. Gertrude knew it, but wished passionately that she could be sure what it boded for her daughter. Peter walked away into the house without telling her, and she was left in anxious peace with her roses.

Josephine was not in the west range, and Lucy was no longer making up beds. For the moment all that could be done *was* done; she could sit pretending to admire the rocking-horse that still lorded it over the day-nursery. It was a little the worse, now, for the wear and tear of several generations, but surely small London children who might

348

never have seen such a thing would be enchanted by its handsome black tail and mane, and the stirrups Victoria had polished until they shone?

Lucy had passed the days since Anita's last telephone call in a frantic round of activity. She would allow herself to think of nothing but the hundred and one tasks needing to be done before they were ready to receive ten children and a teacher from Harry's dockland constituency in London. In the cold watches of the night when there was nothing to stop thought rushing in she struggled to remember that Anita might have been mistaken. Even the gift of his mother's ring might simply have been Peter Hoffer's way of saying that something beautiful should be cherished, no matter by whom. She gave a little sigh, unaware that she was being watched by a man who thought she looked thin and tired, and beautiful in the particular way that comes from unhappiness somehow survived and transmuted.

'Lucy . . . I am sent to tell you that it is time for you to stop working. Your mother insists, and she is always right, is she not?'

She ducked her head against dizziness, doubting that he actually stood behind her . . . imagination had conjured him up, and if she turned her head the sunlit corridor would be quite empty.

'Won't you even look at me . . . perhaps say *"guten abend, meine freund"*?'

He was real and perfectly remembered, and she didn't have to turn round, because he came to stand in front of her . . . Her eyes, staring at the floor, took in only what was in her line of vision – the familiar sight of cracked, polished shoes, frayed trouser cuffs – the shabby dress of a man too poor to spend money unnecessarily on clothes, and too unconcerned about himself to care. His hands hid themselves in the pockets of his old tweed jacket; nothing to be learned there except that he didn't seem to want to touch her. Nothing to be learned from his face, because it was under stern control now. If Anita had been wrong . . . She clung to the knowledge that he'd been told about

Frank's will, and finally forced her voice to reach across the sunlit space between them.

'I have your mother's ring . . . Anita gave it to me, and I shall never give it back to you. It's *my* treasure now.'

He didn't smile, didn't move, or do anything but stare at her. Dear God, Anita *had* been wrong, after all . . . The sapphire ring on its chain about her neck felt cold against her skin, but she made one last attempt at happiness. 'I can never put it on my finger, of course, unless you say that I may.'

'How *can* I . . . Lucy, how can I say anything at all?' he cried suddenly. 'Here, you are Frank Thornley's widow, with wealth, a beautiful home, and children who love you. I have nothing to offer you – no money at all except the small salary that I allow Jane to pay me, no home but the couple of rooms she is kind enough to set aside for me at Bicton. I might be able to do better than that elsewhere, but you know that my work is at the Institute; if I left it you would despise me for turning my back on it. Even if none of *that* worries you as it does me, there is something else that does trouble you . . . Your husband rejected me as a friend; Charles feels obliged to do the same, and I am obliged to admire him for his loyalty.'

'Only one thing in life terrifies me,' she said quietly, 'the prospect of living out the rest of my days without you. In time I think we might make Charles understand, or his own life will teach him about the mistakes people make; if not, we must manage without him and he without us . . . but, please, my dearest, don't let *us* waste any more time.'

They moved at the same moment through the space dividing them, Peter's arms suddenly outstretched, Lucy safely home at last. Their hands, lips, bodies, clung, desperate to be assured that nothing could separate them again. The loneliness and despair had been so terrible that only absolute closeness could convince them now.

At last he held her away from him, breathless and trembling, so that he could see her face. 'Things were bad in Austria, *liebchen*. We couldn't get Jakob across the frontier legally and in the end became, Harry and I, the most unlikely couple of desperados you ever saw, looking for a place where we could cross at night! I promised myself then that if we got back at all I would ask you to marry me, because nothing mattered but being alive and happy. But the nearer we got to England, the more I became afraid again that other things mattered as well. You must be absolutely sure that they do not.'

Lucy's transfigured face answered him even before she put it into words. 'Being together . . . that's *all* that matters, apart from mending the children at Bicton.'

She was kissed again, but when Peter lifted his head to smile at her the happiness in his face was suddenly quenched. 'My God . . . children *here*, you said . . . how can that be managed, my dear one, if you live with me at Bicton?'

'Easily, apparently! Sybil's daughter, Josephine, is already here to help my mother and Mary. You scarcely know her yet, but she has Henri Blanchard's intelligence, Sybil's stubbornness, and a supply of energy worthy of her Great-Aunt Louise! I think she'd cope with twenty children without turning a hair.'

In the weeks that followed there were times when it seemed less simple than that to cope with the ten who actually arrived. They came quietly, to begin with – crop-headed boys and wary small girls, with unfamiliar accents and gas-masks in boxes slung round their necks. Most of them hadn't seen fields before, and they were nervous of animals at close range; they missed the safe, rough street life they knew, and the large families left behind. The strangeness of the country was hard enough to get used to, but it took them longer still to accept Providence itself. How could it ever seem like home? They were happier outside, or in the slightly more familiar atmosphere of the classroom in the village school.

With autumn came the sort of rain London never seemed to have, and there were no friendly street-lamps to break up the night-time darkness between Haywood's End and the strange place they'd been left in. They were homesick for what they knew and, as the quiet weeks of the 'phony' war went by, there seemed no reason to be in the country at all. By the end of October eight of the children had been reclaimed by their parents and gone back to London. Only the youngest two, Billy Andrews and his sister Eliza, were still there because they no longer had a home to return to.

Gertrude listened obediently when Louise Trentham explained that she must be firm and point out to the authorities that evacuee children orphaned unexpectedly were *not* the responsibility of their country hostess. She agreed with her sister-in-law that there must be relatives who should be traced, and went on hoping in her heart that Mary would be allowed to keep and mother the lonely little pair the war had wished on them.

Lucy was married to Peter Hoffer at Haywood's End on a soft, grey November morning when they walked through the wood to the church with falling golden leaves for confetti. No crowds of guests this time, or fancy dress. Just Lucy's family and old friends like Maud Roberts back there to see her happy.

Anita and Harry took Kate home with them afterwards, but Josephine still stayed at Providence, as if she had forgotten any other life. With Victoria enrolled at a veterinary college thirty miles away, and Tom back at Rugby for his last year at school, Gertrude felt obliged one morning to be more firm with her grand-daughter than she intended to be with any evacuee authority.

'Darling Jo, we love having you here, but are you quite *sure* you don't want to go home?'

Josephine considered the question gravely, then nodded her head. 'Yes, I'm sure. I hate London, and this seems as if it *is* my home.' Her grandmother looked unconvinced and she rushed into speech again. 'I know Mary can look after Billy and Liza perfectly well without me, but Emmy's teaching me to cook, and she and Ethel really *need* help here now . . . I thought you could show me how to mend things, and apart from all that I'm not a quarter of the way through the indexing yet . . .' She ran out of breath, stared at her grandmother, and took a fresh gulp of air. 'Do you and Grandpa mind if I stay?'

Gertrude wondered whether in some Elysian field Henri knew and was smiling at what had finally happened – the sombre-faced child who had roamed about Providence like a wild creature pining for its natural habitat had discovered that she belonged there after all.

'We should miss you sorely if you went away,' she confessed after a moment or two. 'I was being amazingly unselfish because I thought I should encourage you to go back to London. What does your mother say?'

Josephine's face relaxed into the rare grin that lit her face with mischief. 'Oh, it's quite agreed that *one* of us must be here to keep an eye on you and Grandpa. *She* is busy learning to drive an ambulance about London, so looking after you and Providence is going to be *my* war-work!'

'Then I shall give in gracefully, and leave you to take the good news to the studio. Your grandfather is there pretending to work, but more probably staring out of the window, trying not to mind the thought of you going away.'

She was given a sudden shy kiss, and then left alone to consider among other things why her grand-daughter so hated London. It was wicked to think that the war, terrible though it might have turned out to be, had brought them nothing but good, but Lucy was deeply happy at Bicton, Mary had been given some children to love, and she and William had been given Josephine. Blessings usually had to be paid for, but there was no hard and fast rule – perhaps *this* time God Almighty would allow the war to sputter out altogether without leaving Europe torn in pieces.

It seemed so for a little while longer, at least to anyone who hadn't lived and died in the ghettoes of Warsaw. In England the war was an inconvenience that required people to blunder about at night in the dangerous obscurity of the black-out; in France the army sat behind its impregnable Maginot Line; and at sea the Royal Navy began the blockade that was to starve Germany eventually into peace. But in Finland at the end of November came the Russian advance. The League of Nations, in a final death-throes twitch, expelled Russia from the League, and the Finns fought their invaders for months through bitter Arctic weather. They were forced to capitulate in March of the following year, and scarcely anyone then foresaw that the war was about to become real for England and France as well.

When the moment finally came, with Hitler's lightning invasion of Denmark and Norway, Josephine was making a rare visit to London. She got to her mother's flat in Pont Street to find Christopher Wyndham already there, looking very much at home. Sybil was lying on her white sofa, swathed in the becoming folds of a turquoise silk dressing-gown. She was perfectly made up as usual, and not even the plaster cast and sling on her left arm could lessen the effect she made. When she smiled at the unexpected sight of her daughter Josephine was suddenly reminded of her grandmother – age made no difference to either of them because their power to enchant lay so little in mere flesh and bone.

'Darling . . . this is lovely provided there's nothing wrong at Providence. I was feeling sorry for myself half an hour ago, then Christopher arrived, and now you.'

Josephine nodded at the man who hoisted himself to his feet and immediately sank back into the chair as if nothing would prise him out of it again; he looked so tired that she thought he would probably fall asleep if they were kind enough not talk to him. His clothes were crumpled, but it wasn't because of them that she could no longer think him effete or dandified. With medical training nearly complete, he had somehow moved beyond her reach. The languid young man who had been provoked into kissing her in the Library at Providence had become *this* tired, adult, thin-faced man who still found time to come and sit with her mother.

'Nothing's wrong,' Josephine said abruptly. 'I just

thought you might need a little help until your arm mends.'

'Sweetheart, if he could rouse himself sufficiently after a night on the wards at St Thomas's Christopher would tell you that I'm *walking* wounded, but please stay if Grandma can spare you . . . it's so lovely to see you.'

'There was a news placard on the street corner, Maman . . . the Germans have invaded Denmark and Norway . . . that sounds very bad, doesn't it?'

'It sounds the beginning of real war,' Christopher put in slowly, opening his eyes. 'Harry *said* it would happen if we didn't move first. The Germans can't afford any threat to their supplies of iron ore from Sweden. When the Baltic freezes over they bring them out from the Norwegian port of Narvik and down the North Sea. Now the Government will *have* to do something at last, but it will probably be too little and too late.'

'Because we can't do *anything* right, according to you?' Josephine asked angrily.

'No, because we don't yet seem to understand that we're going to have to do some real fighting. Chamberlain's powers of decision have been exhausted by the effort of declaring war, and making up his mind to issue ration-books! It's not quite enough in my humble, *American* opinion!' He smiled suddenly at the expression on her face, but heaved himself to his feet and leaned over Sybil to kiss her goodbye. 'I shall tactfully disappear before I enrage your daughter with my usual unfailing skill! Get her to make sure you don't go falling about in the black-out again, my dear; we might be needing good ambulance drivers soon!' He glanced at Josephine, apparently considering whether or not to kiss her as well. 'Perhaps *not*,' he murmured, 'discretion being much the better part of valour!'

There was a moment of silence in the room after he'd gone before Sybil ventured a question. '*Does* he make you angry?'

'Usually . . . for one reason or another,' Josephine muttered. 'We don't see eye to eye about Providence . . . I suppose that's the main thing.'

Sybil watched her daughter's flushed face, and wondered whether it *was* the main thing. 'He has so little free time that it was kind of him to make sure I was all right.'

'Why shouldn't he come . . . you made sure *he* was all right when he was hurt. Anyway, it's obvious he's . . . he's very fond of you.' Josephine jumped up suddenly, brushing the subject of Christopher Wyndham aside. 'I came to be useful . . . what can I do?'

'Hear me when I explain something I didn't make clear enough once before. I hope Christopher *is* fond of me . . . because he seems like the son I might have had. It's why he's so kind to me – because he understands that.' She would mention Patrick if she had to but, even to be reassured about Christopher, her daughter might never forgive her for loving any other man but Henri Blanchard.

Josephine's mouth suddenly tilted in a sweet smile. 'You're lovely, like Grandma Gertrude . . . everyone should always be kind to both of you.'

They didn't see Christopher again for as long as she stayed in Pont Street, but as the days of April went past it seemed as if individual personal dramas no longer mattered. From the time that the Allied expeditionary force sent to Norway had to be ignominiously brought home, the headlong pace of disaster seemed to gather momentum every day. The Prime Minister survived a vote of censure when the Norwegian debâcle was debated in the House, but he couldn't survive the German invasion of Belgium and Holland immediately afterwards.

Josephine was visiting her godmother when Harry came home and gave them the news of Neville Chamberlain's resignation.

Anita stared at her husband's sombre face. 'You've been convinced ever since the war began that we needed a different man . . . in fact, needed the man we've now got . . .'

'. . . so why am I not happy? I suppose because it's hard to crow when any well-intentioned man comes a cropper; but the manner of his going was terrible . . . Amery delivered the *coup de grâce*, as it happened, and chose

Cromwell's words to do it – "Depart, I say, and let us have done with you. In the name of God, go!" Effective, but I can't bring myself to believe that Chamberlain deserved quite *that* farewell.'

In the weeks that followed, even that small individual tragedy ceased to matter. By the time the Dutch capitulated, German tanks were already pouring across France, simply outflanking a Maginot Line that might have been invincible if only it had been long enough. The troops that made up Britain's small regular standing army were still fighting in the north when the Belgian King surrendered as well. Cut off by the German advance behind them, they could only fight their way down a dwindling, hellish corridor to the sea.

The evacuation of more than three hundred thousand men from the bomb-torn beaches of Dunkirk seemed miraculous enough to become the stuff of legend afterwards, and to be counted almost as a victory at the time. But before the June hay harvest was in at Providence, Italy had entered the war on Germany's side, and the French Government under Pétain had accepted Hitler's armistice terms. The war was real enough now. Around the coasts of England unarmed civilians watched the sea, and listened for the sound of church bells to signal that the German armada had arrived.

During the feverish summer of 1940 even Jakob Lindermann's age and scholarly reputation might not have been enough to protect him from internment as an alien, but the old man was left in peace with Jane Thornley and Lucy, and they suspected that Harry had something to do with it. He enjoyed watching the children who slowly mended under his friend's care, and made a last late friendship with William Wyndham.

Tom Thornley left Rugby as the air battles over southern England began, and immediately volunteered. Charles accepted his stepfather enough to visit Lucy occasionally at Bicton, and reported with tired triumph that Thornley's were now working three eight-hour shifts a day, in order to replace the equipment that the army had had to leave behind at Dunkirk.

Sybil began to drive her ambulance in earnest, and Josephine learned to cook and clean and mend and help Ned grow vegetables. But, thanks to Great-Uncle James, her war-work in the end became not quite what she'd anticipated. One of his multifarious activities since Christopher's return from Spain had been to meddle in the running of several orphanages for blind children. They had been left undisturbed at the beginning of the war in their familiar surroundings, but by the late summer of 1940 the Luftwaffe switched from attacking RAF airfields in southern England to bombing London itself; the children had become too vulnerable now not to be moved.

On a morning in late August a small bus-load of them, driven by Dr Christopher Wyndham, arrived at Providence. The arrangement had been made so hastily that the gardener was still helping Ned to fix the last stretch of improvised fencing intended to prevent blind children from falling into the moat. Christopher climbed down from the bus, and found Gertrude Wyndham waiting on the bridge, smiling a welcome.

She nodded in the direction of the water. 'I'm afraid it took us a little while to remember something we take for granted.'

'Do you mind what Ned's doing? A line of chestnut fencing isn't exactly an adornment.'

'These children won't be troubled by the look of it; why should we?'

His smile acknowledged the rare note of rebuke in her voice. 'Sorry, Aunt; but my grandfather was in one of his Napoleonic moods when this was arranged; he didn't give you much choice, or remember that you've devoted a lifetime to preserving the beauty of Providence.'

'In the last war a sea of potatoes and cabbages round the house wasn't much of an adornment either, but they seemed more important at the time, and may do so again. At the moment it's the children who matter. Our previous evacuees didn't settle down here, because Providence seemed to overpower them; these poor mites won't see it, only *feel* it; so perhaps we shall do better with them.'

She was shy of saying anything more to this cool and self-sufficient young man. He had never been over-powered by anything as far as she knew, least of all by the charm of the house that his grandfather would one day bequeath to him. She admired him and thought she might have loved him if he'd given her the chance, but he still resisted them, just as he'd always done.

'Shall we introduce the children to their new home?' she suggested after a moment. 'They must be tired of sitting in that bus.'

Before Christopher drove away again the following morning, he rose very early, with the intention of going out for a walk. He was accustomed now to being awake when the rest of the world still slept, and although he would accept no attachment to Providence itself, he admitted to himself that its park in the dawn of a summer morning was a better place to be in than London.

He walked quietly along the corridor, but stopped abruptly at the top of the wide, wooden staircase leading to the hall. Ahead of him Josephine's slender figure was groping its way so hesitantly that he'd have imagined her to be sleep-walking if she hadn't been fully dressed. The slight sound he made caused her to waver, miss her footing, and land spread-eagled at the bottom of the flight.

When he reached her she was already sitting up, gingerly rubbing her ankle. He knelt down and ran his own hands over the ankle she'd been holding.

'What it is to have a doctor in the house!' she muttered, then ducked her head against sudden dizziness.

'Sprained probably, but not broken, and the doctor recommends the cup that cheers but not inebriates. Can you hop as far as the kitchen, or do I have to lug you, fireman-fashion?'

'I think I'll hop as the lesser of two evils.' She was helped upright, but quickly released, and left to hop along wondering whether his briskness was habitual, to prevent impressionable, silly nurses from falling in love with him.

In the kitchen he wetted one of Emmy's clean tea-towels and wrapped it round her throbbing ankle, then made tea with calm efficiency. No male fumbling with crockery for Christopher Wyndham, no hesitant search for things he couldn't find. Nor had his hands been hesitant, either; she remembered their cool touch on her skin, as she knew she would remember the rest of this early-morning moment in the quiet dimness of the kitchen.

'Do you always get up with the dawn?' he asked suddenly.

'No, although I don't like to miss anything if I can help it.'

He smiled because the answer was characteristic, but thought of something else. 'I thought you were sleep-walking . . . you looked so odd.'

'I'd covered my eyes so that I shouldn't cheat and look – I wanted to know how it will feel to these blind children, learning to find their way about. I'm familiar with the house, but it was still horribly difficult.'

Again he realized that it was what he might have expected of her – no treacly, self-indulgent, useless pity; instead, she would try to understand what it *felt* like to be blind.

'If you'd fallen from the top of the stairs you might have damaged yourself seriously.'

'So I might.' She ignored a sharpness in his voice which obviously had more to do with her stupidity than his own concern. 'Will you bind it up for me, please? There'll be a lot of work to do later on.'

'Blame old James, not me – it was *his* idea; one of his rare mistakes, I'd say. Your grandmother told me the previous intake had been overpowered by this house, and I'm not surprised.'

Josephine clasped her hands tightly round the mug he'd put in front of her. 'You still don't understand . . . I doubt if you ever will. The mistake was to bring normal children here from dockland tenements . . . what could you expect *them* to make of Providence? But children who can't see must feel, and smell, and *sense*.'

'What don't I understand that they will sense?'

'Something you're incapable of seeing – that they've come to what Providence has always been, a place of refuge.'

Her eyes challenged him across the table, and he knew that he must deny the truth of what she'd said. If not, Providence would win, and he would be trapped into believing that a house was more than a collection of bricks and stone.

'The refuge is very temporary in this case, and I hope you can stop them falling down polished stairs and wandering into the moat for as long as they're here.' It sounded so weak even to him that he was forced to assert himself. 'Stay where you are while I fetch a bandage from my bag . . . Oblige me by doing *that* without an argument.' He walked out of the room without looking at her, for fear that she might be smiling.

The strapping was put in place swiftly, as if he had no wish to linger. He stood up to go and she broke the silence that had fallen on them.

'Is it very dangerous, what my mother is doing?'

'Yes! Ambulance drivers on duty don't sit in air-raid shelters – they drive their ambulances to where they're needed.'

She accepted his bluntness, sensing that it was born of an anger he could do nothing about. He was enraged by the knowledge that refugees were being machine-gunned to death as they straggled along the roads of France, and children suffocated under the stinking rubble of their bombed homes. The world had gone mad, and all he could do was help to mend those who weren't beyond mending.

'Rest your ankle when you can, and for God's sake keep your eyes *open* in future.'

The curt instruction was flung at her, and this time she didn't understand that his anger was suddenly confused by longing. He wanted to carry her away to some green, private place outside where they could forget the hateful world and all the bitter differences that kept them arguing. He would stop her mouth with kisses, her ams would comfort him, and they might learn to love each other. Longing and need burned in him like a strengthening flame. She was aware of it too, because her eyes and mouth told him that she was ready to be loved. He moved towards her, only to be shocked back to reality by the sound of Emmy's clock on the wall behind him. Its preliminary asthmatic whirr destroyed the tension linking them, even before it ponderously chimed the hour of six o'clock. It was just the start of another day after all, a day like any other, and his only duty was to get back to London.

'Must you go back this morning?' she asked softly.

'Yes. The hospital was bombed two nights ago . . . there's a lot to clear up still, even if the sods didn't come back last night.'

She accepted the finality of what he said. He didn't need a refuge, he wanted to slay the barbarians.

'Give Maman my love when you see her. Tell her to . . .' She stopped – tell her what? To take shelter and forget the people who needed help? 'Tell her I'd like to be with her in the ambulance.'

Christopher's tight mouth relaxed a little. 'All right, but if you really want to be useful, stay here and start learning Braille. These children will need teaching, apart from everything else.'

He walked out of the room leaving her still sitting there. Emmy would be down at any moment and there was a lot to think about and arrange. But her mind wouldn't relinquish its vision of hospital buildings crumpling, and clouds of dust rising in the silence that followed destruction.

Chapter Thirty

The invasion didn't come, because for the first time since the war began the Germans couldn't win in the air. Radar, and the Spitfires and Hurricanes that Lord Beaverbrook's demonic energy forced into production, and the men who flew them, were more than the Luftwaffe could beat. But although the Armada assembled across the Channel didn't sail, it was the only mercy to give thanks for in the terrible year of 1940. Italy's invasion of Egypt started the interminable swings of fortune of the North African desert war, German submarine attacks on Atlantic shipping began to seem enough in themselves to bring them victory, and the nightly bombings went on – London still, but other major cities as well.

In December the remaining members in the House of the old Independent Labour Party brought a motion that Britain should beg for a negotiated peace. It was defeated – by 341 votes to 4. Ian Nicholson abandoned his attachment to the Party as a result of it, and Harry Trentham entered the Government for the first time. Victoria proudly wore the cream breeches and green sweater of the Women's Land Army, and Tom sweltered under a desert sun that seemed composed of different, fiercer elements from the one he knew at home.

At Providence Josephine led her blind children up and down and round the house until they knew the feel and sound and smell of it as well as she did; they learned where uneven floorboards were and didn't stumble, and walked confidently across Gertrude's courtyard garden from their wing of the house to listen to William playing the piano for them in the drawing-room. They tore about like any other children in the safety of Ned's gardens, and when it was time to walk to the sweet-shop in Haywood's End Mary's refugees, Billy and Eliza, with their life in London almost forgotten, shepherded them to the village without fuss. Much of what was happening was terrible, but there were small triumphs to be counted as well – acts of kindness, and shared laughter on black days, and the courage of ordinary people as well as that of heroes.

Winter gave way to spring and, although there wasn't much else but the season itself to encourage hope, at least the nightly raids were slackening. There were still occasional massive attacks on one industrial city or another, but the Germans were beginning to learn the cost and the futility of air-raids that didn't break morale, or seriously harm the war effort. Before the lesson had been fully learned, Birmingham was singled out for attack one night in May. In case they hadn't heard the siren up at the House, Matthew Moffat, on duty in the ARP post at Haywood's End, rang the telephone that now sat by Ned's bed.

'Bad 'un, by the looks of things, Mr Ned . . . lot of them bastards on the way, seemingly.'

'Thanks, Matthew – we'll rouse the children. Better ring Dr Hoffer too, if you will; they're nearer to trouble than we are.'

Mary, pulling on slacks and sweater as she went, was already waking Billy and Eliza next door, and Ned left her to run along the corridors that veined an old and inconvenient house. There were occasions when he thought Providence could have been better-planned, and hurrying round it at night in a black-out was one of them. In the west range where Josephine and the other children slept, she had heard the siren and was dressed by the time Ned knocked on her door. The air-raid routine hadn't been much used recently but the children hadn't forgotten it, and they had no need to be troubled by night-time darkness. Five minutes after Matthew's call they were being lifted down into the shelter on the other side of the kitchen yard beyond the moat. It had been the ice-house in what were once called less civilized times.

With the children safe, Ned stood outside watching the sky over Birmingham, meshed with the white pencil beams of searchlights vainly trying to protect the city. The sinister hum of bombers on their way and the thud of anti-aircraft guns, made his temples throb with memories of another hateful war. Already, a lurid glow in the sky spoke of fires begun by incendiary bombs, and he shivered at the thought of one of them landing on the sprawling roofs of Providence.

He went back inside the house and climbed the staircase to knock on his parents' door. Gertrude appeared at once, as if she had been expecting him.

'Do you want us to come, Ned?'

'Please, my dear . . . things are looking rather bad over the city.'

He shepherded them downstairs and outside, William gently bemoaning the unseemly necessity of it all until the sight of Josephine sitting on the floor among the children made him smile; she was teaching them to sing the French words of 'Frère Jacques'.

'Everyone here, love?' Ned murmured to Mary.

'Yes . . . except for Emmy. She'd forgotten her handbag and went back for it!'

Ned grinned in spite of himself, remembering the huge black compendium containing all Emmy's treasures, and which now went with her everywhere. 'She *must* have been flustered. I wish she'd stayed put, all the same.'

'Don't worry . . . she'll be on her way back by now.'

'Yes, but I think I'll just go and make sure.' He kissed the tip of his wife's nose, then smiled at her. '*You* oblige me by staying where you are.' He saw no reason to say that incendiary bombs were on his mind, rather than the need to look for someone who knew her way about the house blindfold after forty years.

The high-explosive bomb fell as he was running up the back staircase. He heard its whine, and dull roar, and was thrown against the wall as the old house lifted on its foundations and shook with protest at the hurt that had been done to it. Emmy's cry reached him a moment later from her bedroom on the corner where the south and west ranges of the house met. It had been a pleasant place but he stepped through choking dust and falling plaster into a ruin. The wall between it and Josephine's room next door had disappeared, and the floor now canted at a mad angle down towards the black hole where Jo would usually have been sleeping. Thank God in Heaven, and Matthew for his telephone call.

The narrow beam of Ned's torch found Emmy lying almost underneath the heavy oak door that had connected the two rooms. It had been blown outwards on top of her and probably saved her life. She was conscious, and able to whisper when he knelt beside her, 'Sorry, Master Ned . . . wanted my bag, stupid old fool.'

In the faint torchlight glimmer she seemed unhurt, but her body was held fast by the angle of the door, close to where the floor threatened to give way.

'Emmy love, it's not very healthy to stay here. If I try to lift the door a little, will you do your best to crawl out . . . carefully? Try to move when I say . . . try *now*!'

The weight he braced himself against shifted a little, then settled again. 'Again, Emmy . . . go *on*.' The drag on his arms and back was cruel, as if the weight of Providence itself hung on them, but the door moved and so did Emmy. He could hear her gasp as she crawled away from him over the rubble-strewn floor. 'Keep going . . . I'll be coming behind you.'

The floor was giving way, with a terrible, slow inevitability, but she had reached the comparative safety of the door into the corridor when a rushing sound behind her spoke of some final calamity she could hear and sense but not see. Choking with dust, she began to crawl through the blackness of the corridor, dimly aware of the direction in which she must go to find help; but pain she'd been unaware of was gaining on her, making each effort to move more agonizing than the one before. She was unconscious at the top of the stairs when Sid Moffat and his grandson arrived and found her.

Ned was dug out alive from the wreckage on the floor

below, but died in Warwick Hospital two days later. All the people of the valley crammed the churchyard when he was buried alongside his friend, George Hoskins; only Tom was absent, still somewhere in the Western Desert. At his grandmother's request, Charles read the lesson, with his burned hands hidden by bandages. A Thornley factory had been one of those set alight on the night of the raid, but Charlie had made sure that with a superhuman effort it was in production again by the time of his uncle's funeral. Victoria had kissed him warmly for once, understanding why the effort had been made.

Afterwards, Gertrude insisted on walking back with William along the path through the wood, just as they'd always done from church. She appeared not to see the huge tarpaulins that covered the shattered corner of the house; her slender black-coated figure led them home, and they stumbled after her.

'I couldn't understand at first why she didn't weep,' Lucy whispered to her husband, 'but now I know . . . She's buried herself with Ned. It won't matter at all, except to us, when she dies – she's dead already.'

Peter Hoffer's arm tightened its clasp on her shoulders but he shook his head. 'You're wrong, my dearest. She's frail, but not dead; in fact, still stronger than the rest of us. She knows that she must live without Ned because William needs her – we *all* need her.'

Lucy was forced to agree with him. Only the knowledge that she was indispensable as well as greatly loved could have enabled her mother to bear what had happened.

Gertrude's calmness held, even during a day that seemed interminable to the rest of them, but her face quivered at the sight of Christopher Wyndham, wearing the uniform of the Royal Army Medical Corps. She wanted to weep *then*, not for her darling left in the churchyard, but for another generation of young men and women whose lives were being wrenched so terribly out of shape.

'I can't find anything to say to you . . . I tried, all the way here.' He made the confession with difficulty because the taste of hatred was in his mouth. His oath had been given to the service of healing, but he wanted to kill the people who had hurt her so terribly. It was a strange moment to discover that he loved her very much, but when she smiled he thought she knew what he was feeling.

'There's no need to say anything at all,' she said gently, 'but there's something I should like to tell *you*. Ned loved Providence, but understood in the end that owning it didn't matter; the only important thing was for it to survive. After the last war he was afraid that he wouldn't be able to fight for it again; he was content for it to go to someone who *could* fight for it.'

'He died saving Emmy, wasn't that enough?'

Gertrude smiled luminously. 'I think he knew that it was.'

She moved away to greet someone else, and Christopher walked out of the house, suddenly desperate to escape. He knew that she had wanted to make him a gift of Ned's understanding, but the gift was a burden he found intolerable. His life was his own, or would be when this damnable war was over. He was a free man, with no particular reason to be attached to the Wyndhams, and a very particular determination *not* to be attached to a house he didn't want. If need be, he would refuse the inheritance James was so anxious to foist on him. What became of Providence would be no concern of his.

He took a deep breath of relief, and walked on, along the far side of the moat. From where he was he could see the hideous gash that disfigured the corner of the house. He didn't want it, but it had been beautiful. There wasn't so much beauty in the world that they could afford any of it to be wantonly destroyed.

'How helpful of the Germans to have made things easy for you.'

The sound of Josephine's cold voice made him spin round. It was the first time she had spoken to him all day, and he'd had the impression that she'd deliberately avoided him. For once her clothes didn't become her; a black jacket and skirt made her sallow skin seem lifeless.

She looked tired and sad and too old for her nineteen years, but her eyes were alive, and fiercely accusing.

'In what way – easy?'

'They've done what they can to destroy Providence . . . you'll be able to leave the rest to fall down.' Christopher stared at her in silence, and she was goaded into shouting at him. 'It *is* what you want – admit it, can't you?'

He closed the gap between them and fastened his hands on her thin shoulders, shaking her in a sudden flare of anger that matched her own. 'Stop shouting at me . . . I don't know *what* I want.'

Her mouth close to his own trembled, but not on the brink of tears. He knew she was about to fling some fresh defiance at him and, as clearly as he'd known with Gertrude Wyndham a few minutes before, the certainty was born in him that here was someone else he would love all the days of his life.

'Dear God . . . I *do* know what I want. Josephine, marry me.'

He hadn't proposed to a girl before – told himself afterwards that he'd had *that* much excuse for making such a deplorable hash of it. But even if the timing and the wording had been less disastrous than they were, she would still have believed that he was making fun of her. She pulled herself free of his hands and backed away from him out of reach.

'You're mad, and I wouldn't marry you if you were the last man left on earth.'

'Definite, at least,' he said, with a wry smile. 'You don't think you might ever come to change your mind?'

'I never change my mind.'

'You did about Providence.' That was a mistake, too. He saw grief overtake anger in her face as she turned and fled, running like a wild creature across the grass. It was the last he saw of her for the rest of the day. She stayed with the children in the other wing, and he was left to do his duty by the others – by Ned's white-faced widow and the silent pair of children who shadowed her, William, who held Gertrude's hand as if he dared not let it go, and his friend Sybil, who had loved Ned so. He went back to London without speaking to Josephine again, and found awaiting him there the news that his unit was to be sent overseas immediately.

Chapter Thirty-One

He didn't return to England again for eighteen months, until after the Battle of El Alamein had signalled the beginning of the final German retreat across North Africa. In Europe and the Far East, where the war mattered most, 1942 had been a terrible year, but at least there was now a spark of hope in the desert fighting.

Christmas leave returned him to a land of hoar-frosted trees, and fields lying under the cold, pure whiteness of snow – the stuff of magic after what he'd grown accustomed to. He stayed a night in London with Anita and Harry, and explained briefly that his next destination was Providence, not Dublin. During the slow train-ride and the lifts he hitched from Warwick, he observed countryside and people, talked when conversation was necessary, and smiled at anyone who smiled at him. But everything about the journey was unreal; he no longer belonged to the life he'd left behind in the desert, and belonged even less here. Walking along the drive leading to the house, he couldn't remember why it had seemed so imperative to come; but it wasn't until he was across the bridge that he realized with a sickening shock what Gertrude Wyndham would think his reason had been for coming. He was on the point of turning away, but it was too late – the door opened and she was there, looking at him.

'I was just about to turn tail and run,' he said jerkily. 'Is it a frightful nerve, turning up like this?'

'Christopher . . . how lovely; Sybil arrived an hour ago, and now you. I didn't raise William's hopes, but when your last letter hinted at leave, I think I half-expected you.'

The smile that lit her thin face held only warmth and welcome; it ignored so completely everything she considered unimportant that for the moment, at least, he must ignore it too. She led him into the Great Hall, and the same warmth and the same welcome enfolded him there as well. He stared round the room, then at her. 'I'm afraid it will dissolve if I breathe too hard – like the snow-scene in the paperweight I had as a child . . . shake it and it was gone.'

Gertrude busied herself with the waiting tea-tray, afraid that if she didn't do something else she might weep for the strange longing and pain in his voice.

'Not what you've grown used to, but not a mirage, I promise you!'

He accepted the tea-cup she offered him without knowing that he did so.

'Your letters kept me very well informed, but all the time I had the feeling that I was reading about a place that didn't exist – only the life I was living out there was believable. Now that I'm here, and it *is* real, I can't understand how you manage at all.'

'Like everyone else, we manage because we have to. Mary and Victoria have become experienced farmers now; Josephine runs the orphanage and teaches the children although, like Lucy at Bicton, she insists that they teach her more than she teaches them. She also helps me take care of William and Providence.'

'Nothing to it, in fact!' Christopher said gently. 'God be thanked for the people we leave in England.'

Gertrude found it harder to put into words what had to be said next. 'James saw to it before he died that the damage to the house was properly repaired. When the time comes for *you* to think about such things, you must just tell us what you want to do with Providence.'

Nothing to that, either, she seemed to say. Christopher remembered that he'd fled out of the house once before, in a pitiful attempt to shrug off his inheritance, but he'd left it too late to tell James that he didn't want it at all.

'The time to think may never come,' he said after a long

pause. 'Even if this war ends, *we* may not win it.'

He thought she looked disappointed in him.

'My dear Christopher, of course we shall win. William tells me that things must get worse than they are now before they get better, but even *he* has no doubt about the outcome. Hitler ensured his own defeat by invading Russia instead of us, and Japan's madness at Pearl Harbor brought America into the war. We couldn't have won alone, but we *shall* win, eventually.'

'On which trumpet-blast of hope, dear aunt, I shall indulge myself in the luxury of getting out of uniform!'

'The others will be here when you come down. William and Sybil are attending a carol rehearsal in the other wing. Our children are like Peter Hoffer's – they love to sing and play musical instruments.'

She led him upstairs to his bedroom, accepting that he'd chosen not to be drawn on the subject of Providence; he knew that she wouldn't refer to it again until he did.

He changed into comfortable old clothes, but instead of going downstairs afterwards stood for a long time at his open bedroom window. The air tasted cold and clean, and the last gleams of a winter sunset painted purple shadows on the whiteness of the park. They were slowly overtaken by darkness, in which there now hung the thin crescent of a new moon flanked by one attendant star . . . the English countryside and sky at night – no dust, no glare, no obscene noise of gunfire.

When he finally went downstairs the Great Hall seemed full of people – William was settled by the fire, with Mary Wyndham on the hearth-rug talking to him, and the two London waifs who were now hers by adoption advised Victoria and her aunt Sybil on the decoration of the tree that filled the room with the scent of pine-needles. They had all to be greeted and talked to, but the girl he still watched for didn't come until they were about to sit down to dinner.

She looked tired, and very thin, but her black hair still shone in the lamp-light, and she wore her dark-green sweater and skirt with the unconscious grace that had always been a part of her. He'd been waiting for her, and now couldn't find anything to say. Josephine could, apparently.

'Granny told me you were here. Have . . . have you grown? You seem very large.' She could have added that he was unfamiliar altogether – a tall, powerful-looking stranger, with a deeply bronzed face and fair hair bleached almost to whiteness by the sun. To Christopher he sounded painfully casual; if she remembered the suggestion he'd flung at her on the day of Ned's funeral, it had clearly not troubled her since. Then Gertrude summoned them to the dining-room next door, and with eight of them seated round the table it was only noticeable to him that she made no further effort to talk to him. When dinner was over she kissed her grandparents, said a general good night, and disappeared.

He and Sybil sat on alone by the fire after the others had gone to bed. They were old friends and there was much to talk about, but she thought he was choosing not to talk about what was uppermost in his mind. It was she who broached the subject in the end.

'In case you're wondering, it was Josephine's turn to be on duty in the other wing – that's why she left so early.'

'Is that also why she did her best to pretend I wasn't there?'

'No, there was another reason for that,' Sybil explained carefully. 'My daughter finally gave her allegiance to her grandparents and to Providence. She knows that you don't share that allegiance; so the reason for your visit must be to stake your claim to something you now have the right to destroy.'

Christopher heard her words die on the quiet air, listened to a log shift and settle on the hearth before he said anything. 'Is that what you and Gertrude think, too?'

Sybil smiled, and shook her head. 'My mother is unshakeably convinced that Providence is indestructible.

All *I'm* certain of is that she has the habit of being right.'

'A vote of partial confidence, at least, *not* shared by Josephine!'

'Perhaps I should also mention that she got a wrong impression when you came back from Spain needing help. My fault, but I eventually found an opportunity to explain that I loved you like a son!'

'Not your fault – mine. But I should like to have been your son.' He smiled at her with Patrick's smile and she couldn't be sure whether that was pain or comfort.

'Go to bed,' she suggested gently. 'You look as if you'd been short of sleep for years. There's no need to worry about the future for a long time yet.'

He did as she said and fell asleep to the sound of an owl hooting from its perch above the stables. The clatter of hooves woke him the following morning, and he got out of bed in time to see Victoria riding off on some early-morning duty.

Disinclined to return to bed, he shaved and dressed, although it was much too early to go downstairs in search of breakfast. He thought of going to look at the rooms his grandfather had had repaired, changed his mind and walked along the corridor in the other direction instead. The door of William's studio stood open, and on an impulse he went in. It was icily cold, and lit by the first faint shaft of the morning sun. He didn't immediately see that he wasn't alone until Josephine moved out of the shadows and went to stand in the embrasure of the huge window, as if in need of what little warmth the sun offered.

He had only time to think that she was too thin, and to remember why *she* would think he was there, before she spoke to him.

'Good morning . . . there's tea brewing downstairs – we keep farm hours here.'

'And you'd rather get rid of me . . . get rid of me altogether, in fact, if you could only bring yourself to say so.'

Her dark eyes inspected him gravely, making clear what needn't be said at all, but her next effort at conversation took him by surprise.

'I'm not going to quarrel with you in here. Instead, I'll thank you for your long letters to my grandmother – she and William looked forward to them; I suppose we all did.'

'But *you* didn't ever feel inclined to write back?'

'Our war has become rather humdrum now – a matter of small daily problems – monotonous food, darned clothes, not enough petrol, and the everlasting black-out; too quiet to be written about.'

'Quiet . . . with fourteen children in the house, twelve of them blind?'

For the first time he saw her smile, and even in her shabby sweater and corduroy slacks she was beautiful. 'Twenty, now! When Great-Uncle James died my mother took his place on various charitable committees. She sends us another addition to the family from time to time.'

His expression didn't change, and she misinterpreted it.

'There's no need to think we shall be a permanent nuisance here. Your grandfather was kind enough to set aside money – "Trust in Providence", he called it! We shall be able to find another home when the time comes . . . when you tell us to go.'

'You were going to live in France – look after your father's paintings. What became of that idea?'

'I had a better one – looking after children who need help,' she said tranquilly. 'But I *shall* go and look at the paintings one day, when the Germans have been cleared out of Paris.'

She had learned serenity from her grandmother, but even so he resented it – she had no right to be so composed and sure of herself when he was not; he was a churning, shameful mess of emotions that threatened to get completely out of hand, and she stood waiting politely for him to leave the room – damn it, *his* room.

'Why did you say you wouldn't quarrel with me *here*?'

376

She turned the question aside, with a sudden, charming smile. 'It's nearly Christmas – not the season for quarrelling at all.'

'Then in that case I'll push my luck a little more. If it's the season for universal love, you might not be so deplorably definite as you were the last time I asked you to marry me! Do you think you could change your mind about accepting me and Providence?'

She had the frozen stillness of a wild creature trapped by its own carelessness, but she was silent for so long that he had to go rushing on, incapable of knowing whether he was making a lamentable performance worse.

'God damn it, Jo, you *love* Providence. You must want to help me take care of it.'

He strode across the room, and pulled her hard against him; fearful that she would still refuse, half-aware that he could kiss her into a kind of surrender, wholly certain that he needed *her*, even if she didn't need him. She struggled to free herself, and his self-control finally snapped. His mouth found hers, demanded and gradually received a response that startled and delighted him.

He lifted his head a little to smile at her, and murmur, 'My darling one – I *wasn't* wrong – we need and love each other . . . we do . . . oh God, we do.' His lips were soft on hers again, then urgently insisting on surrender.

She tore herself free at last, and stood an arm's length away from him, trembling and desirable, but struggling to gain control of herself. Christopher's smile was full of tenderness and triumph.

'Dear heart, you can't pretend that what's just happened *didn't* happened.'

'I know that,' she muttered unevenly, 'but it doesn't change anything. We lost our heads for a moment, that's all, and there's always been this . . . this feeling that we had something in common.'

'And I mucked it up by seeming to be besotted with Sybil? Sweetheart, she was kind when I needed kindness, and we're true friends; but it's you I love with all my heart and soul and body. Now will you stay with me here, for ever and ever, so that we can take care of Providence together?'

It was bitterly hard to resist him, with his eyes bright as jewels in the brownness of his face, and his mouth so tender. 'I'd stay if I could, but you still don't understand about Providence,' she said hoarsely. 'It isn't a matter of the two of us enjoying a happy little life together, while we make sure that we hand on a useless house intact to another generation. No, don't touch me, Christopher . . . *listen* to me, please. After Ned died Emmy nearly went mad believing that *she* had killed him. My grandmother brought her back here to be mended, because that's what Providence is – a healing-place, a sanctuary for people who need help. If my blind children can't stay here I shall find another home for them, and we must take with us as much of the grace that's here as we can manage. God knows it will be needed more than ever after this war is over.'

She stopped talking, waiting to see him leave her; when he turned away, the faint glimmer of hope in her heart died, and she shut her eyes so as not to have to watch him go. Then his voice reached her from across the room, and he was still there, standing in front of William's painting of spring.

'Do you remember bringing me in here one day, Jo? You were quite right, then, to say that I didn't understand, but you're not right now. Whenever I've thought I was going mad during the past eighteen months I only had to remember these paintings to step back inside peace and sanity; I *know* what we have to preserve.'

He turned to smile as she slowly walked towards him. 'Can't we *all* stay here, my darling – Gertrude and William, and you and me, and *these* children, and *our* children, and however many more Sybil finds who need cramming in . . ?'

She wasn't sure yet, because there was one more question to ask. 'We spoke of choices one day; you weren't going to make any.'

'I still won't take sides, Jo – England against Ireland, or the other way round. But I've *chosen* all right, between happiness here and unhappiness anywhere else.'

He just had time to glimpse the radiance in her face before she flung herself into his arms and mumbled into his tweed jacket, 'You'd better hold me tight, or I shall faint at your feet.' After a moment she lifted her head and stared at him with questioning eyes. 'I'm almost afraid to believe you mean it . . . but you do, and I could die of contentment.'

'Yes, but not just yet, sweetheart; we have to live a little first!'

A smile lit her face, then she grew serious again as she pointed to William's painting in front of them.

'I don't think he will ever work in here again – there's no need now; everything he wanted to say has been said.'

'The resurrection of life over death – it's Gertrude's vision, too . . . no wonder she rebuked me yesterday for a lack of faith and hope.'

Josephine turned to look at him. 'She's right, isn't she – good *will* defeat evil . . . there *will* be spring, and a time for happiness?'

'My darling, it's coming . . . it's on the wing.' He smiled as he leaned towards her to kiss the tip of her nose. 'Even William says so!'

They went downstairs together, hand in hand, unprepared to find Emmy's kitchen already occupied. Gertrude, wrapped in her husband's old Jaeger dressing-gown, was pouring tea while Sybil sat working out how to make a table-decoration of sprays of holly and ivy and Christmas roses. Josephine kissed them both, but looked imploringly at Christopher. He smiled at Sybil, then spoke to the frail, silver-haired woman who seemed to embody the good that was to triumph over evil.

'Your grand-daughter seems to think that you and William might let me stay here with the rest of you . . . always,' he said simply.

Gertrude's thin, veined hands trembled but her face was suddenly transfigured with joy.

'Oh, my dears, it sounds a very . . . *perfect* arrangement!'

Sybil lifted her cup in an eloquent silent gesture, while Christopher stared at the three of them.

'It's taken me all this time to realize how alike you are. I shall drink a toast of my own . . . to the lovely women of Providence!'

THE END

THE WOMEN OF PROVIDENCE
by Sally Stewart

'Long-shanks Gertie' the village children called her, chasing her all the way to school. It was because she was different, with her long legs and long dark hair and clean pinafore. And, as the daughter of the land-agent on Providence, she accepted that she didn't belong anywhere – not part of the village, and not part of the Squire's family at the Big House.

But she was always fascinated by Squire Wyndham's family – Louise, the arrogant daughter of the house who never missed an opportunity of snubbing her. James, who was handsome and wonderful and charming – and who was one day to break her heart. And William, the heir, quiet, bookish, and almost as much of a misfit as she was. But above all there was Lady Hester. It was Lady Hester who saw something in Gertrude that no-one else had perceived – a quality of strength and endurance that would serve the family well.

Between them, Lady Hester and Gertrude Hoskins were to be the salvation of Providence.

0 552 13637 9

THE QUIET WAR OF REBECCA SHELDON
by Kathleen Rowntree

The Ludburys were a clannish and dominating farming family – Rebecca was the new young bride they didn't like.

Rebecca first met George Ludbury when she was eleven years old. Her mother had died that morning and George was the only one to give her comfort. She loved him from that moment on.

But George's family were a different matter. The Ludburys – an affluent Midlands farming family – were snobbish, possessive, malicious, and in the case of Pip, downright mad. The matriarchal Mrs Harold Ludbury was enraged when George – for whom she had planned better things – insisted on marrying Rebecca. From that moment on the family did their best to wreck the marriage, win George back to the family farm, and alienate Rebecca's children from her.

It took thirty years of gentle compliance and evasive pleasantness before Rebecca won her private war and achieved exactly what she wanted.

0 552 13413 9

THE MOSES CHILD
by Audrey Reimann

Oliver Wainwright was sixteen when he first set eyes on Florence Mawdesley. He was hiding in the water of the lake on Sir Philip Oldfield's land – taking refuge after stealing a mallard duck.

She was standing at the water's edge, silk-gowned, sheltered by her parasol, the privileged, aristocratic granddaughter of Sir Philip Oldfield. Oliver thought he had never seen anyone so lovely.

That same day he ran away – left the estate and the life of servitude that had killed his father – and took the first steps towards his future – as a self-made cotton king, a mill owner, a man of property. It was in the mill he met Rosie, dark, warm, beautiful, who began to cast her spell over him, even though she was a married woman.

But even as he rose to power – fighting Sir Philip Oldfield's vicious and vindictive revenge every inch of the way – he never forgot the vision of the beautiful girl at the water's edge.

0 552 13521 6

A SELECTION OF FINE TITLES
AVAILABLE FROM CORGI BOOKS

THE PRICES SHOWN BELOW WERE CORRECT AT THE TIME OF GOING TO PRESS.
HOWEVER TRANSWORLD PUBLISHERS RESERVE THE RIGHT TO SHOW NEW
RETAIL PRICES ON COVERS WHICH MAY DIFFER FROM THOSE PREVIOUSLY
ADVERTISED IN THE TEXT OR ELSEWHERE.

All Corgi/Bantam Books are available at your bookshop or newsagent, or can be ordered from the following address:

Corgi/Bantam Books,
Cash Sales Department,
P.O. Box 11, Falmouth, Cornwall TR10 9EN

UK and B.F.P.O. customers please send a cheque or postal order (no currency) and allow £1.00 for postage and packing for the first book plus 50p for the second book and 30p for each additional book to a maximum charge of £3.00 (7 books plus).

Overseas customers, including Eire, please allow £2.00 for postage and packing for the first book plus £1.00 for the second book and 50p for each subsequent title ordered.